The Hokey Pokey Man

The Hokey Pokey Man

ANITA ARCARI

y Lolfa

Anita Arcari was born in Wales to a Welsh mother and an Italian father. She works as a computer science lecturer in a Carmarthenshire college. She has been writing fiction for as far back as she can remember and her love of the written word shines through in her debut novel. She has drawn on her own family history to produce this evocative and moving story, which will appeal not only to Welsh-Italians everywhere, but to anyone who enjoys romantic fiction.

First impression: 2010

Cover design: Anita Arcari and Michael David

ISBN: 9781847712578

Printed on acid-free and partly recycled paper and published and bound in Wales by
Y Lolfa Cyf., Talybont, Ceredigion SY24 5HE
e-mail ylolfa@ylolfa.com
website www.ylolfa.com
tel 01970 832 304
fax 832 782

For my brother Roy
'Sabatino'
Always an inspiration to me
But never more so than now.

'Un uomo veramente notevole'
'Dyn gwirioneddol arbennig'
'A truly remarkable man'

Acknowledgements

There are many, many people who deserve thanks for their encouragement and support, both before and during the writing of this novel. In particular, I would like to give special thanks to my husband and children, who have always had confidence in my work. My sister and brother, who read and loved this work, and my other close family members, are worthy of a special mention, too.

I would also like to pay tribute to family no longer with us. Many of my ancestors, some no more than names, others immortalised in a few faded photographs, lie at the heart of this story and were its inspiration. As a child, I would listen, mesmerised, to the story of how my grandparents came to Wales as poor Italian immigrants at the turn of the 20th century. Like others of their kind, their indomitable spirit and flair for enterprise ensured their future as well-liked and respected business people.

Sincere thanks must go to my many friends, old and new, especially in Wales and Italy. It was in Immoglie, Italy that I first discovered the family *cappella*, sowing the seeds of curiosity that became the very essence of this novel.

Thanks also to Michael David, my friend and colleague, who worked with me on the cover for this novel and valiantly responded to my constant requests for changes.

I am deeply indebted to Eifion Jenkins for his wonderfully empathetic approach in guiding me so skilfully through the editing of this novel. I believe he now knows the D'Abruzzo family even better than I do.

May I also thank Eirian Jones and Lefi Gruffudd of Y Lolfa for their help, support and encouragement.

Finally – to use a well-worn but appropriate cliché – last but definitely not least, my love and thanks go to my little grand-daughter Sophia Rose, for being my own special little miracle.

There are so many others I would love to mention by name, but I'm sure if I did, the sheer volume would almost constitute a novel in itself. So, if I have not mentioned you individually, it does not mean that your support is not appreciated, simply that space will not allow for it.

Thank you – Diolch – Grazie

Prologue

CARLA WAITED AT the top of the winding path, maintaining a discreet distance between herself and the old man. A lump came to her throat as she watched the frail, slightly stooped form labouring upwards, leaving the mountain cemetery behind him. He paused now and then to take off his hat, wiping away the shiny droplets of sweat as they merged into little rivulets on his forehead: futile, for just moments later, they reappeared in the unforgiving heat of the sun. Since he had heard the news, Carla thought, he seemed to have shrunk in stature, retreated inside his own body.

She could never remember seeing him like this before, he had always been so brave, whatever life had thrown at him. It was almost as if a light had gone out. He was nearer now, one last effort and he would be alongside her. But it was all far from over for him. Earlier, Carla's heart had almost broken, watching him as he stood forlornly at the edge of the little group, head bowed in resignation and silent regret as the coffin slid into place. Things were done differently here, in this remote, mountainous region of Italy; some graves in the ground, but mostly, slots in the wall, three or four high, where ancestors slept side by side in eternal peace. Carla's throat had constricted when she saw the old, weathered face crumple as he turned away from the graveside.

But no, it wasn't over yet. Carla knew there was one more thing he had to do, one last ghost to lay to rest. He had to make his peace. She reached out her hand to him as he came alongside, gently guiding him towards the car. He sat in silence and she made no attempt at conversation, knowing instinctively he would prefer to be left alone with his thoughts. They drove a short distance up the rough-made road that led towards the village before turning off sharply to the right, crunching and bumping alarmingly along a narrow lane that gradually petered out into a stony, dry-crusted track. The wheels fought with the rutted dry earth, kicking up clouds of pale yellow-orange dust as they bounced along, testing the car's suspension to its limits. The whole journey took just a few minutes. Carla stopped and turned off the ignition before looking around. She knew this was the right place, though there was nothing much to see; three steps, partly obscured by gnarled and ancient olive trees, led upwards to nowhere, standing in ever-hopeful anticipation beside an untidy heap of rubble. Nearby, at the end of an overgrown path was a small *rustico* a ruined farm cottage, roof dipping ominously, window-shutters rotted and drunkenly askew. A few lizards clung lazily to its thick stone walls, basking in the warmth of the blazing sun. Just to the side of the same path stood a little cappella, or shrine. This too had suffered the ravages of time and war; roof open to the sky, and the once cornflower-blue plaster now peeling and faded to a dingy, mottled grey. On the back wall, a metre-high alcove curved gently as if to embrace the statue of a Madonna long since gone. Carla sighed softly.

For the second time that day, she stood back and watched the old man heave himself out of the car; she knew her presence would not be welcomed beyond this point. He stood motionless, quietly taking in his surroundings; things had changed so much in the intervening years, and yet, somehow, they hadn't changed at all. Slowly, he turned his attention to the cappella. Someone had bolted a thick stone slab onto the wall near the top; it carried a rough-hewn inscription, a curious combination of Italian and the local Piciniscani dialect. With shaking hands, he adjusted his glasses, pushing them right to the top of his nose. Squinting against the dazzle of the sun, he read:

Built for my dear son, Sabatino, in penance and atonement for all he was forced to give up for his family.
May God and Our Lady grant me forgiveness.
Built in this year AD 1900.

A tear trickled from the corner of the old man's eye and he sank to the ground as his legs gave way beneath him. Kneeling before the cappella, he buried his face in his hands. Hunched shoulders, once broad and strong, shook uncontrollably and the single tear became a torrent as he wept like a child.

Chapter 1

SABATINO AWOKE TO the sound of birds squabbling and a shaft of bright sunlight streaming through the one and only window in the barn. In truth, it wasn't even a proper window, but a gap that had been left deliberately at the apex of the rough *Majella* stone, to provide welcome ventilation for stored crops and farm animals. Little had changed in the countless years since it had been built by long-forgotten ancestors; certainly the barn itself remained the same, good, local stone, still solid and timeless despite enduring the rigours of several earthquakes and extreme weather conditions. The surrounding land rolled into the infinity of the valley below, wild and untouched. Eyes still heavy with sleep, the boy blinked a few times and rolled lazily onto his back. Raising his arms above his head, he inhaled the comfortingly familiar smell around him.

It was a good smell; a heady mix of warm, sweet earth and hay mixed with the musky scent of animals – goats, pigs, two donkeys and numerous chickens that shared the barn with him; the pigs, together with a small flock of sheep, stayed outside in the warmer weather. At the height of summer, when the heat became intense, the sheep would be driven even higher up the mountains, to the coolness of greener, sweeter pastures. He smiled lazily as his outstretched hand made contact with the soft body of another living being – his favourite goat, Tina – which, of course, he would have named Tino, like himself, had it been born male. He had hand-reared it almost from birth, after its mother had become sickly and died. The goats especially were his pride and joy, it was his job to look after all the animals and for him it was a labour of love. Papa often laughed at him for being too soft – '*molto sensibile*,' he would mock, especially when it was time for one of Tino's precious charges to be slaughtered for the table; but Sabatino did not care and would just shrug his shoulders nonchalantly, so that Papa would not notice the tears in his eyes. He absently tickled a sensitive spot just behind the goat's ear and was rewarded when a wet nose gently nuzzled his hand.

'Tino, Tino! Time to get up!' Mamma's voice penetrated his thoughts, as she called across from the little house where the rest of the family slept. Sabatino's name had long since been shortened into a more manageable form by everyone except the local priest up at the village, and Mara. Ah, Mara! A smile flickered across his lips as he thought of the lovely young daughter of one of the neighbours. So far, just a smile here, a shy glance there; but one day, he promised himself, one day, Mara would be his wife.

'Tino! Get up, you lazy boy! *Ragazzo pigro! Poltrone!*'

'Coming, Mamma, coming,' he called back, swiftly pulling on his rough cloth trousers not a moment too soon, for the stocky figure of his mother was already rapidly approaching the entrance to the barn. He fumbled hastily with his clothing. All this familiarity was fine when he was a little boy, but he was thirteen now, approaching fourteen fast, and almost a man, growing taller and stronger by the day, the hard work on the land tightening his muscles and turning the colour of his skin from olive to a deep, golden brown. It was late summer, the weather stayed hot despite the cooling mountain breezes and Sabatino slept on a thick bed of hay, naked and without covers. It really wouldn't do for his mother to see him like that; a faint flush of pink coloured his cheeks at the thought.

Lena D'Abruzzo was a handsome woman, a tiny yet imposing figure framed in the doorway, a faceless outline silhouetted against the dawn sky. It was uncanny how so small a woman could convey such a remarkable presence that it seemed to envelop everyone and everything in sight, and that included Tino. Hips swayed and plump arms folded menacingly over an ample bosom. Tino knew that pose well and realised he was in trouble. 'Well, hurry up now, Tino – it's late and I need you to get water from the spring,' she grumbled, head bobbing up and down comically like a marionette. 'Trouble with you, *ragazzo mio*, you're always too busy day-dreaming to do your work properly.' Tino felt a bubble of laughter welling up inside him, but he wouldn't dare give vent to it. 'Those smelly goats, that's all you care about. Never mind that your Mamma needs her water! Paah!' She snorted out the last word and stamped her tiny foot comically, reminding Tino of a stubborn mule and it was all he could do to keeping himself from laughing.

'*Mi dispiace*, Mamma, I'm sorry', Tino mumbled, still struggling with his trousers. 'I will go right away.'

Grabbing two battered pails from against the barn wall, he sidled warily past his mother and out into the open air. He skirted a little stone well to the right, near the farmhouse itself. Yes, there was water there, but it was not supplied by a free-running source during drier spells, standing for days or even weeks and forming a slightly greasy scum on the top. Mamma insisted it was not pure enough for her cooking, only good for the animals and irrigating the crops. He would have to go further down the mountain slopes to reach the spring, where the water always ran crystal clear and on certain days, when the air was still, it would sound like tinkling bells as it tumbled over pebble and rocks.

He did not dare look at his mother; he knew the deep brown eyes would be even darker with menace. No one could afford to sleep late when they lived off the land, there never seemed to be enough hours in a day to do all the tasks as it was. Maddalena herself worked as hard as anyone else, too, doing more than her fair share of the chores. She was a good wife and mother to her family. There had been nine children in all, but of those only six still survived – Tino was the fourth oldest, after Francesco, Carlotta and Emilia. She had taken the death of her children hard and it showed in the deep furrows imprinted on her forehead and the fine streaks of silver that stood out in stark contrast against the blue-black hair. She was still a long way off forty but looked much older. Arms still folded, she watched her son running barefoot down the hill; if he had stopped for just a moment to glance back, he would have seen the corners of her mouth curling upwards in a smile, and the unadulterated love that lit up her eyes.

Once out of his mother's sight, Tino gradually slowed his pace to an ambling walk, and his thoughts turned to other things. He wondered idly whether he would see Mara today. Sometimes, he would see her with her Mamma at the spring. He hoped she would be there today. It was not yet Sunday, so he knew he could not see her in the little church at the top of the hill, as he did most weeks. He began to whistle, a little out of tune, but even so he was proud of his whistling ability, because when he really tried, it could be heard from quite a long way off. He and his friends would have competitions to see who could whistle the loudest and more often than not, he would win.

He smiled. Today was Friday. Even if Mara was not at the spring, there was just tomorrow to go and then it would be Sunday anyway. His spirits lifted, they always did when he was out in the open air. He loved this land. It was still very early, but already the sun was climbing higher in the sky, bathing the mountains in its soft pink glow and swathes of woodsmoke hung in the air like ever-shifting silken ribbons. The warmth seemed to penetrate his very being and little droplets of moisture appeared on his forehead in response. He looked back up the path; right behind, Colleruta, where his family had farmed for centuries; renowned for its olive groves, fruit orchards and the fattest, ripest figs and cherries anyone could wish for. Further back, hidden by trees and higher up the mountain the little walled village of Picinisco, with its pretty mediaeval churches and towering castle; and across the valley, hidden by dense trees, San Gennaro, with Villa Latina nestling sleepily just below.

Dotted all around were other villages and hamlets – Le Serre, Il Cervo, Vallegrande, Immoglie – often no more than a few *rusticos*, farmhouses huddled together intimately. When he had been very small, Tino had the strangest notion that these little houses were talking to each other, whispering age-old secrets, especially when the chill winds blew through the mountains and made all kinds of strange, creaking and groaning noises. Some people said the mountains were haunted, but Tino didn't believe that for one moment. There were wolves and snakes though, and despite the warmth, he shuddered slightly at the thought.

Some of the older villagers, who had travelled in the past, told tales of how, on a clear day, from the top of the towering Monte Meta behind him, you could even see Vesuvius in the far distance. He wondered if that was true; he didn't really know much about Vesuvius, except the little he learned from the priest, who taught, or at least tried to teach, most of the children in the village; that it was a volcano that had erupted and buried a whole town of people beneath molten rocks and lava. It all sounded a bit too far-fetched to him, fire and rocks coming out of the top. Tino had never been right to the top of Monte Meta, but it did sometimes feel like it was very high up in the world even here, and the summit was much higher again. The furthest he had ever been was to the little market in Atina, where he and Mamma sometimes loaded up the donkey and took along cheeses and other food items to exchange for clothing. Tino loved it all, the sights, the smells, the sounds; his love of this beautiful, primitive land was buried deep inside, an integral part of him. He didn't want or need anything beyond his immediate surroundings, and although he was sometimes curious, why worry about places he would never need to go?

Tino's pace picked up again as he came closer to the spring. Despite the early hour, there were already quite a few women gathering around, not just from Colleruta and Picinisco, but from other villages too. The people of the area were renowned for their good looks and these women were no exception – generally small in stature but mostly with the same abundant dark hair and velvety brown eyes. In most cases, though, the hair was well hidden beneath a headscarf, usually brightly coloured, but exchanged on special days or feast days for fine white cloth edged with delicate lace, which they painstakingly made themselves. This was tied in a triangle and knotted securely at the nape of the neck. This was tradition for the people of the area, the headscarf, together with the wide-sleeved blouse and *sciareca*, a long dress with the neckline fashioned to allow the bodice of the blouse to peep out at the front and back. Over this, a voluminous yet practical dark apron covered the front of the skirts.

As Tino neared the little group, he dropped the wooden pails under a tree and raising one hand to shade his eyes, carefully scanned the faces gathered around the spring. His heart plummeted. There was no sign of either Mara or her mother. Disappointed, he sank onto the ground, leaning back idly against the rough bark of the tree. He knew he should be busy filling those containers at the spring, and he would probably get a row from Mamma for taking too long, but why should he care? What did it matter, anyway? He was not quite sure how long he sat there like that, downhearted and dejected, elbows resting on his knees. Eventually, though, the prospect of being at the receiving end of his Mamma's temper pulled him back to his feet – he swore her tongue was sharp enough to slice meat. He reached out to pick up the pails but stopped dead in his tracks. Out of the corner of his eye, he caught a movement just ahead and to the right of him, on the stony path leading to the spring. His heart seemed to skip a beat as he recognised the distinctive figures of Mara and her mother – he knew, he was sure, because even at that distance, Mara's hair shone like spun gold in the sunlight, rebelliously escaping from the confines of her scarf.

It was her hair that had first caught his attention, even when they were both very small. He still remembered sitting behind her in church one day when he was about four or five, watching, fascinated, as she knelt piously in front of the little altar – eyes closed, hands clasped tightly together in prayer. The thought had gone through his head at the time that she must be an angel. What Tino did not know even now was that her father, Mario Fonte, had come from Northern Italy where fair hair was not quite so remarkable. He had been sent all those miles to the village many years ago with a message, fell in love at first sight with Rosa, his bride-to-be, and never returned home. At the time, he had been as golden fair as his daughter, but now, despite being a relatively young man, his head was completely bald. Tino had often eyed it in amazement, marvelling at its smooth, hairless sheen. In fact, he often stared at it through screwed-up eyelids in church, especially when they all knelt down to pray and he could get a better view. This had been a good way to pass the time until the day Lena finally realised what was going on, and gave him such a resounding crack across the ear that it seemed to echo and bounce off all four walls simultaneously, and much to her mortification, attracted disapproving glances from everyone around them.

Tino quickened his movements, slithering and sliding over parched earth and pebbles as he neared the spring. Mara stood just behind her mother, carrying two small containers. When their turn came, Tino seized his chance and rushed forward.

'Let me help you with that, Signora Fonte,' he offered, bounding eagerly towards the woman. Dropping his own containers on the ground once again, he took hold of the large one that Mara's mother held out instead. He then helped her with another large, earthenware jug, which up to this point, had been expertly balanced on top of her head.

'*Grazie*', she smiled. 'Thank you. You are a very polite young man, Tino.' Rosa Fonte's eyes showed a glint of amusement, aware that although Tino was addressing her, he could not drag his gaze away from her daughter. 'And that might not be such a bad match, either,' she thought to herself. Everyone knew the boy's family was one of the better-off ones in the area. Even her own home and little parcel of land were rented from the D'Abruzzo family, as were many of the other dwellings in the area. Yes, Mara could do a lot worse for herself than Tino. Nodding to herself, she made a mental note to talk to her husband about this matter, they would make a good match.

Tino nodded. 'Mamma tells me I must always help where I can, *signora*,' he answered shyly, flashing a smile that seemed to light up his face. For once, he was grateful that Mamma had always insisted the whole family must clean their teeth with a rag and the foul-tasting soot from the chimney of the enormous fireplace, where chestnut logs burned fiercely in the cold winters of the mountains. He hated doing it, the soot was cloying, and stuck to the roof of the mouth and tongue in a thick black sludge. But it had paid off, for not only were his teeth sound but brilliantly white, too. 'I am young and strong, it is far easier for me to do this than you.'

'Well, the next time I see your Mamma, I will tell her what a good, kind son she has.'

Tino's chest puffed up with pride and not a little embarrassed by the compliment, he bent his head to position the containers. By this time, most of the other women had drifted away, carrying pots and other containers gracefully on their heads as Rosa had, backs ramrod straight. He was acutely aware of Mara's proximity and risked a shy glance in her direction. Sure enough, eyes the colour of dark sapphires were fixed on him and she smiled as she realised she had caught his attention. He smiled too but quickly turned back to his task. He was painfully aware of her presence. The only sounds disturbing the silence were the stirring of the leaves on a nearby chestnut tree and the tinkling and gurgling of the spring. He was quite sure she must hear the thudding of his heart above them. Mara was so close now; he knew if he put out his hand he could touch her. He would have liked that, but would she? Without warning, the thought made him blush furiously.

'I don't think you'll get any more water in those.' Signora Fonte laughed. In his confusion, Tino had allowed the water to spill over from the container, where it had spread out and darkened the parched earth beneath.

'Oh. I am sorry, signora,' Tino blustered. 'I wasn't thinking…' That wasn't quite the truth, he knew – he had been thinking, but it had nothing to do with anything as mundane as water; his thoughts had been of soft golden curls, and wondering what it would be like to kiss those full rose-red lips. His cheeks, already pink, deepened to scarlet.

He put the containers gently onto the ground. He wasn't quite sure what to do next; should he take Mara's containers too, or allow her to get the water herself? He didn't want to appear too forward. His mind working away furiously, he decided to try a different approach.

'Signora Fonte,' he gulped, turning to the amused lady, 'shall I fill Mara's as well as yours?'

'Yes, thank you', she replied with a knowing smile and just a hint of a twinkle in her eyes. In that instant, he was convinced she had read his mind, and in his discomfiture, almost dropped the pot Mara was already holding out to him. Somehow, he managed to catch it just in time, but as he did so, his hand brushed lightly against hers; he could only compare it with being struck by a bolt of lightning; his hand was on fire. He glanced up to see a flush of pink matching his own softly colouring Mara's cheeks.

'*Mi dispiace*', he mumbled, though he was anything but sorry. That simple, innocent touch had caused all sorts of feelings that his rapidly awakening body did not yet quite recognise. All he knew was, he was most definitely *not* regretting it; what was more, he had enjoyed it; and even worse, he knew he would like to do it again. He was not entirely sure the priest or Mamma would have approved but surely he could not be blamed for his feelings when they were way beyond his control?

'I'm very hot, I think I'll go and rest in the shade of that tree over there.' Tino's head jerked up towards Signora Fonte. Was she deliberately giving him the chance to talk to Mara – not exactly alone, since young girls were rarely, if ever, allowed unchaperoned, with members of the opposite sex – but at least, out of earshot.

'It will be fine, I'm not far away', she reassured him, 'and I can tell you're a good boy, not like some of them'.

Tino couldn't believe his luck. At last a chance to talk to Mara properly, after years of longing from a distance. He watched in silence as Signora Fonte settled herself beneath the tree. White petticoats and impossibly tiny dark leather sandals, *le ciocie*, peeped out from beneath the hem of the bright red *sciareca*. The straps of the sandals twisted and wound their way upwards from her ankles until they were hidden from sight.

He looked first at Mara, who stood quietly alongside, eyes downcast, then shot a swift glance in her mother's direction. She was leaning back against the tree, eyes closed. His first chance to talk to Mara – and he was tongue-tied. Head bent, he stooped forward towards the spring ready to fill the container, all the while desperately searching for something interesting and intelligent to say.

It was Mara who finally broke the silence. 'It is still very hot for the time of year, isn't it?' she said, squinting against the brightness of the new day.

'Yes'. His voice was in the process of changing, and although it promised to be as rich and deep as his father's and brother's, it still sometimes fluctuated wildly between a gentle bass and a girlish falsetto. On this occasion, to his utter dismay and embarrassment, it shot up a whole octave and the sound that came out was little more than a pathetic squeak – even pigs could do better.

'Oh, no,' he thought, heart sinking. 'My big chance and not only do I sound like a girl, I can't even think of anything to say'. Desperately gathering his wits about him, he took a deep breath and tried again.

'We will be...' There it was again and now, not only was he mortified but he could feel the first faint stirrings of panic. He would, he must, try one more time. Plucking up all his courage, he took yet another deep breath and coughed gently, clearing his throat.

'We will be starting the harvest soon; Papa says we'll have to take on more help this year.' Oh, yes, that was better. At last he sounded like a man, not an excited pig about to get its food. Encouraged, he went on, 'Although it's been hot, we've had enough rain this year to keep the land watered; it should be a good crop, one of the best in a long time.'

Mara watched as Tino began filling the second container. To any onlooker, it wouldn't have been difficult to see that his admiration was reciprocated, her eyes shone as she tilted her chin upwards to look at him. Although she was slightly older, he was much taller and she was fascinated by the way his hair clung damply to his head in a mass of shiny, blue-black curls. She suddenly had the ridiculous urge to run her fingers through them and she caught her breath audibly at the idea. She was not too sure that 'good' girls should have thoughts like that.

Not recognising the significance of the sharp intake of breath, Tino turned to her, immediately concerned. 'Are you all right?' he asked, reaching out a hand to steady her.

Embarrassed at being caught out, she cast her eyes downwards. 'Yes. Yes, I think so,' she said. Her heart raced as the heat of Tino's fingers burned through the thin cloth of her top; she really did feel faint.

'Look, rest under the tree for a little while with your Mamma, while I finish here.' He guided her gently to the tree, genuinely worried as she settled down on the grass. Those wayward strands of spun gold seemed to form a hazy little halo around her face and once again, Tino was struck by thoughts of angels. She was beautiful, he was quite sure he loved her, even more so now that they had finally spoken. Carefully positioning the next container where the spring gushed out from the rocks, he wondered idly if Mara felt the same.

Everything suddenly seemed more beautiful, colours brighter, the birdsong sweeter; even the water coming from the little spring seemed to be scattered with tiny flecks of gold and silver as it sparkled in the morning sun. Tino's heart soared. He was completely oblivious to the fact that Signora Fonte and Mara were now alongside him, until the older woman spoke.

'We'd better get back home now, we have plenty to do

and I know you will have, too. I don't think your Mamma and Papa will thank me if I keep you away too long,' she smiled gently. Taking the containers, she carefully balanced the now full pot on her head and steadying it with one hand, picked up the remaining container with the other.

'Mara tells me your Papa is going to need some help with the harvest.' Tino nodded in silent agreement, sad that Mara would now be going back home, away from him. 'Well, tell him that some of my family can help, if he likes. I have good, strong sons and my Mario is still fit and strong, too'

'Yes, I will tell him. *Grazie,*' Tino answered. 'Thank you, Signora Fonte.'

'No, I should be the one thanking you for your help today. You're a good boy, Tino.' The mother and daughter waved and started walking away. Mara stole a final glance over her shoulder as Tino picked up his own pails and went in the opposite direction to the stony path that led upwards and homeward, downcast for he was not sure when he would be able to speak to the girl again. He had gone just a few steps when Rosa Fonte's voice spun him around once more.

'Oh, and of course, Tino,' Rosa called out, eyes gleaming wickedly, 'I'm sure my little Mara here could help your Mamma and sisters with all the extra work they will have, too. Goodbye for now. And don't forget to tell your Papa!'

'No, I won't forget, I promise!'

His spirits soared again. Papa would be glad of the offer of help and knowing that Mara would be there, Tino could hardly wait. He breathed long and deeply, the sweet scent of late summer flowers and wild herbs and garlic filling his nostrils as they bruised beneath his feet. He smiled. It was so good to be alive. Tino headed for home with a renewed spring in his step.

Chapter 2

'AH, TINO, AT last! Where have you been, Atina and back?' Mamma's sarcastic remark drifted down towards Tino as he rounded the last bend in the stony path. 'We've been waiting for you.'

'Sorry, Mamma,' Tino sighed. He always seemed to be saying 'sorry' these days, but at least this time he had a good excuse. 'I was talking to Signora Fonte, she asked me to give Papa a message.'

'Well, you'd better come in and give it to him, then,' Maddalena conceded finally with a smile. She could never be cross with him for long, he was such a gentle and kind boy. One look from those velvety eyes and she was lost.

Tino bounded up the steps and followed his mother into the cool of the stone-built farmhouse. By local standards, the D'Abruzzo family were well off and instead of sharing their living quarters with the animals, as most families did, the opening to the barn had long since been blocked off, by Tino's great-grandfather. As a result, the rooms were completely separated. Unlike the poorer families, it was only in the depths of winter now that the animals were brought inside and then only to generate additional warmth for the house through their body heat.

Although the weather was still hot, a wood fire burned brightly in the huge open fireplace and a big black cauldron of polenta, made from the rough-ground flour of maize from their own fields, hung from a hook suspended above the flames. It bubbled and gurgled ferociously, interrupted only by an occasional loud plopping sound, like some glutinous, yellow-gold witch's brew. In the far corner of the room, partly obscured by a clean but threadbare curtain, was a raised wooden platform which supported a mattress stuffed almost full to bursting point with the husks of the maize. This was Mamma and Papa's bed and two smaller pallets, also made from maize husks, stood nearby. They rustled and creaked loudly with every turn, but nothing was wasted in this part of the world, where poverty had made people resourceful. There was a use for everything – even maize husks.

The mouth-watering smell of freshly baked bread filled the air and a spotless white cloth covered the table. Apart from the communal oven in Picinisco, and another belonging to their neighbours, the Grillos, they had the only oven capable of baking bread in the region – something Raffaele had skilfully put together with his own hands, much to his wife's delight.

Tino's mouth began to water in anticipation and eagerly took his place opposite his two younger brothers, Angelo and Michele. Francesco, who was four years older, had gone to England to work with Uncle '*Zi*' Giuseppe, a travelling musician who toured the streets of London with a big, brightly coloured barrel organ. They had a little monkey called Chico, too, who could dance and do tricks. Francesco was a good boy, he sent a lot of the money he earned back home. When he had left, Tino wondered what it would be like to go away like that, almost to the ends of the earth. He just couldn't even begin to think how far it was, it was way beyond his imagination. Some people said the streets there were paved with gold, but Papa said it wasn't really true, and he should know. Hadn't he often told them tales of how, many years ago, he too had walked the streets of London with Zi Giuseppe, where they tramped along in their 'one man band' costumes, singing old folk songs to the accompaniment of a huge banging drum and cymbals that clapped loudly as they knocked their knees together? This was how, through sheer guts, determination and hard work, he had saved up enough money to buy the land they worked, how he had earned the respect, and sometimes envy, of their neighbours.

Papa Raffaele sat at the head of the table as Mamma, together with Tino's sisters, Carlotta and Emilia, brought over plates laden with crusty black bread, polenta and thick slices of black sausage. The latter had been selected carefully from several that hung invitingly from a row of hooks on the ceiling, alongside curing hams and bunches of fragrant wild herbs. There was fruit too, and figs freshly picked from their own trees.

Carlotta placed the bread on the table and brushed her hands together, wiping away a few crumbs.

'We helped Mamma with the baking, so you'd better eat it all up!' She smiled at her little brothers and ruffled their hair affectionately. She was a gentle girl and at sixteen, the elder of the girls – a miniature version of her mother, short and stocky with a round face and shiny blue-black hair. She was just saved from plainness by enormous liquid brown eyes flecked with gold, and framed exquisitely by impossibly long, black lashes.

It was fifteen year old Emilia though, who held promise of real beauty to come. She too shared similar features, but more refined, softer and more sensual, not sharp or angular, like those of her mother and sister. Hair the colour of wild chestnuts fell down to the slim waist in a cascade of shiny curls. The only thing that marred her looks was a slight cast in her right eye. It wasn't always noticeable, but whenever something upset or worried her, it would become much more apparent.

But a turn in the eye like that was considered a bad luck omen, and the villagers were very superstitious people. They were afraid of being given the *malocchio* – the evil eye – and it worried Mamma that it might be difficult to find a willing husband. She had become a little argumentative recently, too, and Mamma was often heard wailing in despair as she tried to reason with her wayward daughter.

The smell of the warmed bread wafted across the room and Tino suddenly realised just how hungry he was – the early morning walk had whetted his appetite and, after waiting for Papa to start first, he tucked in avidly to the feast before him.

'Here's your favourite,' Lena smiled, handing him a mug of goat's milk. 'Carlotta had to milk the goats this morning, too, they couldn't wait for you any longer, they were almost dancing, poor things!'

The milk was still warm and tasted sweet. He gulped down almost half of it in one long draught, then hastily used the back of his hand to wipe away the damp white moustache around his lips. 'Oh, I nearly forgot!' he said quickly. 'Papa, I have a message for you.'

Papa tore a hunk of bread off a loaf and chewed quietly before replying. 'Ah, a message,' he answered, head nodding up and down. Raffaele's hair was as dark and wavy as in his youth; he was still a handsome man, though a few furrows now lined his face, the legacy of a life spent outdoors. 'So, *mio figlio*, what is this message you have for me, then? Is it good news?'

'Well, in a way, Papa. From Signora Fonte,' Tino explained. 'She offered to help us again with the harvest, this year.'

'What, just Signora Fonte?' Papa teased. 'Now, that will be such hard work for her, on her own.'

His long-running fascination with Mara hadn't gone unnoticed by the astute Raffaele D'Abruzzo. But of course, it would never come to anything; it was nothing more than a childish devotion, like a dog to its master. In any case, he and Grillo, his friend and neighbour, shook hands a long time ago on a union between Tino and Grillo's daughter, Serafina. Since his wife's untimely death some years before, Grillo had doted on the girl, whatever she wanted, she got – and now, she wanted Tino. She told her father in no uncertain terms she would either have Tino for a husband or she would have no husband at all. He had made sure that the ambitious Raffaele D'Abruzzo wouldn't turn him down, either, for he made the offer conditional – it was nothing more than a bribe, but he would take Emilia off his hands, a wife for his son, Marco – a very generous offer which Raffaele wouldn't get elsewhere, he took pains to point out, given the condition of the girl's eye.

As yet, though, except for Serafina, none of the young people involved had been told – plenty of time for that. Raffaele hadn't even told Lena, it was probably better she didn't know. The thought suddenly struck him that even after all these years, no-one knew Grillo's first name; he had always been called plain 'Grillo'. Nor did anyone really know where he came from; some said France; some said Napoli, and that he had turned up many years ago to trade goods and never gone back home; others said even further away. Grillo himself said that he had lived in another part of the region, but no-one believed him. What Raffaele did know, though, was that Lena despised the family, and thought they were coarse, rowdy and show-offs, except for the son Marco, who was quite unlike his father and sister; but Raffaele would win her round, given time, of that he was convinced. They would be good, profitable marriages, uniting the adjacent land of the two families, as well as their offspring – and Grillo was a very wealthy man, he owned far more land that he himself did, raking in an enviable revenue from renting out to the desperately poor *contadini*. Although payment was usually in goods grown on the land or other items such as fine lace made by the families, Grillo had secured outlets where he would get the best possible returns. Tino's reply interrupted Raffaele's thoughts, bringing him back abruptly to the present conversation.

'No, Papa, of course not just *la Signora.*' Tino recognised the amused glint in Papa's eyes and flushed with embarrassment. 'All of them. Signor Fonte, the boys…' dark lashes brushed his cheeks as he dropped his gaze, 'and she said perhaps Mara might be able to help Mamma and the girls out, too.'

'Ah! The lovely Mara, too.' Papa nodded once again, enjoying teasing the boy. 'Yes, the help would be good, and at least this time we should have a crop worth harvesting, not like the paltry bits and pieces we've had the past few years, what with all those droughts.' He turned to his wife. 'The Grillos have promised to help as long as we help them in return, Lena. They've offered to lend us that big ox of theirs to pull the cart.'

'That's good.' Lena sipped thoughtfully at the goat's milk. She had an idea something was going on in her husband's mind. Lately, he was always thinking up trivial excuses to bring that Grillo girl over to the farmhouse, contriving ridiculously implausible situations that would inevitably throw her and Tino together. He may not have said anything, but she knew him well enough to guess when he had some scheme or another fomenting inside that stubborn head. And in this instance, she rightly guessed that it involved the two young people. What she hadn't guessed yet or anticipated were the plans involving Emilia and Marco, too.

Lena disliked that swaggering Grillo with an intensity that shocked her; she hated the slow, lumbering movements and his greasy, slimy, unwashed appearance. He disgusted her with his fat belly, bulbous lips and piggy little eyes; the way the coarse tufts of hair stuck out from the sides of his head, and sprouted copiously out of his ears and hooked nose made her feel sick. She despised the way he squeezed every last drop of blood from even the poorest people who rented their little plots of land from him; nor did she like the way he always overstepped the bounds of propriety, squeezing the arms and shoulders of the women-folk around here, and letting his hands slip lower to their breasts, apparently by accident, yet grabbing and mauling eagerly at the flesh with soft, pudgy fingers. And worst of all, he dribbled. It turned her stomach, especially when she caught him casting sidelong, drooling glances in the direction of her daughters. It hadn't escaped his notice that they were fast becoming women. Lena's flesh crawled at the thought.

Serafina was most definitely her father's daughter, there was no doubt. She was pretty enough, yes, but that girl was forward, too forward for comfort, and what was more, she was thoroughly lazy and spoilt by her indulgent father. Maybe they would not be so smug if they knew how the locals made fun of them, calling the blustering show off *Signor Milionario*, because he was forever bragging to anyone who would listen about how much money he had, when he knew full well that most of their neighbours lived from hand to mouth. The only one Lena had any time for was the son, Marco. He was completely unlike the others and was a good friend to Tino. He was similar to look at, too, though where Tino was already showing signs of being broad and thick-set, Marco was tall, gangling and thin as a rake. But he was a quiet, good-natured and sensitive boy, much to his father's disgust. Her thoughts were interrupted by the two younger boys squabbling.

'Mamma, he stole my sausage,' Angelo babbled, pointing an accusing finger towards Michele. Approaching four years of age, it was easy to see he was Tino's brother, as the huge dark eyes brimmed with unshed tears. Angelo was a good name for him, too, he looked almost cherubic with his plump little face and dimpled cheeks. 'Mamma, I want my sausage back.' He began to sob.

'I didn't touch his sausage,' Michele protested loudly. He was older, eight next year, but quite different in appearance from anyone else in the family, except for his hair, which was a lighter version of Emilia's. It was strong and springy with a distinct reddish-brown tint and his complexion was much fairer than the others; Papa insisted his looks came from his grandmother's family, they had similar colouring.

'Yes, he did, Mamma. He did! He stole my sausage and ate it all up.'

'Now, stop it both of you!' Lena cried, throwing up her hands in despair as Carlotta rushed to comfort the younger child. 'Emilia, cut him another slice, would you, please?'

'Why always me, what's wrong with Carlotta? Why do you never ask her?' Emilia retorted, her voice sulky.

Lena raised her eyes to the heavens – she never asked Carlotta, because she never needed to, the girl did things without being asked. But she was quite sure this was just a phase her daughter was going through, she was normally a good, biddable girl but at the age when girls sometimes behaved out of character. She would soon come out the other side, a normal human being again. However, Raffaele's reaction was rather different.

'Don't you dare speak to your Mamma like that!' he interjected crossly, and the argument stopped in an instant. He stood up quickly, sending his chair clattering onto the stone flags beneath. 'I've had enough of this quarrelling and noise, I'm going outside, there is plenty of work to be done and at least a man can get some peace out there.' He stopped just long enough to snatch a battered straw hat off a nail at the back of the door and left, slamming it behind him.

'Now look what you've done!' Lena remonstrated sharply. 'He will have a head like a raging buffalo for the rest of the day now.'

Emilia's reply was to flounce away from the table and begin to clear the breakfast dishes away with exaggerated movements, interspersed with lots of theatrical puffing and panting. While all this was going on, Carlotta had quietly and efficiently cut another slice off the long sausage and given it to Angelo, who was now snuggling up on her lap, sucking contentedly on his thumb. His eyes drooped and he began to snore softly.

Lena sighed heavily. 'Tino, you'd better go and help Papa,' she said, handing him two cloth bundles, each containing a hunk of bread, some cheese and her own special meat pies, together with a flask of water. She knew they would be out in the fields until dusk began to fall, and would be hungry later on. Afterwards, she would send the girls up to the woods to collect the wild mushrooms that grew there in abundance.

Taking the bundles from his mother, Tino obediently followed his father out into the fields.

It was always Raffaele's answer, walk away from a row, that was his way. She was the woman of the house, it was up to her to keep her daughters in check. There were times when Lena was tired of the rows, she wished he would give her a little more support. To make matters worse, for some reason he favoured Emilia and their son, Francesco, above all the others. He would avoid a confrontation with her at all costs, when in fact he should have been putting her in her place. It was time they thought about getting a husband for Emilia, that was what she needed. It might be difficult, but surely someone would take her on?

Tino found his father a little way down the track, mending a wall. He watched him for a few moments, marvelling at how deftly his fingers worked with the rough stone.

'What can I do to help, Papa?' he asked quietly, handing him one of the food bundles. Papa stopped and looked up from his work, tipping the straw hat to the back of his head. He was calmer now, working on the land always had that effect on him.

'Take the sheep further along the mountain, son,' he said.

'The grass here is still too dry and sparse for them, even with all the rain we've had this year. They need better pastures than this.'

Tino nodded. He was always pleased to be working with 'his' animals, he preferred it to anything else, even the wine making, which he also enjoyed. Papa was right, the grass was thin and patchy here, and lacked nourishment. But he knew the exact spot where he would find excellent pastures, thick and lush, that would fatten the sheep, so the ewes would give good, rich milk for Mamma to make the pungent Pecorino cheese that was his favourite.

Whistling for the two dogs, Tino made his way down the mountain for the second time that day, though now with a small flock of sheep and a couple of goats for company, bells tinkling as they went. He passed the spring, pressing onwards towards the valley and the river, driving the sheep onwards before him. The Melfe was one of several rivers that ran here, making its way ever-downwards over rough rocks and boulders. Right now, it was little more than a benign stream, gently washing the stones on the bed until they glistened in the sun. There were a couple of gnarled tree trunks straddling the narrowest part, providing a crossing point, but the river was so low that its bed was clearly visible and one could walk across quite easily, rendering the makeshift bridge redundant. It was different in the winter months though, after heavy rain, and even in the early spring, when the snow in the highest regions started melting; then, the river could become a raging torrent and no-one Tino knew would dare to cross when it was like that.

Guiding the sheep towards a shady bank alongside the river, he waited until they began to chew, watching fascinated as their jaws worked from side to side, pushing stray bits of grass out of their mouths. Yellow, black-slitted eyes glazed over with pleasure. Tino settled down in a hollow against a low hedge, calling the dogs away from the river, where they were cooling themselves off. There was a strong scent of wild garlic permeating the air and he felt content. He sat there for some time, thinking of nothing in particular, though Mara was never far from his mind. Later, the rumbling noises coming from his stomach announced it was time to eat. The food was good, and he ate avidly, throwing the occasional crust towards the ever-hopeful dogs who hovered around nearby. He settled back again, comfortably full. The only sounds were the occasional bleating of the sheep answering the calls of others in the far distance, and the monotonous buzzing of bees as they gathered nectar from a profusion of wild flowers. His eyes became heavy and his lids drooped.

When he woke up, the sun was already dipping in the sky. With a start, he knew he would have to begin the return journey straight away if he was to be home before dark, he certainly didn't relish the idea of being out here alone with just the sheep and wolves for company. Rubbing the sleep from his eyes, he splashed his face with the cool water from the river. Putting two fingers between his lips, he whistled in various pitches and volumes, as he instructed the dogs to round up the protesting sheep. Then with a sense of urgency, he drove them back up the stony track towards home.

After supper, Raffaele settled himself in one of the rickety old chairs that flanked either side of the fireplace. He puffed lazily on a cheroot, a habit he had acquired in England, and one which Lena hated.

'Those things stink!' she grumbled.

Little Angelo settled at his feet on a faded rug his grandmother had made and which now bore no trace of the original multi-coloured patterns which had once brightened up the room.

He was playing with a little wooden bird which Tino had skilfully carved for Michele, but who now pronounced himself far too grown-up for such things and passed it on instead to his younger brother. Lena sat in the chair opposite, fingers moving dexterously as she patched yet another hole in Michele's trousers. Tidillia, a fat black and white cat, purred contentedly, curled up in a furry ball near the hearth.

Tino dragged the wooden settle away from the table, so there was room for the whole family to sit in front of the fire. Despite the intense heat earlier in the day, darkness came suddenly in the mountains and the temperatures would drop dramatically at night, so they were glad of the warmth from the flames. The fire gave additional light, too, for the only other source in the room was a couple of old lamps, which were far from efficient and smelly.

But they enjoyed these times together, after a hard day's work. Tino waited for the ritual – he knew exactly what would happen next. Papa would clear his throat, then expertly direct a gobbet of spittle straight between the bars in front of the fire. Only then would the stories would begin. Sure enough, Papa D'Abruzzo was true to form.

'Now, then,' he began, leaning back in the chair and puffing away on the cheroot. 'It was very hard work in England in those days, out in all winds and weathers, carrying that huge drum and all the other bits and pieces.'

'What other bits and pieces, Papa?' Michele asked eagerly. He knew exactly what other bits and pieces, because they had all heard the story time and time again, but they never tired of hearing Papa's tales because there was always something a little different. He was a natural story-teller.

'Well, now, let me see...' he paused for effect, puffing thoughtfully now at the black stick as it dangled perilously out of the side of his mouth. 'There were those big, enormous, gigantic cymbals tied with leather straps to my knees, so they would clatter and bang as I walked along. Oh, yes, and the shepherd's pipes that would whistle a strange tune when I blew into them.'

'Yes, Papa, go on...'

'And, of course, the drum. Huge, it was, enormous! It was so big I could hardly lift it, let alone carry it around all day. And it would go 'bang, bang, bang, boompety bang bang bang!''

'What about your clothes, then, Papa? What did you wear?

'Let me see, now, bright red coat – too small for me, of course, and I couldn't do all the buttons up – not that there were many left, anyway – and baggy yellow trousers that flapped above my ankles. All patched and wrinkled, of course...'

'Tell us about the hat, Papa,' Michele asked excitedly. His face was beaming with anticipation.

'Ah, yes, the hat!' Again, Raffaele paused for effect, smiling benignly. 'Oh, Michele, *mio figlio*! If only you could have seen that hat! Everyone who saw it wanted my hat! Like a big, upside down cone, it was – you know, like those big wicker ones we use for carrying the cheeses – with little pom-poms and golden bells that would tinkle when I shook my head from side to side, or nodded up and down. Ah, but it was my lucky hat. Now, one night, I had settled down under a tree just outside a big town, tired after a long day, and I put my precious hat on the ground beside me, thinking it would be safe enough there. I was very tired and before long I was snoring like a great fat pig.' He mimicked the sounds, which brought a roar of laughter from the family, for they all knew how loud his snores could be and it was almost an insult to a pig to compare himself with one. He waited for the laughter to die down, then paused for effect before going on.

'Well, next thing I knew, there was this big commotion around me, shouting and screaming and yelling. A gang of thieves had seen me with my hat and the leader wanted it for himself, so they had followed me. They crept, closer and closer, so as not to wake me, and just as they were about to steal it … well, what do you think happened?'

They knew what was coming next, but even so, they shouted, 'Tell us, Papa. Go on, tell us!'

'Well, just as they reached out to steal my lovely hat – at that very same moment – it began to move! Right in front of their eyes, it began to move. Crept along the ground, it did.'

There was a gasp from Michele and his eyes widened like two saucers. 'All on its own?' he breathed.

'Yes, all on its own!' Papa nodded. 'Now, by this time I was wide awake and watching everything that went on, though I didn't let on to the robbers, for they might have killed me – it was very dangerous out there, then! Anyway, each time they tried to grab the hat it would move further away from them. But … what they didn't know was my little secret! Giaco, my little monkey, used to sleep under that hat, it was his very own bed. And of course, he did not take kindly to being disturbed from his sleep, so he kept running away from them across the field. In the end, they ran off terrified, as fast as their legs could carry them, tripping up and bumping into trees as they went, screaming to their friends that the hat was cursed, and it must have evil spirits inside.' He paused, taking a deep puff of his cheroot. 'And do you know,' he paused dramatically, 'they never, ever bothered trying to steal my hat again!'

Lena smiled wryly to herself as they all clapped in appreciation, begging for another tale. Raffaele began to tell them about the time he and his brother Giuseppe played what they thought were their best tunes outside a very big house, only to get a chamber pot emptied over their heads for their troubles. 'Full it was, too,' he told them. 'And smelly.' He pinched his nose with his fingers to emphasise the fact, resulting in more howls of laughter from his audience.

He was unaware that Lena was studying him intently. She knew her husband better than anyone, but she observed him now with an unaccustomed feeling of detachment. Raffaele was a good man underneath, a good father, and the children worshipped him. So why did she feel so irritated by him lately, so angry? In her heart she already knew the answer. Since Grillo had come along, Raffaele's driving force was no longer the love of his family. Instead, he was consumed by a lust, an obsessive passion for wealth and power.

Lena sighed heavily. She loved him, of course she did, he was her husband yet she wasn't blind to his faults. 'He's lived through bad times, but so have most of us – times of real poverty, ruined crops and empty bellies. But now he seems to think it's compensation time, and why?' She shook her head sadly. 'Because somewhere in his mind, he thinks money will buy him respect. If only he would realise that he already has the respect and love of the people who count most – his family.'

Chapter 3

IT WAS NEARING the end of August. Soon, it would be the Feast of the *Madonna di Canneto*, when the village priest would lead a procession of the Faithful up the winding path that led to the church of San Lorenzo in Picinisco, the village above. Tino was especially excited this year, because he and his friend, Marco Grillo, had been specially chosen to carry the two enormous candles that flanked the cart which carried the statue of the Madonna, resplendent in golden robes and a crown of flowers. The cart, too, would be decorated with flowers, usually by the women of Picinisco and the surrounding hamlets. It was a tremendous honour to be allowed to carry the holy candles and Tino was hoping that it would not go unnoticed by Mara.

He had seen her a few times since that day at the spring, mostly after Mass, when small groups of young people would gather and talk about nothing in particular. Tino was good-looking and many of the young girls would get shy and giggly when he was around. Serafina Grillo, though, was much bolder in her approach and would unashamedly flutter her lashes or lean boldly against him at every opportunity, much to the shock of observers nearby and to Tino's embarrassment. His mother had noticed how she played up to him, too and would shake her head in disapproval. Tino, though, had eyes for the other girl only and Lena did her best to encourage that. The Fontes were good people who made an honest living, unlike the Grillos – the origins of their fortune were dubious.

Everyone looked forward to the *festa*, it was a time to relax and celebrate the fruits of the dying summer and welcome in the autumn and impending winter. Soon the harvesting would begin – first, the fruits from the vines that appeared in places to cling precariously to the thin soil that supported them; and the maize, the staple basis for the flour, coarse and unhusked, from which polenta, bread, and pasta were made. Some had tried to grow wheat, but it was hard, if not impossible in this thin, alien soil and most farmers gave up after just one attempt. Gathering the maize was often the hardest work, especially for those who were too poor to have their own donkey or ox, but families often helped each other out. Even then, more work followed, for the corn had to be ground and stored.

Plump ripe tomatoes were gathered and washed, spread out to dry in the sun. Afterwards, they would be bottled and stored. Plums, too, would be left to dry until they shrunk and withered into juicy purple prunes.

Finally, the olives would be gathered, first the loose ones shaken from the trees by a dozen sturdy men who would rock the silver-grey trunks until the fruit fell into nets held below by the women. Those olives that clung resolutely to the branches would be picked by hand later. No-one here had their own press and families would take it in turns to have their sacks of olives pressed between two stone wheels which were pulled around in endless circles by a reluctant donkey, at the communal press in Picinisco. Tino loved to watch as the huge rutted stones squashed the olives hard and the rich liquid oozed out, oily and sweet. The fleshy pulp and anything else left over from the pressing would be used to fertilise the soil.

Strangely, though, much of the fruit except the figs, went to waste – the family would eat as much as they could, but all kinds of fruit – peaches, pears, apples, lemons, limes, plums, oranges, cherries – grew in such abundance there was a glut, too much for anyone. They even tried loading up the donkey one day and taking it to the market in Atina, but everyone else had the same idea. By the time they walked the miles to the market there, everyone had bought or traded all the fruit they needed; firmer and fresher than theirs, too, after the long walk. But the animals would feast on the windfalls from the trees so they didn't entirely go to waste. Now, there was much to do before winter set in; but first, it was time for celebration.

The day of the *festa* dawned and Tino awoke excitedly. He hadn't slept much anyway but, pulling on his trousers, he went over to the well and washed. It promised to be another hot day, but the water was icy cold and Tino shivered.

He bounded up the steps that led into the house but was quickly shooed away by Lena, who was fussing around like a startled hen.

'No, no, you can't come in yet,' she cried, flapping her hand at him. 'Your sisters are getting ready for the *festa*, they're not decent.'

Just behind her, Tino could make out the battered old bath in front of the fire, steam rising up to the wooden beams. It was not practical here to bath too often, but Lena insisted they did 'at least once a week, unless you want to get covered in filth and vermin'. The only other time the bath came out was on special days and holidays. Tino should have remembered. Little ones first, then Mamma, then the girls; they would take it in turns and share the water. But even if it wasn't too dirty, by the time the last one got in, the water was always cold. Tino remembered how some years ago, after working all day in the fields, Papa took the first bath, followed by Francesco, who was still home at the time. Tino was last and by that time, not only had the water become so cold it made his teeth chatter together, but even worse, a slimy scum had formed a thick dark rim around the top. He hadn't wanted to get in, but Papa made him. At least now, with just Papa and himself, it wasn't quite so bad.

It was some time later that the whole family emerged from the house, shining like new pins. Tino was dressed in his best clothes – an old suit Lena had traded for some cheeses in Atina. It had been made for a much bigger man, but she was clever with a needle and had altered it to fit. But that was a few years ago, he had grown since then and it was much too tight for him now. The buttons fought with the buttonholes and the sleeves finished several inches above his wrists; bare ankles protruded like two little sticks from the bottom of the trouser legs.

Mortified, he protested. Surely Mamma could do something. But she waved her hands about in agitation, replying, 'Mother of God, save me! I'm a good needlewoman, yes. But Tino, a miracle-worker I am not. How can you expect me to make cloth from nothing, eh? I can't put back what's been taken away. If you want a miracle, you'd better go and ask the Madonna, not me!'

Tino was sorry he'd spoken. He was lucky to have a suit at all and felt ashamed for being so ungrateful. He may not have realised it, but everyone would be looking at him, not his suit. His eyes were shining with excitement and his hair glistened blue-black through droplets of water that had not yet dried. He looked more handsome than ever.

Lena and Raffaele, too, were dressed in their best; the coarse black working apron Lena usually wore was replaced with a spotless white one. She had made it herself, including the fine lace which ran all along the edges. The two youngest boys had been scrubbed until they shone; little Angelo clung tightly to his mother's hand while Michele trailed obediently behind.

The two sisters were transformed, dressed in the traditional costume of the area – long red skirt, white blouse with puffy sleeves and a black bolero embroidered with brightly coloured flowers. Their white headscarves were edged with hand-made lace. They chattered nervously as they discussed their forthcoming duties in the procession.

Tino and his two sisters raced on ahead of the family, for the procession could not begin without them.

The procession started at the very bottom of the hill, collecting people from the surrounding villages on the way, a multi-coloured snake with the priest at its head, wending its way up the narrow path toward the church in Picinisco. Behind the priest came Tino and Marco, each supporting a large candle in a long, carved wooden holder, followed by the platform carrying the Madonna. No-one could possibility have guessed that it was made of simple wooden planks; for weeks before, the villagers had worked on the decorations, covering the rough wood with coloured cloths and countless bells that tinkled with the slightest movement. There had been several squabbles and heated rows as arguments broke out about exactly where each ribbon and decoration should be placed. As a final touch, that morning, the villagers had placed a thick carpet of wild flowers in every imaginable hue at the feet of the bejewelled Madonna.

From her great height, she smiled down benignly on the gathering below, swaying gently on the shoulders of the six men who had been given the honour of carrying her to the destination. Next came the young girls of the villages, followed by the rest of the faithful, all craning their necks to get a glimpse of their beloved Madonna. Everyone sang and some of the locals played various instruments in honour of their beloved

Madonna. Tino knew that Mara would be among these and his heart skipped a beat at the thought. Soon, they reached the little church at the top of the hill, where it nestled serenely in the shadows of the ancient castle above. The Madonna dutifully followed the padre and the candle-bearers into the cool dimness inside. Gently, she was placed into the alcove above the altar, where everyone could get a good view of her. There wasn't room for everyone to get inside the church all at once, but later, they would file past, making the sign of the cross before pressing their lips to the feet of the Virgin, pinning all their hopes and wishes for the future on her generosity and beneficence. For some, this would be something as basic as having enough food to put on the table; others had more ambitious or selfish requests. But Tino's hopes were simple enough. And it was afterwards, when the fun and feasting began – that Tino would see the object of his dreams.

In the piazza, long wooden tables had been pushed together and covered with brightly coloured cloths. Countless platters of food beckoned invitingly, bread, olives, fruit, sausages – *le salsiccie,* – and cheeses of all descriptions, all piled high on huge dishes. There was a whole pig, too, roasting on a giant spit above a fire, and jug upon jug of wine, red and white, each with its own taste unique to the region. Long trays of trout, freshly caught from the rich stocks of the Rava or the River Melfe below and liberally sprinkled with herbs, cooked just long enough for the flesh to fall away from the bones and melt in the mouth. Everyone had contributed something to the feast, even the poorest among them.

Women fussed around, making sure everything was perfect and toothless old men gathered in small huddles, some leaning heavily on sticks, others more agile, ready and waiting to dance with anyone who would let them.

Tino stood alongside Marco, staring in wonder – every

year it was the same, gaily coloured banners and streamers, food piled high, but it never failed to cause his jaw to drop in amazement. Just then, he caught an unmistakeable glimpse of fair hair among the dark-headed peasants. It could only be one person and grabbing Marco's sleeve, he almost dragged him across the piazza to where he had seen her.

By now, the band had started to tune up – accordions, shepherd's pipes and *zampogne*, or bagpipes, strove to keep time with each other. Someone had dragged a battered, out of tune piano, with several keys missing, from somewhere. Soon, the dancing would begin and Tino hoped to have the pleasure of Mara's company.

Marco knew what Tino had planned, and when he hesitated, swallowing hard as he desperately tried to pluck up courage to ask Mara's father permission to dance with his daughter, he gave him an encouraging little shove in the small of his back.

'Go on!' he remonstrated with a little laugh. 'If you leave it any longer, you'll be like those old men over there, too old to dance!'

Giving one last nervous glance towards his friend, Tino stepped forward. 'Signor Fonte,' he nodded, '*Signora*.' He inclined his head politely to each of Mara's parents in turn. 'May I dance with your daughter, please?'

Signora Fonte gave a swift, knowing glance towards her husband. She had already told him of her hopes where Tino D'Abruzzo and Mara were concerned; she hoped he would remember.

He hesitated a moment, as if thinking it over. 'Well, why not, young Tino?' he said after what seemed an age. 'But you look after her, now!'

Dusk had already begun to fall and the candlelight on the tables cast shadows, so Tino did not see the mildly amused look that crossed his face. He was painfully aware, though, of the interesting effects the flickering candles had on the bald pate, lighting it up so that it shone like a beacon, and he was glad he hadn't taken a moment longer to answer, for he had been terrified his nerves would make him laugh out loud.

Mara, resplendent in her costume, lowered her lashes modestly, but Tino could sense she was every bit as pleased as he was. Custom and etiquette wouldn't allow him to hold her hand but he guided her towards the centre of the piazza, where other couples were preparing to dance. He saw his sister Emilia with his friend Marco – he knew that Marco liked her, he had told him so, and she seemed more than happy to have engaged his full attention too – head tilted back, abundant chestnut curls spilling from her headscarf, she was looking up at him and smiling with something akin to adoration in her eyes. This came as a revelation to Tino; he had never seen his sister look like that before.

The band finally struck up a tune. Mara offered Tino a white lace handkerchief and he took hold of one corner; during the dancing, no physical contact was allowed, even their hands must not touch, but it excited Tino to know that it was only the width of that thin, gauzy piece of cloth that kept their hands apart. The music started, at first a slow, even tune, and the couples danced and swayed gently around in a big circle as the onlookers clapped in time; Mara raised her lashes, gazing into Tino's eyes and he was lost. He had dreamt of her many times since that day at the spring, but he knew now beyond all doubt, as she looked up at him with a longing that matched his own, he wanted to marry her. And her eyes told him everything he needed to know – she felt the same. He made up his mind there and then. In a year or so, when he was a little older, he would approach his father and hers, tell them of his intentions. As the pace of the music increased the clapping got faster, too. The dancing became more sensual, the couples moved within inches of each other, painfully close but never, ever touching. Faster and faster they whirled around, heads spinning until they were dizzy.

Tino suddenly lost his grip on Mara's handkerchief and before he realised what was happening, it was no longer her face looking up at his but Serafina's. How did that happen? She stood before him, hips swaying provocatively, and her hand grasped his tightly before he had time to snatch it away. Tino flushed with embarrassment as he noticed how she had deliberately tugged the lace-edged scarf down to where the neckline of her blouse sat low over her breasts, exposing an indecent amount of flesh, defying all modesty and convention. He didn't know what to do. As they spun around, ever faster, Tino desperately tried to pick out Mara's face in the blur of the crowd. But he couldn't see her.

His mother had watched the scene in utter disbelief; how Serafina had slyly bided her time, waiting for her chance to grab hold of Mara's abundant fair hair and spitefully drag it backwards, causing the girl to stumble and lose her footing. As she struggled to retain her balance, Serafina seized the opportunity to step in quickly, taking her place in the dance with Tino.

Lena's face was dark with fury as she watched that shameless, disgusting girl making up to her son, the lovely head thrown back brazenly in wild abandon. How dare she, she and that low-life father of hers? She turned to Raffaele, opening her mouth to voice her displeasure, but stopped in her tracks. It was pointless; he was already full of food and wine, joking and laughing jovially with the pig-eyed Grillo. All she could do was grit her teeth and wait until the dance ended to rescue her son.

★

The maize harvest had begun and several families came to help the D'Abruzzos. Grillo, in return for a promise of help when their turn came; but in most cases, the people helped out in return for some of the fruits of the harvest, since their own plots of land were so small they couldn't hope to produce enough to feed their families themselves.

True to his promise, Grillo had lent them the big ox to pull the cart. They had two donkeys, but they were getting old and lazy, and the ox was much stronger, able to carry a full load of sacks at a time. The work was hot and hard, for the sun still shone brightly – not with the fierce heat of the summer sun, but still high enough in the sky to bring warmth to the earth. Working quickly, they picked the golden maize, placing it into big baskets until they were full to overflowing. Women and girls worked alongside men and boys; the young children would have competitions, see who could fill the baskets quickest. Marco Grillo and Tino helped his young brothers by slipping them some of the corn they had gathered themselves.

Tino put a warning finger to his lips. 'Now, this is our secret,' he smiled, eyes glistening. 'You mustn't tell, or they won't let you win!'

'But isn't that cheating?' Michele asked, a puzzled frown crossing his brow. 'Mamma says we shouldn't cheat!' He had been working hard and his forehead was damp, flushed with heat and excitement. Marco burst out laughing.

'Of course it's cheating!' Tino grinned. 'But do you want to win, or not?'

The conversation was interrupted when Tino became aware of a shadow falling across the rows of corn. Mara was standing there, holding a jug of a lemon drink which Mamma had made from their own lemons. For a moment, he was tongue-tied. She spoke first.

'Your Mamma asked me to help her with these drinks,

take them around to everyone,' she explained. 'But she said I should come to you and Marco first, because you have the young ones with you and she was afraid they would be getting very thirsty by now.'

'Thank you.' Tino took the small mug she offered and took a long drink. The taste of lemons was strong, but it was cool and refreshing. Michele and Angelo, too, drank greedily, holding out the empty mugs and demanded, 'More, please!' much to everyone's amusement, and they laughed out loud as Mara refilled the mugs.

'I would really like to talk to you later.'

It was only when Mara answered shyly, 'Yes, I would like that, too,' that Tino realised with embarrassment he had spoken aloud. He blushed furiously.

'I… er… I'm sorry, I didn't mean…' he stammered.

'Perhaps we will get a chance to talk later, when the work is done,' she spoke softly, a little smile curling up the corners of her mouth. At the end of the day, when the sun lowered in the sky, everyone would sit down and strip the leaves from the corn, talking and laughing and generally making merry whilst they did so. Usually, some of the men would bring their musical instruments, and sing and play – not always in tune, especially after they had downed several jugs of wine; but no-one really cared, it was the camaraderie that was important. Some people, especially the younger ones, would dance too, making a real occasion of the aftermath of hard work.

'Yes.' Tino's eyes shone. 'We will talk later then, and that's a promise.' He watched for a few moments as she threaded her way gracefully through the other workers. It was a busy and vibrant scene; some were to-ing and fro-ing, carrying full baskets on their heads to where the ox waited patiently, then emptying their load into big sacks on the back of the cart. He couldn't wait until evening, but meanwhile, he turned back to his task, though now with renewed vigour.

'Maybe your girl should talk to you more often; it's certainly got you moving a lot faster!' Marco teased mercilessly.

'She's not my girl!' Tino muttered.

Determined to have the last word, Marco replied, 'Ah, but she soon will be!'

From the shadows of the barn, Serafina had been watching every move and was not happy. Her eyes darkened with unspent rage. She would tell her Papa, she would! He would make sure that nothing happened between that girl and Tino. Tino was hers!

That evening, Lena D'Abruzzo and her daughters, together with Rosa Fonte and Mara, and a few other willing hands, prepared food and drink for the workers who were now ready for fun, reaping some of the benefits of their hard work in the fields. Lena and Rosa made sure that they took up the greater part of a small bench, spreading themselves as far as they could across the seat, leaving just enough room for two people at one end. Mara and Tino were the only ones not yet sitting down.

Lena threw a smug, self-satisfied look in Rosa's direction as the two young people sat self-consciously next to each other. The wine flowed and the music played. The older people chattered and laughed, raising their voices to be heard above the music.

'Tino, why don't you and Mara go for a little walk?' Lena suggested. His head snapped around as if it were on a string. Had he heard correctly? If he didn't know better, he would swear their mothers were trying to push them together. 'Go on!' she flapped her hand daintily. 'What do you young things want listening to two old hags like us, eh? It's a beautiful night, the moon is shining; take her to see those new kittens our Tidillia's just had. Ah, that cat, she is so brazen, every tomcat in the neighbourhood chasing her and even worse, she let's them catch her.'

Rosa Fonte's reply was heavy with sarcasm. 'A bit like that one over there,' she whispered, making sure only Lena could hear her. She nodded towards a tree where Serafina stood, unmistakable by the silky length of black hair reaching well beyond her waist. She tilted her head back shamelessly to receive the kisses of one of the local men, at least fifteen years her senior, all the while stealing sly glances in Tino's direction, checking whether her ploy to make him jealous was working.

But Tino's eyes never left Mara, as he guided her towards the barn where their cat had unexpectedly given birth to four mewling kittens.

'They are beautiful!' Mara cried, clapping her hands together in delight. 'And so tiny! Can I hold one?'

Her eyes shone as Tino placed one of the wriggling furry scraps into her outstretched hands. He watched as she gently stroked its soft tabby coat and the kitten responded with the beginnings of an immature purring sound.

His breath caught in his throat. 'Beautiful!' he whispered.

'Yes, you're right. They are so pretty, Tino.'

'No. I mean you. You are beautiful,' he breathed, and although he knew he shouldn't, he couldn't stop himself from lowering his lips to hers. Gently, ever so gently. It was the first kiss for both of them, pure and innocent. But in that moment, they both hoped it would be the first of many.

Chapter 4

JUST OVER A year had passed since that harvest. The following year's crops hadn't been as abundant what with poor weather and widespread droughts, though what the family had was adequate and more than most, where many struggled from day to day to put food on the table. It was characteristic of Lena that she often took little food parcels to some of the poorer families, especially where there were elderly or sick people, or where there were young children. Lena D'Abruzzo was known as something of a guardian angel, when it came to such matters, though Raffaele often chided her for giving away the very food out of their mouths.

Many other things had happened in the intervening time. Marco and Emilia now spent every possible moment together and it came as no surprise when he called on her father to ask permission to marry his daughter. This pleased Raffaele and Grillo immensely and they all agreed that the couple should be married before too long, when Emilia was just a little older.

What did not please the two men, though, was Tino's continued infatuation with the Fonte girl. Raffaele insisted that was all it was, an infatuation. But Grillo was getting more and more restless over it. Serafina constantly flaunted herself in front of Tino, always finding some reason to turn up at the D'Abruzzo house, even to the point of befriending the quiet Carlotta so that she could spend time in his home. She was beginning to grind Grillo down, too, with her constant carping and nagging, setting his nerves on edge.

'You have to do something, Papa,' she whined. 'I just can't bear it any longer, watching him with *her* instead of me.'

'I'm warning you, D'Abruzzo,' Grillo hissed afterwards, stabbing an accusing finger into the centre of Raffaele's chest. 'I'm warning you now, if my Serafina doesn't get Tino, you can forget about all these fancy wedding plans for Emilia and Marco!'

'Oh, come on now,' Raffaele replied unhurriedly, superficially calm but desperate to placate the agitated Grillo. 'You should know me by now, *amico*. Do you really think I'd let anything happen to spoil that?'

He would never let Grillo see it, but he was starting to get worried himself; this thing between Tino and Mara had gone on much too long for his liking and he couldn't risk his favourite daughter losing her young man because of it. He would have to do something before it was too late.

'Well, you just remember this!' Grillo spat, so close that Raffaele recoiled in disgust as a shower of saliva spattered his face. 'No Tino – no wedding for Emilia!'

Tino and Mara, encouraged by the two mothers, continued to seize every opportunity to be together and he often wrote her little love notes. It was true he did not write very well, but even so he knew all his letters and could put together a few simple sentences quite adequately. The only schooling he had received was very intermittent; Papa said he was more use on the land and what good would all that reading and writing nonsense do, anyway? He himself had never found the need, and if he needed to sign his name, well – he could just put a cross! It was only since the 70s this nonsense about school came about, before that the priests provided all the education they needed and that was good enough for them. Even the priests weren't happy about it, people in high places interfering in their lives, telling them what to do, taking over the role that had long been the sole province of the priest. Tino, though, proved to be an able pupil, he was bright and learned more in the few odd times he'd attended school than most.

It was he, then, who read out the letter that came from his brother Francesco, in England. It was delivered by the son of a neighbour who had himself only recently returned from London. Francesco could write very little, with even less schooling than his brother, so Tino knew he must have got someone to help him with it. Laboriously, he spelt out the words that were scrawled on a scrap of cheap paper, dog-eared and grubby after months of travel.

Dearest Mamma, Papa and my dear sisters and brothers.
Soon I will be home for a short visit, not long after you get this.
I am going to Rome to join the Army.
Your loving son, Francesco'

The D'Abruzzo family were thrown into confusion. Their first reaction to the news that Francesco was on his way home was one of elation and excitement, but this was quickly tempered with fear. There had been widespread unrest since Garibaldi and the unification of Italy some years before. More recently, news had reached even these remote parts of the shocking collapse of the big banks and of course, the huge scandal with the Banca Romana, which had printed enormous sums of money illegally, and arranged dubious 'loans' for many high-profile politicians. Italy was in financial crisis with widespread political unrest; there had been revolts and riots in Sicily. Francesco Crispi, the Prime Minister, had recently sent Italian troops to a place called Ethiopia, but they suffered many setbacks. The country was in a fragile and volatile state.

These things didn't often touch the remote Colleruta and other, nearby villages, life tended to go on the same, day after day as it had done for centuries. Now, though, Francesco

D'Abruzzo was talking about joining Crispi's army, probably going to fight in the war, facing who knew what? They had lost children already. And they were frightened for him.

Every day, Lena would scan the rocky path leading up the hill to Colleruta, her hand shading her eyes against the sun that sunk lower and lower in the sky as Christmas approached. Then one day, her patience was rewarded. The weather had turned decidedly colder and a few flakes of snow had begun to fall. She wrapped her woollen shawl tightly around her shoulders, giving a little shiver as she stopped to scrutinise the road. She could just about make out a dark shape heading for the house, no more than a speck in the distance. But as it got nearer, she soon recognised the familiar shape of her eldest son.

'Raffaele, Tino, everyone…' she called loudly. 'Come quickly, it's Francesco! Francesco's coming, he's home!'

Her excited cries brought everyone running from the house. 'Francesco, Francesco,' they called in unison, waving their hands to welcome him. Tino could hardly wait. This was his big brother coming home. After Papa, the man of the house. The brother he looked up to.

They were soon rewarded as Francesco returned the greeting. Angelo had only been a tiny baby when his eldest brother left and he didn't really remember him, but realising something special was happening, he began to jump up and down excitedly.

At last, Francesco reached the little party comprising his closest family members. After many weeks of travelling from England, he had managed to hitch a lift on a cart for the start of his journey that day, but he had still had to tackle the last few miles from Atina on foot. The sheer pleasure of being home at last overcame exhaustion, though, and after hugging everyone in turn, he picked up little Angelo and swung him high in the air.

'Hey, bambino, you have grown so big,' he laughed, a deep rich sound. Francesco, too, had grown up since he had left, no longer the gawky young lad Lena had watched tearfully disappearing into the distance with his Zi Giuseppe. And he was more handsome than ever, too – a lot like Tino, in fact.

Angelo suddenly became shy and tucked his head into his big brother's neck. The few flakes of snow that had settled there tickled his nose and made him sneeze.

'*Avanti*! Let's go in!' Francesco said. 'It's freezing out here and this little man will catch his death of cold if we don't get him inside.'

The house was warm and welcoming, with a huge log fire burning in the grate. Many people didn't have the foresight of the D'Abruzzos, they collected wood all through the summer, storing it in a corner of the barn to keep it dry, ensuring they had a good supply of fuel for the winter. There were sacks of olive stones, too, saved from the pressings, and dried – these made excellent, slow-burning fuel to supplement their wood stocks.

Lena fussed around, making sure Francesco had everything he wanted. For days, she had kept a constant supply of soup bubbling in the pot above the fire, anticipating his homecoming and the first thing she did was make sure his belly was full. Tino too, desperate for his brother's approval, rushed to meet Francesco's every need.

The soup was hot and wholesome, made with lamb and vegetables into which Lena sprinkled slivers of Pecorino cheese from their own sheep. It was Francesco's favourite, he liked the texture, the way the cheese went stringy and chewy in the hot liquid and he ate hungrily, tearing at the hunk of black bread and dropping small pieces into the soup to soak up the juices. He hadn't eaten properly for some time and now, stuffing his stomach to the point where he felt he might explode, he left the table replete.

Papa gave up 'his' chair at the side of the fire to his son and they all sat together, drinking one of Lena's warming cordials which she had made from wild berries, and roasting chestnuts over the bright flames. Tidillia the mother cat and her now fat offspring, huddled together on the rug in a sprawling tangle of paws and tails. They listened, eyes wide, as Francesco recounted some of the things that had happened to him in London and beyond.

Tino was fascinated, wondering what it would be like to experience all those strange sights and people in a foreign land. He loved his big brother and longed to be just like him. Even when Tino was very small he would follow him around and try to copy everything he did. Now, he was hanging on to his every word intently.

They all listened and laughed until they reached the point where none of them, especially the younger ones, could keep their eyes open a moment longer.

'I think it's time we slept,' Mamma suggested, and was met with cries of, 'Oh, not yet!' and, 'Do we have to?' from the younger children. 'Yes, we do!' Mamma replied. 'Poor Francesco, he must be exhausted and you're not giving him a moment's rest! Don't worry, he'll still be here tomorrow.'

Francesco became quiet. 'I won't be staying very long, Mamma,' he said, almost apologetically. 'I've already joined up with the *Bersaglieri* in Rome, if I hadn't volunteered now, they would have called me up for service sooner or later, anyway. But I have to go back soon after Christmas. Oh, and that brings me to another thing.' Turning to his brother, he explained, 'Tino, now I've left, Zi Giuseppe is all on his own, there's no one to help him with the business in London. He asked if you would go in my place.'

There was a stunned silence. Everyone in the room had been taken by surprise and Tino didn't know what to say.

'I… I don't know,' he stammered. 'I've never been further than Atina and that only a few times, with Mamma or Papa, taking things to market. And on my own, well…' his voice trailed off uncertainly.

'But it would be a good opportunity for you!' Raffaele interrupted, enthusiasm sending his voice a pitch higher than usual. He had prayed for days for an answer to his prayers and God had now sent him this golden opportunity. 'Of course you must go! Zio needs you and apart from that, just think of it – you will travel, see the world! And just look at all the money you will make.' He turned back to his eldest son. 'Isn't that so, Francesco?'

'Well, yes, I've seen so much and it's true, I have made good money. Even with the money I sent home, I still have some savings.'

'There, then, it's settled!' Papa Raffaele's eyes gleamed triumphantly. Send Tino away for a few years, he'd soon forget about the Fonte girl and be more than ready to accept Serafina as his wife on his return. Two years should do it, they could have a double wedding then, with Marco and Emilia. 'You will go and help your uncle.'

'Raffaele, let the boy have his say! He has a tongue in his head!' Lena's voice was sharp and her brows were drawn together in annoyance. She was cross, she had seen her husband push people into making decisions against their will before, he would make up their minds for them before they even knew where they were. 'Let's hear what Tino wants to do.'

'Mamma, I don't know,' Tino began hesitantly. In most things, he loved nothing better than to emulate his brother, follow in his footsteps. Francesco had always been his hero and nothing would ever change that. Conflicting ideas raced through his mind. 'I could earn lots of money like Francesco, make Papa proud of me,' he thought excitedly. Then the doubts came rushing to the fore. 'But London! It's so far away from everything, everyone. They don't even speak the same language.' Panic began to set in as the full implications hit him. London might have been the moon as far as he was concerned.

'What's there to think about?' his father butted in. 'It's too good an opportunity to miss!'

'Raffaele!' Lena chided and shot a withering glance in his direction

'I'm not sure,' Tino said quietly. 'I would miss you all so much. And what about Mara?'

'If she really loves you, then she'll wait for you!' his father cajoled. Realising that his son was beginning to waver, he pressed the point home. 'Look, go and see her tomorrow, tell her you're going away but you'll come back for her, a rich man who will be able to provide everything she could ever want. Come on, Tino,' he coaxed. 'Do it for Mara! Two years will fly, you'll regret it for the rest of your life if you give up this chance.'

Lena shot a glance in her husband's direction. To her dismay, she noticed the sly glint, an unnatural brightness in his eyes and her heart sank.

Christmas Eve arrived, bringing with it the first real falls of snow of the winter. Despite this, though, the D'Abruzzos and other villagers from around braved the cold weather and trudged up the hill to attend Midnight Mass, making the sign of the cross as they walked past the nativity scene, marvelling at the look of serenity on the Madonna's face as she gazed lovingly down on the baby Jesus. It was with mixed feelings that Lena realised it was the first time the whole family had been to Mass together since Francesco had left for England.

The announcement Raffaele had made earlier that day, though, made it clear that her happiness would be short-lived. In a few days' time, Francesco would be leaving to become a soldier. But that was not all. This time, he would not be leaving alone.

'It broke my heart when Francesco went before,' Lena thought in despair. 'How will I bear it, parting with two of my boys at the same time? How can I stand by and watch them go?' She turned to the statue of the Virgin Mary as hot, unshed tears stung the backs of her eyes. Hadn't the Madonna been a mother herself? She knew above all the pain of losing a son, she would understand.

'Madonna mia,' she prayed. 'Why is this happening? I'm so afraid for my sons, yet all Raffaele has done is encourage them. I can't bear to think of Francesco in some wild, war-torn country, not knowing what horrors he might have to face. And Tino, my gentle boy, trudging the streets of England. Please, I beg you, make them change their minds. Let them stay.'

Pearls of tears slipped down her cheeks as she turned away. She dashed them away hurriedly before Raffaele noticed. He would only tell her not to be so silly.

The more she dwelled on the situation, the more uneasy she became. She would talk to Francesco again, at the first opportunity. Despite her love and fears for him, she was angry with him, too. He should at least be supporting her over Tino, not siding with his father.

Her thoughts turned to Tino. Lena had watched helplessly as Raffaele and Francesco had finally worn him down, all the time impressing on him what a wonderful opportunity he was being offered.

'Going to London will be the making of you,' Francesco had assured him. 'It will make a man of you and a wealthy one at that, someone people will look up to.'

'Then Mara's father will welcome you with open arms as a son-in-law, a man who could provide for all her wants and needs,' Raffaele had interjected.

But despite this, Tino still felt huge misgivings and had lain awake at night, wondering what to do. He dreaded leaving his homeland, his family and Mara and he was afraid he would not cope.

He hadn't even yet plucked up the courage to tell Mara he was going away. 'I'll tell her after Christmas, I don't want to spoil it for her,' he had hedged, though his mother suspected the delay was as much about his own uncertainty as it was concern for the girl. As if these thoughts had conjured her up, Lena noticed the girl and her family taking their places just ahead of them. Mara waved cheerily, her cheeks flushed with cold. Lena had grown fond of the girl, Tino could do a lot worse – that Grillo girl, for instance, though she knew Tino had more sense, he could see beyond Serafina's pretty face and would recognise her for what she was. But this other girl would make a fine daughter-in-law and give her beautiful grandchildren.

The next day, Christmas morning, the family went about the usual tasks, seeing to the animals before anything else. Few people in these poor regions could afford to buy presents, though the D'Abruzzo family had rarely gone without – Papa, Francesco and Tino were all skilled at whittling useful or attractive little novelties out of wood and Mamma and the girls would sew little gifts for everyone, or cook some special treats. The younger children were sitting on the floor playing with their new toys – mostly recognisable as the animals that lived on the farm. There was even a model of Tidillia and the other cats, the wood smoothed and polished until it shone golden brown.

The girls made a new woollen shawl for Lena and she in turn had made skirts for them out of wool she had spun and dyed herself, boiling up a concoction of wild berries and other plants to produce a rich burgundy red colour. There were other gifts too – Francesco had brought some of the deep brown, pungent cheroots Papa favoured from England, keeping them until now; and a little ornament for his mother's mantelpiece. To Tino, he gave a small book – he had drawn in it directions to all the best places to go with the barrel organ, the places where most money could be made.

'You'll find this good, it will help you find your way,' he explained. 'It is easy to get lost there, it is bigger than you would ever imagine. I know I got a shock when I first went there, but you soon get used to it.'

Raffaele had given him money, too. 'To help you on your way to England,' he had announced proudly.

The day wore on and a veritable feast was cooked and served up by Lena and the girls. Tino, though, refused to eat any meat, except for the chicken, much to his mother's dismay. It wasn't that he was ungrateful, but it was the young, suckling pig he had reared by hand after the mother's milk had dried up. He had become so attached to it, it was truly upsetting to see it now, nothing more than a charred carcass instead of an appealing little animal with a character all of its own. It was inconceivable that he should now be expected to sit down and eat it as if it were any old pig. Afterwards, though, there was fun, laughter and merriment all round, with Papa and Francesco trying to out-do each other in the story-telling arena.

Later, as the day wore on, Tino announced his intentions to go to see Mara. It was a fair walk away and his mother insisted he wrapped up well; it was getting colder by the minute. It also gave Lena the chance to approach Francesco and see if she could change his mind. She wheedled, she begged, she pleaded, but to no avail.

'Mamma, I've made up my mind,' he told her quietly, but with such firmness that it brooked no argument. 'I'm going and nothing will stop me. And Tino is coming, too'

She was distraught, but realised any further pressure would be pointless. Francesco was like his father, single-minded; when his mind was made up, nothing on earth would shake his resolve. She shook her head sadly.

Some time later, after a brisk walk, Tino arrived at the Fonte home.

'Come in, Come in!' they all cried together. He was always welcome in their home. He accepted a warm drink and listened to the family chattering on, about Christmas, the weather and nothing in particular. He was uncharacteristically quiet, and a little restless, but no-one really seemed to notice. Eventually, when he announced he would have to leave for home before it got too dark to see his hand in front of his face, Signora Fonte and Mara walked to the door with him.

'Thank you, *signora*, for the drink,' he said, then, 'Would you allow Mara to walk to the gate with me, please?'

'Yes, of course!' she replied with a smile. 'But only if she puts on a nice warm shawl first!' She handed Mara her own shawl which was thrown across a chair.

The young couple walked in silence to the gate. Tino did not know how he was going to tell her he was going away, but it had to be done. He had to be strong for both of them.

Turning to her, he handed her a small packet, wrapped in a piece of brightly coloured paper. 'What is it?' she asked.

'Open it, and you'll find out!' Tino smiled gently.

Mara carefully unwrapped the tissue, extracting from its folds a small carving in the shape of a heart, with two love birds holding a ribbon between their beaks. On each side of the heart, were carved the initials T and M, surrounded by a circle of flowers. Mara looked up at him with tears in her eyes.

'Tino, it's beautiful!' she breathed. 'It must have taken you so long to make!'

A lump formed in his throat, preventing him from answering. Instead, he reached out and took her hand in his, gathering his courage.

'It's to remind you of me when I'm away,' he whispered.

'When you're away?'

'Mara, I have to go away. To England. Francesco is going to the army and Zi Giuseppe has no-one to help him.'

'No, Tino, NO!' she cried. 'I couldn't bear it without you!'

'Mara, listen!' he begged. This was going to be harder than he'd thought. 'I didn't want to go either, but Papa made me see sense. He talked to me, made me realise! If I go to England, I can earn good money, plenty of money.'

'But I don't want money, I want you!' The blue eyes filled with tears.

He kept his voice steady. 'I didn't want to go, either, at first,' he went on. 'But I need the money – to marry you!' Defying all convention, he put his arms around her and hugged her tightly. 'Mara, say you'll wait for me, please. When I come back, I want to make you my wife.'

'Tino, Tino!' Her emotions were in chaos; how could someone be so sad yet so happy at the same time? 'Of course I'll marry you. I love you!'

'I love you, too!' he said. 'Please don't forget me when I'm away. And I will send you messages whenever I can.'

'Yes, you must, or I'll think you've forgotten me!' Mara teased.

Tino held her even tighter. 'How could I possibly forget the beautiful girl I'm going to marry?' he smiled.

A few days later, just after the first light of day dawned to reveal a still, white landscape, the whole family gathered to wave goodbye to Tino and Francesco. They were subdued as they watched them slipping and sliding down the snow-covered slopes of the hill; Lena had trouble holding back the hot tears and Raffaele was quiet, feeling a few pangs of something that might have been the stirrings of a guilty conscience, but he soon brushed those aside. He was thinking of the boy's future, of course he was. He would thank him in time. Serafina was there too, despite not being invited to what was obviously a private family farewell party. But early as it was, she was thick-skinned enough to walk over to the D'Abruzzo house on the pretext of visiting her friend Carlotta. She was shameless, and threw her arms around Tino as if she would never let go, crying hot tears against his cheek until Lena pulled her away sharply. She had no time for the girl at all and made no attempt to hide it.

Lena was not fooled by Serafina's tears and she turned away abruptly, releasing her vice-like grip on the girl's arm as she did so. Her emotions were in turmoil. She had a desire to take Serafina by the shoulders and shake her until her perfect little teeth rattled. She was shocked by the small voice in her head that kept telling her that Francesco was as much to blame for Tino going as his father was. He had encouraged him every bit as much as Raffaele. She had a right to feel angry with him. Yet overshadowing this was an overwhelming ache, so intense it became a physical pain as she watched her sons move further away. She was frightened for them, frightened for their safety and a wave of panic washed over her as she realised there was nothing she could do to change things now.

Mara had said a tearful goodbye to Tino the night before; she swore she couldn't bear to watch him go. He consoled her with the promise of marriage on his return. Lena was trembling as she watched the forms of her two sons get smaller and smaller as they disappeared into the distance, wondering what the future held for them and praying to God to keep them safe from harm.

Raffaele's mood, though, had changed. Any discomfiting thoughts had been relegated to the back of his mind and now he was becoming increasingly hopeful, convinced now that in time, the plans he and Grillo had made together would come to fruition. All they had to do was sit back patiently and bide their time.

The weather was bitterly cold, and the boys were grateful for the extra layers of clothing Lena insisted they wore, including the warm, woollen mufflers made from lamb's wool which she had spun herself, then skilfully weaved on the loom in the corner of the farmhouse. They had soft, if well-worn, cloths wrapped around their feet, especially their toes, to help prevent blisters on their long journey. Tino's feet were hardened and tough after all the years of walking barefoot, preferring to feel the grass between his toes rather than wear *le ciocie*, the local leather sandals that tied onto the feet and lower legs with thin straps – it felt strange, now, to have them encased in a pair of his father's old boots that Lena traded for some eggs in Atina a few years before. Francesco had already experienced the luxury of shoes given to him by Zi Giuseppe in London, albeit a few sizes too big with holey soles, so that he had become adept at stuffing them with layers of cardboard to keep out the rain and cold.

The boys were fortunate enough to hitch a few cart rides on the road to Rome, walking briskly in between to keep warm. Even so, progress had been slow and as dusk began to fall they were forced to stop in a small village some miles away from their destination. They handed over a few coins each for a just-palatable bowl of hot but thin soup, and a hunk of stale bread. They also had the dubious privilege of a bed of straw in a stone outbuilding, for their money. One or two resident sheep bleated softly at the interruption, lifting their heads in a half-hearted greeting.

There was a basic transport system in place, particularly in the northern regions. Railways had sprung up in various places since the 1870s with much of the wood needed for the tracks taken from the forests on the southern slopes, severely denuding those areas and creating landslides in their wake. But as yet the railway system was intermittent and unreliable, with tracks often ending in unexpected places; and travellers were often forced to continue their journey by foot, cart or carriage, as their pockets and stamina would allow, until they reached the next link in the rail network. Francesco explained to Tino that often, it was probably quicker and cheaper to travel on foot, only using the railways when it was absolutely necessary; otherwise the money Papa had given him would soon be swallowed up and there would be nothing left for food. It was true, he said, that many of the previous generation, including their own father and Zi Giuseppe, had walked all the way to London, – except, of course, for the boat, – a journey that took many, many months, busking and doing other odd jobs on the way to earn a crust of food or some money. No need for it to be as bad for Tino, but he should still be prudent. Lena had already taken the precaution of sewing hidden pockets on the inside of his coat, so that most of his money could be kept out of sight, for 'there are ruffians and robbers out there who wouldn't think twice about slitting your throat for next to nothing.' she had warned. He was a big, strong boy who could put up his fists along with the next one, but this talk of knives had scared him. How could fists compete with a knife?

Casting a disapproving glance in his mother's direction, Francesco reassured him. 'You'll be fine, but you must keep your wits about you.'

The next day, the brothers reached Rome. Soon, it would be time for them to part, each going in opposite directions – Francesco, to the barracks where he would proudly wear the uniform of the *Bersaglieri*, resplendent with its plume of black cockerel feathers in the hat; Tino, in contrast, would embark on his long journey to London. Tired as he was, and given the fact that he had spent much of the night picking off sheep ticks which had hungrily attached themselves to him, he had still been excited and overawed by the sights in the centre of Rome, things he had only every heard about or seen pictures of in the one-room school in his home village. It was loud, and noisy, and boisterous, and colourful.

'A bit like London,' Francesco informed him knowledgeably.

'Now, don't forget, Tino,' he urged as they said their final farewells outside the gates of the barracks in Rome. 'Keep your eyes and ears open and keep your money well-hidden. When you get off the boat in Dover, Zi Giuseppe said you must go to this address.' He handed Tino a piece of paper. 'They will take you to Zio, then, in London. And don't look so serious, *mio fratello*.' He had caught the glimmer of a tear in Tino's eye. His younger brother might have the body of a man but he was still very young and naïve, and Francesco was eager to reassure him. 'They are good people, friends of Zio, and me, too. They will look after you, I promise.'

Tino nodded, not quite convinced. Someone in uniform

appeared at the gate behind Francesco, and murmured something to him which Tino didn't quite catch; Francesco replied then turned back to his brother.

'So, this is it, *mio fratello*,' he said, his own voice husky with emotion. 'Time for me to go!' He hugged his brother and for a brief moment, neither of them could speak.

'Take care, Francesco. I'll say a prayer every night for God to keep you safe.'

'And I will do the same for you,' Francesco promised. The guard behind spoke again, urging him to get a move on. '*Si, si*!' Francesco nodded vigorously. 'Now, I really have to go, Tino, they are waiting for me.'

Tino watched as his brother was led away, not sure when, if ever, he would see him again. Like Lena, he was frightened for him. Sad and alone, he took the first few steps that would eventually lead him to London, his home for the next two years.

Chapter 5

TINO'S JOURNEY HAD for the most part been uneventful as he travelled through countries like France and Switzerland, names he had only ever heard of before. Few people took notice of one young peasant boy among all the others. The boat trip, though, had been the one thing he wouldn't forget in a hurry. The crossing had been rough and overcrowded, with everyone jostling, elbowing and pushing for space. The rank smell of unwashed bodies in close proximity became overpowering, especially for someone used to the clean, fresh scents of the mountains of Italy. His head spun relentlessly and he felt more sick than he had ever imagined possible. He had spent most of the crossing fighting to keep the contents of his stomach where they belonged and when the famous White Cliffs came into view, he heaved a sighed of relief. He staggered gratefully off the boat, the pale olive skin taking on a decidedly greener hue.

It hadn't been hard to find Zio's friends, the Bartolomeo family, who lived very close to the port of Dover. About the same age as Lena, Signora Bartolomeo was thin and wiry, with shiny black hair that was tied into two braids crossed over each other on top of her head. Tino thought she looked austere, but when she smiled, all traces of hardness and severity were swept away in an instant. Signor Bartolomeo, in contrast, was shorter than his wife, fat and round, with loose floppy jowls around his chin. His hair too was black, but he had a thin area on top over which was carefully arranged a few strands of longer hair from the back of his head, slapped down with scented pomade to keep it rigidly in place. His eyes were bright and kindly, two shiny black buttons that nestled deep in the plump folds of his face.

Tino already felt comforted by the reassuring presence and familiarity of his own country-folk after his long, lonely trek across Europe. They embraced him, and greeted him in his native dialect as if he were a long-lost friend, then immediately offered him food.

'*Grazie, ma non per me*,' he replied, even the thought of food causing his stomach to begin its gymnastics routines again. 'I'm not hungry. But I'd like a drink, please,' he had added.

Later, although it was already well in to the day, Tino and his few belongings were bundled onto a rickety old cart pulled by an equally rickety old nag. Signor Bartolomeo made a meagre but sufficient living as a rag-and-bone man and he was proud of the cart – he had painted it himself, with bright red wheels with blue and yellow sides and his name proudly emblazoned in big black letters that he couldn't read.

They set off after saying goodbye to Signora Bartolomeo. Although it was not the smoothest of rides, compared with the boat it was heaven and Tino even managed to doze off a few times. It was a long journey and Giuseppe had arranged for them to stop overnight at an inn. They started out again at sunrise next morning after a hearty breakfast and the addition of a fresh young horse. Although the weather was good, progress was not as fast as Tino had hoped and they were forced to spend a second night at another inn, this one closer to their destination.

Tino was still feeling the effects of the long weeks of travelling and once more, on the final part of their journey, he kept nodding off. Eventually, he fell into a deeper sleep, only to wake with a start when a nauseating, acrid smell of something unrecognisable filled his nostrils. 'Ohhh. What is that smell?' he asked the older man, holding his nose.

'What smell?' came the puzzled reply.

'Well, I don't know. It's horrible. Like fish, and stuff rotting.'

'That is exactly what it is!' replied Bartolomeo, his plump jowls shaking with laughter. 'They say it's better now than it used to be, but London still stinks, especially the poorer parts and around the Thames. Trouble is, the drains block and the stench comes back up onto the streets. And that's even before you begin to take into account the piles of horse shit on the roads everywhere. But don't worry, a day or so here and you won't even notice it.'

Tino hurriedly pulled himself up in the cart, looking around in astonishment. Already he was beginning to regret his rash decision to come here and an image of the gentle, scented slopes of home, with his family and Mara, popped unbidden into his head. Hot tears readily pricked the backs of his eyes. Where were these wonderful 'streets of gold' everyone back home spoke about?

The sky was grey and a fine drizzle began to fall. A light mist swirled about them. The streets were grey. The lofty, dark buildings were grey. All around was dirt, filth and squalor, worse than anything he had witnessed in Rome, which seemed entirely civilised by comparison. Everywhere he turned were the unmistakeable signs of deprivation and poverty.

To the left, ragged, grubby children played with wooden hoops on the cobbled street, while a snotty-nosed little girl sat on a doorstep watching, all the time scratching enthusiastically at a mop of brownish, matted hair. A mangy dog hurtled out of the door and past the child, coming to a sudden stop and yelping loudly as its cornered quarry, a cat of indeterminate colour, defended itself heroically by scramming ferociously at its adversary's nose. To the right, a small group of three or four men, clothes filthy and in tatters, swayed drunkenly, singing something which Bartolomeo identified as a well-known Irish ditty. The people here were clearly as poor as those in the remotest parts of Italy; but at least there they had open, blue skies and clean, mountain air. Tino was horrified at the scene unfolding before him.

'Nearly there, now,' Bartolomeo announced brightly. The sombre look on Tino's face hadn't escaped his notice and he sympathised. He had felt the same when he had first come to these parts of London, but Tino was young, he'd soon adapt. That's how it was with young people. Bartolomeo nodded in silence, more to reassure himself than Tino. 'We're in the Holborn district now – you'll soon get to know the area. We're making for Leather Lane, there's a side street off there, that's where your uncle is staying.'

Tino couldn't bring himself to answer. His mind was working overtime – how could he possibly stand this for the next two years? He was strong, he was determined, but he hadn't expected this.

Ignoring the absence of a reply, Bartolomeo went on, 'You'll meet lots of other Italian boys around here – you might even know some of them.' He was trying his utmost to keep his voice cheerful and encouraging, but it was useless denying it, this was not the most savoury place to be.

The population of Holborn and Clerkenwell consisted mostly of immigrants mainly from the various regions of Italy. As their numbers increased, an Italian church and a hospital were built, though as in Italy, many families didn't take advantage of the schools that had been provided and classes were often poorly attended. There was a significant Irish and Jewish presence there, too. Accommodation was mostly dirty and overcrowded, but cheap. The location was ideal for the organ-grinders and ice-cream sellers, because it was just a stone's throw away from the centre of London, where they would often do a roaring trade.

Tino still hadn't replied and Bartolomeo decided it was best to give up his attempts at conversation; they were only a few streets away now, in any case. They turned off into a series of narrow back-streets. The only sound was the rhythmic clip-clopping of the horse's hooves until they pulled up with a loud, 'Whoa, boy! Whoa!' outside a several-storeyed building with tattered paper at the windows, through which a few vestiges of yellowish light escaped.

'This is it, then,' he smiled at Tino, whose eyes were wide with horror. '*Avanti*! I'll come in with you, we'll find your uncle together,' he patted him reassuringly on the shoulder. He handed over the horse's reins to a young stable lad who held out his hand in return. Bartolomeo knew this was his cue to press a coin into the small fist, which he did with a wry smile - this would ensure the safety of his horse and cart.

It was dim inside the lodging house and it took Tino's eyes some time to adjust. It was noisy too, and crowded with men, women and children of every imaginable shape and size. At one side of the room, someone was cooking over a huge metal slab with holes in the base. From it came a plethora of cooking smells which vied with each other for attention, and a thick haze of bluish smoke swirled merrily in concentric rings about the cook's head. The smoke made his eyes sting and he was relieved to make out the tall, lanky shape of Zi Giuseppe coming towards him from the opposite side of room. He had been very young when he had last seen his uncle, but he hadn't changed at all – thick, wavy black hair, overly large nose and full mouth over which nestled a moustache that was so thin, it looked as though it had been drawn in pencil. Tino was comforted by the knowledge that he was with a relative and his uncle slapped him heartily on the back in welcome.

'*Mangiamo*!' he invited Tino and Bartolomeo. 'Let's eat, you must be very hungry.'

Tino was surprised to discover that indeed, he was and he tucked in greedily to a dish of greasy fish, bread and cheese. The cheese was hard, not like the good stuff they had at home, but it was edible, despite the edges being flecked with small spots of green-grey mould.

They sat at the table on a long, wooden settle and Tino could not understand why the knives and forks were chained to the tables. He said as much to Zi Giuseppe, who promptly burst out laughing.

'Because, if they are not chained up, they will get up and walk away all on their own!'

Tino's eyes widened as he thought of some of the frightening tales he had heard back home. 'Zio,' he asked in a quiet, trembling voice. 'Are you trying to tell me there are evil spirits in this place?'

Zio and Bartolomeo bellowed with laughter, rocking back and forth and holding their sides, until the tears ran down their face.

'Oi! Wha's all this noise, 'en?' a slurred voice with an indeterminate accent demanded. They turned to see a short, pugnacious looking man with a long, black beard and a small scar above his right eye swaying alongside their table.

'What's it to do with you?' Giuseppe answered, still laughing at Tino's naiveté. It would take a long time to exorcise the centuries-old superstitions of his homeland, where legends of ghosts, curses and evil spirits roaming the mountains were rife.

With lightning speed, the man's hand shot out and grabbed at his collar, bodily lifting him off the settle. The room suddenly went quiet.

'Are you bloody-well laughin' at me?' he accused. The

scowling face was so close that Giuseppe smelt his breath, fetid with stale beer; he could even see tiny red blood vessels bursting with anger, flooding the whites of his eyes and turning them pink. Without further warning, the man threw his head back, then forwards, in one swift, continuous movement, butting him full force in the face. There was a loud crack and blood streamed from Giuseppe's nose. Tentatively, he wiped it with the back of his hand, and studied the crimson rivulets for a few seconds in stunned silence. Suddenly, the room erupted.

Giuseppe was well-known in this lodging-house, he had many friends who raced to his defence, vaulting over tables and leaving wooden benches upturned in their wake. Tino was petrified. He hadn't understood a word of the exchange, but he had eyes, he saw the way things were going. His first thought was to help his uncle, but he knew he was tired and weary from the long journey and would not come out of it too well. Instead, some primitive instinct for survival came to the fore and he pressed himself hard against the wall, well out of the way of the brawling. The fight was short-lived, though and ended with the bearded man being thrown unceremoniously into the street, amidst strict instructions from one of Giuseppe's friends 'never to come back unless yer want yer balls cut off wiv a blunt knife an' fried fer me supper wiv onions'.

Still dabbing at his bloodied nose, Giuseppe apologised to the landlord. 'I didn't start it, he just came at me.' he explained.

'Don't worry, I saw what happened,' he replied, patting him on the shoulder. He reminded Tino a little of Mara's father, with his shiny head and fair features and, shaken up by the fight, a pang of longing for home hit him unexpectedly. 'We're better off without the likes of ruffians like him here,' the landlord continued.

Giuseppe heaved a sigh. 'Time for bed, I think,' he

announced. Bartolomeo, too, was staying until morning, it was too late now for him to start the return journey home, he would never get there in one piece.

He led the way up a dark, narrow staircase filled with eerie shadows that danced and moved in the dim light of the lanterns. Tino shivered.

Their 'bedroom' was in fact a dormitory, consisting of one long room, with around twenty to thirty narrow beds squeezed in tightly against each other. Some people had already retired and in the dimness, Tino could just about make them out. They were crammed three, four and even five to a bed. There were heads, feet and arms everywhere. It reminded Tino of Tidillia and her kittens.

Giuseppe indicated a bed to Tino. 'For tonight, because you have had a long journey, you can have the luxury of a bed to yourself, I paid extra for you.' His voice was not unkind. 'I couldn't afford to do it all the time, though, it costs four pennies a night each as it is.'

Despite the day's events, Tino was snoring within moments of laying down his head. He was by nature an optimist and his last thought had been, 'Maybe things will be better in the morning.'

Giuseppe looked down at him thoughtfully, noticing even in the semi-darkness how much he resembled Raffaele and Francesco, with his black curls and finely shaped features. His brother's son was turning into a handsome young man but he had a lot to learn yet. There was poverty in England, as there was in Italy, but life here was hectic, with dangers he would need to be told about. The chaos of the London streets couldn't be more different from the slow, simple way of life he had known in the remote mountains of Italy. Francesco had learned quickly; hopefully, Tino would do the same.

Tino awoke early. Snores, in every imaginable pitch and tone, struggled for supremacy over a variety of loud grunts and groans that emanated from every corner of the room. Why had he woken? he wondered. His left leg was itching and he scratched it idly; then his hand moved up to his arm, and he scratched again. Sitting bolt upright, he suddenly remembered picking off the sheep ticks in the barn in Italy. Oh, no, not here, too? Diving off the bed and running to the window, he pulled up a corner of the yellow paper and inspected his arm in the faint light. He found a small, red bump, like a little pimple, which was swelling up before his very eyes, but there was no sign of any ticks. Panicking, he checked his leg; sure enough, several more bumps, but not a tick in sight.

Puzzled, he turned back to the bed and immediately recoiled in horror. A whole army of dark, scaly bugs were scurrying around, frantically trying to relocate their now absent source of food. Their flat, ridged bodies were swollen and bright red with fresh, human blood – Tino's blood. He shuddered, fighting to resist the urge to scratch his body until it bled.

He shook Giuseppe frantically, calling out his name to wake him. There were cries of, 'Shush!' – a sound universal enough for even Tino to understand, but right now, he didn't care.

'What is it?' Giuseppe mumbled, still half asleep.

'There are things in the bed, they are horrible!' he cried, shuddering again. 'Look, look!' he pointed to a series of red bumps that were now prolific enough to be called a rash. 'They bit me!'

By now, half the room was awake, shouting and cursing at being woken up well before their normal time. Bartolomeo raised his head up to see what all the fuss was about. If Tino hadn't been so preoccupied, he would have been highly amused to see the long, pomaded strands of hair standing to attention at least six inches above his naked pate. Giuseppe sighed heavily.

'Madonna!' he muttered under his breath. 'They're just bugs. Bed bugs, that's all! Have you never seen a bug before?' He delivered this in their own dialect, in spite of his unspoken resolution to talk to Tino in English so that he could learn, too; for he was angry and irritated at being woken up over nothing. He had been there for many years now and although he still spoke English with an accent, he was proud that he could speak more of the language than most of the other Italians he knew.

'Ticks, yes! I see plenty of those!' Tino nodded. 'Fleas, too. But bugs – no!'

'Well, you'd better get used to them then, cos you won't find many places without them! And it's a miracle you got off that ship without picking up a few yourself.' He paused accusingly. 'Maybe you even brought them with you!'

Seeing the offended look on the boy's face, Giuseppe relented slightly, lowering his voice. 'Look, if it makes you feel better, I'll take you to the public baths later, you probably need one anyway. But it'll cost, an' it's extra if you want soap, so it'll come out of your wages!'

Mollified, Tino agreed. The closest he'd ever got to a bath was the one that Mamma used to drag in front of the fire, or running and swimming into the cool waters of the River Melfe, splashing himself all over. Francesco had told him these public baths were huge and quite amazing. Even so, the thought of sharing his bed every night with those disgusting creatures was unbearable – he'd thought ticks were bad enough, but these disgusting vermin were a thousand times worse – and even the promise of a real bath was little comfort.

Chapter 6

AFTER A SCANT breakfast of weak tea and bread, they said their goodbyes to Bartolomeo before making their way to the baths. As Francesco had promised, the washhouse and baths were like nothing Tino had ever seen before. A mixed bag of men, women and children lined up in separate queues, and if they'd paid their ha'penny each, they were handed a sliver of slimy carbolic soap and a towel, before they disappeared one by one through big doors that led into areas segregated according to gender.

'Tuppence for a second class tepid bath an' a penny for a cold 'un!' a skinny, uniformed superintendent proclaimed theatrically. The superintendent had the most luxuriant, bushiest whiskers Tino had ever seen; it was quite impossible to see the man's mouth and instead, the thick, unmistakeably Cockney accent seemed to emanate from the depths of the whiskers themselves. 'Or o' course, you can go first class, if you're willing to part with fourpence fer 'ot an' a shiny thre'penny bit fer cold!' Tino didn't understand a word, and turned to his uncle for guidance.

Zi Giuseppe had no intention of bathing himself, hadn't he had one just two weeks ago? 'We'll-a take-a da secon' class, cold-a!' he announced imperiously, with an Italian accent that was as thick as the other man's Cockney one. He had lived here for many years, but there were times when it suited him to exaggerate the sing-song lilt, usually when he wanted to avoid opposition or to get out of a tricky situation. This was one of those times. 'An' just-a da one. I no wanta bath today!' Zio hadn't filled his pockets to bursting by wasting money.

Why pay a penny extra, just for a drop of lukewarm water, when cold would do the job just as well?

Tino joined the queue, complete with bright pink soap and rough towel, and was soon swallowed up behind the big door. He was amazed at the sight of the huge baths, shielded behind wooden panels in rooms lined with shiny white tiles. He hesitated for a few moments before getting in to the water, terrified he might drown in its beckoning depths. However, he finally took a deep breath and plucked up the courage to test it out, first with his toes, then quickly followed by the rest of his body. It was icy cold and the shock made him gasp for air. Soon, though, he was scrubbing away enthusiastically at his hair and body with the pungent carbolic soap, in an effort to remove all traces of the vermin he had encountered the night before. He emerged eventually feeling clean and refreshed, though the bites still stood proud from his skin and itched mercilessly.

'Soon, the work begins!' Zi Giuseppe promised him. '*Avanti*! Let's go and meet the boys you'll be in charge of.'

They walked for some time, through a maze of narrow streets leading off each other like a rabbit warren, all flanked by the same tall, grubby buildings either side. Tino was quite convinced they were going round and round in circles and said as much to his uncle.

Giuseppe laughed. 'No, Tino, I know my way around here like the back of my hand, I promise you.'

'Are you sure, Zio?'

'*Sì*! Quite sure! Won't be long now.'

They emerged out of the dark lanes suddenly; it was as if someone had lit a giant lantern. Tino blinked. Here, the streets were wide, with an expanse of sky and a wintry sun above; everything suddenly seemed lighter and brighter. There were public trams and big, smart carriages pulled by fine horses.

Rows of more lowly carts and drays lined up at the side of the road as they made their deliveries; flat-capped errand boys ran at full pelt, and scores of people milled around; some stopping to admire the wares in shop windows, or going about their daily business. Many simply strolled along, enjoying the freshness of the winter's day.

The men were either sporting tall hats or wearing round ones with a brim which Tino later learned were called bowlers; others wore flat, cloth caps and mufflers, the latter not dissimilar to his own; many ladies wore plain, flat-brimmed hats while the more extrovert and wealthy among them displayed amazing concoctions resplendent with flowers, feathers and bows. Across the street was an open square with several other streets leading off. A small crowd had gathered and Tino could hear music; it was towards this area that Giuseppe guided him, pushing him none too gently ahead of him as they dodged numerous vehicles that seemed to be coming at them at breakneck speed, from all angles. Tino tried his best to hurry, but he wasn't used to traffic like this and his feet flapped around loosely inside the overly-large boots. He decided he would rather brave the traffic than Giuseppe's temper, which was legendary, and valiantly tried to put on a spurt. In his haste, though, the toe of one boot caught the heel of the other and he stumbled, pitching forward and sprawling flat onto the road, right in front of a drayman's cart. The man pulled frantically on the reins, causing the horse to rear up with a frightened whinny, its eyes rolling back in its head; then moments later its hooves came crashing down again, missing Tino's head by inches. The round wooden barrels on the back of the cart shook and rolled ominously, causing it to overbalance. It tilted first one way, then the other and narrowly avoided toppling over before settling to an abrupt stop. A torrent of abuse followed.

'Yer a bloody loonytic, or what?' yelled the red-faced man,

shaking a fat fist at Tino, who was still struggling to get up from the road where he had landed. His face was pale and he was trembling; his knuckles were skinned and bleeding and his knees hurt, but the look on the man's face terrified him. 'Tryin' ter get yersel' killed, that's wot. Oughta be locked up, you did, that's wot!'

Tino threw up his hands in submission. '*Mi dispiace, signore. Dispiace!*'

The man clapped his forehead with the flat of his hand, as the penny dropped. 'Ah, that s'plains it all, then. No wonder yer's a bloody looney.' The dray-man put a finger to the side of his head and wiggled it backwards and forwards. 'Course! Ah should'a know'd. All the bleedin' same, you bloody foreigners. Bloody 'ead-cases!'

Giuseppe grasped Tino's elbow, and helped the shocked boy to his feet. He wasn't an unkind man, not like some of the other *padroni* around these parts. He treated all the boys who worked for him well – he might shout and yell a bit now and then, that was his way – but he never ill-treated or hit them. He didn't like the way this man was talking to Tino and although he knew the boy couldn't understand a word of English, the dray-man was a big fellow and his whole manner was threatening.

'Why-a you no bladdy clear-a off an' leave-a da boy alone, eh?' he retorted.

By now, the disturbance was causing gridlock, with other carts and drays held up behind. The other drivers started calling and shouting to the dray-man. 'Gerra move on, will yer? Some o' us got work to do.' 'Fer Gawd's sake, we can't wait 'ere all bloody day!' The dray-man opened his mouth as if to reply, but the shouts from behind stopped him in his tracks. Snatching at the horse's reins, he gave them a quick shake, and with a cry of 'Giddyup!' went off down the road, muttering something about 'those Bleedin' Eye-talians' under his breath.

Tino's dark eyes were bright with tears. His first time in a foreign land, his first day in London and all he had achieved so far was to incur the wrath of the dray-man. He was upset and embarrassed.

'Don't worry, Tino!' his uncle told him. 'Likes of him are not worth worrying about, all mouth and no guts. Come on, let's take you to meet the boys.'

Giuseppe led him towards the square where the crowd was gathered. As they pushed their way through, Tino soon forgot the altercation with the dray-man. The scene was incredible; there were young boys and men everywhere selling hot chestnuts and potatoes; a young girl, pretty but shabbily dressed, offered brightly-coloured paper flowers, lace and other trinkets for sale out of a wicker basket. 'Ah made all 'em flahs mesel', mind,' she assured her customers. 'All by me own fair 'and, an' all.' Competing with her for custom was an older man, displaying a host of almost transparent coloured wax figures of birds and animals. There were one or two religious statuettes too, mostly of well-known saints. Tino was fascinated.

'*Si*, they are nice. That man is from Italy, too, but not from our area, much further north,' he explained. 'Used to be a lot of them around a few years ago, but only a few left now; some of them have gone and found jobs, others have gone back home.'

Just beyond the figurine seller Tino noticed three boys, a bit younger than himself, grouped together in a scruffy little band. He immediately recognised one of them from his home village but knew him only as Beppe. Beppe was playing the *zampogne* bagpipes, more or less in tune, fat cheeks puffing up to become even fatter with the effort; the second boy was thin and pale, with long, slim fingers that ran skilfully up and down the length of a shepherd's pipe; the sound produced was haunting. The third had a wooden music-box strapped around his neck, steadied by a long thin pole that rested against the ground. A colourful painting of two lovebirds surrounded by flowers adorned the front, a swathe of ribbon between sharp little yellow beaks, which was a poignant reminder to Tino of the carving he'd made for Mara. The boy's black eyes grew large with pride as he proudly informed Tino he had painted them himself. While he talked, he continued to turn the handle furiously, producing a series of melodious notes that collaborated effectively to form a faithful rendition of an old Italian folk song.

Their clothes were almost a uniform, greasy mufflers around their necks, well-worn jackets and trousers that were either too big or too small, and round bowler-type hats, so big they fell over their ears. All except the hurdy-gurdy boy, who's thatch of coarse, black hair stood away from his head in spiky tufts. His hat had been placed strategically on the ground in front of the band and was already almost full to the brim with coins.

'Madonna!' cried Zi Giuseppe impatiently. 'Haven't I taught you? Eh?' He scooped up most of the hat's contents and shoved it into the capacious pocket of his coat before shaking an admonishing finger at the boys. 'You mustn't let the hat get too full! I tell you, people won't put money into a hat that's too full or too empty. If it's too empty – they think you're no good, so they won't give to you. If it's too full – then they think you are rich enough already!' He heaved a loud sigh in feigned exasperation. He was in fact quite the reverse, gleeful even, for the hat had been full not just with ha'pennies and farthings – there were several sixpenny bits and a couple of shilling pieces, too. He could have sworn there was even a half-crown, but he couldn't imagine for one moment anyone being quite so generous. It had been a good day and it was still early, yet.

'Come on, Tino, you'll be looking after these boys, so you'd better get to learn their names now.' Another dramatic sigh. 'I just hope they'll do a better job for you than they do for me.'

One by one, Giuseppe introduced the boys; there was of course Beppe and, even if he didn't know him that well, Tino was grateful for a familiar face; Donato, whose face was as thin as Beppe's was fat, on the *zampogna* and lastly Salv, with the mass of spiky hair, on the hurdy-gurdy.

'Not too hard to remember, then,' Tino mused. 'And I'm pleased to see someone from home; I know we'll become good friends, I can tell' he added to Beppe.

Giuseppe, pleased with the takings of the day, sauntered off to buy some hot potatoes and chestnuts for the boys, leaving Tino to make their acquaintance. 'They've worked hard today, they deserve a treat,' he decided with uncharacteristic generosity.

The boys' eyes widened in disbelief as he returned with his cache of food. 'Hurry up, mind!' Giuseppe warned. 'You haven't got all day, there's a good afternoon's music left yet.'

They sat down on the ground, carefully placing their instruments nearby. It was a bit harder for Salv with the hurdy-gurdy and Tino helped him.

'You'd better be careful, you can't take your eyes off your belongings for even a second around here,' Beppe advised shrewdly. 'Or they'll disappear before you know it. Just like magic.' After delivering these words of wisdom, Beppe's chubby cheeks puffed up even more as he attempted to cram in as much food as he could in one go. Zi Giuseppe took the opportunity of explaining to Tino and the other boys what his latest plans involved.

'You see, Tino,' he began, 'usually the boys go out in ones or twos. Especially when they go around the houses to play.

Yes, they can make good money as a band and they are good boys, good enough to compete with any of these German ones that have been hanging around our territory lately. But I have a big idea! Better!' He finished with a theatrical sweep of the hand.

The boys watched him intently, waiting for the revelation, but he was silent, determined to eke out the suspense.

'Come on, Zio, tell us! What idea?' Tino asked after what seemed an age.

Giuseppe tapped the side of his nose, and winced audibly. In his excitement, for a split second he had forgotten his nose was still a swollen pulp, sore and bruised from the fracas the night before. 'That would be telling!'

'Oh, come on, Zi Giuseppe! Please!' Tino persisted.

Again, another long pause before he finally relented. 'I will tell you, then. I have been here now for a long time and what I have noticed in the past few years is that there are fewer and fewer of us musicians left. Yes, you did good, today, my boys, I can't deny that – but that's because I trained you to be good, you make good music and the rich people will happily pay to hear it. But the fact is, I think our kind of music is on the wane, it's dying!'

The boys looked at each other fearfully. Donato finally put their troubled thoughts into words. 'But how will we live?' asked the boy, brows drawn together in a serious face. 'We need to earn money to send back home.'

'Ah, but this is where my plan comes in!' Giuseppe was quick to reassure them. He knew only too well that the money these boys sent back home to their families bridged the thin line between plain hunger and starvation; it was the very reason why, all those years before, he and Tino's father had first come to this country, walking every step of the way, except for the sea crossing.

'The music will still be good for the winter months, especially with hot chestnuts and potatoes to sell, too. And you, Tino, you can take my big barrel organ out, from now on. But for the summer,' he paused for a few moments for effect, 'I am going to buy us some ice-cream carts. The boys were looking at him open-mouthed yet unable to utter a word. His flow uninterrupted, he continued, 'So! In winter, we will have music and chestnuts and potatoes; and in summer, we will have... ice-cream.' The boys stared at each other incredulously, then looked back at Giuseppe as if he had just lost his mind.

Giuseppe suddenly became more serious. 'I've noticed – as the musicians like us are getting fewer, so there are ice-cream sellers everywhere taking their place. And that's not all!' he added, leaning towards the boys conspiratorially. He was in full flood now, not giving the boys time to get their breath, before stealing it away again with his next statement. 'Today, we are moving out of our old lodging-houses off Leather Lane.'

Beppe piped up this time. 'Where are we going, then, Signor Giuseppe?'

'Over Notting Dale way. I'm renting a lodging-house over there for a fair price, it's all fixed up. And it's got a huge cellar, nice and cold, to make our ice-cream when the season comes. I can just see it now!' he said. 'Lovely bright carts with *G. D'Abruzzo* painted on the side.'

'You mean you are renting other rooms for us, then? In another lodging house?' Donato piped up, clearly puzzled.

'No, I mean I'm renting the lodging house!' Giuseppe beamed. 'The whole house!' His chest puffed up with pride.

'You will be a real landlord, then?' Tino asked incredulously. 'But won't that cost a fortune?'

'No, I've already thought about that,' his uncle explained. 'I've already got plenty of other lodgers ready and willing to take up the spaces there, because I don't plan to charge as much as the places like we've been staying up 'til now, the ones around Holborn and Clerkenwell. It's only fair, Notting Dale's a bit further away from the centre of London, so they'll have further to travel. Course, they could use the rail now, not like a few years ago. But then, that costs, too. It's money out of their pockets'

'Notting Dale?'

'Yes. Not that far from The Potteries.' Giuseppe replied. 'But it'll bring in a bit of extra money and I'm getting too old these days to go tramping the streets any more. So, instead, I will now be landlord of my very own lodging house!' he announced proudly. He gave the boys instructions on how to get to the lodging house; it wasn't too difficult for them, for they knew many of the landmarks anyway. His parting shot was, 'Don't come back 'til the hat's full again, though!'

With a quick wave to the ragged little band, Tino obediently followed his uncle through yet another maze of streets – past a school and a grey, forbidding place that Giuseppe, eager to show off his local knowledge, informed him was the Mary Place workhouse. 'Last place anyone would want to end up!' he warned Tino.

Further along, near the towering railway arches, he pointed out the Kensington Public Baths

'But I haven't tried that one, myself, yet. I've heard it's very nice.'

Tino noticed the overpowering smell of something he didn't quite recognise. It was strong, but not unpleasant.

'Hops!' Giuseppe told him. 'From the breweries. Where they make beer.'

He knew the area well and proudly named some of the streets as they passed through – 'Silchester Road, left into Bramley Road, then take the second on the right into

Bramley Mews.' They walked along the block for a few yards. 'Here we are, then. Number 9!' he announced.

Tino's heart sank. Bramley Mews, was every bit as narrow and dark as the other streets he had already seen in Holborn Hill and Notting Dale, with the same reek of poverty. Like all the others in the street, the door of Number 9 had peeling brown paint and grimy windows. There seemed to be hordes of children hanging around the street, a few sitting on doorsteps, others gathered in small groups, others playing. A few scruffy-looking women, arms crossed over drooping bosoms, watched Giuseppe and Tino's every move intently, eyes following in silent vigil. His uncle informed him quietly that there were quite a few gypsy families living in the area and a lot of Irish folk, too. There were often fights between the Irish and the English, especially when the beer had been flowing freely; these often started in the same way, with one of the Irish accusing the English of oppressing their people, or conversely, the English accusing them of being lazy good-for-nothings.

'If they start, just keep well out of the way, and don't get involved,' Giuseppe advised wisely. 'They're quite happy to fight dirty, with knives, even.'

Tino shuddered. He didn't have the heart, though, to dampen his uncle's obvious pride in his achievement at being master of his own lodging house, so he kept his thoughts to himself.

However, he was pleasantly surprised as he stepped over the threshold, for the walls had been freshened up with a new coat of green paint, covering up the greasy marks and fingerprints of goodness knew how many previous tenants. There were three floors plus the cellar. Unlike the common lodging house in Holborn, where the beds in the multiple dormitories had been crammed in until they almost touched, the upper floors of Giuseppe's house had been divided into neat, individual units separated by wooden partitions. They were small, but each partitioned area had its own mattressed bed, with clean sheets and a chamber-pot peeping out discreetly from beneath. Some even had tiny stoves, too.

'What do you think, then, Tino?' Giuseppe asked, after taking him on a tour of the ground floor, where he had allocated Tino and the boys their own areas – slightly larger than those of the lodgers. Giuseppe's was separate from all the others, at the other end of the room, and much larger again than theirs.

There was even running water straight from a tap, something Tino had never encountered before, in a roomy kitchen-cum-sitting-room with a high ceiling. A few plain upright chairs, wooden settles and tables, similar to those he had seen the night before, lined the walls but it was the enormous, black-leaded cooking range and fire grate that dominated the room. Papers and a few sticks had been laid neatly in the grate, but no light had been put to it yet and Tino shivered with the sudden realisation that he was cold.

Long lashes swept upwards. 'It's much better than I thought from the outside,' he answered truthfully. 'I thought it was going to be like the dirty one we stayed in yesterday.'

'Well, I'm trying to attract a better class of person here. Although I'm trying to keep the prices down to some other places, the better rooms with their own stoves are a bit dearer, a shilling a night, but at least we might not get some of the really dirty buggers.' he went on. 'We might have been poor in Italy, but we had our pride, not like some of the stinking vagabonds you get here. And the funny thing is it's some of these who've got the cheek to call us people from Italy "low-life" and "filth" and spit on us.' He shook his head. He paused, then added, 'Anyway, I've got one last surprise for you.' he said.

'What?' Tino asked, curious.

He pointed towards the door, grinning bashfully. Tino turned to see a small, buxom woman dressed in a long brown coat and matching hat, with a few silk flowers pinned off-centre at the crown. Her smile was wide, exposing a neat row of teeth with just one or two missing, and even then, the gaps were towards the back of her mouth where it hardly mattered. Tino immediately liked the look of the woman – brown hair, piled high beneath the hat, framed a round, fresh face spattered with freckles; a snub nose tilted slightly upwards and blue eyes, paler than Mara's sapphire coloured ones, twinkled merrily. Her smile widened and her cheeks dimpled fetchingly.

'Yer mus' be Tino, then,' she assumed correctly and it wasn't hard even for Tino's as yet untuned ears to guess that she had been born within the sound of Bow Bells. 'All the way from 'em forrin parts, like yer uncle.'

Tino couldn't understand a word, but her demeanour was one of friendliness. He simply smiled back in reply.

She walked over to Giuseppe's side where he took hold of her left hand and extended it towards Tino. There was a plain gold band on her third finger.

'This is Janey,' he explained. '*Mia sposa!*'

Tino's brown eyes flew open, and his jaw dropped. 'Your wife?' he gasped.

'*Si*. We only just got married, we didn't have time to send a message home.' He seemed a little embarrassed and uncomfortable, lowering his eyes to avoid Tino's, fearful of being met with reproach. Most Italian men married Italian women, it was a simple as that. It was very unusual for them to take a foreign wife. As it happened, Tino had taken to this cheerful-looking little woman instantly and was truly pleased for his uncle.

'About time, too, Zi Giuseppe!' he grinned daringly, and

his uncle laughed at his cheek. He translated for Janey, and she laughed too, a pleasant, tinkling sound that made Tino smile.

'Well, I betta get the fire goin' an' sum food cookin', those other little urchins'll be in fer their supper, soon!' Janey announced in her no-nonsense way that Tino would soon get to know well. 'An' they'll 'av ter sing fer it, too, at this rate, if I don't get a move on!'

When Tino went to sleep that night, it was in a clean bed – a rarity in these parts, but Giuseppe was right, they belonged to a proud race that endeavoured to keep that pride intact at all costs and he was determined to improve his lot. Unlike many of the common vagabonds and beggars that trod the streets of London and other large towns and cities, they refused to beg outright – they always gave something in return, whether it was music, or chestnuts, or carvings or ice-cream. You could pull yourself out of poverty if you kept your pride but it would be harder to drag yourself up from the depths of degradation.

A muddle of thoughts ran through Tino's head before the warm comfort of sleep finally engulfed him. He liked Giuseppe and was pleased for him; he liked Janey, too.

'Giuseppe reminds me of Francesco – strong, handsome, determined. And a good man,' Tino reflected. 'I want to be like him one day, to get on in life.'

Tino knew things had to change, knew he would need to change. He had a lot to learn, but it was still early in the year, a good time for fresh beginnings. Mara's face drifted in front of his closed eyes and he smiled. 'I'll miss her, of course, but I can face anything, as long as I know she is waiting for me. I'll save every penny for the next two years, and make her proud when I return. Make them all proud.' He slipped into a deep sleep, a smile still lingering on his lips at the prospect.

Chapter 7

WHILE TINO WAS starting out his new life in London, things in Italy were undergoing ominous changes. It was 1895 and there were rumblings of trouble flaring up yet again in Ethiopia.

'That Crispi, I don't care if he's Prime Minister or not, his policies are going to cause us trouble, just you wait and see!' Raffaele D'Abruzzo announced indignantly. His face was grim and he was visibly upset by the latest developments in his country.

His friend Grillo nodded agreement, fat jowls shaking enthusiastically with every movement. 'I think you're right, Raff. In fact, hasn't he already caused us enough problems? You've only got to look at those riots in Sicily and all that scandal with the banks a few years' back. There's absolutely no doubt in my mind he was involved up to his neck, what with all that "dirty money" flying round.'

'But I'm really worried about Francesco, though,' his friend answered slowly. 'This situation in Ethiopia, I tell you, it's heading for more trouble. And he's only just completing his training. But you can bet on it, they'll send them all out there, new boys or not, they won't care.'

'Well, nothing would surprise me after that other fiasco a few years ago,' Grillo replied. He ran fat, stubby fingers through hair that was non-existent, except for the dark wispy tufts either side of his head. 'If Italy hadn't double-crossed them with the Ucciali treaty, then Emperor Menelik wouldn't have got so angry, anyway.'

'That was done deliberately, no doubt about it.' Raffaele

rubbed his chin thoughtfully. It felt rough and stubbly beneath his fingers. 'Writing such an important agreement in both Italian and Amharic, it was bound to cause confusion. Little wonder things got muddled in the translation. And no wonder either that Menelik went mad when he found out they'd tricked them into agreeing to an Italian protectorate.' He paused, mentally assessing the situation, then sighed wearily. 'And now, here we are again, Italy about to dive headlong into Ethiopia and try to take it by force.

Once more, Raffaele rubbed his hand across the stubbly chin. His eyes were heavy, underscored with deep shadows and lines that seemed to have appeared almost overnight.

'But after last time, sending all those brave boys out there, with no proper equipment or trainin…' he continued, his voice heavy with concern. 'Feeding them all those lies, about how they were bound to win. And look what happened there, at Dogali? All those killed, at least five hundred …' his voice trailed off and he swallowed hard. His adam's apple bobbed up and down convulsively in his throat.

Grillo threw back his head, draining the contents of his mug. 'Well, if you ask me, it's about time we got rid of Crispi. And King Umberto, too – he's not much better than the rest of them, he's supported this venture all along.'

'That may well be,' the other man agreed. 'But they're determined to press on out there, keep the attack up. And where does that leave my eldest son?'

'It might not come to that.' Grillo, for once in his life, was attempting compassion. 'They might not send him, you know. And by the time he finishes his training, it could all be over.'

'I hope you're right!' his friend replied. 'But somehow, I don't think so.

Tino woke up the next morning, refreshed after a good night's sleep in a bed that was blissfully devoid of vermin. It took him a few moments to gather his thoughts and remember where he was, but a mouth-watering smell of cooking soon helped his memory – crispy bacon, he guessed, and perhaps eggs.

Jumping out of bed, he splashed his face and head with water from a jug placed on top of a small chest of drawers at the side of the bed. It was freezing cold – so cold he could have sworn there was a thin skin of ice on the surface, and goose bumps erupted all over his body in response. He dressed quickly and went out into the kitchen area. It was much warmer there, with a good fire burning in the grate. Tino stretched his hands out to the flames, rubbing them together gratefully.

'So, yer up, then?' Janey smiled, stating the obvious. 'You 'av a good night?' Tino looked puzzled and quick to catch on, Janey closed her eyes, and tilting her head to one side, rested it on her hands. She opened her mouth wide and pretended to snore loudly, making a series of exaggerated grunting and whistling noises, reminding Tino of his father's impressions of a pig.

'Ah, *si*!' Tino immediately understood and nodded in assent, a big grin on his face. This Janey really was nice; funny, too.

Zi Giuseppe was already sat at the table with an enormous culf of bread on a plate together with, as Tino had rightly guessed, a mound of bacon and eggs. There were sausages, too, though nothing like those they had in Italy. He laughed out loud at his new wife's acting skills and Tino's initial discomfiture; his eyes crinkled up attractively at the corners and the pencilled moustache moved upwards.

'Don't worry, Tino,' he spluttered through a mouth full of bread in his home dialect. 'You'll soon learn the language. Anyway, it won't matter a bit this morning.'

'Why not?' Tino asked. By this time, the other three boys

had joined them and were all sat around the table, eagerly awaiting the plates that Janey was piling high with food. None of them had ever eaten like this back home; their eyes grew round and their mouths watered at the prospect. They, too, were beginning to take a real liking to Janey!

'It's Sunday,' Giuseppe went on, as if that explained everything.

'Yes?' said Tino expectantly.

'Now, didn't your Mamma always tell you what good people do on a Sunday?' he laughed, eyes twinkling.

Tino wasn't quite sure which road this conversation was going down and a bemused expression crossed his face.

Giuseppe raised his eyes to the heavens. 'Holy Mass!' he replied at last in mock exasperation. 'At least we can all understand the Latin Mass and that includes you, too. But it's back to work afterwards, don't forget.'

It was true that, unlike many people who celebrated Mass, even those from other areas of Italy, they could indeed understand much of the service. The dialect of their home village was much closer to Latin than it was to Italian, a direct legacy of the Roman influence hundreds of years previously. It was only in more recent years that a few Italian words had crept stealthily into their village, usually brought in by migrant workers, returning from the bigger towns they visited on a seasonal basis in an effort to boost their meagre income.

Later, Tino and the other boys headed for St Francis of Assisi Roman Catholic church, led by Giuseppe and Janey, who had dutifully adopted her new husband's religion on their marriage.

'You will not be married in my church, otherwise,' Father Delaney had insisted and went on to issue a dark warning of an afterlife in perpetual hell, if they failed to comply. Father

Delaney, almost as broad as he was tall, epitomised everyone's idea of Hellfire and Brimstone. Most of the parishioners were terrified of him; with his huge wide-brimmed hat and black cassock that billowed around him in a dark fury, he resembled a carrion crow in full flight. Others, though, saw the kind, sensitive man beneath the hard exterior – the man who fed the hungry, ministered to the sick, even giving up his own food for those he thought were in greater need.

As a result of his dire warnings of hell, though, Janey had endured many hours of instruction in the 'True Faith,' designed to ensure she would become a good and dedicated servant of God and someone who would be fit and pure enough to receive the Holy Sacrament. However, Janey was bright and had quickly learned that as long as she knew when to make the sign of the cross and chant a few semi-recognisable words in the appropriate places, she could get away with murder. Father Delaney would never have admitted it in a thousand years, but he was deaf and didn't have a clue if her responses were correct or not.

On one occasion, when he had asked her to bring Giuseppe along, he announced imperiously, 'My dear Giuseppe and Janey, let us begin with a prayer to Our Lady.' He closed his eyes and solemnly clasped his hands together in prayer.

Janey was overcome with the sudden urge to rebel. Her eyes twinkled with suppressed mirth as she began to ad-lib the words of the prayer, all the while discreetly kicking the ankle of her husband-to-be with a stout-booted foot.

'Hale an' merry, Full o' grapes,' she murmured meekly, and Giuseppe gave a little snort. Relentless, she continued, 'The wine is in thee...' Well, no-one could deny, they'd both had more than their fill of drink in the tavern around the corner before they got there, and a second snort rent the air, louder this time. '... Playful as sinners, now an' at the 'Half a Penn'orth, Ah, Men," she recited piously. The formidable Father Delaney was greatly impressed at how quickly she had familiarised herself with the prayer and nodded his smiling approval.

Giuseppe almost choked. The 'Half a Penn'orth' was the nickname given to a local hostelry, well-known for its free-flowing ale downstairs and its bevy of willing beauties upstairs – you could get either for a half-penny, so it was said. He tried unsuccessfully to stifle the impending laughter and instead, feigned a severe coughing fit. Father Delaney was no fool though, and he shot him a glance worthy of Medusa herself.

'Giuseppe,' he uttered imperiously. He drew up already broad shoulders and somehow seemed to grow to twice his normal size. Giuseppe wondered if this was one of God's minor miracles. 'This good woman here is trying her best to become one of Us. The least you can do is behave yourself, and set a good example; you should know better! Perhaps it's time for you to go now. And make sure you come back in a more suitable frame of mind next time!' Impatiently, he almost pushed Giuseppe out of the room, and ushered him none too gently towards the panelled oak door, the heavy bolts creaking in protest as he drew them open.

As the door slammed shut behind them, Giuseppe and Janey both burst out laughing; they were still laughing when he left her at her home, where she had lived at the time with her mother and father.

The boys chatted merrily as they headed towards The Potteries; many others were travelling the same road, some they vaguely recognised from Bramley Mews and others they knew by sight from the surrounding streets – Silchester Terrace, Martin Street and Lockton Street. They had tried playing their instruments around the area a few times in the past, but were usually moved on. Even so, they knew the area quite well. All the faces were unfamiliar to Tino though, except for a few of the ragged children he had noticed on his arrival, clothes still shabby as ever and perpetually running noses. These poor families had clearly made an effort to make themselves presentable, and their faces had been scrubbed until they shone bright red, with nit-ridden hair slicked down flat to their heads with water.

One young girl in particular caught Tino's eye; he was sure she had been sitting on the doorstep opposite Number 9, with another little girl, when he'd arrived – a pale, thin girl who looked as if a good meal would knock her sideways. Her cardigan, several sizes too small and missing its buttons, sported big holes at the elbows, and several threads of unravelled wool trailed down like crinkly little worms. Despite this, she was undeniably pretty in a fragile way, with hair not quite light enough to be called blonde yet too light to be mousey. Huge, greenish eyes fringed with long, dark lashes openly surveyed him. He judged she was probably about thirteen or fourteen. She smiled shyly at Tino and he smiled back. He hoped they would be friends.

The Church of St Francis of Assisi was relatively new, with a presbytery, a school and an adjoining baptistery, later additions to the original building. As they turned into the small courtyard, Tino thought how different this church was from the tiny one at home; St Francis's was much bigger, constructed of plain red brick broken up by bands of black, strategically placed to form a simple geometric pattern. It was bounded on three sides, with Pottery Lane on the west and Hippodrome Place to the north. The east side backed onto the rear of the houses in Portland Road. The area all around the church displayed the unmistakeable signs of dire poverty, yet many of the inhabitants still came faithfully to Mass, confident in the knowledge that by doing so, their place at God's right hand would be assured and their promised eternal life would make up for their miserable existence on Earth.

It was all new and strange to Tino and he felt a little apprehensive. Once inside the church, though, he soon slipped into a comforting sense of déjà-vu – the sweet smell of burning incense, the poignant ring of the bell as it invoked the presence of the Holy Spirit and the mesmerising chanting of Father Delaney, followed by the monotone responses of the faithful. Everything contrived to engender familiarity and a sense of solidarity, every soul present – young or old, rich or poor – joined together in communal prayer.

Tino was strangely moved by the knowledge that somewhere in a little church in Southern Italy, his family and his sweetheart would be praying together at around this time, too. He made sure he remembered them all in his own prayers, going through the names one by one – Mamma, Papa, Carlotta, Emilia, Michele and little Angelo. His friend Marco, too. He said a special prayer for Francesco, to keep him safe if he went to war. But he saved his very last prayers for Mara.

Chapter 8

THE WEATHER HAD slipped off its chilly winter mantle and replaced it with a gossamer shawl of cherry and apple blossom. A profusion of spring flowers had seemed to appear overnight – but only in the green areas and parks. The sun always lost its battle as it struggled to penetrate the gloom of the smog-filled alleys and streets of the London slums, and they stayed as drab and grey as ever.

Tino had now been in London for almost three months and with the passage of that time dawned the realisation that he was actually beginning to enjoy the experience. Giuseppe and Janey's lodging house had fast gained a reputation for comparative cleanliness, and excellent food and value for money – even the new inspectors, who were now monitoring all the lodging houses, were impressed and had said so. While they weren't exactly taking in high class lodgers, they did have a few regulars, travellers and salesmen who were a class above the level of the average vagabond and thief that frequented most other establishments.

Tino had soon learned that, although he and the boys were far from wealthy, and their clothes were as shabby as the next person's around these parts, they were very fortunate to be working for someone like Zi Giuseppe. He treated them with respect and made sure their bellies were full; unlike many of the *padroni,* the Italian men who sent home to Italy for young boys to work for them, with the alluring promise of a wonderful and prosperous life, then went on to treat them with unparalleled cruelty and contempt, regularly beating them and keeping them hungry if they didn't bring in enough money.

The sight of some of these boys, scared out of their wits to go back to their *padrone* with less than their set quota of takings, had already prompted Tino on more than one occasion to slip them a few coins of his own, saving them from a certain thrashing or even whipping with the buckle-end of a thick leather belt.

One in particular, a boy of about nine or ten, he had helped a few times. Tino felt so sorry for the boy, who told him his name was Paolo – he found him one day, sitting at the roadside, crying pitifully. He explained that his *padrone* had forced him to walk miles with stones in his boots, so he would limp and gain the pity of passers-by. The stones had dug so deeply into the balls of his feet he couldn't walk another step and Tino had almost carried the lame boy back to his lodgings.

Although home – and Mara – were never far from his mind, Tino had adjusted well; his friendship with the other boys had flourished, especially the mischievous chubby-faced Beppe, who was almost like a brother to him. Beppe had shown infinite patience in teaching him a few words of English at a time, so that he could now both speak and understand many of the things he needed to. Early on, with Giuseppe's permission, he had taken the time to show Tino some of the sights of London – the Houses of Parliament, Tower Bridge, the Thames and the docks area – the latter a dangerous place, at best unsavoury by day and somewhere to avoid by night – and Tino was enthralled.

Sights like these were unprecedented for a young peasant boy from the remote mountains of Italy and he had viewed them with awe. He had made another friend too – the young girl from across the road had, in fact, befriended all the boys. It turned out her name was Kathleen, one of the daughters in a family of impoverished Irish immigrants. She was from a family of ten, with their ages ranging from four to twenty-four and she was somewhere in the middle, with only one other sister, Mary, who was younger, and two little brothers. The older ones had already left home and some had families of their own, although others were in service. Her father, known as Paddy, worked in the Phoenix brewery, down by the Latimer Street junction and her mother, Bernadette, took in sewing to supplement his meagre earnings. Despite their poverty, and unlike the majority of the residents in the area, they were proud people and did their best to keep themselves and the house clean. 'The price of soap is a small price to pay for cleanliness, an' cleanliness is next to Godliness,' Bernadette insisted.

Kathleen was as sweet-natured as her gentle countenance promised. They had all grown fond of her, including Giuseppe and Janey. With her pale, almost transparent skin and air of fragility, they were all very protective towards her and her little sister, Mary, especially. It was comical, wherever Kathleen went, Mary toddled behind.

'I tell yer, I don't like the sound o' that cough the little un, Mary's got,' Janey told Giuseppe quietly, well out of earshot of the boys. 'Her Ma says she got croup, but I don't know, don't sound like that ter me. An' I used ter work in the Infirmary, so I should know!' She shook her head, frowning.

It was a lovely evening and after supper, Giuseppe dragged out his old barrel organ on its cart, inspecting it thoroughly. He had rented it at first, until he carefully saved up enough to buy it outright. Now, it was old and well-used, but fully paid up, so why should he swap it for a newer one, even if they were on wheels and easier to push around? He ran his hands over the instrument, checking for signs of wear and tear, and woodworm, all the while emitting a series of 'Hmms' and 'Ahs'. He stood up at length, letting out a groan as a twinge of pain shot across the small of his back. 'Must be getting old!' he muttered, pausing for a few moments to rub vigorously at the offending area with the palm of his hand.

'It's looking a bit shabby,' he announced at last. 'Salv, you are good with a paint brush, how about working some of your magic on this?'

Salv jumped at the chance. 'Yes, yes!' he agreed immediately. 'Now, let me see – how about fitting some nice bright wheels and maybe painting some lovebirds, like the ones I did on the little hurdy-gurdy?' His eyes were bright with excitement.

'Gotta right little artist, there, we 'ave!' Janey interjected, amused by Salv's unstoppable enthusiasm.

'That sounds good to me, and I've already got some old wheels and paint here somewhere, down in the cellar, I think,' Giuseppe said, running his fingers thoughtfully through dark wavy hair as he tried to conjure up a mental image of where he had last seen the small tins of brightly-coloured paints and the rusty old cart wheels. 'I'll look for them now, if you start straight away it'll all be dry by tomorrow, then. It's not warm enough yet for ice-cream, another month or two maybe,' he added. 'So Tino, you and Salv can take the organ out tomorrow – special treat for Salv, since he'll be doing all the hard work on it and it'll need two of you, anyway; it's too heavy for one to push around. When it looks nice and new, it should get a bit more attention – and more attention means more money. You should know the best places to go by now, try some of the parks and big houses. Just make sure you go in the opposite direction to Beppe and Donato, we don't want you in competition with each other!'

In less than four hours, Salv had indeed worked miracles on the instrument and its cart. Whereas before, the paint had been faded and nondescript, it now gleamed brightly and a beautifully crafted, life-size version of the miniature hurdy-gurdy lovebirds flew gracefully across the front of the box, feathers flashing blue, green and blush pink. He had cleaned up the two rusty wheels until they shone, then painted the spokes in matching colours.

'Eeh, them birds, they're so real, I can almost hear 'em singin'!' Janey exclaimed. 'Cor, Salv, you should be an artist, you should!'

'Yes, they do look real!' Tino breathed, truly amazed at the boy's artistic talent.

Half the neighbours in the street had come out to look at this work of art and Salv beamed widely at the never-ending succession of 'Oohs!' and 'Aahs!' He stood proudly as they all admired his craftsmanship, oblivious to the comic picture he made; the thick tufts of hair were now tipped with the same greens and pinks and blues as the organ, and a smudge of crimson red paint adorned the side of his nose.

Kathleen giggled to herself, while Donato looked on forlornly, longing to catch her attention. From the first time he saw her, he recognised something of himself in the girl, a certain vulnerability that was endearing. He smiled shyly, a little lop-sided grin which brought dimples to Kathleen's cheeks. A flush of warmth added colour to his face. He was ecstatic, overjoyed that she had noticed him at last and he hoped with all his heart that this would be just the beginning of a long and happy friendship.

The following morning, Tino and Salv raced through breakfast, eager to take the organ out and show off its new artwork, convinced the pair of lovebirds would make them a fortune. Donato and Beppe were more than a little envious; Beppe especially felt hard done by, he was already Tino's best friend, after all.

'How about going to Hyde Park?' Giuseppe suggested, pressing his fingers hard into the corners of his eyes and rubbing firmly. He had woken up with a headache and the boys' chatter and laughter, together with that of some of the louder new lodgers, was beginning to get on his nerves. He couldn't wait until he was on his own with Janey, he'd be glad to see the back of the lot of them today. 'It's a fine day, it'll probably be busy there, today. Young sweethearts, that sort of thing …'

'Yes, that's a good idea. We'll do that.' Tino agreed. 'But what about Donato and Beppe, where should they go?'

'Madonna! Didn't I tell you yesterday?' Giuseppe clapped a hand to his forehead, his frustration evident in his voice. It seemed to come from the very bottom of his boots and he heaved a loud sigh of exasperation. 'Anywhere! Anywhere but in the same direction! And don't you forget what I've always taught you, don't go too clean. The scruffier and poorer you look the more sympathy you get – and sympathy means money!'

The four boys shot each other a warning glance. They knew the signs – Zi Giuseppe was in one of his famous 'moods' – he didn't get them very often, but when he did, you could look out. Just like a volcano, he would erupt without warning and God help anyone who got in the way of the molten lava. Better to keep out of his way!

As one, they beat a hasty retreat towards the front door, grabbing their instruments and almost knocking Mr Reedy, one of the regulars at the lodging house, off his feet in the process.

'Sorry, sir!' they apologised in unison as they hurtled out into the street. Out of earshot, the boys giggled wickedly. The travelling salesman, James Reedy, was undeniably gaunt and as thin as a snake, and the moment they clapped eyes on him, Beppe had christened him Mr Weedy, a name which had stuck.

Salv and Tino ran down the street at full pelt, laughing all the way and dragging the cart on precarious wheels, resplendent with freshly-painted organ bouncing up and down precariously at every step. They kept on running until they were well away from Bramley Mews.

They all went together in the direction of Hyde Park, laughing and joking, until they reached the entrance at Marble Arch. 'You two had better go off and find your own pitch somewhere,' Tino instructed Donato and Beppe. 'We'd better do as Zi Giuseppe says. But we must meet here afterwards.'

'Pity we can't all stay together, though,' Beppe said. His chubby face was downcast. He was still miserable, sulking because he couldn't stay with Tino and the masterpiece organ.

'Well, we can't, so that's that!' Tino replied firmly, but not unkindly. He and Salv watched as their friends disappeared into the distance.

'Come on, then, let's go!'

Hyde Park was a place of welcome escape, where rich and poor alike could relax and enjoy the recreation; where ladies and gentlemen would take a leisurely stroll together and even the poorer people from the dismal slum areas could sometimes forget their everyday toils and troubles, if only for a little while. It was a large park which Tino found fascinating. He loved watching the ducks on the pond. He often saw people throwing in crusts of stale bread or cake for them and he wondered how many of the poor people living around Bramley Mews would have fought over those bits of leftover food.

It was particularly attractive now, in the spring sunshine – many of the trees were covered in a froth of pink and white blossom, while others sported fat buds that looked fit to burst. Flowers had been carefully planted to produce a riot of spring colour. There was a children's playground too and even a bandstand where musicians were already tuning up their instruments. Tino was careful to keep well away from that though, because they could do without the competition.

They finally found a suitable place and stopped. There was a cloth cover on the organ, which they removed with a flourish to display the instrument in all its newly-painted glory.

'Put your hat on the ground, for the money,' Tino instructed. Salv missed the mischievous gleam in his eyes and dutifully obeyed. His hair, no longer restricted within the confines of the too-big bowler hat, shot up in tufts as if blessed with a life of its own. The multi-coloured ends still bore testimony to his artistic work the night before and the smudge of red paint, which had initially marked just the side of his nose had now spread all over it, no doubt as a result of his habit of using the back of his hand to wipe his snotty nose. Tino stifled a giggle and gave the signal to start winding the handle of the organ. The music flowed sweetly and harmoniously, but still loud enough to be sure to attract the attention of passers-by.

Before long, quite a crowd had gathered and already the hat held quite a few coins. Tino found himself making a mental calculation of how much money he and Salv would make, if everyone watching gave a penny or two. He had always been good at his sums, although his schooling had been limited. An unwelcome thought suddenly crossed his mind that he was getting as bad as his father and Zi Giuseppe. He resolved to stop counting, there and then. Although he loved them both, the last thing he wanted was to inherit their obsession with money, 'enough' would be sufficient. Providing he earned enough in the next two years to go home to marry his girl, he would be a happy young man.

Just then, he was dragged from his reverie by a small boy tugging at the sleeve of a lady, whom he judged to be about twenty-five years of age. She bent down to the boy who whispered something in her ear; then she led him over to the front of the audience. Like everyone else, they had been attracted by the newly-decorated organ and tinkling music. It was quite obvious she really was a lady too; her whole demeanour gave away the fact that they were from the upper echelons of society; she was attractive rather than pretty, with a smile that softened her expression whenever she looked at the boy. A flower-sprigged gown peeped out from beneath her coat and a beribboned hat decorated with a bunch of tiny roses framed a heart-shaped face. Tino had rightly concluded the boy must be her son – he bore a strong resemblance to her, with similar colouring and features. Suddenly, the boy started laughing and clapping his hands with glee.

'Look! Mamma, look!' The childish, high-pitched voice carried, to the amusement of everyone else in the crowd. 'A clown! Is'sa silly clown!' He pointed a tiny, index finger straight in Salv's direction.

The audience and Tino immediately doubled up with laughter, while Salv continued turning the handle of the organ frantically, as if his life depended on it. For a split-second, he hadn't realised all the hilarity was directed at him; then a sudden vision of his own reflection that morning, peering into the broken piece of mirror which served the whole household, sprang to mind. Much of the silvering had come off the back of the mirror, so the surface was foxed and mottled brown instead of shiny, but it was good enough to see that the paint had stuck to him like fish glue. But it hadn't worried him at the time, his hat would cover it all up, anyway – or so he had mistakenly thought.

As the awful truth dawned on him, a flush crept upwards from his neck until he was as red as the paint on his nose. Some odd, nervous reaction had also caused his left leg to stamp involuntarily on the grass like an impatient horse, but in perfect time to the music. The harder he turned the handle, the faster the music played; the faster the music played, the faster his leg went up and down to match.

He was so ashamed he wished the earth would open up beneath his feet and swallow him whole. A mental image of the Bible story about Jonah and the whale flashed into his head and he realised dismally he would trade places with Jonah right now without a second thought. However, he was about to change his mind. The sound of laughter had carried and the small audience had now become a throng of people thoroughly enjoying the antics of this supposed young comic. Before long, they began to show their appreciation in a more tangible way.

Someone shouted out, 'Bravo! Bravo!' and threw a handful of coins into the hat. Others started to join in. 'Encore!' 'More!' they cried, laughing all the while at the supposed clown's antics. Coins, silver ones too, began to flood in from all directions and the hat was filling up fast. So fast, that Tino was forced to take off his own hat and went around the crowds, giving a neat little bow of thanks to the benefactors.

Salv couldn't believe his eyes. They actually liked what he was doing, they thought it was all part of the act. The next tune was slow and sad, and Salv, realising what he was achieving, was now beginning to enjoy all the attention and decided to play up to the audience. His let his eyes droop and turned down the corners of his mouth, assuming a grossly exaggerated melancholy expression. He turned the handle slowly and his bobbing leg went slower, too; then with remarkable timing, he feigned a loud sobbing. 'Boo-hoo!' he cried, then progressively 'Boo-hoo'ed' louder and louder until it became a manic wailing. 'Waaaah–hah!' he cried and the leg shook convulsively in sympathy. The audience loved it and applauded enthusiastically. The coins flooded in even faster.

This was the pattern for a few more hours, until the hats

could be filled no more. The boys stuffed as much of the money as they could into the 'secret' pockets that were sewn to the inside of their jackets and trousers. Tino knew they'd never made as much money before, not even when the four of them pooled their takings. Zi Giuseppe would be pleased – he might even give them a bit extra this week. There was nothing else for it, the clown act was so successful it would have to stay.

'Tell you what, let's go and get something to eat,' Tino suggested.

'There's a hot pie 'n eels shop down the road,' Salv replied. 'They're nice, too, I had some there before.'

'I could eat a horse right now, I'm starving,' Tino said. He grinned wickedly, casting a sidelong glance in Salv's direction to gauge his reaction. 'As long as its kick isn't as bad as yours.'

Salv burst out laughing, too. 'Come on, let's go get our hay, then.'

They walked along the streets of London, laughing and joking, each taking it in turns to eat their pie and peas, while the other one pushed the heavy cart and organ in a leisurely fashion; through Hyde Park and St James' Park, and passing the old Queen's residence at Buckingham Palace.

'Wouldn't like to be her servants, cleaning that lot,' Tino remarked, nodding in the direction of the Palace.

'And what about the poor gardeners?' Salv added. 'I'll stick with the barrel-organ, thanks!' he added with a laugh.

They walked along in companiable silence for a while. At length, Tino said, 'Why don't we go and see if we can find Beppe and Donato?'

'Why?'

'Well, we've had a good day, we made more than enough money for the four of us so we could all go back early,' he explained. 'I've got a pretty good idea where they've gone, I went there with Beppe before. And with a bit of luck, all this should bring the smile back to Zi's face!' He jingled his pockets to demonstrate.

Tino led the way; they walked in the opposite direction from the parks, then turned off the main roads until they reached a crescent of tall, grand-looking town houses with gabled roofs and painted iron railings. There were lacy curtains at the windows and neat shoe-scrapers embedded into the ground near the flight of steps.

Just then, they heard a commotion in the distance and Donato came running towards them as if the Devil himself were on his tail.

'Tino, Salv, come quick!' he shouted, his voice filled with fear. 'Quick!' His breathing was heavy from running and his usually pale face flushed with colour.

'Slow down!' Tino tried to calm the younger boy down. 'What's wrong?'

'We haven't got time to slow down, just follow me!' Donato had already started to run back the way he had come and sensing the urgency of the situation, they dropped the organ and cart at the side of the road and ran after him, wondering what was going on. They soon found out.

Around the next corner, where the end of the crescent opened out into a grassy expanse, they found Beppe curled up into a ball in the middle of the street, arms folded tight above his head in an effort to protect himself. A rough-looking, thick-set man was bringing down a leather belt onto his back again and again, cutting though the air with a crack like a whip. Behind the man, the young Italian boy, Paolo, who Tino had helped before by giving him money to take back to his *padrone*, was tugging frantically at his jacket in a futile attempt to drag him off Beppe. The boy, too, had fresh red weals scarring his face. He had no jacket but the shirt on his back was rent in two, revealing even more weals forming a lattice across his back

Tino quickly summed up the situation; he knew Beppe had taken to the boy and would have run to his aid if he had seen him being beaten. Without hesitation, and with no thought for his own safety, Tino ran towards the fracas and jumped straight on to the man's back. Taken by surprise, he turned round but Tino was ready. He slammed his fist straight into the man's face.

'*Bastardo*!' the man cried, as blood spurted from a cut on his cheek. Tino took advantage of the fact that he had caught the man unawares and caught him a second blow at the side of the head. The man reeled for a moment but he was strong and quickly regained his balance.

His arm shot out and grabbed Tino by the collar. '*Bastardo*!' he screamed again manically. Tino was well-built, strong and courageous from his work on the farm, but he was still young and no match for this evil man. Almost lifting Tino off his feet, he began to shake him like a terrier with a rat. Beppe had scrambled to his feet and Tino remembered shouting to the others, 'Run, quick! Get help!' before being butted full force in the face. He heard a crack and saw red as the blood trickled into his eyes from a deep cut above his brow. A second head butt followed.

Donato and Salv, unsure what to do, had paused momentarily, but they realised that, even all together, they couldn't overcome this great hulk of a man. They ran off and began hammering on someone's door, desperate for help.

Meanwhile, Tino was slipping in and out of unconsciousness; the only reason he was still on his feet was because the man still had him by the collar. He suddenly released his grip and Tino fell to the floor in a crumpled heap. The young boy was crying hysterically, and rivulets of tears streaked the dirt on his cheeks. Beppe was desperate and yelling for help.

The man, still not satisfied, turned the belt on Tino. Down it came, again and again, on his head, his arms, his legs, until Tino could feel it no more. Mercilessly, the *padrone* started kicking at the lifeless body.

Beppe knew if he waited a moment longer, it would be too late. Ignoring his own pain, he found a big stone on the ground. Drawing his arm back as far as he could, he brought it down with full force onto the back of the man's head. For a split second, he stood there, a shocked expression on his face. Then the light seemed to fade from his eyes and his legs buckled beneath him. He collapsed to the ground, in a crumpled heap.

Beppe was motionless, the stone in his hand now dark with blood and hair. He stood for a few moments, watching the man in a curiously detached way. Then he burst into action. He ran over to Tino, unsure whether he was alive or dead, searching desperately for signs of life and listening hard to find out if he was still breathing.

The two other boys came back on their own. No-one took any notice of two urchins yelling for help and Donato had been sent packing with the threat of the contents of a full chamber pot being emptied over his head, for his troubles. They stopped in their tracks at the scene before them – the young boy, Paolo, was still sobbing uncontrollably; Beppe leaning over Tino, who was ominously still, showing no signs of life whatsoever. Alongside, the man lay prostrate, one leg at an awkward angle to his body. From the pale lifeless eyes, slightly open but seeing nothing, the boys were sure he was dead.

At about the same time in the lodging-house in Bramley Mews, Giuseppe received news from Italy. He was dreading Tino coming home, he didn't know how was going to break it to him. Most of the lodgers had gone out, except for one or two who had opted to stay in their little rooms. Giuseppe sat quietly at the table, his head buried in his hands. He stayed there for a few moments, trying to block out the inevitable. At length, he lifted his head beseechingly to Janey. The voice that came out was unfamiliar, heavily accented and thick with emotion. He was pale, his mouth dry and set in a grim line. Brown eyes, bright with unshed tears, met his wife's.

'Janey, how am I going to tell him?' he begged. 'How?'

Chapter 9

THE WINTER MONTHS in Picinisco had been bitterly cold, living up to an early promise of snow-covered mountains, and rivers and streams that had frozen over, mid-flow. As soon as darkness began to fall, the animals would be locked up safely for the night, some in the stone barn which Tino had once shared with them and the weaker ones, together with the old and the young, would be brought inside into a makeshift pen in a corner of the house. The area was notorious for wolves, which were bold and brazen enough to come right up to the houses. Any animal or fowl, whether sheep, hen, cat or dog, left outside or in an insecure building would be nothing more than skin and a few scattered bones by the following morning, and no-one could afford losses like that.

These long, dark nights had prompted the family to spend most evenings huddled around a welcoming fire, which would burn merrily, stoked up with logs from the forest. Sometimes they would add some of the dried olive stones, which were long-lasting and would give off a bright glow rather than burn fiercely. In these times, with her family around her, it never failed to cross Lena's mind that although they were not really rich, they were so lucky compared with others, who had little food, warmth or even decent shelter. Many of these already large families would increase every year or two with the addition of yet another new baby; many looked after elderly mothers and fathers, too. Every extra mouth to feed was an additional burden on their already overstretched resources and yet they would never turn anyone away from their door, if they thought their need was greater than their own.

Wealth was all relative – to those poor people, the D'Abruzzos were apparently well-off; but to the really wealthy people in the cities, they were nothing more than illiterate peasants who were just managing to scrape a living.

Lena and Raffaele were quite an odd couple, the product of a marriage of convenience. But while she was a kindly, generous woman, whose good deeds in the neighbourhood had gained her the love and respect of the poor and sick, Raffaele's greed and ambitious ideas now overshadowed the fact that he was in fact a loving husband and father. 'Well-intentioned, but very, very misguided,' she often thought sadly, though she would never dare to question his motives aloud. He was her husband, after all.

Since the day they waved goodbye to Tino and Francesco, the D'Abruzzo family had carried on their lives in Colleruta more or less as normal, a quiet haven set against a backdrop of unrest and rebellion throughout the rest of Italy. They knew that Tino was well, for Giuseppe and Tino had sent messages through the son of a mutual friend who, having completed his contract to a *padrone,* was returning home to the nearby village of Villa Latina, his pockets stuffed full with money for the first time in his life. They knew if they sent messages via friends, they would get through, unlike a postal system which was slow and unreliable. This was a great comfort to Tino, because he would always make sure he sent a little message or note, or perhaps a little gift, for Mara as well as his family. At least she would know he was thinking about her.

Recently, though, as the snows had begun to melt and the spring sun shone once more, disturbing news of other events had begun to reach them. Francesco, having undergone a brief period of training, had been sent out with his regiment to join other troops in Ethiopia. Raffaele had once again discussed his concerns for his son and the Italian army with Grillo. 'It seems to me that after last year's disaster, when our armies tried to occupy the provinces and failed, that damn Crispi's stirring things up again,' Raffaele had remarked. 'He and his government, there's no stopping them.'

'Well, it's down to the fact that they won't accept defeat easily, Crispi especially,' Grillo replied lazily. 'Look what happened in Dogali a few years ago, they were beaten hands down. They're just not going to let that go, now, are they?'

Raffaele nodded seriously. What Grillo said made a lot of sense. Now, regular skirmishes between the opposing armies led to heightened tensions and a resultant promise of new threats and bloody battle. Raffaele was very worried for his eldest son's safety.

Lena, too, was worried and her stomach felt as if it were permanently tied in a constricting knot that prevented her from breathing properly. 'I'm so frightened for Francesco,' she confided to Mara's mother, Rosa. She seemed to have aged in a matter of weeks. The few streaks of grey that had once peppered the black hair now seemed to merge into solid blocks of silver and deep ridges lined her eyes and mouth, where once the skin had been smooth.

She knew Rosa would understand her concerns, hadn't one of her own sons joined up in the same regiment not long after? This common ground had brought the two women even closer together.

Rosa reached out and patted her hand. 'I'm afraid too, Lena,' she said. 'But in my heart, I know God will bring them back to us.' Her words and smiles were reassuring, but inside, she too was worried sick. Crispi didn't care who he sent to war, it was fine for him and his government, holed up in their own safe little world; they didn't care whose sons died for their country.

Lena heaved a sigh. 'I hope you're right,' she whispered.

At that point, Carlotta, Emilia and Serafina Grillo came into the room, carrying bundles of cloth, which they had spent hours embroidering and edging with lace. Angelo and Michele, who seemed half the time to think that Carlotta was their mother, trotted dutifully behind. Earlier, Mara had come to visit with her mother but had returned home alone not long after, when Serafina had turned up unexpectedly.

On the surface, Serafina treated Mara with honeyed kindness; it was when she thought no-one was watching or listening that the spiteful remarks and digs would start and she had begun to keep well out of her way.

'Tino's mine!' she would hiss in Mara's ear through clenched teeth. 'Don't you think you're going to get him because you're not, my father will make sure of that.' Or, on this occasion, when she had been left alone while the other two girls went to fetch their sewing, 'Tino loves me, not you! Why do you think he hasn't sent any messages to you yet, eh?'

Mara, sick of her malicious inferences, began to walk away, but Serafina, immediately sensing the other girl's discomfiture, seized the chance to drive the point home with a blatant untruth.

'He sent me a message, anyway!' she taunted.

Mara's face blanched as she spun around to face Serafina. She fought to resist an almost irrepressible urge to swipe the smirk off the other girl's face with the back of her hand.

'What do you mean?' she asked, her quiet, controlled voice and calm manner belying the inner turmoil she was experiencing.

'The boy from Villa Latina,' Serafina lied. 'He brought me a message from Tino, a note.'

'Saying what?'

'That he was well and having a lovely time.' More lies tripped easily off her tongue. 'And that he was missing me.'

She was so convincing that for a moment, Mara wasn't sure what to think and had to bite her tongue hard to stop herself from asking if he had mentioned her at all in the note. Then her mind went back to the last time she and Tino had been together; how he had held her and told her he loved her; how in two years' time, he would be back for her with money in his pocket to make her his bride.

'You're lying, Serafina!' With one last look of contempt, she turned her back on the other girl, and headed for home.

But the seeds of doubt had been planted and the blue eyes were troubled. 'It is strange, though,' she thought, as she left the D'Abruzzo household behind. 'In a way, she's right. Tino could surely have got a message to me by now.'

Raffaele D'Abruzzo had an old, battered tin, which he kept hidden under the bed. No-one was allowed to touch it, not even Lena. It contained all the things he treasured – small items that had been passed down through his family for generations, from father to son – an ancient hunting knife, which, it was said, his grandfather had bravely used to kill a brown bear in the forest; a small dark nut, skilfully carved into a miniature Madonna by someone whose name had long been forgotten, and a few private papers relating to their land, none of which he could read, but knew nevertheless were important. The latest addition to the box had been a small piece of cheap lined paper, folded up into four quarters, and bearing even more words he couldn't understand. The boy from Villa Latina had given it to him, with express instructions from Tino about its intended recipient. The outer quarter bore a rough drawing of two inter-twined hearts and one single word: Mara.

*

The daylight hours were already getting noticeably longer and the sun dropped behind the mountains a little later with the fall of each consecutive dusk. The ewes had started lambing and it was time to start thinking of sowing the new seed on the land.

The day started off as any other, Carlotta had taken over Tino's job of looking after the animals and Emilia helped her mother with the rest of the chores, spending any spare moments either with Marco, making plans for their wedding or sewing little items for her new home. It was customary for a bride to go and live with her new husband in his family home, so she knew that in a year or two, she would be moving over to the Grillo house. She knew how her mother felt about Grillo and, if she were truthful, she would have to say she didn't like him either. He always made her feel uncomfortable but she could never quite put her finger on the reason why. But she loved Marco and he loved her, so she was quite prepared to accept his father, too.

Carlotta came out of the barn, carrying a pail full of steaming milk from the goats, with her younger brothers in tow, as usual. Michele chased a laughing Angelo around in circles, panting loudly and his plump face flushed red with the effort. Emilia and her mother had just returned from the river where they had washed clothes, pounding them with a rock to clean them and dipping them in and out of the water. Now, they were busy spreading them out over low bushes to dry, chattering idly about everything and nothing as they did so.

It was Raffaele, just leaving the house, who first noticed the figure in the distance. He raised a hand to shade his eyes against the sun, which still hung low in the sky. The figure got closer, but he still couldn't make out who it was.

'Lena,' he called. 'Lena, look! Down there.' He pointed in the direction of the figure. She draped the last item of clothing neatly across a bush and joined him on the top of the three steps.

'Who is it?' she asked, brows furrowed together.

Raffaele shrugged his shoulders. 'I don't know. Perhaps someone has got lost…?' He didn't want to admit even to himself what he suspected. Surely not! It couldn't be. There was an oddly heavy feeling in the pit of his stomach.

'Funny place to get lost, Papa.' Carlotta and Emilia were now at his elbow. The whole family stood together in silence, unwelcome thoughts racing through their heads. Even the two young boys had gone quiet.

They lost sight of the figure for a moment or two behind a bank, then he came into view once more. They could see now he was wearing a uniform, the uniform of an officer of the *Bersaglieri*. But it wasn't Francesco. Lena began to sway.

'Oh, Madonna!' she cried. 'No, please, God! Not my son! But I told him, he should never have gone, it was too dangerous.' She began to sob and leaned heavily on her husband's shoulder. She knew instinctively it was not good news.

'Can I come in?' asked the man. Once inside, he introduced himself as Sergeant Fusco, from Francesco's regiment. Then he went on quickly, in an attempt to reassure the family.

'It may not be as bad as you think,' he explained.

'Is my son dead?' Raffaele asked, his mouth set in a grim line. Hearing her worst innermost fears spoken aloud brought a renewed bout of sobbing from Lena.

'We just don't know,' explained Sergeant Fusco truthfully. 'There was a battle, a big, bloody battle in Adua. The first day of March 1896. That will be written on my mind forever. You must have heard about it, surely, even here?' He shook his head and stared down at the stone floor, unable to continue. He finally regained his composure, but his voice was heavy with emotion as he went on, '*Signore*, we've lost thousands of men there, thousands. Many of those were killed and others taken prisoner. But there were rumours that some made a run for it and others managed to hide. We really don't know what happened to your son; we just don't know.'

Lena and the girls were inconsolable. The two little boys, not fully understanding what was happening, looked on wide-eyed and pale. Raffaele, though, was the first to seize onto the faint ray of hope.

'But you say some are prisoners?' He looked to the other man for confirmation and was rewarded with an almost imperceptible nod of the head. 'And others escaped, so Francesco could easily have been among them. Lena, don't you see?' he shook his wife roughly. 'He may be safe; we don't know that he's dead. He may be safe.' He made a small, choking sound that was somewhere between a laugh and a sob.

The girls latched onto his optimism and immediately wiped at their eyes, each cuddling one of the young brothers. Lena, though, was devastated. She would never rest until her eldest son was back home with her and she knew for sure he was alive.

The coming weeks went by in a haze. Raffaele and the girls did their best to keep cheerful and optimistic but Lena went about her daily tasks with mechanical routine, neither thinking nor caring about anything except the whereabouts of her eldest son. Was he lying dead, rotting somewhere on a bloodied battlefield? Or was he being ill-treated, a prisoner at the mercy of the enemy? It was not knowing that caused the greatest hurt and distress. The family were almost as worried about her as they were about Francesco – she cried all the time, her skin seemed almost transparent and the weight seemed to be falling away from her bones. Rosa had kept away too, full of guilt because she had been elated when news had arrived that her own son was alive and well and on his way home.

A few weeks' after Fusco's visit was Francesco's birthday. Lena felt particularly despondent. It was odd, few people bothered to remember birthdays here, but his had coincided with a feast day, so it was hard to forget. She collected the laundry, throwing it carelessly into a woven basket. She steadied the over-full basket on top of her head and made for the river.

It was the first fine day for some time after weeks of heavy rain. The level of the stream had risen, it was swollen and fast-flowing. It was at its most dangerous when it was like this – most women would have gone back home, or not even have gone in the first place, but Lena stayed. She stared straight ahead as she reached for the clothes. Taking the biggest rock she could find, she began thumping and pounding in a methodical rhythm; slowly, slowly at first, then gradually becoming faster until she brought down the rock with such force and speed that it that was frightening to watch. She caught her fingers more than once under the rock but felt no pain. Again and again, the rock slammed down until her fingers bled and stained the water red, but still she seemed oblivious.

She hadn't noticed little Angelo, either, as he slipped out of the house and followed her. The day before, Michele had been showing him how to stalk rabbits, how to keep perfectly quiet and creep along so lightly on bare feet that not even the tiniest sound could be heard; Mamma surely wouldn't hear him. He knew in his heart he was being naughty and he should have stayed at home, so he kept a discreet distance slightly upstream and on a higher level than the spot where Lena was beating frantically at the clothes. He couldn't see her, but he could hear the loud rushing of the water and the continuous 'bang, bang' as she brought the rock down onto the clothes. He leaned his upper body over, but she was still out of sight. Slithering down further, he leaned out as far as he could over the bank. Without warning, the ground slid from beneath him as little stones dislodged under his feet on the wet, muddy riverbank. He pitched forward, rolling head over heels until there was nowhere else to roll. He went headfirst into the river, cracking his head on something hard as he fell. Dazed and confused, he didn't stand a chance. He tried calling Mamma for help, but the thin, reedy voice was lost in the roar of the water as it rushed over boulders and stones, ripping up small trees and plants in its wake. For a few moments, he thrashed around, desperately trying to keep his head above the level of the water, but it was impossible to stop it from filling his mouth and lungs. His puny efforts were futile against the ferocity of the angry river and finally, overcome with exhaustion, he stopped fighting and slipped quietly beneath the relentless foam.

Lena's eyes were dry as she climbed the last gentle slope to the house. Arms stretched out before her, she held the still, lifeless form of her youngest child as if he were made of the most precious, delicate porcelain. Droplets of water still clung like heavy dew to the baby-fine hair but his face was the colour of parchment.

'*Mea culpa, mea culpa.* My fault, my fault.' The words rang out over and over in her head. It was all her fault. She should have put her foot down, tried to stop Francesco and Tino from going away, looked after her youngest baby son Angelo properly. She had neglected him, forgotten he was still just a little boy, a baby who still needed his Mamma. How could she ever forgive herself? Her preoccupation with the fate of her two eldest sons had made her forget the needs of the rest of her family. And now, because of her selfishness, yet another of her children had died – her angel with the dark, gentle eyes and cherubic smile, her bambino, her little Angelo. '*Mea culpa, mea culpa.*' The sound pounded away erratically, echoing louder and louder. And why hadn't Francesco listened to her? If only he had taken notice of her begging him not to go, instead of being so stubborn. Yes, this was as much his fault as hers, he should never have gone away to fight, not when everyone knew it was getting so dangerous. It was madness. If he hadn't gone missing, Angelo would still be alive. No, she would never forgive herself – but she might never forgive Francesco, either. She stopped as she reached the rise near the farmhouse and stood still as a statue. '*Mea culpa.*' The sound was no longer erratic but had settled in perfect rhythm with the wild pounding of her heart.

That was how Raffaele found her – motionless and silent, as if by saying the dreadful words, 'Angelo is dead,' it would turn the nightmare into reality. He took in the situation in an instant and let out a growl of sheer terror, pain and disbelief.

'My God, woman, what have you done?' he screamed. 'What have you done?' Oh, *Madre di Dio*, my little son, my bambino.' Tears ran unchecked down his cheeks as he lifted the lifeless form from his mother's arms and gently carried him into the house. He could almost hear his son's laughter ringing in his ears, squealing with excitement as he did when he used to carry him into the house just like this, pretending he was going to be the meat for that day's dinner. He turned back to Lena, his eyes dark. 'This is all your fault, I'll never be able to forgive you for this.'

'Mea culpa, mea culpa.'

An unexpected sound cut cruelly across the stricken man's thoughts – a quiet, choking that came from the very depths of Lena's soul. Soon, the sound of sobbing rent the air, becoming progressively louder until it culminated in an ear-shattering crescendo which seemed to encompass every misery that had ever been ever suffered since the dawn of time. She was inconsolable with grief. And above all a guilt that could never be assuaged.

Chapter 10

THERE WAS A loud knock on the door of the lodging house.

'I'll get it,' Janey offered in her good-natured way. 'Probably someone looking for somewhere to stay.'

She came back into the room, the freckles standing out in stark relief against the pallor of her skin. She was accompanied by a plump, ruddy-faced police officer from the X Division, which served that area of London. He looked vaguely familiar and Giuseppe struggled to remember where he had seen him before. It came to him that he had often seen him on his patch. He was a kindly man and had never moved him on, as some of the other bobbies did. The policeman removed his helmet to reveal coarse brown hair, thick except for a bald spot on the crown. He was turning the hat round and round in his hands, obviously uncomfortable with the task he had been given. Giuseppe looked from the policeman, to Janey, and back again.

'Is this about my family in Italy?' he asked.

'No, sir,' the policeman answered quietly.

Just then, Giuseppe caught sight of the three boys behind him – Donato, Salv and another younger boy he didn't recognise. He noticed the bruises and dried blood on the unknown boy and quickly put two and two together.

'If you boys have been up to no good, fighting, you can look out,' he began. 'I will not have you bringing trouble to this door…' His voice trailed off as the boys began to cry, making fresh tramlines on already tear-stained faces.

'Now, sir, let's not blame these boys. They 'ain't been

fightin' or anyfink else, fer that matter,' the policeman admonished gently.

Giuseppe slammed his fist hard on the wooden table, his features tight with fear. 'Then you must tell me your business!' he demanded, his breath coming fast. He turned to the boys, 'And where are the other two?'

The boys looked at each other helplessly.

'I've bin tryin' ter tell yer, sir,' the policeman's voice was quiet. He hated being the bearer of bad news. 'Them boys are in the infirmary, taken a bit of a hidin', they 'av.'

Giuseppe shot out of the seat, resisting the temptation to grab the man by the neck. 'Hiding? What do you mean, hiding? Are they alright? Which infirmary?' The colour had drained from his face. As if the news that had just come from Italy wasn't bad enough, with Angelo dead and Francesco missing; now it seemed there was even more to cope with.

'One question at a time, sir!' the policeman answered. 'The younger boy – Beppe, is it?' he sought confirmation of the name and everyone else in the room nodded. 'Beppe, 'e ain't too bad, a few marks on 'im, but 'e'll live.'

'Thank God for that!' Giuseppe said. 'Tino is staying with him, then?'

The policeman hesitated slightly and the boys went deathly quiet.

'For God's sake, out with it man!' Giuseppe brought his fist down on the table with a bang.

'I'm sorry.' It took him a moment to pluck up the courage to meet Giuseppe's eyes. When he did, he saw naked fear reflected in the soft brown depths. The policeman shook his head. 'E's real bad, that un.'

'But he's going to get better?'

'As I said, sir, 'e's bad. You better get ter the infirmary, I fink, an' ask 'em there, they'll be able ter tell yer more.' He coughed discreetly. 'I take it you got the means to pay, sir? P'raps an insurance fund? I doubt the Board will…'

Giuseppe rounded on him. 'The boy is that ill and all you can think about is money?' he spat out.

Usually, the policeman would not have put up with Giuseppe's apparent lack of respect, but he recognised that he was in shock and for once, was prepared to overlook it. 'I on'y asked…'

Giuseppe sighed heavily. 'I'm sorry,' he ventured apologetically. 'We've already had bad news and now this on top… But yes, I can pay, you needn't worry about that.'

Then, not even stopping to grab his coat, Giuseppe ran all the way to the infirmary, with Janey hurrying behind. She had given the other boys strict instruction to stay put until they got back. The light was starting to fade and if the area was unsavoury in the daytime, by night it could be treacherous, especially to the weak or unwary.

When they arrived, they found Beppe first; the doctor was still tending to Tino, they would have to wait to see him, and even then only if the doctor allowed, they were told by a nurse whose face was as starchy as her apron.

Beppe's mouth was split and a few teeth were missing; his eyes were puffy, rimmed with blue-black bruises. It was painful to talk, but he recounted the full details of what had happened; the way they had come across the man beating the boy and how Beppe had gone to his rescue and was himself beaten. Then in turn, Tino had come to his aid. He ended with an account of how they had managed between them to lift Tino onto the cart with the barrel-organ and pushed him all the way to the infirmary. Someone had called the police, who had then gone in pursuit of the boys. Luckily, an elderly man, Jack Cooper, who lived nearby had seen everything from start to finish and had spoken up for them, told the police how they were just defending themselves from the evil, cruel brute. It was just as well he had witnessed it, because very often, the 'Eye-ties' would be blamed for things they knew nothing about and thrown into prison without a second thought. Jack had never had a problem with them himself, always found them to be very polite and respectful. And in any case, in this instance, the evidence had disappeared, so he doubted anything would come of it.

Shortly after the boys ran off, Jack had watched in disbelief as the *padrone* stirred then struggled to his feet, all the while holding the sore spot on his head. He looked around blearily, muttering curses under his breath when he suddenly realised that he was being watched intently by an audience of young boys and a few adults who had gathered to see what all the commotion was about. The *padrone* felt very hot and uncomfortable under their accusing gaze. He had a lot to hide, he was already well-known to the police. As his head began to clear, he realised it would be in his best interests to clear off as fast as he could and he scurried along the road, swaying from side to side like a drunken man, accompanied by a torrent of abuse from the onlookers.

Beppe began to cry. Although he knew now the *padrone* was not dead, he was still scared. Janey rocked the sobbing boy back and forth. 'What if Tino dies?' he wailed. 'Just because he tried to save me.'

'We won't let him, Beppe,' Janey reassured him.

But she needed reassurance herself when they were finally shown into a tiny cubicle to see the boy. Tino was lying motionless, his skin beneath the surface as white as the bed linen he was lying on, the stark pallor relieved only by fresh purple bruising and numerous bloody cuts, which appeared to meld into each other and become one. This lump of raw flesh did not even look like Tino; blackened eyes no more than slits lost in the puffy tissue that surrounded them and the mouth beaten to a red, swollen pulp. One arm had been immobilised, strapped to his side and almost his entire chest had been bound with some kind of strapping. The only thing that gave a clue to his identity was the thick, black, curly hair, still sticky with blood.

Giuseppe was so angry, he could feel the bile rising in his throat and his stomach heaved convulsively in response. He pressed his fist hard to his mouth to stop himself from vomiting. How could anyone do this to another human being? That vile man had not only ill-treated his young charge, Paolo, but had turned on these boys too when they went to his aid.

It was at times like this his faith in God wavered – how could He allow all these bad things to happen to one family in such a short time? He vowed there and then he would keep this from Lena and Raffaele, for the time being at least. Better to wait first and see which way things went. If the unthinkable happened and Tino should die, then he would go back home himself to break the news. But no, Tino must not die, he couldn't. Yet when he looked at the broken, battered body on the bed, his confidence began to waver.

For weeks, Giuseppe and Janey went either together, or in turns, to the hospital and sit at Tino's bedside for as long as the strict nurses would allow. Sometimes, Father Delaney would go with them. The first time, when he had given Tino the Blessed Last Sacrament, had been unbearable; no-one really expected him to live. But Tino was a true fighter and against all odds, had so far survived the beating. His physical appearance had even improved a little; the swelling had gone down and the bruises faded, turning over time from blue-black and purple, to marbled green and yellow. His breathing seemed less laboured, but still he remained unconscious.

The weather had become much warmer, but they hadn't really noticed.

Giuseppe stared for some time at the young boy, watching the thin chest rise and fall with each breath. Tino's weight had dropped and his once full cheeks had hollowed out.

'Is he ever going to come back to us?' Giuseppe looked beseechingly at Janey, eyes glittering with unshed tears.

She put her arms around her husband's shoulders and held him tight. She was concerned for him, she knew he was blaming himself for Tino's situation.

'Well, 'e's still here with us, ain't e?' The reply was non-committal. She had been a nurse herself, but she had seen this sort of thing time and time again. Sometimes the only thing you could do was leave things in God's hands and pray – and that was something she had done a lot of lately.

'Still here.' The voice was weak, but enough to cause Giuseppe and Janey to stare at each other in disbelief. Had they imagined it?

'I'm thirsty.' The voice came again. The rushed over to the bed, tears running down their cheeks. 'Thank God! Thank God!' A nurse came to see what all the commotion was about. When she realised what was happening, she too had bright tears in her eyes.

A few weeks later, amid great rejoicing, they were told Tino was well enough to go home 'but only because you are used to nursing the sick, Mrs D'Abruzzo,' they had conceded. The road to recovery, though, was long and hard. The physical scars were healing, but Tino was very weak.

'Don't yer worry, we'll soon 'ave you 'ale an 'earty again!' Janey promised. She worked hard with the boy, giving him little exercises to strengthen the arm which had been broken and feeding him up with her home cooking. She swore by good home cooking, especially her special chicken broth.

Beppe had become his constant companion, quietly blaming himself for his friend's condition and swearing he would never be able to repay the debt he owed this brave boy who had come to his rescue. What he seemed to forget was that he himself had shown just as much courage in running to the aid of the little boy, Paolo, in the first place.

As it happened, Paolo was now a permanent fixture in the lodging house, and worked for Giuseppe now, as dedicated in his gratitude to Beppe as Beppe was to Tino. He and Janey had felt sorry for the boy, either they must look after him or it would be the workhouse and they refused to be responsible for condemning him to that final indignity, on top of everything he'd already suffered. He was a quiet and subdued boy, but gradually beginning to trust his new carers. It transpired that he had no family left in Italy and the *padrone* had taken advantage of that, for he knew the boy had no-one to turn to. What happened the day the boys had gone to Paolo's rescue was nothing new – he was regularly beaten, sometimes with the back of a hand, or a clenched fist or kicked viciously with a heavy boot, depending on how much alcohol the *padrone* had been drinking. Other times, he would be leathered with a strap until the blood ran. Paolo did not miss him at all.

As Tino gradually began to feel better, many of their regular, working lodgers asked after him and Mr Reedy had even brought him some playing cards and games. Many of the neighbours popped in and out constantly to see how he was getting on, they had all quickly become fond of the gentle, amiable Italian boy. Much to Donato's delight, Kathleen, her little sister Mary and their mother, Bernadette, had also become daily visitors. They all liked Kathleen, it was impossible not to, but Donato more than liked her and looked up to her with something akin to worship.

Tino had developed a taste for Bernadette's porridge – he said he liked the skin she got on the top when it went cool – and now, there was always an extra dish for him, whenever she made it, which was more frequent than it had ever been before.

It never ceased to amaze Janey and Giuseppe; the people in Bramley Mews and the surrounding streets were looked down on by some as little more than animals – and it was true that there were many out there you wouldn't want to meet in a dark alleyway – yet these people, so poor that the threat of the workhouse constantly loomed over many of them, were willing to share what little they had with this boy who was nothing more than a stranger and had not even learned the language properly, yet. They were rough, yes, but in times of trouble, she would prefer to have these humble people for her friends than royalty.

It was late summer before Tino was well enough to even think of going out onto the streets again. The beating had weakened his lungs, he wheezed and coughed constantly and easily became short of breath. The doctor said it might improve with time, but there were no guarantees. It was Sunday morning and after Mass, he had gone across the road with the other boys to see Kathleen. Apart from the lodgers, who were all either in their own rooms, or had gone out, Janey and Giuseppe were alone in the house.

'Yer got ter tell 'im, Gio! Now!' Janey shouted. The easy familiarity of the pet name she had given her husband seemed strangely incongruous with the tone of her voice.

It was their first real argument. Most of the time, they got on so well there was never any question of dissent or bad feeling, each so sensitive to the other's feelings, they seemed to know instinctively what to say or do to keep each other happy.

Whether or not to tell Tino about Angelo's death, and the missing Francesco, though, was a major sticking point on which they could never seem to agree. Almost every day, it was discussed and as soon as Janey stood her ground, Giuseppe would go silent, refusing to say another word on the matter. This time was different, though.

'Why?' he yelled, his face suffused with rage. 'Why should I spoil the boy's happiness, after all he's been through?'

'Cos the boy's got a right ter know, that's why!' Janey was more exasperated than angry and she sighed deeply. 'It's bad enough that you didn't tell them in Italy about 'im being so bad, left for dead an' in 'ospital. But Angelo and Francesco are 'is brothers, what gives you the right to keep it from 'im, eh?'

'I will tell him in my own good time!' He paused then walked over to the window, deliberately turning his back on his wife and leaning heavily on the sill. He pretended to peer out through the scrap of lace Janey had picked up in Petticoat Lane, but his staring eyes saw nothing. They were focused too intently on a scene thousands of miles away.

The voice that shattered his thoughts was quiet but firm. 'If you don't tell 'im, I will.'

He spun around. 'You wouldn't dare!' His eyes challenged, glittering hotly with a potent combination of anger and fear. Then without warning, his voice dropped down to a mere whisper and he begged, 'Janey, no, you mustn't! Please!' He knew in his heart she was talking sense, he had always admired her for her wisdom and common sense. She was right, the boy deserved to know. His shoulders slumped wearily as he finally acknowledged defeat. 'I'll tell him. As soon as he comes back.'

Tino took it badly. He had still not completely recovered from his ordeal; his recuperation had been slow and he had not yet regained his full strength. Giuseppe had broken it to him as gently as he could, but how could he possibly prepare his nephew for this dreadful news? As he had predicted, he was inconsolable.

Tino just couldn't imagine never seeing his bright, lively little brother again. Why Angelo? He was such a good boy, he had never been any trouble, with his sweet, loveable nature. And there was even more to contend with than Angelo's death – it had now been months since Francesco was reported as missing in action and still no-one knew if he was alive or dead. Nobody even knew what had happened to him – there was a glimmer of hope that he could be alive and taken prisoner. But he could also be lying dead somewhere, his mortal flesh slowly rotting away in some alien land. That thought hurt more than anything, for if it were true, his family would never even know where he had died.

Chapter 11

For Lena, the unbearable pain of losing her youngest son Angelo was unlike anything she had ever experienced before, to the extent that it completely and utterly overshadowed the conspicuous lack of news about her other son, Francesco. She had lost other children, too, but never had she felt such an intense feeling of utter emptiness. Whether it was the loss itself or the deep sense of guilt, she neither knew nor cared. At first, she had searched for reasons why, running obsessively through the tragic scene over and over in her mind, thinking up all the possible different outcomes that might have been. What if she had noticed him following her? What if Francesco hadn't gone away, then she wouldn't have been worried about him and would have been paying more attention. What if Michele hadn't taught him to stalk rabbits? The questions were alive, spinning around in her head like a whirlwind. The only thing she was sure of was that she wanted to join him.

Raffaele, too, had found it hard to come to terms with the loss, but at least his shoulders had escaped the awful weight of the burden of guilt that tormented his wife day and night, with never a single moment's peace. The neighbours, including the Grillos and the Fontes, had rallied around the bereft family and the two D'Abruzzo girls, Emilia and Carlotta, had been wonderful. Carlotta, as always, was the strong one in the family, the one who made sure there was plenty of tasks for everyone to do, including her Papa, and giving some of Tino's old jobs to Michele. She knew instinctively they should all keep busy; somehow it seemed to numb the pain.

The nights were the hardest, though, when they lay in their beds with nothing but memories to fill their minds.

But no-one could get through to Lena. For most of the time, she sat motionless in the chair at the side of the fireplace, her dull, vacant eyes staring into space, oblivious to everything and everyone around her. Other times, she would rock back and forth for hours on end, humming the poignant little lullaby she had always sung to her babies to get them to sleep. It was heart-rending to watch and now, even Rosa Fonte had stopped visiting, she couldn't stand seeing her friend like that.

It had taken Carlotta weeks to get anything more than water past Lena's lips and even then, she would only accept small amounts of soup. Now, she was a thin, bony shell of a woman, locked inside her own little world.

In desperation, Raffaele had come to the decision to call the doctor from Atina. It would cost, but he had to do something. He went to the box where he kept his keepsakes and took out a few coins. His eye caught sight of the note written on lined paper, and now there were two more joining it. For a moment, his resolution wavered and he wondered whether he was doing the right thing. Then, he put the lid back and clicked it firmly into place.

The doctor turned to Raffaele, and shrugged his shoulders. He was old, he'd seen most things before, but never the deep, trance-like state this woman seemed to be in. 'You can try some herbs, if you like – maybe an infusion of chamomile, give it to her to drink,' he suggested. 'But Raffaele, I've known you all your life, and your father before you, and I won't lie to you.'

'Is it serious, then?' Four anxious pairs of eyes fixed apprehensively on the doctor's face.

'Physically, she is well enough,' he announced and they breathed a sigh of relief. 'She is thin, yes, that's understandable. But it's not the physical we are talking about here. This state she is in, it's in the mind and there's nothing you or I can do for that. We just have to be patient and wait. She will only come out of it in her own good time.' 'If ever,' he added to himself silently. He might never have seen it for himself, but he had heard of cases like this before, and some people never returned to normality.

'How long will that be?' Raffaele was desperate for words of hope.

The doctor picked up his hat from the table and firmly planted it on top of his head, despite the warm, outside temperatures. 'Let's just wait and see.'

It was some months later and the vines had been stripped of their fat purplish fruits. Already, layers of ripe tomatoes had been laid out to dry in the fast-waning warmth of the sun. Autumn was quickly setting in and still Lena showed no signs of improvement, staying firmly locked away in a solitary world that no-one else had permission to enter. Raffaele would often sit in the opposite chair in silent observation, viewing her with a mixture of pity and anger. She had lost her son, yes – but Angelo was his son, too. She shouldn't be doing this to him, leaving him to cope with everything on his own. It was selfish and there were moments when he resented her, even hated her for it.

The girls and Michele were outside, and Grillo's son Marco, and Mara had joined them. Mara had spotted Marco on his way over and he quickly told her his Papa and sister Serafina were not very well and had been sneezing and coughing all night. He was a thoughtful and sensitive young man and it was his way of diplomatically telling Mara that his sister wouldn't be going to the D'Abruzzo household that day. He wasn't blind; he knew how the land lay between the two girls.

Carlotta, Emilia and Michele had already dragged the big

wooden tubs out from the barn and now they were piling them high with plump, juicy grapes. In the past, this had been a happy, joyous occasion when they would all have fun treading the grapes. Now, though, it was rather more subdued, but even so, the girls were determined to put on a brave face, for Michele's sake, if nothing else.

Marco and Mara joined in until the vats were overflowing with fruit.

'Come on, who's going in first?' Marco laughed, then daringly gathered his sweetheart Emilia up into his arms and dumped her unceremoniously into one of the vats. She struggled to get up in the slippery vat and her headscarf slipped to the back of her head, revealing a swathe of glossy chestnut tresses.

'You are wicked!' she shouted, but was too overcome with laughter for him to take her seriously. She began pelting him with grapes, which he promptly pelted back at her. Soon, the other two girls and Michele were joining in. Then Mara and Carlotta clambered into the tub and throwing caution to the wind, all three girls hoisted their skirts up to their knees, showing more leg than would be considered decent and would no doubt cause some of the neighbours to have an apoplexy if they could see. But they didn't let that stop them. For the first time in many months, they were actually starting to enjoy themselves, pushing their troubles to the back of their minds.

They trampled and trod, moving their legs up and down rhythmically to squash the grapes, releasing rich purple juices that flowed pleasantly under their bare feet and ran between their toes. As the level in the tubs went down, the boys piled in more grapes to replace them. Michele was laughing. Really laughing, Carlotta noted with pleasure. He was only a little boy himself, everyone had seemed to forget about his needs.

Raffaele sat opposite his wife, wondering what all the

hilarity outside was about. After a while, he pulled himself up from the chair, leaving Lena softly humming her lullaby to herself. It was starting to get on his nerves; much more of that, he thought, and he would become as twisted and crazy as she was.

He stood on top of the steps, looking down the hill. How could so much have happened in less than a year? He was vaguely aware of a donkey pulling a cart in the far distance, but quickly dismissed it from his thoughts. He went around the side of the house, near the barn, where all the laughter seemed to be concentrated.

'Papa, Papa, look at all this!' Michele excitedly dragged his father by the hand to see the tubs which were quickly filling up with the juice that would soon be turned into wine.

Raffaele felt a pang of guilt that he hadn't helped earlier. Even picking the bunches of grapes from the vines was hard enough, it all had to be done carefully by hand and was a time-consuming business. It suddenly occurred to him that, in his own way, he was ignoring and neglecting his family as much as Lena. Wasn't he too wrapped up in his own little world? He made a promise to himself there and then, that no matter what, from now on he would try his utmost to get things back to normal, for their sakes. His looked at what was left of his family and his heart ached for them. Poor Emilia, she and Marco were supposed to be marrying in not much more than a year and they hadn't even talked about it properly yet.

'Well, this is marvellous!' he smiled. 'You've done very well. But don't stop now, there are plenty more grapes where those came from!' He too began throwing grapes into the tubs and joining in the fun.

Emilia was the first to notice the figure in the distance – tall and thin, ethereal in the shimmering haze of wood smoke and autumn mists. He was leading a small, flat cart on top of which was perched another figure, legs dangling down over the side. It was to this second person that Emilia's attention was drawn. There was something vaguely familiar about the set of the shoulders, the slight tilt of the head. She stopped treading, standing motionless in the wooden tub and the colour drained from her face as realisation dawned. Carlotta turned to her sister, wondering why she had ceased the rhythmic movements so abruptly. Registering the shocked expression in Emilia's eyes, she followed her gaze. Soon, they were all silent, staring into the distance beyond Papa Raffaele. He continued to face them, perplexed as the last murmurings of laughter died away.

'Aren't you pleased to see me?' The voice was weak and thin, but nevertheless unmistakeable.

Raffaele shook his head in disbelief, desperate to turn around but scared in case he was dreaming. Slowly, he turned to face the other way and the tears that had until now remained unshed sprang readily to his eyes.

'Francesco! *Mio figlio*! *Mio figlio*!' he cried, holding his eldest son in a tight embrace and the tears now flowed unchecked down his cheeks. 'We thought we would never see you again.'

The girls scrambled out of the tub, feet and ankles stained red from the juice of the grapes, but they didn't care. Their brother had come home. They rushed towards him, the whole family striving to hug him and throwing their arms about him. Even the farm dogs seemed to sense the importance of the occasion and ran around in circles, jumping and barking excitedly.

Mara and Marco stood back at first, waiting quietly until the family's excited greetings had been said. Only then did they move forward and Marco shook Francesco's hand heartily. There were tears in Mara's eyes as she looked at him and welcomed him back home.

He reminded her so much of Tino – he and Angelo had all looked alike, with the red-haired Michele the odd one out. But he had lost so much weight, the handsome features now honed and chiselled so finely that the skin seemed to be stretched tight, transparent where it covered the cheekbones. She was the first to notice he was leaning heavily on a stick and looked weak and tired. It was clear he was not a well man, and her heart went out to him. She resolved to do everything she could to help him get better, it would help her cope with the time until Tino returned. She always felt closer to him when she was with his family and now, she felt she could do something really useful in return, especially since his mother was not well enough to see to him. She was sure her own Mamma wouldn't mind, she had always been fond of Francesco.

Her train of thought had led her once more to Tino. He was never far from her mind anyway, but lately, she was getting concerned; she hadn't heard a thing from him in all the time since he had left, not even when Angelo had died. And yet she knew he had sent messages to his family. She just couldn't understand it.

'Papa, can we go inside, now?' Beads of perspiration stood out on Francesco's brow. He was swaying slightly on his feet, as though he might be about to drop in a dead faint and his father cursed himself for his lack of consideration. He was worried too, for he didn't know what Lena's reaction would be when she saw her son; he should prepare Francesco for her catatonic state of mind too. And of course, he did not know about Angelo's tragic death, either.

It was only then that they realised they had paid no attention to the second man, who up to this point had been hovering in the background, near the cart which had pulled Francesco up the hill. He stepped forward sharply, grasping Francesco by the elbow.

'Papa, this is my friend, Giac,' he explained wearily. 'We were together in the war; we looked out for each other.' He paused briefly. 'Now, can we go in before I drop?'

They all exchanged brief but polite greetings with Giac and at the same time, Carlotta caught her father's eye. Her eyes begged silently for him to be gentle with her brother, to make the inevitable blow as soft as possible.

Mercifully, as they entered the cool dimness of the old stone building, Lena was fast asleep in her chair, snoring softly. Francesco somehow summoned up the strength to drop a light kiss on her brow before almost falling into the old chair at the other side of the fireplace.

'What's wrong with Mamma? Has she been ill?' he queried, a deep frown causing his forehead to crease into deep furrows which certainly hadn't been there when he had left almost one year ago. He looked quizzically around the room. 'And where's the bambino? Why hasn't Angelo come to see me?'

Raffaele heaved a sigh and dropped to his haunches beside him. 'Son, there are things you need to know.'

As gently as he could, he told Francesco all that had happened in his absence.

The boy was distraught; he was in no fit state to tell his own story. Instead, his friend Giac took Raffaele to one side, taking it upon himself to explain what had transpired in Ethiopia and since; how they had come under attack in Adua, where thousands of their fellow soldiers were killed or taken prisoner. Francesco had been recommended for a bravery medal, for he had stayed to protect as many of his comrades as he could, acting as a decoy so that they could escape, until eventually he himself fell to the ground.

'*Signore*, he shielded me and another soldier with his own body, and they left us alone – they thought we were all dead, anyway.' He spoke directly to Raffaele, but everyone else there was listening in silent awe, proud and amazed at the courage and fortitude which Francesco had displayed. 'He saved my life. The other man – he wasn't so lucky, but I swear to you, I wouldn't be here now if it wasn't for Francesco.' He nodded towards his friend and swallowed hard, overcome with emotion as the stench of the battlefield seemed to fill his nostrils once more. 'But they found us and we were taken prisoner, we were beaten, tortured. We bided our time and managed to escape eventually but it took us a long, long time to get back to safety. It was impossible to let anyone know where we were.'

Giac leaned forward and dropped his voice to little more than a whisper. 'We lost a lot of good men there, *signore*, and he ...' he broke off, jerking his thumb towards Francesco, 'well, he took it badly. He is weak and gets very bad dreams, where he wakes up screaming. Forgive me if I am being forward, Signor D'Abruzzo, but he will need nursing until he is well again, he has suffered injuries it would be better for him to tell you about himself. I brought him home, because he wouldn't have made it on his own – and even that is only a tiny part of the debt I owe him. But now, I must go home myself, I haven't seen my own family yet and Sora's a long way off from here, hours away.'

Raffaele's shoulders were bowed, as if he carried a great weight upon them. 'Thank you, son. You are welcome in this house at any time.' He put his arms around the younger man and held him tight. But please – you must be tired. Won't you stay with us a while, have something to eat? Or you can rest here for the night, carry on with your journey tomorrow?'

'*Grazie, signore*,' he replied. 'I'm grateful for your offer, and a cool drink would be welcome. But I won't stay long, I want to get home before evening sets in.'

Carlotta appeared in an instant, holding out a flask to Giac.

'Then at least take our mule, it's rested and fresh.' Raffaele offered. 'It's the least I can do, after all you've done for us. You've brought my son home. I will always be thankful to you for that.'

'Thank you, Signor D'Abruzzo.' He handed back the now empty flask to Carlotta. 'I will call in again, if I may, to see Francesco.'

'Any time, son, you'll be welcome in this house any time.' Raffaele hugged Giac fiercely. 'Now, go home to your own people and put their minds at peace. And may God go with you.'

Shortly after he left, Lena's eyes flickered open. They fluttered and closed, then opened once more. Her gaze settled for a full minute on the chair opposite, where Francesco had fallen into a deep sleep of exhaustion. It was just as well he had, for at least he was spared her reaction to his presence. It was the only animated response to come from her since Angelo had died. Her eyes glittered with something akin to hatred as she leaned forward and drew in a deep breath that seemed to come from the very depths of her stomach, then spat on the floor near her eldest son's feet. Some of the thick, sticky globule sizzled as it hit the warm hearth, then dripped wetly off the edge. The only way she could cope with her own guilt was to direct some of it at her eldest son – if he had stayed home, none of this would have happened. Then without warning, she slumped back hard against the back of the chair, eyes dull and lifeless. And once more, she began to softly hum the familiar, unrelenting lullaby that haunted them all.

Chapter 12

IT WAS ALMOST Christmas – nearly a year since Tino and his brother had left home together – before the news of Francesco's safe return reached England, amid much rejoicing.

Father Delaney had been carrying out one of his home visits when the news came through. Every so often, he would march into the lodging house unannounced, engulfed in yards of flapping black cloth. He was a creature of habit, and they knew his every move off by heart – first, he would nonchalantly throw the wide-brimmed hat onto one of the pegs in the narrow hall; he would walk over to the fireplace, rubbing his hands briskly in front of the fire – it didn't matter whether it was summer or winter, he never deviated from his course of action. Then he would turn around, hitch up his cassock and let the flames warm his ample buttocks for a minute or so. Finally, he would hurl himself into one of the chairs, crossing his long legs as if they were made of rubber. It never ceased to amuse them. Giuseppe was wise to him now though – he knew when the Father appeared out of the blue, it was usually with one thing on his mind – he was after money, a donation for the church. The Italian man made a point of never having more than a few shillings in his pockets now.

'Father, this is all I have,' he would offer the coins held in his outstretched hand with an air of feigned sincerity. 'But I know how lucky we are, and the poor of the district need this much more than we do.' Giuseppe was always so plausible, Tino often wondered how he managed to keep a straight face in the presence of the formidable Father.

The inevitable reply, which the boys would mutter along with him in a hushed chorus, was, 'Thank you, my son, you are a good man. God will surely reward you in Heaven.'

It was no different that day, except he explained that he had just come from the family opposite, and that Kathleen had asked him to tell the boys that she'd be over to see them later. At that moment, Mr Weedy came into the room, accompanied by a young boy and Kathleen bringing up the rear.

'This young man tells me he has an important message for you,' he indicated to the boy at his side. 'I hope you don't mind, I let him in… Kathleen from across the road, too.'

They knew the boy, he had brought messages before. He was beaming, grinning widely in the knowledge that he was about to deliver very special and important news. As soon as they heard the words, 'Francesco is safe,' a huge cheer went up in the room. Even the normally dour father was beaming, a big grin spreading across the craggy features.

'There, what did I tell you?' he said smugly, determined not to be left out of the celebrations. 'I said, didn't I, God looks after his own, and already he is rewarding you for your generosity to His causes. Now, you can look forward to a really happy Christmas.' he stopped for a few moments, but never one to miss a golden opportunity, added slyly, 'and I'm sure you will want to thank God in the best possible way. We will be taking donations tomorrow in St Francis' towards the excellent work done by the Sisters of Mercy, with the most needy in the parish. Now, I'd better be going, so I'll leave you all to it.'

He unfolded his bulky length from the depths of the saggy old chair and lumbered across the room towards the door. As Father Delaney turned his back to them to pick up his hat from the rack, he was quite oblivious to the dolly pegs that decorated the back of his cassock, like a neat little row of wooden soldiers. Even worse, at the dead centre, a fluffy strip of brown fur flecked with grey swished back and forth like a fat, wayward pendulum. Tino's eyes and mouth flew wide open simultaneously. He was desperate to look away, he could feel a bubble of laughter rising at the back of his throat, but he couldn't, he was transfixed. He registered that the 'tail' looked vaguely familiar, then it hit him – the last time he had clapped eyes on it was yesterday, on Kathleen's mother's kitchen table and at the time still firmly attached to the body of a rabbit she was skinning for their supper.

Up to this point, Kathleen had remained quietly in the background but now, positioning herself carefully so that she was just out of sight of the adults present, she caught the boys' attention by twitching her nose and putting one hand either side of her head, wiggling her fingers like rabbit ears. Her eyes twinkled merrily, leaving them in no doubt as to the identity of the culprit.

As the priest left, everyone dissolved into gales of laughter, and tears streamed down their faces.

'Yer'll never get ter 'eaven, gal!' Janey wagged an admonishing finger in Kathleen's face. 'But yer've given me the best laugh I've 'ad in a long time. That crafty ol' Father Delaney, no more an' no less than 'e deserves. Just wait til 'e gets 'ome and finds that bleedin' lot stuck on his arse. Oooh, I wish I could be a fly on the wall. I'd give anyfink ter see 'is face!'

Chapter 13

TINO HAD NOT been out with the other boys properly since his attack. He still suffered the occasional nightmare and apart from feeling generally apprehensive, it was taking him a long time to come to terms with the loss of his young brother, although he was thankful that his older brother had been spared. He made sure he thanked God and the Holy Mother every time he went to Mass for keeping his older brother safe, though he could never quite understand why it had had to be at the expense of his younger one. The Father had said that God moved in mysterious ways, but it seemed cruel for Him to expect to trade one brother's life for another.

At first, he had wanted to return home to be with his family, but Giuseppe realised he would be even more distraught if he saw Lena in her present condition, and wisely persuaded him that nothing would be accomplished by it. He would be better off seeing out his contract with him until next year – the time would soon pass. So instead, Tino contented himself with sending home notes and messages. At least they would all know he was thinking of them. And of course, he sent home special notes to his sweetheart Mara, telling her how he was counting the days until they were together again.

Another Christmas had come and gone and now it was April, the musical instruments were put away and Giuseppe's new venture was about to take off – or so he hoped, at least. Today, he had taken delivery of three ice-cream carts in readiness for the spring and summer. He had thought of making them himself, but in the end decided he wanted his to be the best around – he wanted people to buy his ice-cream, not someone else's and what better way to attract them? He had bartered a fair price with Seamus, a friend of Bernadette's husband, Paddy. Paddy had told him that Seamus could work wonders with a bit of wood and paint and he had been right – the carts were a sight to behold, painted yellow with bright red wheels and his name emblazoned along the sides in a fancy script – *G. D'Abruzzo*. That made him really proud. Perhaps one day, he thought, he would be able to add, 'and son' to the script. That possibility made him even more proud.

Tomorrow, though, Seamus was coming to collect his money. Giuseppe was investing a substantial part of his savings in these new carts and he knew he was taking a big risk. Even so, he was determined to make it work, what could be better in the hot weather than a nice, cooling ice-cream?

Earlier, they had started to prepare for the next day. They had boiled up huge pans of milk, and Giuseppe had shown Janey how to measure out the other ingredients – the pods of vanilla, sugar, egg yolks and cream together with one or two secret additions; all essential to making the custard that would form the basis for their own, unique ice-cream. They carefully stirred these into the milk. The mixture had been taken down to the newly white-washed cellar, where it was now cooling in big metal pails covered with clean muslin, wafting its delicious, mouth-watering scent through every floor of the house. Early tomorrow morning, the freezing and churning would be carried out, transforming the thin, creamy-white liquid into real, thick ice-cream.

The lodging house itself was doing well, its reputation spreading farther afield and bringing in good, regular lodgers, even in this rundown corner of London. The inspectors had been several times now and never failed to comment on its cleanliness and value for money. But it was not enough for Giuseppe, he needed to excel, to be the best at everything, to be a real businessman. Then he could go back home and buy land in his native country, make his family and friends proud, even jealous, of him. However, this resolve to do even better for himself and his family wavered when he saw the cost of the carts laid out before him on the kitchen table, in real, solid piles of coins. It seemed an awful lot of money.

'I don't know, Janey.' It was late, well past midnight and the rest of the household were sleeping soundly. Giuseppe and Janey had counted out just enough money from their savings to cover the cost of the carts. Giuseppe rubbed his chin thoughtfully. 'I hope we're doing the right thing, this is going to leave us with almost nothing. What if something goes wrong?'

Janey put her arms gently about his shoulders. 'It won't!' she assured him. 'Look at yer, already a successful man, an' here you are, worryin' you won't do well this time. I got ev'ry faith in yer.'

He returned her hug, resting his head gratefully against the softness of her bosom. She smelt clean and fresh, so unlike many of the other people they came across. She had the uncanny knack of making him feel better, no matter what.

'*Mia cara*,' he whispered, his voice low and thick with love. 'Why is it you always seem to say the right thing to your grumpy old husband, eh?'

'I dunno!' she giggled like a young girl and there was a mischievous twinkle in her eyes. She tweaked the end of his little pencil moustache playfully. 'But ain't it about time yer did the right thing instead an' took yer wife ter bed?'

The next morning, Tino got up at four to help Giuseppe make the ice-cream. It was still dark outside and Giuseppe had to shake him to wake him up out of a deep slumber. He had already been up for some time himself, having collected buckets of ice from the ice-house. It had surprised him to see how many carts were lined up, an array of different colours and designs, all waiting their turn patiently, or impatiently in some cases, before the piles of ice could be shovelled in.

It took Tino a few minutes to come around fully and he padded out of bed, rubbing the sleep away from his eyes. Although his physical recovery was now almost complete, he was still feeling very anxious about going back out on streets. Even so, it would take more than that to daunt him, he just needed a bit more time. Giuseppe, at Janey's suggestion, hadn't pushed the point and instead, assigned other duties to his nephew for the time being. The other boys could take out the carts, and Tino could help with the preparation and cleaning up afterwards, as well as general duties in the lodging house. He was eager to do as much as he could, and he felt it was only fair after all, that he should do his share of the work, somehow.

Giuseppe had bought in a hand-cranked wooden tub for the freezing and churning. There were newer, more efficient ones coming out on the market now, but he would wait until later to get one of those, when his savings started to grow again.

'Now, it's important to get the mixture of salt and ice right,' he explained to Tino. He hacked a chunk off the thick slab of salt he'd got the previous day, itself part of an even bigger block. 'Then we must pack it like this.' He demonstrated, piling the ice-salt mixture into the outer skin of the freezing tub. Tino watched first, then helped. He was a quick and eager learner.

Giuseppe finally stepped back, only satisfied when the receptacle was tightly packed around the inner tub. 'Now for the really hard work,' he warned, picking up one of the metal pails. 'This is where we pour in the milk mixture and start turning the handle as if our lives depended on it!' He began to crank the handle, quietly singing an old Italian ballad in time to the motion, and only looking up when he heard the sound of Janey's footsteps as she came down the steps into the cellar. Her eyes were bright, her cheeks still carrying the pink flush of recent sleep. She looked fresh and sensual, and what with the rhythmic movement of the churning and the memory of a passionate night before, Giuseppe instantly became aware of the first signs of arousal creeping over him once more. But his needs would have to wait. There would be plenty of time for that later; for now, he must concentrate on making good ice-cream, the best!

Janey dropped a light kiss on his cheek. 'How are you this mornin', me darlin'?' she asked brightly, and Giuseppe grinned like a shy young schoolboy. It was as much as he could do to stop himself from making love to her there and then and if Tino hadn't been with them, he might have been tempted to do just that.

'I am well,' he whispered. 'And even better now you are here. But this is hard work, *mia cara*, and I shall be expecting a very big breakfast today.'

His wife laughed. 'Well, that's no different ter normal, then. Reckon between you all, it's a wonder there's any food left in them cupboards.'

Beads of sweat were beginning to form on Giuseppe's forehead and Tino stepped in to take over from him. Between them, they took it in turns, cranking and turning until the sounds made by the contents started to change. It was a subtle difference, but nevertheless detectable, even to the untrained ear. As a solid mass of ice-cream began to form, the soft swishing sounds made by the original liquid mix had now turned into a denser, heavier slopping.

'Ah, now we are almost there!' Giuseppe announced, pleased with their progress. 'Pass me a spoon, Janey, *per favore*.'

He dipped a wooden spoon into the mixture to test it. It was still not quite firm enough, and would need a bit more time yet, but he scraped a little off the spoon and tasted. He nodded, satisfied, and offered some to his wife and nephew.

'That's really good!' Tino cried, eagerly tasting the thickening mixture. He was so excited, he had helped to make his first batch of ice-cream. He almost wished now he was going out with the boys, but immediately stopped at the thought. 'Not just yet,' he decided. The thought never crossed his mind that this would be just the first of countless batches of ice-cream to come. In that little cellar, the first seeds of ambition and drive that would one day lead to his becoming a wealthy and well respected man had been sown. But the price he would pay would be high.

That first day had been unbelievably successful, way beyond Giuseppe's wildest dreams. Donato was the first to come back, his cart lighter than when he left – he had completely sold out. Kathleen and her little sister Mary had gone with him after he had invited them, saying they could help by washing the penny-lick glasses in between customers. It was a good excuse for him to spend some time with Kathleen. It was a similar story with Salv and Beppe, they came back with the ice-cream tubs scraped clean.

'We 'ad a bit of an argument with some boys, though,' Kathleen volunteered brightly. 'Pretended they wanted a penn'orth then grabbed some stones an' went to chuck 'em in the bucket soon as we lifted the lid.'

'Ah, I should have warned you,' Giuseppe apologised, cursing himself for not remembering to tell them. 'That's an old trick, *si*!'

'Oh, don't worry, I saw 'em off, the cheeky little buggers,' Kathleen grinned widely. Her language was colourful to say the least and having been brought up in the slums of London, she showed no signs of the pleasing Irish lilt her mother and father had. 'I bleedin' soon got rid of 'em, said my farver was in the police an' 'e was coming to meet us any minute. Told 'em 'e'd give 'em a bloody clip around the ear'ole. You should 'ave seen 'em run, yer couldn't see their bleedin' arses for dust.'

Giuseppe smiled in spite of himself. This was the real Kathleen, not the one who lowered her eyes meekly, saying, 'Yes, Father, no Father, three bags full, Father,' whenever the priest or the Sisters of Mercy were around. Giuseppe wondered idly how she had never forgotten herself and been caught out when she had gone to school; the nuns there didn't miss a trick. But then again, she had been more out of school than in it and the man from the Board had visited their house more than he'd had hot dinners. Bernadette kept her home to help out and look after the younger one, and would stick up for her.

'Sorry, sir, but she's got a real bad cold today,' or 'Ooh, she had such a gippy tummy last night, I wouldn't want her to give it to someone else.' There was always some excuse and the man would leave exasperated but never believing a word of it.

'Well, let's go and count our takings!' Giuseppe suggested, 'and if we've done well, I think maybe we can get some special treat tonight for supper, to celebrate. And Kathleen, if it's all right with your mother, perhaps you and Mary would like to stay, too. You did "see the buggers off" after all!' He raised his voice up by an octave, doing his best to mimic Kathleen. He didn't quite pull it off, the sound of an Italian accent attempting to emulate a London one was hilarious but Giuseppe was perplexed when the whole room erupted, not quite grasping what it was they had found so funny.

'Oh, just stop it, will yer?' Janey groaned at last, holding her hands to her sides. 'Now look what yer've gone and done, I've laughed so much I got a bleedin' stitch in me side, now. I'll be fit fer nothing, at this rate, let alone making more ice-cream.'

The ice-cream business really took off as a warm spring quietly slipped into summertime. It was June and the whole of London was making preparations for the forthcoming Diamond Jubilee of the old Queen. Miles and miles of bunting had been put up around the city and some people were using the event as an excuse to hold a street party. Goodness knows, many of them rarely saw a bright moment in the day; this was something to take their minds off the mundane chores and scrabbling for the last pennies when the rent man was due on a Saturday. And if they couldn't find enough pennies to pay up, they would conveniently be out. Giuseppe had often smiled as the dapper little rent man, complete with bowler hat and cane, made his way along some of the family occupied homes in Bramley Mews; the door would usually be opened about three inches by a grubby child with a snotty nose. 'Me Ma says ter tell yer she's not in,' was the usual message that came through the narrow gap between the door and the doorpost.

'Well, you tell her to come out here and give me the message herself, then!' the man would reply. The children would see his persistence as the signal to adopt more drastic measures – some would feign a hacking cough, others would scratch heartily or dig at their nitty heads – all strategically designed moves to make sure the rent man didn't hang around too long. Invariably, the tricks worked and he would step back in disgust. 'Well, just you tell your Ma – er, mother – I'll be back next week. And I'll be expecting two full weeks' rent waiting for me then.' By the time he got to the end of the street, there would be a whole row of children, poking their tongues out at his disappearing back, not to mention the occasional missile, which by now he had learned to dodge quite adeptly.

The ice-cream sales had been so good that Giuseppe had been toying with the idea of buying another cart, a horse-drawn one that could carry even more ice-cream.

'What shall we do, then, Janey?' He ran his fingers through his pomaded black hair, then began to fiddle with the ends of his moustache. He was thoughtful, but he never did anything these days without consulting his wife. She was a wise woman and he valued her opinion. 'Tino could come and help me for the time being,' he continued, 'and when he goes back home at the end of the year, I can get someone else in his place. Or maybe Kathleen would like to help.'

'I think we should go ahead an' do it!' Janey said firmly. 'I can manage the house an' the lodgers in the day, cos most of 'em will be out workin' anyways, an' Bernadette can come an' 'elp me if it gets too much.' She paused, looking at her husband adoringly. It was easy to see they doted on each other. 'Let's do it!'

Later that day, Giuseppe went to see Peter the Smithy about a horse. He had good contacts and he knew of one straight away. 'A good, strong 'un, pull yer cart along wiv no trouble,' he had assured him. Paddy's friend Seamus would do the honours with the cart again; he'd be glad of the extra money with all those mouths to feed, eight in all and another one due any day. With a bit of luck, the new cart would be ready just in time for the jubilee celebrations. Giuseppe rubbed his hands together at the thought of all those extra customers.

Sure enough, the cart arrived in all its glory a few days before. Seamus had surpassed himself, it was a sight to behold. He had even made a little wavy canopy, supported by four hand-turned barley twist poles, to go over the top. Over this was spread a large striped awning, the bottom of which was heavily fringed. This was Bernadette's contribution and not only did it look attractive, but it served a useful purpose too, keeping any direct sunlight off the freezer compartments. Along the sides and the canopy were the familiar words, *G. D'Abruzzo* with the legend *Pure Cream Ices* written in crimson scroll lettering beneath. The beautiful hand-painted script was surrounded by a border of coloured scrolls. All it needed now was the horse to slip between the harness, and he duly arrived on June 21st, the day before the big jubilee parade. He was a bit on the old side but still strong and very docile, and the youngsters thought he was wonderful.

'Oooh! Ain't 'e lovely?' Kathleen had been watching in the window, dragging the clean but ragged curtains to one side. But she heard it before she saw it, and trundled across the road as the sound of the first 'clip-clop' in the distance reached her keen ears. 'Can I touch 'im?' she asked.

'Yes, of course you can,' Giuseppe smiled.

''E won't bite or anyfink?'

'No, Peter the Smithy said he's very gentle.'

The girl reached up and stroked the horse's shiny black mane. She was rewarded with a soft, contented whinnying.

'Where's Mary today, then?' Janey asked.

'Her cough's a bit bad today, Ma says she'd better stay in fer a couple of days. She really wanted to go to the parade tomorrow too.'

Janey was concerned. The girl's cough had seemed to worsen lately and she was losing weight fast. Only last week, Bernadette had taken the thin little waif down near the potteries, there were some workmen down there putting tar on the roads, it was always a good way to treat a persistent cough. A good sniff of those fumes would kill off any old germs. ''As yer Ma got a doctor to take a look at 'er?'

'Nah, can't really afford to an' she don't really trust 'em anyway.'

'Well, I'll pop over meself later, see if there's anything I can do,' Janey offered, then turned towards her husband. 'Do you need any help with the 'orse?'

Giuseppe shook his head. 'No, I can manage, thank you.'

They were lucky, they had a small back yard where they had kept the carts and now, the horse would be joining them. There was a small shelter at one end too; it would be ideal. He led the horse back down the road and around into the narrow lane that separated the houses at the back, until he reached the back entrance to Number 9. Tino had already gone before him to open the wooden gate and put out some hay for the horse – animals' needs always came before his own and he'd had plenty of practice back home.

'There you are, boy!' he whispered gently, stroking the horse's flanks. He turned to his uncle.

'What shall we call him, Zi Giuseppe?'

Giuseppe rubbed his chin thoughtfully. 'I haven't really thought about it,' he admitted. 'How about Nero? His coat is black, it would suit him.'

'Yes, that's good!' Tino agreed enthusiastically. 'Nero it is, then!'

The next morning, every door in the street opened, one by one, as whispers of Giuseppe's new horse and cart passed along the neighbours like a daisy chain. It didn't take long for a crowd to gather, and a wealth of 'oohs' and 'aahs' filled the air. They stood around in admiration, some reaching out to stroke the docile, friendly horse, others staring open-mouthed at the gaily painted cart with its fluted canopy, the likes of which they all swore they had never seen before.

'Me mate, Seamus, made it!' Paddy boasted loudly, eager to take some of the credit for this incredible ice-cream cart. He casually pushed the flat cap to the back of his head. A dog-end, which had long gone out, dangled from the corner of his mouth, bouncing up and down with every word.

'Dad, shurrup!' Kathleen admonished, cringing as all eyes turned on them.

Giuseppe smiled, uncharacteristically embarrassed by all the attention, but even so, his chest swelled with pride. He had come from the poverty of an Italian village to the poverty of the slums of the metropolis, yet at last he felt he was beginning to get somewhere, to make something of himself. He was not a rich man, but compared with these people around him, and the peasants back home, he wanted for nothing. He had a roof over his head, never shied away when the rent man called and above all, a lovely wife who made sure there was always a fire in the grate and food on the table. What more could a man want?

Just then the sound of voices drifting down the street brought Giuseppe back to earth with a jolt. The unhappy realisation suddenly hit him that not everyone was pleased at his success.

'Trust a bloody Eye-tie!' came the snide remark. All heads turned to see John Timmings and his wife, Daisy, leaning against the door jamb of their house, legs crossed at the ankles and surrounded by an assorted variety of snivelling children. The pair of them were as skinny as rakes but Daisy towered a good foot above her runt of a husband.

'Aye, they steal our jobs an' as if that's not enough, they try to rob us of the last of our money, temptin' our little 'uns with that ice-cream an' stuff.' Daisy joined in with her husband's verbal assault. Everyone knew that she was always the one who stirred up the trouble and her husband just went along with it. Two young children tugged at her skirt while another suckled greedily at the grubby, pendulous breast which hung loosely over the top of a ragged blouse.

Paddy thought a lot of Giuseppe, recognising the incredibly long, hard hours that this honest, gentle man and his workers were putting in to try to make a better life for themselves. The Timmings' reputation was quite the opposite, lazy good-for-nothings who would prefer to go around begging, thieving and scraping rather than work. How they had kept out of the workhouse was amazing in itself, but it was common knowledge that John would send Daisy out to make a few bob when things got tight. Not that she needed much encouragement. She'd even offered her services to Paddy himself once. 'I'll on'y charge you a shillin' cos I knows yer,' she'd said, dragging her top down to expose her breasts, and he'd turned away in disgust. You never knew what you'd catch from someone like her; she was stinking, filthy dirty. But right now, he could feel the beginnings of a storm brewing up in the pit if his stomach.

'Why don't yer shut your foul, disgusting mouth?' he yelled. 'You're just jealous, the pair o' you, an' if you got off your fat arses an' did a bit o' work, you never know, you might even be a bit better off yourselves. There again, even if you did, you'd likely go down the pub an' piss it all back out again against the wall.'

'Oi! Don't you tell me to shut me mouth!' Daisy shrieked, and dug her husband sharply in the ribs with her bony elbow. 'Tell 'im, John, he's insultin' yer wife, mind! Tell 'im!'

John Timmings nodded, and egged on by his wife, added, 'Aye, you shut yer gob, you miserable Irish sod. Send the bleedin' lot of 'em Eye-ties back 'ome, I say. An' you Irish bleeders can go wiv 'em, too.'

Bernadette was hanging on to her husband's jacket sleeve for dear life, but he was straining at the leash and broke away from her grasp. It was bad enough that they had spoiled his friend's day but now this was getting personal.

'Right, that's it, you bugger,' he shouted, running towards the Timmings house. Seeing the look on his face, John darted swiftly behind his wife, using her greater height as protection. 'Ay, that's it, go an' 'ide behind your wife's skirts like a babby, you bloody coward!'

'You leave me 'usband alone, yer ugly Irish bleeder,' Daisy

was screaming like a banshee, blocking Paddy's swipe at her husband. 'Ay, go on, 'it a woman instead then, would yer? Yer just get away an' leave us alone.'

The children had started crying and at that point, Bernadette finally caught up with her husband, breathless from running.

'Not so quick to open your big trap now we're all face to face, are you?' Bernadette shouted at John Timmings, then turning towards Daisy, added, 'An' as for you, my husband wouldn't touch you with a barge pole, you stinking bitch.' She was deliberately goading the other woman, she hadn't had a fight in quite a while and it was about time someone taught this old hag a lesson.

'You scabby ol' cow, just who do you think you are? I'll rip yer bloody face off!' Daisy was riled and swiftly shoving the baby into the arms of one of the younger children, she gave Bernadette a resounding slap across the cheek.

'Why, you lousy, filthy prossie, God help me, I'll swing for you.' Bernadette grabbed a handful of lank, greasy hair and dragged Daisy's head to one side with an audible snap.

'Leave 'er alone!' John whimpered pathetically and at that point, all hell broke loose.

Paddy took a well-aimed swing at John, catching him on the side of his head and sending him reeling into the wall. Before he could retaliate, another punch caught him in the same place on the other side and he slithered to the ground, whimpering.

Meanwhile, Bernadette and Daisy were grappling on the floor, spitting and hissing like a pair of angry cats. The crowd that had been gathered around the ice-cream cart had now gravitated further up the street and were enjoying their ringside view of the fight. Shouts of laughter and encouragement went up as the two women fought it out, a confusion of fists and elbows, skirts dragged up around their waists to reveal pale, flabby thighs that hadn't seen the light of day in years. Bernadette grabbed the other woman's blouse and the thin fabric tore from top to bottom, leaving both breasts now swinging wildly from side to side as she fought like a cat. Another round of cheers and a few lewd comments spurred the women on. But in the end, it was Bernadette who emerged the victor, hair straggling limply around her face and deep gouges scarring both cheeks. Daisy realised she was taking a battering with no hope of winning, and seized her chance when Bernadette temporarily lost her footing on the cobbles. She ran off, only just managing to stumble into the safety of the house before Bernadette could catch up with her. Quickly, she slammed the door loudly after her.

Bernadette hammered her fists on the door for a few minutes, cheated of the satisfaction of finishing off her opponent. 'Aye, that's it, you bloody cowards. You 'idin' behind your wife's skirts, an' 'er 'idin' behind the door,' she taunted. As an afterthought, she added, 'An' now I'll leave you to it, cos I'd better be gettin' 'ome and disinfecting meself. Never know what I might 'ave picked up from you lot.'

'Ma, you'd better come quick.' Kathleen was calling her mother from their doorway. 'It's our Mary, she's 'aving one of them coughin' bouts again an' she's throwin' up all over the place an' I got to catch up wiv the boys.'

Chapter 14

GIUSEPPE AND THE boys had quietly slipped away. Salv and Donato, together with Beppe and their newest acquisition Paolo went in pairs with a handcart each, but Tino and Kathleen were going to help on the big cart. They had all worked hard for most of the night to make enough ice-cream to last the day, for the freezer on the new cart held a huge amount compared with the smaller ones. Giuseppe had calculated that, given the amount of ice-cream and the fact that he expected it to be a busy day, what with the jubilee parade, he would be able to serve customers much more quickly if he had help – two to serve and one to wash the licking glasses in between. He had promised them all they could watch the procession. And if it was a good day, he'd give them a bit of extra money to go to the fair afterwards. And of course, there would be fireworks later, just to top it all off.

The sun dutifully shone on the procession, with what seemed mile upon mile of bunting, and flags fluttering from almost every window and rooftop. It was an incredible sight, only rivalled by the Golden Jubilee celebrations ten years before. The Queen rode a full six miles through the streets of London, waving benignly to the throngs of people that lined them on either side. As soon as the magnificent landau came into sight, a fresh bout of cheering and deafening applause from her loyal subjects would greet her amid the bands' enthusiastic and uplifting rendition of *Soldiers of the Queen*.

People's jaws dropped in awe at the sight of the procession; first, soldiers from throughout the British Empire paraded in full dress uniform, some on foot, others on horseback. It was marvellous to watch how the straight rows deviated neither left nor right, while somehow they still managed to keep in perfect step with each other. Then came the landau that carried the Queen herself, ornate and ostentatious, pulled by six perfectly-groomed horses, themselves a pale creamy-white colour. All around, members of the cavalry, splendid in immaculate tunics of blue, grey, buff and bright scarlet, flanked their monarch. They reminded Tino a little of the *Bersaglieri*, with their colourful uniforms and plumes decorating their helmets, though these feathers were quite different from the cockerel feathers of Italy's elite corps.

'She's very old,' Beppe remarked as the Queen approached. 'Nearly as old as *Nonno*. And everyone says that he is at least a hundred years old.'

Giuseppe nearly choked. He knew Beppe's grandfather well and doubted that he was much more than sixty or so.

'Better not tell him that when you go back, home, Beppe,' he grinned. 'I'm not sure he'd be too happy if you compared him with the old Queen.'

They watched in amazement as yet another line of soldiers brought up the rear of the procession, each wearing the different colour and style uniform associated with their own regiment, and from every part of the Empire, including Borneo, West Africa and Jamaica. There were rajahs from India and African chiefs, princes and kings, Prime Ministers and diplomats in the capital that day, all there to pay homage to the Queen, celebrating her long reign, and the omnipotence of the Empire. The boys thought it was a sad contrast in a way, because the Queen herself looked so old and frail, and she was tiny, much smaller than they'd imagined. They overheard someone in the crowd say they had heard she wasn't even strong enough now to get out of the landau and up the steps into St Paul's cathedral and instead, the thanksgiving service would be held outside.

As the end of the procession came nearer, people's attention began to turn to ice-cream. It was a lovely, sunny day, just right for business and Giuseppe sent the handcarts further afield, so that they wouldn't be in competition with each other. As he had predicted, the new ice-cream cart complete with Nero, was a big attraction. It was as much as they could do to keep up with the demand.

'*Ecco poco!*' they would call, tempting passers-by with the familiar cry and sure enough, for much of the time there were queues of people waiting to 'try a little' of their delicious home-made ices. Giuseppe had recently acquired a new bowler hat, tipping it comically towards the back of his head while Tino sported a flat cap. They both wore a clean white outer sleeve over the jacket sleeve of the arm they used to serve ices. There were spotless white towels hanging from the side rails and a pail of water for washing the glasses after use.

There had been a lot of controversy about ice-cream sellers; many were not as clean as they could have been, others were decidedly grubby. The Board of Health had raised concerns, because there were cases reported of people being made ill after eating ices from street vendors. Giuseppe was adamant that no-one could ever make accusations like that about his ice-cream, his was not only the cleanest but the best.

'Look, Ma, the hokey-pokey man!' one little boy shouted excitedly, pulling his mother by the hand towards the cart. It wasn't difficult to see that they were struggling to meet ends meet, for although their clothes were neat and clean, they were well-worn and there were several patched areas on the woman's calico print dress. The boy was dark, with wavy hair and big brown eyes. It brought a lump to Tino's throat as memories of his little brother's tragic accident washed over him.

'Shh!' the mother admonished, checking the few coins she had in her hand. 'I'm sorry, luv, I just ain't got enough money left.'

The little boy's exuberance disappeared at once. 'Never mind, Ma. It don't matter.'

Swiftly checking over his shoulder to make sure his uncle was otherwise occupied, Tino called the little boy over and handed him one of the little glass containers with a dollop of ice-cream piled on top. 'Here, especially for you.' His English was improving all the time, but it was still delivered with the captivating accent of his homeland.

'No, he can't!' the mother pushed the little boy's hand away quickly as he was about to take the glass. 'I'm sorry, we haven't got the money to pay.'

'For the boy, free!' Tino smiled gently and handed a second glass over to the mother. 'And one for you too.'

Others in the crowd had seen what he had done and many were enchanted by the young man serving. He had grown since he first came to Zi Giuseppe, and all childish roundness had disappeared from his face and been replaced by a refined, clear cut jaw-line and high cheekbones. He had always been attractive but now he had matured into a remarkably handsome young man, although he was quite unaffected and unaware of it. More worldly, too, but even so, in his modesty he failed to notice the crowd of girls who had gathered around the cart, giggling and fluttering their eyelashes in his direction, hoping they would be rewarded with a smile or some other recognition of their existence.

'Eeh, reckon they likes you,' Kathleen nudged Tino. 'Look at 'em, can't take their mince pies off yer.' Although she was smiling, an unexpected pang of something she couldn't quite identify crept over her.

Tino glanced in the same direction as his friend. Long black lashes swept upwards, framing the deep brown depths of his eyes and the crowd of girls went weak at the knees.

'Oooh, me Gawd!' one of them sighed. "'old me up before I faint.'

Tino overheard and immediately averted his eyes, embarrassed by the attention. One of the gang, a pretty, petite blonde girl was pushed forward by the rest. She practically threw a small slip of paper towards Tino then beat a hasty retreat. Written in a childish, uneducated hand, it said, '*me an me frends reely like you, av you got a sweet hart? if not wil you be ours.*'

Tino went bright red and, not quite sure what else to do, passed the note to Kathleen – his command of written English was virtually non-existent – but he was even more perplexed when she burst out laughing. Her own reading and writing was appalling, but she knew enough to be able to read the message. She reiterated the contents of the note, giggling all the time.

'Take yer pick, Tino me lad, they all fancies yer!'

He carried on serving the growing queue of customers, fixing his eyes firmly on the ice-cream, and trying his best to ignore the girls who were still hanging around hopefully, waiting for his reply. Most boys of fifteen would have been flattered by all the attention, and in truth he was. He was fast becoming a man and it was impossible to ignore the needs of his burgeoning maturity. But there was only one girl for him, no-one else would do. He remembered the sapphire blue eyes and golden hair and a longing for home washed over him – a real *lontananza*. It wouldn't be much longer now, one more Christmas here and not long after, he could go back to Mara. He would miss Zi Giuseppe and Janey, and all the new friends he had made here, but his heart and soul lay firmly ensconced in the hills of Italy. His savings were growing too, enough to ensure they would make a good start together.

He was relieved when they finally scraped out the last of the ice-cream clinging to the inside of the freezer container. Replacing the metal lid with a clang, Giuseppe announced, 'Sorry, we are sold out. But we will be back again soon, and don't forget us, for ours is the best ice-cream around!'

True to his promise, Giuseppe gave the boys and Kathleen money to go to the fair. Tino had never been to anything like this before. They knew they were getting close because they could hear the music in the distance, but even that didn't prepare them for the plethora of colour, light and movement, a bustling real-life tableau with the fairground as the stage. There was row upon row of different stalls and barrows and rides, ranging from the gentle and innocuous to the absolutely terrifying and apparently death-defying. There was a merry-go-round, where horses of every colour and description spun around dizzyingly.

'Tino, will ya come on that wiv me?' Kathleen begged. They had somehow become separated from the other boys in the swarms of people, some wearing their best clothes and others getting into the spirit of the day with red, white and blue hats, bow ties, rosettes and other royal regalia. She would have asked Donato, but since they had become separated, Tino would do.

'I don't know…' he hesitated.

'Aw, come on! Don't be a spoilsport!' She dragged the boy by the hand towards the merry-go-round and handed over two penny pieces to the attendant.

'This one's nice.' Still tugging, she pulled Tino towards a dapple-grey painted horse and clambered up, giggling and screeching as her skirts got caught in the process. Tino sat stiffly behind her.

'Oh, for Gawd's sake, put yer arms round me, or we'll both bloody fall off!' She guided his hands around her waist, just as they ride began to move. Tino began to feel hot and uncomfortable, yet he could not deny he was also enjoying these heightened sensations, the tingling all over that accompanied this physical closeness to Kathleen. He felt a momentary pang of disloyalty to Mara but quickly pushed those thoughts away. He had never realised before how pretty Kathleen had become and she felt warm and yielding as he leaned forward against her body. He noticed that her hair had lightened to blonde and the green almond eyes reminded him of the cats back home.

The speed began to increase and the horses bobbed up and down. Tino could feel an undeniable stirring in his loins. Faster and faster they went, round and round until they were giddy, and the faint stirrings became an urge that demanded release. The wooden horses swung outwards, up and down, up and down. Tino broke out into a cold sweat. He was sure that Kathleen would feel the hardness of his body pressing against her back, he was convinced he would die of shame. The end of that ride couldn't come fast enough for him and he said a small prayer under his breath as the horses eventually came to a standstill and he could get off.

Kathleen's eyes were emerald bright. 'I really enjoyed that!' she breathed and Tino wasn't quite sure whether she meant the ride or their embarrassing proximity. Before he could decide though, she was already dragging him towards a stall where there were rows of coconuts lined up, begging to be hit off their perches. She was a real whirlwind and it was refreshing; Tino had become used to organising and looking after Giuseppe's other boys and sometimes, he felt it was nice to let someone else make the decisions.

Soon after, and proudly carrying their hairy-shelled prize,

Kathleen then proceeded to drag a not-unwilling Tino on practically every other ride in the fair – a helter-skelter, swings and the ghost train to name just a few. Thankfully, none of them required him to get quite so close to Kathleen as the merry-go-round and he was grateful for that. Eventually, they caught up with the other boys.

'Hey, have you seen the lady over there?' Beppe asked, pointing to a tent a few yards away. 'There's all sorts of odd things in there, mirrors that make you look tall and thin, or short and fat. And there's a lady with this long, long beard.' He moved his hand down from his chin to indicate the length.

'Don't know why she doesn't just get a cut-throat and shave,' Donato added.

'Cos she gets paid for standing there in the tent, showing it off, stupid!' Beppe replied. 'Easy money, really. All she's got to do to earn a few bob is stand there an' let people stare at her.'

They all went together around some of the other attractions. Donato won an ugly toy dog for Kathleen, but she assured him that she thought it was lovely not to hurt his feelings. Tino, though, caused the biggest stir. They stood watching men testing their strength on a machine, swinging a huge hammer down on to the base so that the pointer would move towards the top, to tell them how strong they were. If they hit the bell at the top, they would win a fluffy teddy bear. Up to that point, no-one had managed it though and there was still quite a big stock of bears waiting patiently for new owners.

'How about you?' The stall-holder had noticed Tino, well-built and muscular, standing in the crowds. 'Come on, 'ave a go! 'Bout time I got rid of some of these bears, they're getting lonely!'

At first, Tino shook his head, but encouraged by the crowd and his friends, he paid up his money to try his luck. His first attempt fell short; so did his second, but by then, he was getting a feel for it. For the third time, he slammed down the hammer with every ounce of strength he possessed. The bell rang loudly! His friends jumped up and down excitedly and everyone in the crowd clapped him on the back, cheering and congratulating him. Even the stall-holder was impressed.

'Don't suppose you want a regular job here, do you?' he asked pleasantly. 'Just ter show it can be done!' Everyone knew that half the games in the fair were rigged so that people didn't win too often, and this one was no exception.

Tino declined politely, but collected the bear with a murmur of thanks. Immediately, he handed it to Kathleen. 'For your sister,' he said, 'because she is not very well'.

Eventually, they were spent out, both in monetary terms and energy. They dawdled back to Bramley Mews, nibbling at toffee apples and candy floss and other sweets on the way. Tino and the boys said goodbye to Kathleen. As soon they opened the door to Number 9, they could hear the unmistakable sound of someone retching and heaving. Concerned, they entered the kitchen to find Giuseppe holding a bucket beneath Janey's chin, into which she was obligingly emptying the entire contents of her stomach.

'What's wrong?' Tino asked, alarmed.

Giuseppe turned back to him, his eyes bright and shining. 'Nothing's wrong!' he grinned.

'But Janey… she is not well!'

'Yes, but it is good!'

Tino was decidedly puzzled but Janey looked up too, smiling wanly between the bouts of sickness.

'Tino, you're going to have a baby cousin! A little *cugina* or *cugino*.' Giuseppe explained, his face a picture of delight. 'I'm going to be a Papa!'

Soon, the bout of sickness passed and Janey began to feel

better, amid the excited chatter and words of congratulations. 'Trust me ter do it arse-backwards!' she laughed. 'I ain't getting' mornin' sickness like yer average lady-in-waiting, seems mine comes later in the day!'

Just then there was an urgent knocking at the door. It flew open before they could go to open it and Kathleen stumbled in, practically falling head-first into the hall. She turned to Janey, whose pretty freckles contrasted sharply with the damp pallor of sickness.

'Me Ma says, can yer come quick.' Kathleen's breathing was coming in short bursts, her eyes wide with alarm. 'It's our Mary, she's taken a turn for the worse.'

Chapter 15

MARA HAD BEEN a regular visitor at the D'Abruzzo household for some time, but never more so than since Francesco's return. She missed Tino desperately and longed to hear from him, but her notes had gone unanswered. Raffaele had reassured her that he would probably be kept very busy with Giuseppe and he would not have the time to go sending messages. She knew then she would have to be patient until he returned.

Her heart had gone out to Francesco, he had been so depressed and nervy after everything he had suffered in Ethiopia and the way he reminded her of Tino only served to make her more determined to do everything she could to aid his recovery. He was still very weak and the wounds on his leg were taking a long time to heal. They kept filling up with yellow-green pus; a weeping infection had set in, despite the hot poultices and healing herbs they were using to keep the inflammation and infection down. He spent most of his days resting on a raised pallet stuffed with maize husks, for which Raffaele had made a kind of cushion or pillow at one end by padding it with extra husks.

The family had reached the point where they had begun to accept Lena's condition. Now, all they could do was hope that one day she would snap out of it but with every passing day and no change, even that was beginning to fade. They all did what they could. Carlotta in particular made sure she was washed, fed and made comfortable, but no-one seemed able to penetrate the protective shell into which she had retreated. She was a shadow of the fine woman she had been.

'I can't bear to see Mamma like that,' Francesco confided to Mara one day. They were alone in the house, Mara had offered to look after him and Lena while the others were seeing to the daily chores outside. His eyes filled with pain and regret. 'I keep thinking that if I had been here, maybe I could have done something to save Angelo and then she wouldn't be like this.'

Mara put a comforting arm around his shoulder. 'You must not think like that,' she chided him gently. 'No-one could have done anything, it was just a tragic accident. Nothing more, nothing less. No-one is to blame.'

He turned his head towards the wall, so she couldn't see his face. 'It's easy for you to say!' he snapped, then immediately reached out for her hand. 'Oh, Mara, *mi dispiace*, I'm sorry. I didn't mean to be spiteful to you.'

Hot tears flowed over the thin cheeks, the first real tears he had cried since he had come home. They said he was brave, he deserved a medal. Well, he didn't feel brave right now. The rivulets flowed freely, carrying with them memories of the battlefield. They had been exhilarated, so full of confidence as they went into battle. They were buoyed up by the camaraderie and a sense of immortality peculiar to youth. Francesco recalled sadly how they had charged forward – straight into the hands of an army that was far superior to their own. The sheer number of men, trained to a supreme standard and a range of equipment that far outranked their own, had made them a fearsome enemy.

The Italian army didn't have a hope of winning and they had watched helplessly as friends and comrades went down one by one. It was the sound of terrified screaming, the smell of fear that Francesco felt would never be erased from his nostrils; the sight of the land turning red with the blood of a thousand men. He had endured all this, only to come home to the news of his young brother's death and his mother's disturbed state of mind.

And what for? What was all this fighting supposed to achieve? They certainly hadn't gained the intended control of Ethiopia, and the only thing to come out of it was a huge loss of life. Thousands of Italian men dead and even more thousands wounded or captured, most of them young and newly trained.

At home, there were widespread riots. Everywhere there were signs of political uprising and the people of Italy were coming together in loose-knit groups known as *Fasci.* They were baying for Crispi's head and any respect they had once held for the monarchy had fallen dramatically because of his support for the African mission. King Umberto now sat on a very precarious throne.

As these thoughts flew erratically through his mind, the stream of salty liquid continued to course down his face. Mara, moved to tears herself, put both arms around him and he sobbed on her shoulder until finally, there was nothing more left to cry. It was like this that Raffaele found them, heads bent together, one in sympathy for the other's grief and pain.

At first, he didn't know what to make of it. He knew the girl was besotted with Tino, and he wondered what was she doing like this with his brother, too close for comfort. Then he noticed the young man's tear-stained cheeks. It was Francesco himself who offered the explanation.

'Papa! I'm sorry. I didn't want you to see your son's tears,' he murmured. 'I didn't think you would be back so soon.'

Immediately, Raffaele was at his side. 'Son, you don't have to hide your tears from me. I'm your Papa. I can't even begin to think what you have been through, but I know it must have been unbearable. And remember it is better to let your sorrow run freely; you try to bottle it up and it will find its outlet in other, even worse ways.'

Francesco looked across the room to where Lena rocked back and forth in the chair. 'Like Mamma,' he observed quietly.

'Yes, like Mamma.'

Francesco's head still rested unselfconsciously on Mara's shoulder, as if it were the most natural thing in the world. The girl was good for him, Raffaele observed. He seemed to confide in her in a way he wouldn't, or couldn't, with anyone else, even his own family. She was the one who tended to his needs in the day time, the one who sang to him, or played *scopa* or just talked about this and that. And then, out of the blue, it struck him. The tender look in Francesco's eyes gave it all away. He was in love with the girl. He had fallen in love with the girl his own brother loved.

Raffaele sat down wearily in one of the rickety chairs at the table and leaned forward on his elbows, deep in thought. Tino didn't need the girl in the same way Francesco did, and in any case, his plans for a union between Tino and Serafina Grillo remained as firm as ever in his mind. He was still determined that the wedding between Tino and Serafina would go ahead as he and Grillo had planned. Why shouldn't Francesco have some good luck for a change? The only problem was, how could he convince the girl that this was the brother she should be marrying? He would have his work cut out.

A few days later, Raffaele brought up the subject with his friend, Grillo. He had called over to see him about farm business, but finding him alone, he decided to ask his advice.

'There's no question of it, Francesco is in love with the girl,' he explained. 'She's fond of him, it's true. But that's not enough. Somehow, we need to change her feelings about Tino.'

'Well, you'd better find some way around it, I don't want my Serafina let down, and,' Grillo wagged a warning finger inches from Raffaele's nose, 'I don't suppose you want to spoil things for your Emilia and my Marco, either. *Two* weddings we agreed on, remember?'

'Of course I don't want to spoil things, there's been enough heartbreak already. I just wondered if you have any ideas. You know, just to hurry things along a bit.' Raffaele paused, but his friend didn't offer a reply, so he went on. 'The thing is, Tino is due home early in the New Year, he was only contracted to Giuseppe for two years and no longer. His time will be up then.'

Grillo was silent, but the piggy eyes narrowed, almost disappearing among the ample folds of flesh. 'Hmmm!' He rubbed a piece of rough cloth across his greasy brow, deep in thought. After a while, he said, 'Well, it's simple. Just ask Giuseppe to keep him there for a bit longer.'

'What, you mean renew his contract?' Raffaele was confused. 'What good will that do? Even if I could persuade him, he'd come back sooner or later anyway.'

'Time, Raff! Time!'

'Time?'

'Yes! You'd be buying time.' Grillo's ruddy jowls shook loosely like a dog's. 'If Tino stays there another year, it will give you time to encourage this thing with Francesco... make the Fonte girl see he's every bit as good a catch as his brother.'

Raffaele looked at him and felt an unexpected wave of repugnance wash over him. He suddenly realised he didn't like this side of Grillo very much, this scheming aspect to him. Then he thought of the love shining in Francesco's tear-filled eyes as he looked longingly at Mara. And he thought of his daughter Emilia, so happy with Marco, and any doubts he had about the moral implications melted away. After all, he consoled himself, Serafina wasn't such a bad catch for Tino; she was a real beauty, even with her fiery temper and spoiled attitude.

Raffaele was changing in a way that even he neither realised nor recognised. It seemed the more time he spent with Grillo, the more he was becoming like him, always able to justify even the most unsavoury actions to himself. 'But what would anyone do under the circumstances?' he pondered. 'After all, I'm only trying to do what's best. And it's pointless talking to Lena. The state she's in, I might as well have lost her along with Angelo. But then it's typical of her, taking the easy way and leaving everything to me to sort out.'

Raffaele was becoming increasingly agitated and angry with Lena. It was her fault, she should never have put him in this situation. 'I want to hit her, punch her,' he screamed silently. Even in his head, the voice echoed with venom. 'I want to strike her so hard that it makes her head bounce on her shoulders. Anything, anything to put a stop that noise, that incessant humming, that constant rocking.' He threw his hands over his ears, as if to block out the sound. 'It's enough to drive a man mad.'

Without warning, the burning intensity of his feelings made him tremble. He suddenly recalled how, as a little boy, the priests had told tales of the Devil and Jesus whispering into little children's ears. Bad things. Good things. Was that what was happening to him now? Was the Devil sitting right there on his shoulder, whispering bad things in his ear? He felt uncomfortable with the thought. 'Am I just being spiteful, unfair to Lena?' he wondered. 'She's my wife, after all. Should I try to be kinder, more understanding?' There was an ever-changing conflict dancing around in his head and he didn't know any more how to deal with it. But he soon shook off any feelings of remorse. 'No, it's her own fault, she should pull herself together,' he reassured himself, more ruthless and uncaring than ever. 'Whatever happens, it's her fault.'

'Is he keeping in touch with her?' Grillo's voice broke abruptly into his jumbled thoughts.

'Who?'

'Tino. Is he writing to the girl, sending her presents, or something?'

Raffaele felt a pang of shame as he remembered the growing pile of love letters in his tin beneath the bed. Quickly, he shoved the memory to the back of his mind, justifying it as a necessary evil. 'Yes and no,' he replied hesitantly. 'He has sent notes, yes.'

'Well, you'd better put a stop to that, make her think he's forgotten her already,' Grillo advised sombrely.

'She hasn't seen them.'

'What?'

'I didn't give them to her.' Raffaele muttered the words sheepishly. He had always been an honourable man and in his heart, he knew this wasn't an honourable thing to admit.

Grillo roared with laughter and slapped Raffaele heartily on the back. 'Well, you sly old dog! I didn't know you had it in you. Taking a few lessons off your old friend, Grillo, eh?' He pulled a bottle and two dented tin mugs off a shelf. 'Come on, let us share some wine together, celebrate the forthcoming double marriages of our children!'

The wine gurgled softly as it flowed from the neck of the bottle, jewel-red in the soft light. His lip curled with mischief as he handed one of the mugs to Raffaele, then raised his own. 'To us! And most of all, to the lovely Signorina Mara,' he paused for effect, 'and Francesco!' The laugh was low and unpleasant.

Chapter 16

JANEY AND BERNADETTE spent the night taking it in turns to mop little Mary's brow and wipe away the blood-streaked saliva from the corner of her mouth. Paddy had never been able to stand sickness and had gone out at first light without a word. The girl's forehead was burning with a raging fever and in an effort to keep her cool, they laid strips of cloth soaked in cool water on her forehead. Within seconds, the cloths would dry out and need to be replaced. By the morning, there was no sign of the fever abating and Janey was worried the child would choke on her own vomit. There was no doubt she was getting worse, the girl was hallucinating now, muttering something about a big bird swooping down to take her away.

'Bernadette, you will 'ave to get someone to look at 'er,' Janey advised gently, trying her best to keep calm. She was pale and there were dark circles under her eyes from lack of sleep.

'But I don't want no doctors here,' Bernadette protested. 'You know I don't trust 'em. An' I don't want our Mary to be taken away to the infirmary.'

Janey suspected the aversion to the infirmary was as much about their ability to pay as anything else, but she said nothing. Instead, she looked at her friend imploringly, deciding that honesty was the best approach. She had worked in the infirmary and had carried out nursing duties there, but she didn't have the knowledge or expertise to deal with this. By now, Paddy had returned home and she turned to him for support.

'Look 'ere, Paddy, I don't know what else ter try, I tried all the things I know, from boiled onions ter goose grease. But she just ain't gettin' any better,' she explained as gently as she could. 'An' anyways, I doubt they'd take her to the infirmary, I'd say she's too ill to be moved.'

She knew Bernadette and Paddy had little money to spare at the best of times and had spent much of what they had lately on cough linctus for Mary, so she added, 'I'll send Tino to see if we can get a doctor out, an' you needn't worry about the cost, Giuseppe is fond of your girls, I know he'd love to 'elp out.'

By the time the doctor came, Mary had gone even further downhill. Her breath came in short, ragged rasps and the thin little chest lifted and fell spasmodically in a desperate attempt to get air into her lungs.

The doctor was a young, pleasant man with a bushy fair moustache. He examined Mary and shook his head. 'I'm sure you must already know, she's in a very bad way.' His voice was gentle and cultured. Soothing, Janey thought. He went on, 'All I can say is, keep up what you are doing with the cool cloths. And pray to God like you've never prayed before. It's in His hands, now.'

Bernadette let out a strangled sob. The family were poor, that was plain for anyone to see, but his quick glance around the room told him they were clean and proud, too. They clearly did their best, but the trouble was, in these slum areas with their overcrowded houses and lack of decent sanitation and food, diseases spread like wildfire to those who were even slightly weaker than average. He felt desperately sorry for them; he didn't hold out much hope for this one.

'I'm sorry, but unfortunately, consumption is a hard disease to…'

Bernadette's head shot up. Fear flared naked in her eyes. 'Consumption? You mean our Mary's got consumption?'

The doctor nodded gravely. He couldn't believe that she hadn't realised it before. 'I'm afraid so.'

It was hard for her to hear her worst fears confirmed, put into words. 'But what about me other little 'uns? Holy Mother of God, what about them?'

Paddy was immediately at her side, and tears of desperation welled up in his own eyes as he tenderly pulled his wife to his side.

'Make sure they're well fed and kept as clean as possible,' the young man advised. 'And scrub the place from top to bottom with good strong soap. Cleanliness is vital. Now, I have to go, but I'll call back in to you again this evening.'

He was true to his word, but it was too late. Bernadette was alone with Mary when a prolonged bout of coughing seemed to be dragging the lungs out of her body. Racked with the spasms and in excruciating pain, she had slumped back exhausted onto the makeshift pillow, an old jacket Bernadette had rolled into a soft, sausage shape. She reached out for her mother's hand and smiled, letting her eyelids flutter then drop gently over her eyes. Bernadette thanked God her daughter had finally dropped off to sleep, if only she could get some rest, it would do her the world of good. She laid her head on the edge of the horsehair sofa where Mary lay and fell asleep too.

Earlier, Janey had taken Paddy and the children over to their place, only returning when she saw the doctor's brake pulling up outside. Meeting him on Bernadette's doorstep, they stepped into the house together. One look at Mary's still form, the lips unnaturally white against pallid skin, told them the awful truth. Bernadette raised her head sleepily at the sound of their footsteps.

'Shhhh!' The smile was bright even though her eyes were red-rimmed and heavy. 'Look, she's sleeping! First time in days, an' she hasn't coughed for ages, not once!'

Janey and the doctor glanced at each other. How could they possibly break it to her that this was a slumber from which

Mary would never awake? But in her heart, Bernadette already knew. She just wanted to pretend for a little longer before facing up to the devastating truth.

The next few days passed in a blur. Bernadette would only allow Janey, and no-one else, to help lay out her daughter's body.

'You've been good to me Janey and to my family, too' she said quietly. 'An' above all, our Mary liked you all, as well; she loved it over your place an' when you came over here.'

Janey was moved to tears, and the lump in her throat threatened to choke her. Just yesterday, she had been moaning about a bit of sickness and now, she would give anything for that to be the only thing she had to worry about. She felt so useless. How could anyone ease the pain of these poor people?

Together, they walked hand in hand towards Mary's mortal remains. Gently, they washed the thin, emaciated body and brushed the fair curls into place, to frame the little girl's face. Then they dressed her in a white silk gown which Bernadette had cut down from a ladies' one she had got cheaply from the pawn shop. She had always planned to make a new dress out of it, but she hadn't expected it to be a shroud for little Mary. Finally satisfied, they indicated to Paddy they had finished.

Tears ran unashamedly down Paddy's cheeks as he carried his little daughter into the kitchen and laid her in the simple wooden casket that had been placed in readiness on the table. She looked so small, so young. It didn't seem fair. Huge candles were placed at the head and foot of the coffin in accordance with the way they had been instructed by Father Delaney, in readiness for him to lead the family and friends in prayer.

Over the next day or two, all the neighbours came in to pay their respects, even Bernadette's recent combatant, Daisy.

No-one held grudges in a situation like this. The odd thing was, though, that the element of shock seemed to be damped down. In previous years, people had got used to influenza and cholera outbreaks cutting countless young lives short. And consumption was no different. It seemed the poorest people were hit every time, their systems already weakened through inadequate diets and overcrowding in areas where cleanliness and sanitation were almost unknown. Bernadette and Paddy did their best, especially where cleanliness was concerned, but it didn't put food on the table. They tried their best, but it had not been enough for little Mary.

Kathleen was distraught and sought solace in her friends, Tino and the other boys. Tino in particular was finding Mary's death hard to come to terms with. There was not much difference in age between Mary and Angelo and he felt he was reliving the days when he first found out about his brother's death. He found it hard to understand why God allowed these things to happen.

Giuseppe, although he was usually frugal with his money, insisted that he would pay all the funeral expenses. Paddy and Bernadette refused at first, but eventually succumbed to his persuasion, knowing full well if they didn't accept, the best they could do for their daughter would be virtually a pauper's funeral.

'You have been good to us in the past,' Giuseppe explained. 'When others in the past have spat at us, or treated us with suspicion, you welcomed us here from the very first day and accepted us, not as outsiders or foreigners, but as friends. That meant a lot to me. The boys, too.'

'But Giuseppe, we will never be able to repay you.' Paddy was a proud man, despite his poverty. 'How can we accept such a generous offer?'

'You are not wealthy people, I know that,' Giuseppe said

softly. 'Yet, when Tino was ill, you were willing to share the little you had with him. You brought food for him, sometimes sharing what you were having yourselves, but I know you also made things specially for him, to help him get well. How could I ever forget that?' He shook his head solemnly, reaching his hands out to the bereaved husband and wife. 'It is my turn now to repay that kindness. You would be doing me a great honour if you allow me to pay these expenses. It is the very least I can do for my dear, dear friends.'

The couple looked at each other and moved together towards Giuseppe, enveloping him in an embrace of gratitude.

'We will never forget this.' Paddy's voice was hoarse with emotion.

Giuseppe did not skimp on the arrangements, either, and the neighbours looked on in wonder, they had never seen a funeral like that in the neighbourhood before. Instead of the usual horse and cart, often borrowed from the rag and bone man and draped with black cloth, Mary's casket was placed inside a small glass-sided hearse. The undertaker had his own horse, but Giuseppe had insisted that his own horse, Nero, should draw the hearse for the funeral Mass. The boys had brushed Nero's black coat until it gleamed and Kathleen had plaited his mane neatly along his head and neck. He was resplendent in a black harness and a fine black plume decorated the top of his head.

'Our Mary would 'ave loved this!' Kathleen's voice broke as Nero began to pull the hearse along the street, with the undertaker walking slowly in front, and the family, including the older brothers and sisters who had been given special dispensation from their employers to attend their sister's funeral, walking behind. They were followed last of all by their friends and neighbours whose heads were bent deep in respect. 'Oh, if on'y she could 'av seen it,' Kathleen added tearfully.

Tino slipped his arm gently around her shoulder. 'Maybe she can, Kath. But from Heaven.'

At that moment, the girl gave a little prayer of gratitude for having the support of such good friends. 'Ta, Tino. I 'adn't thought of it like that.'

The mood was sombre as they sat solemnly in front of the richly decorated alabaster high altar, with its marble columns and intricate inlay of mosaics. Bernadette impassively studied the painted panel behind the columns, depicting a vivid image of the dead Christ. Anything to take her mind off what was happening around her and to drown out the monotonous voice of the priest's incantations. But the present inevitably encroached on her thoughts and she reflected how short a time it seemed since they had proudly brought their new-born Mary here to be baptised in the oak-canopied granite font, set upon its columns of marble and alabaster. She wondered if she would ever get over the loss of her little girl.

Later, the girl's body was laid to rest in the small graveyard near the church. This final goodbye was the hardest part of all and Paddy had to support his wife to prevent her from falling to the ground. But it had to be borne, Father Delaney had said so. 'It's God's will,' he'd said, and Paddy had wanted to smack him hard in the mouth, priest or no priest. How could he trot these things out so glibly, a man who had neither wife nor family? What did he know of the loss of a child? The feeling that your very guts were being torn from your body? Paddy felt his faith disintegrate under the strain, but somehow, he managed to keep his fists and his thoughts to himself.

It was that night, when all the mourners had had their fill of food and drink at the funeral wake and the house was quiet, that it really hit home. The couple spent the night hugging each other and their other young children, trying to ease the pain of emptiness and sorrow, and stem the flood of tears that threatened to be never-ending.

The weeks passed and the nights drew in as yet another winter approached. Janey was now getting fatter by the day and the boys took it in turns to help her with the daily chores. Kathleen, too, helped with the cooking and other housework – it was her way of repaying the kindness the D'Abruzzo family had shown towards hers.

When she wasn't helping with the chores, though, she spent more time than ever with the boys. She was finding it hard to come to terms with the loss of her younger sister and had formed a special bond with Tino, knowing he too had lost a little brother he had loved as much as she had loved young Mary. It had really brought them closer together in a way that Kathleen had never dreamt was possible.

Tino, though, was looking forward to the day in the not-too-distant future when he would be going home for good. He would miss them all, of course, and he was sorry he would not be around when the new baby arrived, but he would keep in touch with them and make sure they sent all the news to him from time to time. He often talked about his homeland to Kathleen, describing to her in detail the beautiful, rolling hills and crystal clear streams; how the sun would shine so hot in the summer, they would have to rest in the afternoons and start work again later in the day, when it was cooler.

'I'll really miss yer,' Kathleen said, but preoccupied with his own thoughts and reminiscences, he failed to notice the wistful tone of her voice. It hadn't even occurred to him either that she was now spending more time with him than with Donato, who had placed her on a pedestal from the moment he had set eyes on her and now looked on enviously as she gave all her attention to his friend. But Donato could afford to be generous; soon Tino would be returning back home and he would have her undivided attention once again.

It was a chill November day and a yellow, sulphurous fog hung lazily over the street, swirling and shifting as the wind blew gently into it.

'Still hasn't cleared,' Giuseppe observed. They had gone out the day before with braziers, and sacks of chestnuts and potatoes. They had sold well, the mouth-watering smell had attracted the attention of passers-by and naturally, people liked to have something hot inside them when the cold weather set in. It was still only early evening when they sold out, but even by then, the fog which had started out as a thin and wispy mist, had thickened until they could barely see their hands in front of their faces. The faint haloes around the street lamps were the only glimmer of light penetrating the seemingly impervious darkness.

'If this keeps up, I don't think you'll be goin' anywhere today.' Janey had waddled across the room to where her husband stood at the window and looked out despondently. 'Still, won't 'urt yer to 'ave a day in for once!'

'Ah, but a day in is a day's money lost!' Giuseppe grumbled, and his brow creased into a deep frown.

'Giuseppe D'Abruzzo, philoff… um, philoss…' Janey burst out laughing, she knew the word she wanted but couldn't quite get it out. 'Philosopher!' she burst out proudly. 'There! Got it at last! Couldn't get me tongue around it for a minute.'

Giuseppe laughed too. He was so happy with Janey, and she looked lovelier than ever, radiant, as she waited patiently, though sometimes impatiently, to become a mother. It had taken him a long time to find the right woman, but he couldn't have asked for a better wife.

Just then, a dark shadow passed the window, a swirling eddy of fog enveloping the figure as it ploughed through the dank layers. Then there was a loud rap at the door. Puzzled, Giuseppe went to answer.

'Probably someone looking for lodgings, no doubt,' he muttered.

Janey heard a brief exchange of voices then laughter.

'Hey, Tino!' Giuseppe shouted excitedly. 'Look who it is!' He came into the room accompanied by another man, about the same age and with similar features, but smaller and slighter in stature.

Tino looked up sharply from the table, where he had been playing *scopa* with the other boys and Kathleen, killing time as they waited for breakfast. He was quite oblivious to the fact that Kathleen sat as close to him as possible, hoping no-one would notice the look of sheer pleasure on her face. She hoped he would change his mind and stay, but she knew from the way he talked about Mara that she might as well wish for the moon and the thought hurt her more than she cared to admit.

Now, Tino was on tenterhooks in case the visitor was the priest, for he knew exactly what he would do – stride across the room and sweep the cards off the table with one swift movement of his shovel-like hands. Father Delaney did not approve of playing cards, said they were the Devil's tools. It didn't matter whether they were being used for gambling or not, they were evil.

'Gianni!' he cried in pleasure, rushing forward to greet the newcomer. Immediately and naturally, he reverted to his mother tongue. 'How are you? It's so good to see you again. What has been happening in the village? You must tell us everything. Everything!'

'Hold on, Tino!' Giuseppe chided with a grin. 'Give the man a chance to get through the door!'

Gianni was a cousin of Giuseppe and Raffaele, born and brought up in the same village. In recent years, though, he spent much of his time going back and forth between Italy, France and Great Britain, bringing some of the younger boys over to work and occasionally taking others back when their contracts were up, or they needed to return for some other reason. He was paid quite well for providing this service, but it was a well-known fact that he had some other, very lucrative irons in the fire too. What exactly these activities involved was kept very quiet, but knowing Gianni, it was almost certainly something he shouldn't have been doing, if the immaculate cut and cloth of his suit was anything to go by. Papa and Giuseppe had always laughed it off and embraced him as something of a loveable rogue, but Tino's Mamma had never really approved of him, and her lips would always tighten into a stern little *moue* whenever he called. Even so, Gianni had always been kind to Tino and his brothers and sisters; he had a very soft, gentle side and Tino himself was decidedly fond of him.

'*Mangiamo*! Come and eat with us!' Giuseppe insisted, pulling up another chair to the table. 'Then you can tell us what brings you here.'

Kathleen helped Janey to prepare some extra food. 'Mr Weedy' joined them, too, amid introductions. Most of the regular lodgers now chose to stay in their rooms, where there was adequate heating and a single gas ring in each room, but Weedy liked Janey's home cooking – it reminded him of his mother's he said – and he was happy to pay the few extra shillings for his meals.

They laughed and joked their way through breakfast, Gianni was an entertaining companion and they laughed and cried as he recounted some of his recent escapades. At the end of the meal, he leaned back in his chair and belched loudly.

'I hope you will take that as a compliment to your superb

cooking skills, my dear,' he apologised with an engaging smile that reminded Janey of her husband. They weren't that much alike, she observed, but certain expressions brought home the fact that they were related to each other.

Throughout the meal, Gianni had been shrewdly studying Kathleen's attentiveness to Tino and had come to the conclusion that the girl was very obviously besotted with him. Whether Tino was aware of it was another thing altogether. The boy seemed to be quite indifferent towards her, but it may have been that he was just keeping his distance a little, playing hard to get. Even so, Tino might be needing some company, especially when he got down to the reason for this visit. He had always liked Raff's family, and this boy he liked more than the rest. Still, it wasn't really any of his business, he supposed. After all, he was only doing what Raff had asked – delivering a letter.

'How is Mara?' Tino finally asked, a pink flush creeping up over his cheeks. 'Although, I shall find out for myself before too long!' he added with a smile. He was eager for news of his sweetheart but this was the first opportunity he'd had to get a word in edgewise. They'd spoken of the rest of the family – Papa, poor Lena and the sickness in her head, Francesco's slow recovery, how Emilia and Marco were planning for their wedding – and a thousand and one other things that people ask about their home and family when they've been away for some time. But now, he wanted an answer to the one question that was uppermost in his mind.

Gianni's eyes narrowed and he reached into his pocket. 'She is well, but this will tell you more, I think.' Slowly, he drew out a long envelope and wordlessly, pushed it across the table towards the boy. Pangs of guilt swept over him, even though he was just the messenger, for he knew what the contents of the letter would mean to him; Raffaele had prepared him for that, even though he had only given him the bare facts. There was a single word written on the envelope – '*Sabatino*'.

Tino turned to Gianni, puzzlement clouding his handsome features. 'Who is it from?'

'Your Papa.' Gianni replied simply. 'He asked the priest to write it for him.'

Tino glanced up, his brows furrowed. There was something in Gianni's expression, in the timbre of his voice, which made him feel uneasy. He noticed too, that Gianni could not meet his gaze.

'Everything you need to know is in there,' Gianni added. Then, 'I had better be leaving now anyway, I have an appointment. I just promised to deliver the letter to you safely.'

Giuseppe was disappointed. It wasn't often he had the chance to talk to family from back home, except, of course, Tino. 'Do you have to go so soon?' he asked. 'I was hoping you would stay with us for a day or two, at least.'

Gianni was already in the tiny hall, picking up his hat, overcoat and muffler. 'I'm sorry, I have to go.' The longer he stayed, the more guilty he was beginning to feel – 'I have things to do.'

Tino had moved out of the main part of the room and sat on his bed, turning the letter over and over in his hand. He didn't know why, but instead of excitement, he felt apprehensive at the prospect of opening it. Yet he knew he had to. He took a deep breath and slit the top of the envelope with his finger, leaving a rough, jagged edge in its wake. Slowly, he retrieved the letter from its grubby depths, smoothing out the creases of the cheap paper between his fingers.

Mio Figlio, Tino

I have asked the priest to write this, because as you know, I cannot do so myself. Things are very hard over here. We are finding it very difficult to cope not only with your mother's sickness of the mind, but also Francesco's recovery is taking much longer than we expected. Everyone else here is well and Mara has been a good, kind girl, helping to nurse Francesco and your Mamma through the day when the rest of us are so busy with work. She sends her regards to you, as does the family.

Tino struggled a little over some of the bigger words, but smiled to himself at the mention of Mara; it was just like her to help others out. He was a little puzzled though that she hadn't sent a longer message, but it would be difficult for her to say what she felt to his Papa. There was nothing to be worried about so far, maybe his fears had been unfounded after all. He read on:

The reason, though, I am compelled to write to you is to ask for a very big sacrifice from you. There have been terrible droughts here, our harvest has been ruined and we don't even know if there will be enough food to see us through – we have almost nothing. Without wheat or corn, we cannot make even the basics like bread, pasta or polenta; where bread or wheat is available, the cost has begun to rise so that only the very rich can afford it. People are fighting and there are riots everywhere – di Rudini is proving to be no better for the people of this country than Crispi, who went before him. Son, I do not think it is safe or wise for you to come back just yet and I beg you, no, as your Papa, I order you, to stay there with Giuseppe for just one more year. Believe me, I am only asking this of you for the good of all the family.

Your dear Papa.

Tino read and re-read the letter. Only last night, he had proudly been counting out the money he had saved and for months, he had marked off the days, the hours as to when he would be returning home. Now, all that was gone. All his hopes and plans taken away in a few lines written on a piece of thin paper. Hot tears pricked the back of his eyes and he flung the letter onto the bed. He ran out of the room and the house, eyes unnaturally bright against the pallor of his skin. He did not stop for even a moment to give an explanation or even to grab a jacket in his haste to escape the confines of those four walls, which were threatening to suffocate him.

'Tino, Tino!' Giuseppe shouted after him. 'What's wrong?'

Beppe was concerned. Something had deeply upset his friend and without hesitation or thought for his own safety, he said, 'I'll go after him!'

'Me, too!' Kathleen added, rushing towards the door. If Tino needed comfort, she wanted to be the one who was there for him.

'No, stay put!' Janey shouted rather more sharply than she intended. 'At least we've only got 'im to worry about right now, we don't want the three of yer out there in this weather.' She was right and they knew it. 'An' anyway, apart from that, yer don't know who else is out there, all kinds o' ruffians will use this pea-souper ter get up ter their crafty ol' tricks. Jus' look at that ol' fella down by the brewery a few weeks ago, bashed the poor ol' bugger's 'ed in, an' all fer just a couple o' farthings.'

Kathleen shuddered at her words. 'But why's he gone off like a blue-arsed fly anyway?' Her face was deadly serious as she asked the question, and Janey had to suppress a smile at the girl's turn of phrase, despite the circumstances. She had been brought up in pretty much the same way as she had been herself and she felt a certain warmth towards her.

Janey turned to Giuseppe. 'The letter?'

They hesitated before reading it. Giuseppe's reading ability was limited anyway, and Janey couldn't read Italian at all, although she could now speak quite a few words that Giuseppe had taught her. But it was the moral dilemma of reading Tino's letter without his permission that caused them to step back and think.

'But we got to!' Kathleen's mind was already made up. 'I'm worried about 'im, we 'ave to know why 'e ran off like that.'

'She's right, you know.'

It was Beppe who read out Raffaele's letter in the end. His reading was slow and stilted, but he concentrated as hard as he could, he owed it to Tino.

Giuseppe shook his head sadly as the reasons for Tino's dramatic exit became clear. 'Why didn't he let the boy know sooner? He must have known the way things were going out there, why leave it until now, a few weeks' away from when he was supposed to go home?' he said, almost to himself. He was upset and angry with his brother, but it was typical of Raffaele, thinking of himself first and everyone else's needs would be secondary. Except perhaps for his two favourites, Emilia and Francesco. Giuseppe hardly recognised him as the brother he had travelled through the streets of London with some years before. Then, he had been a pleasant and congenial companion; ambitious, yes; greedy, yes. But never heartless or cruel. He paused for a moment to consider the best course of action for Tino. The weather was bad and if anything, the fog had thickened.

'It's probably best to leave him alone, I think,' he said at length. 'Even if he gets lost, he's a sensible boy, he'll find shelter and come back when the fog lifts.'

'What about when he comes back?' Kathleen asked. Her face looked thin and drawn, it wasn't so long since she had lost her sister, she couldn't bear losing dear Tino, too.

'All we can do is give him our love and support,' Giuseppe said wisely. 'Don't even talk about the letter. If he wants to tell us, he will in his own good time.'

Once outside in the street, Tino just ran and ran. He neither knew nor cared where he was heading, and he was quite sure that on more than one occasion, he had gone around in circles. But all he wanted was to put as much space as he could between himself and that letter, the letter which had smashed his plans into tiny pieces. He only stopped running when the back of his throat burned and his breath came in short, rasping gasps from his chest and he could hardly move another step. Stumbling along, his breathing still ragged, he tried to get his bearings. Every now and then a hole would appear in the fog, just long enough for him to pick up on a few familiar landmarks. He noticed the building before him, with its black-banded red brick. Somehow he had found his way to the church of St Francis. He crossed the courtyard and pushing open the heavy doors, made for the Lady Chapel. Time meant nothing as he sat there, praying to Our Lady of the Seven Dolours for guidance, surrounded by an expanse of marble and painted tiles. A faint light from two pairs of lance windows penetrated the shadows, casting an eerie yellowish glow across the little chapel.

Tino knew that what his father said made sense. There was little point in his returning home when they could not even feed themselves; even the money he had saved would mean little in a situation like this with food in short supply, he would just be another mouth to feed. And yet the thought of having to postpone his plans for another year was unbearable. It suddenly occurred to him that perhaps he could send for Mara to join him in London. But he quickly dismissed the idea, for they would never be able to cope with Lena and Francesco's sickness without her help. He knew he was defeated. But his love for Mara would keep him strong; it might take a bit longer, but the time would come when he could go back home to her. The day had gone full circle, the fog had thinned out and darkness was beginning to fall once more when he finally got up from the hard wooden bench and headed for home, filled with desolation and resignation. Number 9, Bramley Mews would be his home for yet another year.

Chapter 17

RAFFAELE HAD ARRANGED to meet Gianni in Atina, where he was staying for a few days on business. He had ridden over in the cart pulled by the old donkey. It would be a good opportunity to see what provisions he could get while he was there, things were getting harder and harder to come by. They had a few cheeses left to trade with, maybe he could get some flour in return. The weather was cold and a fine drizzle misted the caps of the mountains and settled damply below in the valleys. The journey seemed to take longer than normal, though whether it was because the donkey was getting older and slower by the year or whether it was due to the fact that he was in a hurry to hear what news Gianni brought from England, he didn't know.

There was a small hostelry there, a *cantina,* where travellers, visitors and locals alike could share a bottle of wine or two and get a bite to eat. This was where, hopefully, Gianni would be waiting for him. Raffaele left the cart in a side-street, leaving a small bag of food and a basin of water for the donkey. 'If it doesn't freeze over first,' he thought to himself, rubbing his hands briskly together. He pushed open the door of the hostelry and stepped inside. The light was dim, the air hazy with smoke and it took him a few moments to get his bearings. Then he noticed someone in the far corner waving and beckoning to him and his face immediately brightened.

'Gianni! How are you?' He was pleased enough to see him but couldn't help noticing his cousin's exquisite clothing with a touch of jealousy. His dress was immaculate with attention to detail, even down to the highly polished leather shoes –

not boots or clogs or *le ciocie*, but real shoes – and the ornate, solid gold watch and chain which straddled the centre of his waistcoat. Raffaele couldn't deny he was envious. 'Who said it pays to be honest?' he thought churlishly.

'I'm well enough, Raff,' Gianni replied slowly, pushing a small parcel across the table. 'I know you like these and with the shortages over here …' his voice trailed off.

Raffaele tore off the brown paper covering. Inside were several packs of his favourite cheroots. 'Oh, *grazie*!' It was obvious from the tone of his voice how much this gift had pleased him and after extracting just one, he busily stuffed the rest into the deep pockets of his outer coat. 'Thank you, Gianni.'

Gianni smiled to himself. It was just like his cousin, Raffaele. Did he really think he hadn't noticed the narrow-eyed scrutiny of his clothes, how his eyes had lit up with greed and envy at the sight of the watch and chain? And yet here he was, quite happy to take presents from him.

Raffaele clenched the cheroot between his lips and twisted a piece of paper to form a taper, which he pushed deep into the heart of the fire. The flames licked around it hungrily and when it flared into life, he touched it to the end of the cheroot. His eyes screwed up at the corners as a plume of smoke drifted past them then rose in a spiral towards the brown-stained ceiling.

'Now, tell me!' he whispered. He leaned forwards conspiratorially towards his cousin and for a split second, Gianni felt an unexpected feeling of revulsion wash over him. Raffaele reminded him of a snake about to strike its prey.

'Did you get to see them in London?'

'*Si*. Of course.' Gianni replied slowly. He was deliberately eking it out, teasing and taunting his cousin and what's more, he was beginning to enjoy it.

'Well, out with it, man!' A purplish-red mottling of the skin crept upwards from Raffaele's neck towards his face as he struggled to keep his composure. He could have bitten his own tongue off, it was pointless shouting and ranting where Gianni was concerned, he knew him well enough to realise that if he started pushing the point, he would just get up and walk away. And that wouldn't do at all.

Instead he adopted another tactic and a sly, wheedling note slipped easily into his voice. 'Oh, come on, now, cousin! You know I haven't seen my son or my brother for a long time, I'm eager for news of them!'

Gianni was no angel, making a living mostly by illegal means, but right now, he was filled with contempt for his cousin.

'They are well. Giuseppe and Janey are going to have a *bambino*, soon.' He was determined to make this as difficult as possible for the other man.

'Ahh! Yes! Good! And what about Tino? How is he? Has he got a sweetheart out there?' This sudden interest in Tino seemed rather too quick for comfort for Gianni's liking.

'Well, there's a girl called Kathleen who seems to be very fond of him,' Gianni considered, careful not to give too much away.

'Ah! *Bene, bene!* That's good!'

'But I don't think he's too keen on her, he was more concerned about *la Signorina* Mara.'

Raffaele's face clouded over momentarily. 'Hmmm. We'll see about that!' he muttered, the cheroot drooping out of the corner of his mouth as usual. 'He's not coming back yet, though is he?'

Gianni eyed his cousin with suspicion. There was more to this thing with Tino than met the eye, it wasn't just about food shortages and politics. From Raffaele's reaction, he had a strong hunch it had something to do with the Fonte girl Tino was so fond of.

'Why is that so important to you?'

'Well, you know how it is here, the way things are done here…' Raffaele blustered beneath Gianni's close scrutiny, deliberately making sure his eyes rested on anything but his cousin's searching ones, which he knew were fixed firmly on him and filled with an equal measure of scorn and distrust.

'No, I don't know. Tell me!'

'Well, you know we haven't got enough food for ourselves, let alone Tino as well,' Raffaele protested feebly.

'You know I can get things for you, like I got the cheroots. Do you think I would stand by and watch my cousin's family starve?' 'Even if I might just let my *cugino* himself starve!' he added wryly to himself.

Raffaele shuffled uncomfortably on the hard wooden seat. 'Well, it's done now, he can stay there for another year. It won't hurt him.' His voice held a surly note, he had found out what he needed to know so he didn't care any more whether he offended Gianni or not.

'It won't hurt him?' Gianni spat out. He was shaking with anger by now, his face red above the tight collar, and he pushed his fingers inside and ran them around in an effort to loosen it. He added, 'Then why do I get the feeling that's exactly what will happen as a result of this nasty little scheme of yours?'

Raffaele got to his feet to protest, but he knew Gianni wasn't very far from the truth and his voice lacked conviction. 'Now, don't you go preaching to me, Gianni! You're a fine one to talk, what with all your goings-on and…'

He was interrupted mid-sentence. 'I'm not the one who'd sell my own son's soul to the Devil!' The words came out quietly but carried all the more weight because of it. 'I don't know what you're up to, but I've a good idea it spells trouble.

So, cousin, in future, you can do your own dirty work and count me out. Don't ask me to be your errand boy again; whatever it is, I want no part of it.' The chair scraped across the stone floor as he pushed it away and turned his back on Raffaele. Despite his small stature, he covered the length of the room in a few angry strides, hastily throwing some coins onto the counter as he passed. He went without a backward glance, leaving his cousin and the rest of the customers to stare after him in open-mouthed amazement.

It was getting late when Raffaele finally reached home, softly whistling a tune to himself as he unloaded the few provisions he had managed to pick up in Atina. He was feeling quite pleased with himself and the day's outcome. Suddenly, he stopped in his tracks, lips still pursed, but not a sound escaped from them. His eyes narrowed as he realised he'd been whistling the lullaby Lena constantly hummed. It was really beginning to get to him, and his initial feelings were beginning to evolve into something far less sympathetic. She had kept this self-indulgence up long enough; it was about time she pulled herself together. He'd had enough of it; in fact, he was sick of it. It was about time he started thinking of himself now. It wasn't fair; the burden she was placing on the rest of the family was becoming intolerable. Still, he wasn't going to let her, or anyone, or anything, spoil his ambitions, no-one would stop him getting his hands on his fair share of Grillo's land now. He deserved it.

'Papa!' Emilia's hair shone with rich gold flecks in the dying evening light as she ran eagerly to greet her father. He grimaced as her bad eye wandered off in the opposite direction to the other. He hoped she hadn't noticed his reaction. It seemed wicked that such beauty should be marred, he thought silently – but at least, he would make sure she got her husband, whatever the cost.

He had timed his return well as they were just about to eat. The girls had worked wonders with the reduced provisions they had to work with and so far, the family hadn't gone hungry, unlike many others in the area.

'Did you get any flour?' Carlotta asked, always anxious to make sure the family was well-fed and cared for, despite the present difficulties. She looked up from the corner of the table where she was placing a sticky-looking dough into a deep earthenware dish. Her gentle nature was reflected in the soft brown eyes and rounded features for all to see.

'*Si*! Not as much as I'd have liked, but enough,' he nodded. 'And a few other things, too.'

Francesco was sitting upright, but resting his leg on a makeshift stool which Carlotta had cleverly put together, an old box with a padded cover made from a square of woven cloth stuffed with corn husks. Mara was alongside him and Raffaele noticed with a glimmer of satisfaction that although they were not close enough to touch, Francesco's arm rested in a subconsciously protective gesture just behind her shoulders.

'Did you meet up with cousin Gianni, then, Papa?' He pressed the palms of his hands onto the seat to push himself up higher, and the husk-filled cushion rustled loudly with the sudden movement.

The two girls looked up from the corner of the table where they were now ladling steaming soup into dishes, which they then passed to Michele to place one for each person. They were eager to hear his reply, too.

Raffaele walked slowly over to the fire, completely ignoring his wife who sat, as usual, staring blankly into space. He had long since stopped kissing her on the cheek in greeting. He stretched his hands out to the leaping flames, flexing his fingers before quietly answering his eldest son's question.

'*Si*. Yes.'

'So what did he say?'

'Did Tino ask about me? Or send a message?' Mara asked eagerly.

'One at a time!' Raffaele protested, giving a small, nervous laugh as he played for time. He wouldn't have admitted it even to himself, but he was deliberately postponing the inevitable moment when he would have to drop the bombshell.

'Now,' he began slowly, 'they are all well in England. Your uncle and his new wife are very happy, they're going to have a little one, soon.'

'But what about Tino?' It was young Michele who asked the question this time. 'He said he would bring me something from London when he comes back. Will he be there much longer?'

His father purposefully turned his attention back to the fire, poking and prodding it vigorously with a long bent piece of metal. The fire blazed more fiercely in response, roaring into life, and a shower of orange and red sparks flew up the huge stone chimney.

'Aah! Now, then. There is a little problem there.'

Mara paled. 'But he is well, yes?'

'Oh, he's well enough,' the man replied. Still he kept his back towards them as he continued to concentrate hard on the fire. 'But Gianni tells me he is really enjoying it over there, and he wants to stay for at least another year. Maybe longer.'

'Another year?' Tears sprang readily to sapphire blue eyes that darkened with pain. She didn't know how she could wait another year again, it was asking too much of her.

Raffaele took a deep breath and turned around to face them. It was now or never, he had to keep his nerve. 'Mara, *carina*.' He paused and gave a deep sigh. 'The truth is, I don't know if he is ever coming back.'

'No!' The tears flowed unchecked down her cheeks now,

and glistened on her lashes, running into her mouth. 'Please, *signore*, don't tease me! Please.'

'I'm not teasing you.'

The girl's stricken face crumpled beneath his gaze and he was suddenly beset by an overwhelming sense of guilt. But he noticed too the raw emotion in his eldest son's dark eyes as he looked at her. Then his gaze fell on Emilia, bringing to mind Grillo's bargain, and his resolve was renewed. He tried to defend his actions to himself; he wasn't a bad man, he just wanted what was best for his whole family, including the security of gaining part of Grillo's land. He had to see this through.

'I didn't want to have to tell you this, but I think I must.' He adopted a fatherly expression, putting his hand on the girl's shoulder. 'Gianni told me Tino has another girl over there. Kathleen, I think he said she was called.'

'No! No, I don't believe it!' Pain etched the pretty face and even Raffaele's closed heart softened towards her momentarily. 'Please tell me it's not true.'

But he ignored the feeling, he couldn't back down now. 'It's true. Why do you think he hasn't contacted you?' He was almost brutal in his feigned honesty. 'No messages, no notes. Nothing! He's been gone for two years, and nothing!' The picture of the tin with its growing pile of folded notes, plaster model and a small wooden carving flashed into his head, but he conveniently brushed it aside.

The girl was distraught and no-one objected as Francesco's arm slipped about the slender shoulders to comfort her. He held her close to his side, almost feeling the pain with her, and wishing he could take it away.

'Papa, no more! Please!' he begged. 'Can't you see, she's had enough?'

'I'm just telling it the way it is, Francesco,' the older man replied calmly. 'There's no point in her hanging around waiting for him if he's not going to come back; it's better for her to know the truth now than waste her time weeping and moping, hoping he'll change his mind. She's young and beautiful,' he smiled meaningfully towards his son, 'she'll soon find someone else to take his place.'

The room went silent, except for the young girl's quiet sobbing. No-one felt like food any more and Raffaele was the only one to join Michele at the table in front of the bowls. 'What's the matter with you all?' he grumbled. 'Other people around here are not as lucky as we are, yet here you are, wasting this good food.'

He was feeling extremely smug and self-satisfied. He had successfully planted the seeds of doubt about Tino's return, setting off a trail of other things in motion. If everything went according to plan, by this time next year, there should be celebrations in the family, and judging by Francesco's constant doe-eyed glances towards the Fonte girl, it shouldn't be too difficult to encourage things along in that direction. If they were safely married out of the way, it might be easier then to persuade Tino that Serafina Grillo would make an excellent wife. He would have to win the Fontes over too, soothe their egos when their daughter told them that Tino would not be back after all; the last thing he wanted was for them to come over here causing trouble. For a man to break his promise of marriage was one of the biggest insults not only to the girl, but to her family, and people had been shot for less. Rosa in particular had wanted things to go well in that direction, but Raffaele was confident that he could win them around when he explained that Francesco was available, and a worthy substitute, ready and willing to marry their daughter. Yes, there were a few people that needed to be gently nudged in the right direction, not least Mara herself, but he knew could do it.

In London, Tino had finally accepted his lot. His first instinct had been to send a letter home to say how sad he was at not being able to return, but being a good, obedient son, he would always abide by his Papa's decisions. He knew his father would have had to take it to someone else to read, so he kept his real feelings out of it. But he didn't hold anything back in the letter he enclosed for Mara, he poured out his heart, begging her to wait just one more year for him. Whatever happened then, he would come for her. How could he possibly have known that, like all the other letters he had sent before, Mara would never get to read it.

He didn't know what he would have done without the support of the people around him – Giuseppe and Janey had been like parents to him and made him see that what his Papa had said probably made sense. Things were hard in Italy and it wouldn't help the family at all if they had another mouth to feed. The other boys had been good to him too; Beppe was really concerned for his friend and insisted on taking him out one night to see a new music hall act he had heard about. It was a diversion for a while, and he laughed along with the jokes and sang along with the tunes like everyone else, but as soon as they left the theatre, the memories came flooding back, weighing down on him like lead.

Donato, Salv and Paolo made sure he never had enough time to think too hard. They would invent reasons to ask his opinion of this or that, or even start quarrelling to distract him. Kathleen spent more and more time at the lodging house, trying every trick she knew to cheer him up. She'd tell him in minute detail about the most recent rows between her mother and 'that scruffy cow up the road, Daisy'. She'd describe in colourful words that conjured up all sorts of comical images, the time when Daisy had come up the road one Saturday 'blind drunk an' fallin' all over the place, wiv a man on each arm, one 'anging behind an' not one of 'em her husband!' Anything to take his mind off his home and the beautiful girl waiting for him in Italy.

The first big distraction came on a cold and windy March day, when Janey's first labour pains began.

She had been feeling a bit off-colour for a day or so, with griping pains, but put it down to the stomach complaint that many people seemed to have at the time. But when the first real pain came, she knew this was no ordinary stomach upset. She said nothing for an hour or so, and got up to make the breakfast as usual. The only sign that she was in the early stages of labour was that every so often, she would have to stop to catch her breath as a fresh spasm gripped her, creating tiny pearls of sweat on her brow.

'Is everything all right?' Mr Weedy was at her side; he had noticed how she bent over every so often, clutching at her swollen belly.

Janey smiled. 'Well enough to finish cookin' yer breakfast, don't you worry!' she assured him. 'It's just a little pain, I'll be fine.'

The kindly lodger didn't look convinced but sat down at the table, quietly reprimanding himself for interfering in what was, after all, women's business. Giuseppe and the others sat at the table, eating hungrily and quite oblivious to Janey's situation, but Weedy kept a watchful eye on her. He couldn't help noticing that her face seemed to be screwing up with pain more frequently and eventually, he couldn't hold back any longer.

'Mr D'Abruzzo,' he spoke quietly, so the boys didn't hear. 'I think your wife needs you.'

Giuseppe frowned, looking across the room towards Janey. She was pale and sweating, but two dark red spots brought an unnatural flush to her cheeks. He was across the room in a second. 'Janey, what is it?' He was genuinely concerned and it showed in his worried voice.

Janey forced a smile. 'I think you're goin' to be a Papa very, very soon!'

Her husband broke into an excited smile which seemed to stretch from ear to ear and his eyes lit up. 'You mean the *bambino* is coming?'

'Let's say I think you ought ter call the midwife.' The last words trailed off as another spasm gripped her, contorting her features into a mask of pain.

'Tino, go and get Mrs Thoms,' Giuseppe shouted, then forever the practical businessman, added, 'I won't be coming out with you today, you'll all have to work on your own. So as soon as you get back, Tino, you'll have to be in charge. Now, go – quick!'

Later, the boys met up with Kathleen, preparing the carts for the day and gathering together the braziers, and sacks of potatoes and chestnuts. The day seemed to drag and it was hard for them to concentrate, they were too busy wondering what was happening back home. The miracle of life was no mystery to them, there was little room for privacy either in Kathleen's large family, or in the crowded cottages in Italy. Every one of the boys, except for the youngest, Paolo, had seen many births before, from farm animals to the ever-increasing numbers of their own families. But they knew they would be in the way if they went back too soon, and although they had sold out by mid-afternoon, they made a big effort to hang around the streets just a little bit longer.

'I know, how's about pie 'n eels?' Kathleen suggested brightly, and since the day long ago when Beppe had first introduced him to them, Tino had developed quite a liking for the dubious delicacy.

'Right. It's pie 'n eels all round, then,' Tino agreed enthusiastically. 'I'm sure Zi Giuseppe won't mind us using some of the money, it's a special day for all of us, after all.'

It was dusk when they finally returned to Bramley Mews, eager to hear the news. Giuseppe had been watching out for them, peeping behind the curtains impatiently every few minutes.

'You'll wear a 'ole in the floor, you keep goin' to that window much more!' Janey laughed wearily, but this time, he was rewarded when he saw Tino with Kathleen and the boys tagging along behind.

'They're here!' he grinned. 'At last.' He flew out of the room, pulling the door so hard it hit the wall with a loud bang.

'Tino! Tino!' He was crying and laughing at the same time, and looking for all the world as if he was a man who had just come into a fortune. 'My boys! Kathleen! We have a *bambina*! A little girl and she is so beautiful. Quick, quick! Come and see!'

Immediately, they all broke into a run, shrieking with excitement and falling over each other as they vied to be the first to get a glimpse of the new addition to the D'Abruzzo family.

Kathleen got there first. 'Eeh! Ain't she little?' she grinned as she saw the tiny scrap of humanity wrapped up in a white fringed shawl and held like precious china in Janey's proud arms. Then Tino added, 'But Zi Giuseppe, she is so beautiful. *Una bella bambina*!'

His eyes were moist with tears of happiness. He was so pleased for them, he owed them a lot and would never forget their kindness to him. In many ways, he reflected, Giuseppe had been better to him than his own Papa and he loved him for that.

'You can 'old her if yer like.' Janey's happiness was complete as she held the baby out to Tino. He took the tiny bundle and cradled her gently in his arms.

'She is so beautiful!' he reiterated. Gently, he stroked one of the tiny hands and watched fascinated as it closed into a fist around his finger. 'I think she likes me,' he grinned.

'We've called her Angela,' Zi Giuseppe broke in and Tino looked up quizzically. 'After your little brother. I remember when he was born, too, and this little one looks just like him – a real little angel, even down to the dimples in her cheeks.'

A lump came to Tino's throat. He was really touched by the gesture.

'Grazie, Zio.' He turned to Janey. 'Thank you, too. And it's a very beautiful name for a very beautiful little girl.'

Janey could see the tears welling up in the boy's eyes but true to form, she soon lightened the mood. 'An' to think that only this mornin', I thought I 'ad that stomach thing goin' round, an' I had wind pains,' she giggled. 'I 'ave ter say, our little Angela's got ter be the prettiest lookin' bag o' wind I've ever seen.'

The rest of the year in England passed uneventfully. Angela turned out to be a good, happy child whose cheerful countenance brought a smile to everyone who came in contact with her. Tino became a real favourite with her and whenever he came into the room, her chubby little face would break into a big smile and she would reach her arms out to him, begging to be picked up. He adored the child and would spend hours playing with her.

'You'll make a good father yerself, one day,' Janey would tease and it never failed to bring a shy flush to his cheeks. Sometimes, she would catch the wistful expression on Kathleen's face and began to have strong suspicions as to where her affections lay. She was a good girl, witty and likeable, but Janey knew she was setting herself up for a big disappointment. Janey admired Tino for sticking to his resolve where the girl in Italy was concerned; he had been determined from his arrival in London that he would return to her to make her his wife, and nothing, not even their long separation, had shaken that determination. He was a good boy, a courageous and loyal boy. Mara would be lucky to have him as a husband.

As yet another year passed and the time drew nearer for him to return home, the one thing he regretted was having to leave behind these lovely people who had taken him in and treated him as their son. He loved his uncle and aunt, and little Angela and as before, he felt regret at leaving behind all his friends. But he consoled himself with the knowledge that out there, many miles across the sea, someone else waited patiently for him, just as he had waited all these years for her.

Chapter 18

EVEN IN LONDON, the news of Italy's current state of disarray and chaos was well known; from early on in 1898, there had been street demonstrations against the food shortages and inflated prices with the first rumblings starting in the southern parts of Italy and spreading northwards. By April the whole of the country was in uproar. The government was getting cold feet, convinced that there was some underhanded conspiracy going on, no doubt inspired by the socialists, and they were determined to put an end to it.

A bungled attempt to arrest some newspaper vendors selling socialist literature in Milan ended in riots and the army was brought in to suppress the uprising. But the attempt to quell the riots resulted in the deaths of more than two hundred people and the government became even more heavy handed, insisting that anyone suspected of causing trouble or being involved in inciting riots should be arrested. On the surface, the threat of imprisonment succeeded in quashing the rebellion and silencing the people. But in reality, all it accomplished was to drive the opposition underground, where it fermented and grew, in turn increasing the opposition of the public.

Tino was worried about his homeland like everyone else, but despite this, he was determined this time, nothing was going to keep him from his home for a moment longer than necessary and soon, as the old year gave way to the new, it was time for him to go home. The weather was bitterly cold, their breath turning to mist as they gathered on the doorstep of the lodging house. The threat of imminent snow cut the air and a lowering, pink-grey sky cast eerie shadows on the cobblestones.

He said his goodbyes with a promise to return as soon as he could. 'And next time,' he joked, in an effort to stop the lump in his throat from engulfing him, 'I might just be bringing someone else back with me to meet you.'

Janey guessed at once who he was referring to and cast a hasty glance in Kathleen's direction. The comment hadn't been lost on her either; she couldn't have looked more hurt if someone had slapped her hard across the face. But Tino didn't notice – thoughts of home were uppermost in his mind and he was completely oblivious to her reaction.

The whole street came out to wave him off, and Janey could have sworn she saw Daisy hastily wiping away a tear from her cheek, as she came to wish him good luck. They had all come to love the pleasant, kindly boy from the mountains of Italy, the boy who had turned into a remarkably handsome man during the past three years.

'Don't leave it too long before you come back to see us.' Giuseppe was twirling the end of his moustache, a sure indication that he was sad to see his nephew go.

'I won't, I promise.' Tino hugged his uncle and patted him gently on the back. One by one, they held him close. Beppe could hardly speak; he owed his life to the brave actions of his friend, he would miss him terribly. Kathleen longed to put her feelings into words, but knew she mustn't. Instead, she consoled herself with hugging Tino and giving him a peck on the cheek.

'Now, don't yer go forgettin' us, mind.' Bravely, she tried to laugh and joke, but her voice wobbled as she choked back the tears. 'You gotta come back, even if it's ter see little Angela there growin' up into a big girl!'

They waved and cheered until he reached the corner

of Bramley Mews. Tino was taller now than when he had arrived and his shoulders had filled out, emphasised by the cut of the thick woollen coat. He had buttoned it up almost to the top, leaving the collar open just enough to reveal the checked muffler, crossed over and tucked in beneath. He wore good, strong boots, a parting gift from Zi Giuseppe and Janey. To complete the outfit, a flat cap covered glossy black waves but, rather than detracting from his appearance, it emphasised the depths of the liquid brown eyes, the perfectly straight nose and the fine, sensuous line of his mouth. Recently, he had grown a small moustache, a thin line like his uncle's, but without the twists at the end. A potent combination, but he was still unaware of the melting effect he had on members of the opposite sex. He was committed to one girl only. He turned and gave one last wave before turning into Silchester Road, finally lost from their sight.

The journey would be faster this time, he had been careful with his wages and had saved more than enough to complete most of the journey by rail. In fact, he was heading now for Latimer Road station, past the ragged school and near the Phoenix brewery. The heady smell of hops lingered in the air. He would miss that familiar scent but he did not care, it marked the first stage of his journey home. It wasn't far at all from Zi Giuseppe's lodging house, but he didn't think he could have coped with all the farewells in such a public place and preferred to leave from the platform alone.

He waited patiently until a puff of steam and a whistle told him his train was approaching. He stood back while other passengers alighted, then took one last look around him. He climbed aboard, this time carrying a small, if battered, suitcase instead of a cloth bundle. He had also taken the precaution, as he had before, of sewing most of his money into various hidden pockets in his clothes. The difference was, this time there was a lot more money to hide. A whistle blew shrilly, the signal to depart and he settled back with mixed feelings as his journey began.

After his previous experience, Tino hadn't been looking forward to the sea crossing, but despite the cold weather, it was much more bearable than when he had come in the opposite direction in what seemed to him a lifetime ago. The journey was unremarkable, and as he travelled through the length of Italy, there were few signs of unrest, other than a few skirmishes involving workers at one of the stations near Rome. The mad riots of the previous year had been subdued, though the feelings of resentment still remained and would not be suppressed.

Tino had sent a message home some weeks previously, telling them he would soon be returning. He didn't really know what to expect, with his mother still ill and Angelo gone, but as he journeyed further south, the longing for home came back with renewed vigour and he knew that this country, for all its faults and problems, was where his heart and soul would always lie.

Raffaele had been perplexed when Tino's letter arrived and kept the news to himself, not even telling his family. He had hoped that something would have come of the friendship Gianni had told him about, with that girl in London, Kathleen. He considered replying to him, finding some excuse to prevent him returning. But from the tone of the letter, it was clear that Tino would not be put off any longer. The only person he dared to discuss it with was Grillo.

'What else could you have done?' he asked sympathetically, measuring out an ample portion of the potent home-made wine made from the grapes in his own vineyards. He held it out to Raffaele. The piggy blue eyes narrowed until they almost disappeared in the folds of flabby skin, as he cunningly soothed and massaged his friend's ruffled feathers. He paused a little longer, studying the ruby red liquid as it glowed in the soft light. The words were slow and considered and there was a soothing note in his voice. 'If you are guilty of anything, it's only that you want the best for your family.' Raffaele went home the worse for drink but his conscience was salved.

Now, though, as the time for Tino's return drew nearer, the pangs of guilt and consternation began to return and instead of looking forward to seeing his son for the first time in three years, he was dreading the day he came back home. Finally, he would have to face up to the consequences of what he had done.

'Papa, Papa!' Michele was running as fast as his legs would carry him. 'Papa!'

It was late in the day and Raffaele had been bringing in the animals for the night. The stock was depleted now, the pasture had been poor and they had been forced to use some of them to supplement their diet. His brows drew together in consternation. His immediate thought was that Lena had been taken ill. There were times when he almost wished something would happen to her, he had had enough of listening to that interminable humming, it was driving him mad, and he felt it would be a blessing for the rest of them if the strain of caring for her, day in, day out, was taken away.

'What is it, Michele?' he asked quietly.

'It's Tino!' the boy answered breathlessly. Michele had grown taller and leaner, with no trace of childhood chubbiness left. His shoulders heaved as he panted for breath. 'He's coming up the hill!'

Raffaele's heart skipped a beat and he had to pause to compose himself before he could say another word. Even then, all he could do was repeat, 'Tino,' though the sound that came out was little more than a whispered croak.

'Yes. Papa, he'll be here any minute, hurry!' The boy was clearly excited at the return of his older brother and ran off towards the house. He had been going to tell the others, but by the time he reached the steps, Tino was already there before him. He threw his arms around his brother, knocking his cap askew in the process.

'Tino, it's so good to see you again! We've missed you!' he cried gleefully. 'Come on, let's go in!'

Raffaele stood back, watching the two brothers embrace and his heart began to pound. All his earlier concerns and reservations were back a thousandfold now that he was faced with his son standing there in the flesh before him. He felt uncomfortable, afraid even. Once more he was wrestling with those voices in his head, good fighting evil.

'Papa!' Tino had spotted him out of the corner of his eye and released his grip on the young boy. He was at his father's side in a few long strides, hugging and embracing him with tears of happiness running shamelessly down his cheeks. In his excitement, though, he didn't notice how his father pulled back from the embrace, or see the naked fear burning in his eyes. 'It is so good to see you, Papa.'

'Let's go in,' Raffaele said at length. He sighed heavily. 'We have a lot to talk about.'

It had taken the Fontes a long time to accept what had happened but now things were back to normal between them. Raffaele knew that Francesco and Mara had gone to visit them that afternoon and he prayed silently that they hadn't yet returned. But it wasn't to be. Tino's eyes took a few moments to adjust to the light in the room but Mara's golden hair shone like a beacon in the dimness.

'Mara! *Cara mia*!' he cried and his chest swelled with love and pride. She was lovelier than ever, he would never have thought it possible to improve on what she already had, but time had shaped and refined her features; the face more softly rounded, the lips fuller. But the sapphire eyes clouded and the colour faded from her cheeks as he threw his arms around her and buried his face in the soft hollow of her neck. The room was deathly silent, except for Lena's humming; it was this that caused Tino to look up. He suddenly became aware that Mara stood woodenly, rigid in his embrace and although he was surrounded by people, no-one said a word. The silence was almost tangible. Gently, he released the girl, but still kept his arm about her shoulder.

'What?' he asked, then could have kicked himself as realisation dawned. His mother was sitting there in the chair by the fire, oblivious to the world around her and even to his homecoming; Angelo had tragically gone and here he was, expecting them to jump up and down with excitement at his return. He was filled with guilt.

'I'm sorry!' he said, dropping his arm from Mara's shoulder and going over to his mother, where she rocked herself back and forth, blissfully unaware that her family was about to be torn apart. 'How could I forget Mamma?'

He held the thin frame close, but she remained still and unbending in his arms. Then it suddenly occurred to him that Mara's reaction had been much the same. She too stood there motionless when he held her tight to his chest, as stiff and unyielding as the tailor's dummies he had seen in some of the London shops. No tears. No laughter. No sign of pleasure, or happiness at his return. No elation that her husband-to-be had come to claim his bride. In fact, no reaction. Nothing at all. A feeling of foreboding flooded over him. Something was wrong. Very wrong. He looked at each of the company in turn, searching their faces for anything that would give him a clue. His father stood alongside, white-faced. His two sisters stood hand-in-hand, eyes wide with shock. Even Michele had gone quiet, his initial childish glee damped down as he realised his brother hadn't been told. Tino couldn't stand it, this not knowing, any longer.

'Will someone tell me what is happening? Please!' he cried, desperate to know yet dreading the answer. It dawned on him that his older brother wasn't there and fear clutched his heart. 'Is it Francesco?' he asked, his voice a mere whisper. 'Has something happened to him, too?'

At that moment, the door opened and Francesco himself came into the room, still limping but looking much better now than the man who had come back from the war. Mara still stood where Tino had left her, her body visibly trembling.

He didn't notice Tino, who was silhouetted against the red glow of the fire. 'Mara!' he smiled, and Tino went white as he saw his brother go to her and pull her towards him. 'Come on! Your beloved husband is cold and hungry; I think it's about time we ate.'

Tino went cold. Every last drop of blood seeped out of his face and the room seemed to spin around him sickeningly. It couldn't be! He must have heard it wrong, it couldn't be! He gently released his mother from his arms and dropped down into his father's chair opposite. Mara whispered something, quietly but urgently, to Francesco and immediately, his eyes turned towards his brother. He hadn't even realised he was there.

'Mara, tell me it's not true!' Tino's words were quiet and the pleading note in his voice was unmistakeable. His whole body trembled uncontrollably as fear set in. 'Please, *cara mia*. Tell me you waited for me, like I waited for you! Tell me!'

Mara looked first towards Francesco, then her father-in-law for support. 'I… I thought you weren't coming back. We all thought…' She didn't say the words, she didn't have to. Her expression said it all. The only girl he had ever thought about, dreamt about, had gone behind his back and married his own brother.

'You promised me you would wait.' Tino's voice was dangerously low. 'You promised. But the moment I agree to stay away longer, the minute I try to help the family, you go behind my back and betray me. And worse, with my own brother. As for the rest of you – you're all as bad as they are. Why didn't you tell me?' He turned to his father. 'And you! Why didn't you get a message to me, or something?' he accused. 'You got other messages through easily enough. But I can see now why you didn't want me back.'

He grabbed his suitcase and cap, which he had left behind the door. 'I'll sleep with the animals tonight, at least they have some kind of morality.' His voice was calm now, belying the turmoil going on inside his head, the fact that all his hopes for the future had just been ripped apart. 'I'll be leaving as soon as I can and believe me, I'll never come back here again. Francesco, you are no longer a brother of mine. And to think, all these years, I loved you, respected you. I looked up to you, would have done anything for you.'

'Tino, wait! You don't understand…' Francesco began.

Tino put up his hand. 'Shut up! I don't want to hear your lies, your excuses. I will never talk to you again, not as long as I have breath in my body, you betrayed me,' he shouted, then turned his attention to Mara, who stood perfectly still and wide-eyed, too shocked to weep, let alone to speak. 'As for you,' he whispered. 'I loved you with every breath in my body. Every bone in my body. But I can see now. You are nothing but a slut! And I spit on you.'

He slammed the heavy door after him, unaware of how his words had cut through Mara like a knife. He didn't see her recoil in pain as his accusations tore her apart. It was his sister Carlotta who broke the stunned silence.

'Papa, go after him!' she cried. 'Tell him we thought he wasn't coming back, you can't let him go away again like this.'

Raffaele blustered before answering and cleared his throat, spitting between the bars of the fire. 'He'll come round in the morning,' he muttered, lighting up a cheroot in the leaping flames. 'Leave him alone for now.'

Carlotta rushed towards the door. 'I'm going after him, if you won't!' she cried.

'I'll come with you,' Francesco moved towards her. 'I have to talk to him, make him understand.' His voice was thick with emotion. 'I can't bear the way he looked at me, with hatred in his eyes.' But they were stopped in their tracks as their father's voice boomed out across the room.

'I said, leave it!' he yelled. 'I forbid you to go. I'll talk to him tomorrow.'

In all the shock and uproar, not one of them noticed Lena's increasing agitation as she stroked the cat Tidillia, who had jumped up onto her lap and curled up in a ball. The stroking became faster and faster and the cat purred louder in response. Nor did they see the tears that fell like rain from the vacant eyes.

Tino threw his suitcase onto the floor of the barn and propped himself up in the same place he had always done before he had left for England. He leaned forward, wrapping his arms tightly about his knees. His throat felt as if it was closing up, but he was dry-eyed, the tears wouldn't come. Instead, he sat there, still shaking from head to toe and his head felt as if it would burst, as a plethora of thoughts and memories crowding in to his mind, vying and fighting with each other for attention. He couldn't believe this was happening to him, the worst nightmare he could imagine. He had come back full of love and hope for the future, and what had happened? She had betrayed him, the love of his life had been married while he was away. And as if to twist the knife – to his brother, the man he held in highest esteem and strove to model himself on. No wonder she never answered his letters, no wonder he hadn't heard from her. And all along, his father must have known what was going on. Was that why these last few months he had heard nothing from him, either? He had put it down to the problems in the country, the unrest. He thought it might have been harder for messages to get through. But now he knew the real reason. And oh, his poor mother. She had sat there, rocking and singing right the way through and no-one had taken the slightest bit of notice of her, she might as well have been invisible. She wouldn't have let this happen, not if she'd been right in the head; she would have put a stop to it long before it got to this stage. His Mamma would have made sure…

It was dark in the barn, cold too, but a sudden draught brushed against Tino's face. He didn't know how long he had been there, it could have been minutes or hours; nor did he know if he had been awake all the time or whether at some point he had dozed off into a sleep borne of exhaustion. He turned his head slowly towards the big doors and could see a slit of lighter grey penetrating the blackness.

'Go away!' he said wearily. The last thing he wanted was to talk, he just wanted to be left alone and he shifted position, his back towards to door. But still he heard movement behind him. 'I said, go away! Leave me alone!'

Soft yellow light from a lantern brightened the barn, casting deep shadows against the walls. Tino's eyes picked out a female shadow silhouetted against the far wall. Mara! She had come to him after all! He spun around eagerly. It was not Mara, but

Serafina Grillo, holding the lantern aloft, stunningly beautiful in its gentle golden glow. Her hair hung loose like a black silk shawl around shapely shoulders, brazen in the absence of the traditional headscarf.

She stood over him silently for a few moments, her eyes roaming over the length of his body from head to toe. He felt uncomfortable and embarrassed beneath her gaze.

'What do you want?' he asked sullenly, turning back towards the wall.

'That's not a nice way to greet me after such a long time.' The voice was petulant and mildly irritating.

'You didn't answer my question,' he said bluntly. 'What do you want?'

The girl walked around him, so that he was facing her again and had no option but to look at her. She lifted a bottle of wine out of a small basket and held it up invitingly.

'Look, Tino, I've just spoken to Carlotta, she told me what happened.' Her voice was low and full of sympathy. 'I know I was always jealous of Mara.' Tino winced at the girl's name. 'But I am sorry, truly sorry you've been hurt like this.' She sat down at his side, leaning her body towards him. 'Carlotta and Emilia wanted to come out to you, but your Papa won't let them. So we put some food together for you. And wine.'

'I don't want anything to eat.'

'Come on, Tino!' Serafina coaxed. 'Be sensible. You won't get away from here quickly if you catch some illness, will you?'

He hated to admit it, but she was talking sense. 'Maybe just a little, then…' he conceded.

Serafina drew back a cloth from the top of the basket and pulled out a large dish of soup, thick with vegetables. It was not hot, but pleasantly warm and she handed it to him with a thick chunk of hard black bread, which he broke up and dropped into the soup. It was only when he began to eat that he realised how hungry he was. He hadn't eaten for some time, not since he'd left Sora, many miles away. He hadn't thought he would need to, he'd expected to eat with his family when he got home. A wave of sadness washed over him again and he let out a long, shuddering sigh that seemed to go on for ever.

'See, I told you, you have to eat.'

'Thank you, Serafina.' He felt guilty at being so sharp with the girl, she was only trying to help, after all. He was quiet for a few moments, then asked, 'Why didn't my sisters let me know what was going on?'

'Your Papa stopped them, he said he didn't think it would come to anything.'

Tino was hurt. How could his father have done this to him? He had always felt close to him. Had he been cruel or just blind to what was happening around him? Either way, Tino couldn't forgive him.

Serafina handed him another hunk of bread, but this time with a substantial chunk of cheese and some meat. 'I got the meat from our place, Papa won't even know it's gone,' she said. There was a twinkle in her black eyes as she added, 'Well, at least, not until he goes to look for his supper.' Her laughter was like a tinkling stream and infectious. Tino couldn't help but smile.

Serafina handed him a small flask. 'This came from Papa's cupboard, too!'

He drank deeply, then coughed and spluttered as the golden-brown liquid burned the back of his throat. 'What is it?' he asked, then quickly put the flask to his lips again even before she had chance to reply.

Serafina laughed. 'Papa's best brandy. He keeps it for special occasions, his friend in Sora brought it for him from England, as a gift.'

'It tastes like hell's fires!' Tino remarked. Now he was getting used to it, the drink felt warm, good, and he drank until he had drained the flask empty.

'Plenty more where that came from,' Serafina giggled as she produced a large bottle from the depths of the basket. 'Wine, too.'

Tino grabbed the bottle out of her hand and held it high. The light from the lantern flecked the brown liquid with an array of rich reds and golds. 'To Papa Grillo!' he grinned. 'And to his friend as well, for providing such a thoughtful gift!' He realised his voice was beginning to slur, but he didn't care. What did anything matter now? He drank deeply, this time straight from the bottle, hitting his throat and belly with liquid fire. And yes, it still felt good.

Serafina laughed as she watched him and a deep hunger showed in her eyes. But this wasn't hunger of the body, that could be sated with food and drink. This was something else, some primeval instinct, a mad, insatiable hunger that possessed the soul. She had always wanted him, but Tino, this handsome, charismatic man sitting and drinking here with her now was a far greater attraction for her than Tino, the boy, had ever been. She had to have him, at all costs. And with Mara out of the way, what was there to stop her? But perhaps not just yet.

He tilted his head back to drain the last drops from the bottle, and Serafina shivered at the sight of the taut muscles of his throat and neck. 'Are you cold?' he asked, immediately concerned. He turned quizzically towards her. He was beginning to feel light-headed and his vision was slightly blurred, but he felt much happier now than a few hours ago.

'I'm comfortable,' she answered slowly. 'And look! I've got wine here too. That should warm us up!'

Her face was close to Tino's and he couldn't help but notice how her full breasts rose and fell, voluptuous beneath the woollen shawl and how the luxuriant hair brushed like a silk curtain against his cheek as she leaned across him to reach into the basket. 'She was always pretty, but now she has turned into a real beauty,' he mused. Yes, she was beautiful.

As Serafina drew back up, she deliberately allowed her breasts to rest on his arm for a moment. The sharp intake of breath told her that her ploy had worked and she gave a knowing little smile of satisfaction. Already, she was having an effect on him; soon, he wouldn't be able to resist her. All she needed was a little patience – and to ply him with a little more wine.

She snuggled up closer to him, leaning heavily against his shoulder. 'That's better,' she said quietly and for once, he didn't pull away.

She smelt sweet, like flowers and he felt his body stir in response to her nearness. They sat in silence, and Tino remembered the day at the fair with Kathleen, a hazy memory now, when they had been together on the merry-go-round and his body had responded to hers in a way that had taken him completely by surprise. But Kathleen had just been a girl and now, here in the barn with him, was one of the most beautiful young women he had ever seen. The warmth of her body against his stirred up a longing in him that he had never experienced before. He had imagined and dreamt of this happening with Mara, but now that was never going to be. And the more he drank, the more inviting the prospect of making love with Serafina became.

Suddenly, she jumped up and began singing a tune. It was one of the local songs which accompanied a dance not unlike the tarantella. She started swaying to the tune, moving her body sensuously as she sang, turning this way and that so that Tino could see her from every angle. He smiled as she hitched her skirts above her knees, exposing long, slender brown legs, while at the same time allowing her shawl to fall to the ground. The neckline of the blouse was cut low and her full breasts peeped enticingly above the top, thrusting unashamedly against the thin cloth.

She turned to the side, head thrown back in abandon. The straight black hair fell to the back of her knees, swaying with a life of its own, and he could feel himself becoming more and more excited. His breathing was heavy and erratic and his trousers felt as if they would burst. Then she turned away, hips moving seductively in time to the tune, skirt moulding tightly to the swell of the rounded buttocks. Without warning, she swung back to face him. Her eyes gleamed black in the dim light, but the fire in them seemed to burn into him. With one swift movement, she pulled down her blouse to completely expose the upper half of her body. Tino let out a groan at the sight of her naked breasts, high and firm, tempting and teasing as they thrust back and forth as she danced. Her skin seemed to glow as the light from the lantern threw patterns across her body. He couldn't stand it any longer.

'Come here!' The sound came from somewhere deep in his throat. It didn't even sound like his voice. But she carried on singing and dancing, getting closer and closer, and sending shudders of desire through his body as she leaned forward and pressed her breasts against his face. He groaned once more as he reached out his hands to cup them; but time and again, she pulled away from him at the last possible moment, laughing as she danced and spun away.

'Stop it!' he laughed. 'Stop teasing me!'

Her reply was to turn her back to him and slowly undo her skirt, finally releasing it so that it slid down her hips to the ground; the rest of her clothes followed. She wore no undergarments and she turned around to face him, standing gloriously naked before him. It took his breath away; she was incredibly beautiful, her body full and well-rounded. She reminded him of the statues he had seen in Rome, some ancient goddess whose commands must be obeyed. And he was more than ready to obey any command she chose to throw at him and at that moment, he would have done anything for her. He began to struggle up from the floor, he had an urgent desire to hold her close to him, to experience the sensation of that wonderful body against his. But he was dizzy and fell back against the wall. Serafina laughed lightly.

'Stay there!' she ordered and he was happy to obey. He watched as she slowly came towards him, drinking in every inch of her body. She slid to the floor at his side and put her lips to his. For one blissful moment, he thought he was in Heaven. Then she pulled back with a little giggle and began to nibble gently at his ear. He couldn't stand it, he wanted her now. But every time he went to make a move, she would counter it and pull away. She was determined that when he entered her body, it would be because he couldn't bear to wait for even one more moment. She teased and cajoled, offering herself to him then cruelly pulling away until finally, she slid her hands down his body, reaching for signs of his arousal. She was not disappointed, he was undeniably a man now. And when she herself couldn't stand the waiting and teasing any longer, she gave herself to him with abandon, knowing the one thing she had longed for throughout her life had finally been achieved.

Tino woke up the next morning with a heavy sensation in his head, which threatened to split it apart if he as much as moved a muscle. He tried gingerly to lift his head but the unbearable throbbing sensation made him lie back immediately. As he drifted slowly towards a wakefulness marred by pain, he suddenly became aware of the warmth at his side. He turned quickly to see Serafina's arms and shoulders lying above the top of his coat which had served as a makeshift bedcover.

His first reaction was to pull away; Mara was his girl. Then memories of the night before flooded over him and he groaned deeply, flushing with shame. He couldn't believe what he had done, he had committed an act that was totally anathema to his feelings and the way he had been brought up. It was a cardinal sin, to make love to a girl you weren't married to. He put his head in his hands. She had tricked him, she knew what had happened when he arrived home and she had used his vulnerability to get him drunk and seduce him. What was he going to do?

For the first time since he had arrived home, he put his hands up to his eyes and gave vent to his feelings of utter hopelessness and despair. He let the ready tears fall, overflowing through his fingers and down his cheeks. He sobbed silently, trying not to wake the girl at his side. He looked at her – he wanted to blame her, but he couldn't entirely; it was as much his fault, he should have known better, she was her father's daughter all right. Devious. Finally, the tears dried up and he was left nothing but an empty feeling in the pit of his stomach and a desire to escape from this awful situation as fast as he could.

Then the barn door flew open, waking Serafina up from her slumber and startling Tino into a bolt upright position.

'So this is where you got to!' Grillo roared. He made an imposing figure, with his sheer bulk seeming to fill the opening.

'Papa! I can explain…' Serafina dragged the coat up to her neck, covering her naked body, and her eyes flew open imploringly.

'Explain? Explain what?' his nostrils flared and he looked for all the world like a bellicose bull. 'Explain why you are here, naked as the day you were born, with this – this peasant?'

Tino resented that and he rose to the bait. 'No more a peasant than you,' he retorted sharply.

'That may well be,' Grillo replied with mocking calm, 'but I'm not the one acting like a dog after a bitch on heat.'

The words hit home and Tino hung his head in shame. He couldn't deny it, everything Grillo had said was true. He should have known better than to get involved with the girl, but it was too late now, the deed was done. But what he didn't know was that he was playing straight into Grillo's hands. 'I'm sorry,' he murmured. 'I had too much to drink.'

'Too much to drink? Too much to drink?' The other man had a habit of repeating himself, and this was no exception. 'And you think that excuses spending the night with my daughter? Defiling an innocent girl? Oh, no, young man, that's no excuse. And as her father, I would be well within my rights to blow your head clean off your shoulders. But of course,' his facial expression broke into something bordering on a smile; to Tino, it was more like a snake preparing to strike, 'I'm sure we could come to some arrangement.'

Tino's heart sank as the realisation of what he had done hit him full force. He knew it was taboo in these regions to take a girl before you were married, and he knew only too well the possible repercussions. There was no doubt in his mind that Grillo would stir things up and he would be ostracised by everyone, maybe even beaten or shot dead. He thought about the shame this would bring on his Mamma, his brother Michele and his sisters. The only way he could make up for this, the only way he could appease Grillo, would be to restore the girl's dubious honour. And the only way he could do that would be to marry her. He felt a tide of bitter bile rise up in his throat, accompanied by an overwhelming desire to vomit.

He wanted to shout out that Serafina was far from the innocent girl her father was making her out to be. She knew exactly what she was doing when she had come into the barn the night before. She had come with the intention of getting him drunk; without doubt, she had known how it would end up, she had laid her plans carefully. And she was no virgin, either, as her father had implied. It was well known he was not the only man to taste the sweet fruits of her body, but he was too much of a gentleman to say so. Vulnerable and lonely, still smarting from the cruel blow that had been delivered to him, his only mistake had been to fall for her charms himself. To let her ply him with drink and soothe his battered ego when he was at his most vulnerable. And now, he knew, he was going to have to pay the price. And it was a heavy one.

Chapter 19

TINO REMAINED IN the barn for the following month, refusing to talk to his father or even his sisters, speaking to Michele only, who brought food and drink over to him. Things were happening too fast, he felt as if he'd been hit by a sledgehammer and was still reeling somewhere between consciousness and unconsciousness. One day, he had been ecstatic, returning home to claim his sweetheart for a bride, the next he was being coerced into marrying a woman for whom he had no feelings, for the sake of convention and her supposed honour. But her honour was tainted. He had been duped, tricked and could blame no-one but himself. He thought about running away, but his sense of moral duty wouldn't allow him to shun his responsibilities. He was an honourable man and would not renege on a promise, even if the whole sorry situation hadn't been of his making.

But one thing he had insisted on, was that if he agreed to marry Serafina, she would have to go to England with him to live; as far as he was concerned, he had no family here any more, except perhaps for Michele and his Mamma. And she was blissfully oblivious to everything going on around her, sitting there locked in that private little world of hers, singing and stroking the cat. Much to everyone's surprise, Serafina seemed positively pleased and happy at the prospect of going to live in England, but Grillo had been angry at first, and it had taken a lot more to persuade him. Finally, though, he gave in to Tino's terms and it was agreed they would leave for England soon after the wedding. He conceded that he would have to stay somewhere for that short time, whether he liked it or not, he couldn't expect Serafina to share the barn with him, so it was arranged for them to stay in Grillo's home.

But he didn't know how he was going to cope when the day of the double marriage between the two families would finally arrive. It occupied his thoughts for much of the intervening time. Two weddings – his to Serafina, and his sister Emilia's to Marco Grillo. And how different it would be: Emilia, Serafina and Marco couldn't wait for the day to come, whereas he was dreading it, truly a reluctant and unhappy husband-to-be. According to Michele, both the girls had been revelling in all the fuss and attention they were receiving and Tino was softening towards them. He acknowledged now there was nothing they could have done to change things. But how could he possibly feign happiness in front of their family and guests?

He couldn't sleep the night before the wedding. He tossed and turned and in the end, got up at first light. It was early and the morning was cold; a thin layer of glittering ice floated on the water in the well and he made a fist, smashing it into splinters before splashing his face with the freezing water. Shaking the droplets from his face and head, he walked down the hill towards the stream, breathing in the icy cold air. The grass was white-tipped with frost, and crunched noisily beneath his feet. It was still dark, the high full moon surrounded by myriad silver stars that twinkled brightly against a black velvet backcloth. The moon cast long shadows and glistened on the frost to light the way ahead; he could have done this journey blindfolded, he had made it so many times before – he didn't even need to concentrate.

He eventually reached the spot where he used to take the sheep and sat beneath the familiar outcrop of rock, conflicting thoughts racing around his head. This should have been the happiest day of his life and if it had been a different bride, the girl with the deepest blue eyes and golden hair, then it would have been. But that wasn't going to happen and he would have to make the best of a bad situation. At least soon, he would get away from here for ever, he was beginning to feel as if even the confines of the hills surrounding him were stifling, suffocating him. Just then, he noticed a flash of colour out of the corner of his eye and his head swivelled round sharply to see Mara standing a few feet away, completely motionless. For a moment, he thought he was imagining things – after all, he had dreamt of her enough in the past, seen her laughing face in front of his eyes as surely as if she had been there – and he put the knuckles of both hands to his eyes, rubbing vigorously. But she was still there when he slowly lowered them.

He turned away as he took in the golden hair and unhappy blue eyes. 'What do you want?' he asked abruptly, pain filling his voice.

Her reply was to sit on the grass next to him. Neither of them spoke for a while, but it was Mara who broke the silence. 'Tino,' she began gently. 'I truly thought you weren't coming back.'

He turned to her, anger sparking in the depths of his eyes. 'How?' he snapped. 'Tell me how? With all the letters, the gifts I sent home for you – how could you think I wasn't coming back?'

Frown lines creased her forehead. 'Letters? Gifts?' she repeated. 'What are you talking about? I had nothing from you, nothing!'

'Don't lie to me!' Tino's voice was rising. Her nearness disturbed him in a way no other woman could, he loved her and still wanted her, despite everything. But it was too late, she was already his brother's wife and there was nothing he could do to change that. And today, he himself would take a new bride.

'Tino, listen to me!' she pleaded tearfully. 'I had nothing, I promise you. Nothing!'

He stared at her incredulously. He could see from her expression she was telling the truth.

'But Papa answered my letters, he often sent messages with boys coming over to London,' he muttered, almost to himself. He put his arms on her shoulders. 'Mara, Papa had my letters and messages. I sent everything for you with them.'

She shook her head, not understanding, and he gripped her arms even tighter as an unwelcome and incredible thought sprang unbidden to his mind.

'He wouldn't! No, surely he wouldn't do that to us?' A sinking sensation dragged his stomach downwards as realisation began to dawn. 'But he must have! He must have kept the letters. Mara, don't you see?' Tino was horrified. 'Oh, Madonna! I just can't believe this. Mara, Papa had all my letters, and the ones I sent for you were with them – but he never gave them to you, he kept them.' Things were beginning to fall into place.

The girl too was horrified. 'No. No, he wouldn't.'

'But he must have. It's the only explanation.' His voice held a note of despair. 'Oh, Mara! And now it's too late, it's too late for both of us.'

'But, Tino, I waited. I truly waited, I couldn't understand why you never wrote, but still I waited for you. Then your Papa, he told us all that Gianni said you had another girl in London and you were really happy with her. And you weren't going to come back to Italy, you were going to stay there. He told everyone that – your sisters, your brothers – everyone.'

Tino went pale. 'He told you that?'

'Yes, when he met Gianni after he'd been to London to see you. He said Gianni told him you had another girl – Kathleen, I think he called her.'

Tino was shocked to the core. 'Mara, you've got to believe

me, there was nothing between Kathleen and myself. She was a friend to all of us, someone who lived across the road and used to help out in Zi Giuseppe's business. It's different in England, not like here. I swear to you, you were the only girl I've ever loved. And,' he added quietly, his voice and heart breaking, 'the only girl I will ever love.'

He held her to him and rocked her back and forth. They were both crying, hot tears mingling where their cheeks touched.

'Tino, Tino. I love you, too,' she sobbed. 'I only married Francesco because I thought you weren't coming back. I felt so hurt, rejected, when I heard you had someone else. And Francesco was ill and weak, and he reminded me so much of you, every time I looked at him, I could only see you. He needed me, and I desperately needed someone to take away the pain, the emptiness I felt when I knew you weren't coming back.'

Tino's sigh trembled with emotion. 'It seems we've both been tricked. They've lied to us both and now we have to live with the consequences for the rest of our lives. There can be no going back.' He pulled her to him, resting his lips on hers. He had longed to do this, ached for it. And she responded willingly to him, pressing her soft body against his.

Despite the cold, they made love there and then. It was sweet and tender, the one and only time they would be able to rejoice in the feelings of ecstasy and empathy between two people who truly loved each other. Not like a love born of affection and pity, when Mara obediently gave herself up to her husband's embrace, and a far cry from the mad, inebriated coupling that Tino had shared with Serafina. And the knowledge that this could never happen again made it all the more precious and poignant.

They walked back hand in hand until they came within

sight of the farmhouse. Tino reluctantly released Mara's hand and whispered, 'Mara, I'll always love you, wherever I am. And I will never, ever stop thinking about you.' And she believed him.

Tino went back to the barn so they would not be seen returning together and thought miserably how he and Mara had been deceived in such a cruel and calculating way. He could still sense the warmth of the girl in his arms, and he felt a heaviness settle around his shoulders as surely as if someone had placed a great weight on them. He was overcome with sadness for what might have been. How could they have done this to him? How did it happen? Yet the clues had been there all along.

He suddenly recalled how years earlier, his father and Grillo would whisper and exchange knowing glances, or go quiet when he walked into a room; how they did nothing to discourage Serafina from flinging herself at him at every opportunity, when it was obvious he was uncomfortable with it. His father had done nothing to stop her hanging around their farm and did everything possible to engineer situations that would push them together.

The more he thought about it the more frustrated and angry he became. His father and Grillo, Serafina too, had manipulated them all like puppets. They had been planning this for years, they had set the wheels in motion and in his ignorance, he had been powerless to do anything to stop them. He thought of all the notes he had written, the little gifts he had sent, which Mara had never received. In a moment of blinding revelation, he suddenly recalled something which made his anger reach fever pitch and he could not hold back a moment longer.

He stormed over to the farmhouse in a wild rage, determined to have this out with his father. He barged through the door and in a few strides, reached the corner where his father's bed stood. Apart from Mara, who was helping Lena with her food, the rest of the family was seated around the table, chatting excitedly and eating breakfast. They stopped mid-sentence, shocked by the sudden intrusion.

Tino knew about the tin where his father kept all his important things and he dragged it out from its hiding-place beneath the bed, holding it aloft. It was a hunch, a gamble. His father's face went white.

'What are you doing?' he asked, the steady, quiet voice belying the fear that he was about to be found out.

'What do you think?' Tino shouted. 'About to expose your nasty little scheme, that's what.'

Raffaele shot across the room. 'Give that box to me, it's private!' he shouted, and tried to grab it out of Tino's hands. But Tino was taller now and held the box above his head, just out of his father's reach. But the grasping fingers of the older man were just long enough to touch the small lock. To his dismay, it swivelled around in response, releasing the catch. The box swung open, dangling back and forth on its hinges and hurling its contents to the floor as it did so.

Raffaele's money and other treasures lay scattered on the stone floor. But that wasn't what he was after and he hastily dropped down to his knees in a bid to retrieve several scraps of paper, scrabbling frantically among scores of coins that rolled everywhere in an effort to gather the papers up. But Tino was too fast for him. He'd also spotted the collection of notes and the little gifts he had sent for Mara – every one of them he guessed, including a small plaster statue of the Tower of London, which now lay smashed into a hundred pieces – and quickly gathered them up into a small bundle in his hands. He walked over to the table, dropping them among the dishes. Raffaele remained where he was, still on his knees. He was as pale as buttermilk and his whole body was trembling.

'Yes, you can shiver and shake, Papa.' The voice was icy.

'Tino, what's wrong with you?' Carlotta hissed. 'Leave Papa alone, this is supposed to be a happy day. Your wedding day.'

'Happy?' Tino spat out. 'Happy? He's destroyed every hope I ever had of happiness. Mara's too. In fact, he's duped you all, him and that fat *bastardo*, Grillo.'

He pushed one of the notes towards her, then another to Emilia. He distributed them so that everyone in the room, with the exception of young Michele and his mother, had at least one.

'Read them!' he commanded. 'I wrote to Mara, I sent her gifts – and he stole them. Yes, stole them! Hid them away, so she would think I didn't care. So she would marry him,' he stabbed an accusing finger in Francesco's direction, 'and leave the way clear for his dirty, conniving plans for me to marry his disgusting friend's equally disgusting harlot of a daughter. Just so that he can brag and boast, how the two families are linked, how much land he owns, how much money he has. And you have the nerve to tell me this is supposed to be a happy day!'

Francesco was the first to speak. 'Tino, please. You've got to believe me, I swear to God I knew nothing of this.' He was trembling as he turned to his father. 'Papa, tell him! For once, do the decent thing. For God's sake, tell Tino I had nothing to do with this!'

Raffaele's response was silence. He was still in shock. He knew he should have got rid of those letters. 'Oh, God, what have I done?' he thought miserably. He had achieved what he had set out to do and now there was no way back. But the reality was not quite what he had expected.

'Papa, tell him! I'm as much of a victim of this as he is.'

Tino's laugh was harsh. 'Victim? You, Francesco? A victim?' Anger was causing his voice to quiver. 'You are not the one who lost your girl,' he shot back. 'You are not the one tricked into marrying the village's cast-off, oh no.' There was a long pause, heavy with unspent passion. 'But you are the man who couldn't wait to steal my girl the minute my back was turned. You, my own brother.'

'Tino, please listen to me. It wasn't like that,' Francesco began. He was hurting too, he would never have done that to his brother if he had known, even if it had meant giving up Mara.

Tino's voice broke. He could not take any more. 'I don't want to hear your lies.'

The silence was deathly. Even Lena was silent. The only sound was Mara's soft sobbing. Then the dull thud of the door as Tino slammed it behind him, leaving them all in stunned silence.

They had all seemed to forget that this was Emilia's wedding day too. Pale-faced, she went to get ready in subdued silence, in a quiet corner of the room curtained off especially for the purpose. Her cheeks still bore the flush of pink from crying and her bad eye seemed to work overtime as the devastating truth of Tino's words sank in. She felt guilty too, for she suspected that his marriage to Serafina had been a bargaining point for her own marriage. If she had looked harder, she would have recognised the signs. She felt guilty that she hadn't.

'Come on, Emilia, you can't blame yourself.' Carlotta brushed Emilia's red-brown hair with long, soothing strokes, from root to tip, until it shone. Her own hair glistened dark as night in the shaft of light coming in through the small window. 'Papa has been through a lot, I am worried for him, in a way. It's as if his mind's turned as much as Mamma's, but in a different way. I truly think he's sick too.'

Emilia shook her head sadly. 'Carlotta, I think Papa's always had a nasty side to him. Think of how he slaughtered Tino's favourite little pig for Christmas that year, when he could easily have taken any one of the others. He always used to make fun of Tino because he loved the animals. Papa said he was too soft, he was scornful of him even. But I really didn't think he would go as far as this. Lying to us too, making us think our brother was never coming back.'

Carlotta sighed heavily. 'Emilia, I've got something to tell you.'

'What is it?'

'I've been thinking for some time about going to England myself.' The brown eyes were soft as she looked down at her sister's tear-stained face. 'Mara and Francesco are here now to look after Mamma and Michele, and you'll be going over to the Grillos to live after you're wed, so there's nothing to keep me here any more.'

Emilia's head swivelled round and she stared at her sister, horrified. 'No! Carlotta, you're my only sister, the only one I can talk to.' Then, she suddenly realised the selfishness of her words and immediately felt ashamed. 'I'm sorry. I'm getting as mean as Papa, thinking only of myself. If you want to go, then you must.'

'It's just that after all this trouble blowing up this morning, it's made up my mind for me. I don't think I can look Papa in the face any more after this.'

'Where will you go?' The eye turned in consternation, flicking from side to side in a frenzied dance.

'Zi Giuseppe's, at first. Then… well, I don't know.'

The girls sat in silence, the rhythmical stroking of the brush gently soothing Emilia's rattled nerves. She thought of wedding tradition, where the bride would be dressed in white and sent to her future mother-in-law for approval. She had to be a good, innocent woman to be accepted into her new family, who would then help her to dress in her wedding finery. But there was no mother-in-law and even her own mother was too ill to understand. Instead, it was her sister helping her to prepare for her big day and she was sad. This was nothing like the day she had always dreamt of, but at least, she would have Marco at the end of it. That was the important thing, for she loved him dearly. But she felt so sad for Tino. Francesco and Mara too, for hadn't they been duped as much as the rest of them?

Carlotta led her sister into the main part of the room, where the rest of the family waited. The atmosphere was subdued, and the only additions to the room were Tino, who knew that however hard it would be for him, he had to come back to dress for the wedding. Grillo, who stood with his broad back to the fire, complained bitterly of being thrown out of his own home by those 'interfering women from the village' and Serafina's friends who were helping her to get ready. Encouraged by his presence though, Raffaele was beginning to get back to his normal self and had even started to crack jokes.

Grillo's eyes lit up lasciviously as Emilia came into the room. She looked beautiful; Carlotta had piled her hair on top of her head in a mass of curls, held in place by the same filigree comb and embroidered white lace headscarf that Lena had worn herself on her wedding day. He made no secret of the fact that his steely-blue pin-point eyes were wandering blatantly up and down her body. She cringed and gave a small shiver. He dug his friend in the ribs.

'Lovely daughter you've got there, Raff!' A pool of spittle gathered copiously at each corner of his mouth and dribbled down his chin in a string of frothy pearls. He gave a raucous laugh, 'wouldn't mind changing places with my son tonight, I bet I could teach her a thing or two.'

For once, Raffaele didn't laugh with his friend. He was not in the mood for it and anyway, Grillo was beginning to anger him. He was overstepping the boundaries by a long way. 'Don't you forget Grillo – Emilia is still my daughter,' he answered soberly.

'Ho! Nothing meant, just joking,' Grillo whined. 'Only saying what a good looking girl she is. You should be proud.'

Raffaele was appeased to some degree and nodded in silent assent. Lena, though, sat in her chair staring at Grillo's back. Her eyes blazed angrily as she gently pushed Tidillia off her lap. The cat padded across the floor, tail flicking in disgust and settled instead in the chair opposite. Lena was wringing her hands, fingers entwined tightly as they twisted and turned against each other's iron grip; the pale lips drew away from her teeth in what could only be described as a snarl. Grillo stepped away slightly from the heat of the fire, he could feel it starting to burn through the cloth of his trousers. He glanced towards Lena and stopped in his tracks. He looked away quickly, clearly perplexed and shocked by the pure hatred in the eyes that bore into his. It was some moments before he could bring himself to look again and when he did, he was met with the same dull stare that always filled her eyes. He threw back the wine Raffaele offered him in one go. His was getting too old for this, his imagination must be playing tricks on him.

It was still cold but the sun shone as Tino left ahead of the others, meeting up with Marco on the way; two men who had been friends for many years walking up the stony track to the church to wait for their brides. However, their moods were very different.

Despite objections from the others, Raffaele had insisted it would be pointless taking Lena to the church, she hadn't been outside the door since Angelo's death and it might make her condition worse.

'It might make her better, too,' Tino had mumbled under his breath. He couldn't wait for this all to be over, to return to London, where he would have to make the best of things with his new wife.

Mara would stay at home to look after Lena while the weddings took place. It had almost broken Tino's heart to see the pale, strained face, the blue eyes watching his every movement as he left. He had even thought of asking her to run away with him, but he knew deep down it wouldn't have been possible.

Instead, he waited patiently outside the church with Marco for their brides to arrive. The first hint that they were getting closer was when they heard the shrieks of laughter of the children from the villages, as they ran to catch the treats thrown for them by the brides. Soon, they came into view, the brides Emilia and Serafina in front leading their families and the rest of the wedding procession behind. No-one could deny that Serafina made a striking and beautiful bride; her hair shone like glass, the combs in her hair, unlike Emilia's, made of silver. Tino tried hard to smile as he followed tradition, taking hold of the corner of the fine lace handkerchief she held out to him before walking side by side into the church. But his heart felt as if it would break into a thousand pieces.

Later, the wedding parties returned to the Grillo home. His house was much bigger than anyone else's in the area, with separate rooms downstairs and real bedrooms, not curtained-off areas, upstairs. The fact that they had an upstairs at all was remarkable and spoke volumes about their affluence. Raffaele had been grateful for his offer to host the celebrations; he had always been proud that his home was superior to most others, but when compared with Grillo's, it was little more than a hovel in his eyes.

As the two newlywed couples reached the door, Marco reached for Emilia, proudly showing off his bride to the crowd. Laughing and teasing, they immediately called for them to demonstrate their union. '*Bacio! Un Bacio*!' they cried, demanding a kiss from the couple. Then, satisfied, they clapped and laughed, shouting good-humouredly, '*Vivano gli sposi!*' to wish them a long and happy marriage. Now, they turned their attention to Tino and Serafina. The couple obliged with a kiss, but Tino's was much quicker, lighter than Marco's, though no-one seemed to notice, except Serafina. She wasn't unduly worried, she had made him want her before and once they were alone, she would do it all over again.

Eyes widened at the feast Grillo had provided. In the current economic climate, with food shortages and lack of money, nothing seemed to be missing from these tables. They seemed to groan beneath the weight of dish upon dish of meats, hams and sausages, *salsiccie* and *salame*, cheeses, nuts and fruits and endless bottles of wine, grappa and brandy. But before they ate, Grillo himself led the guests up to the two bedrooms which had been prepared for the newlywed couples. He bent over the large bed in the first room, pinning a small pouch tied up with a lace, onto the embroidered bedcovers. Inside was a substantial amount of money.

He could afford to be generous; he had watched his daughter today get the man she had always hankered for. He had always known that the time would come when he would have to hand his daughter over to the care of another man, it was only natural, after all. At first, though, it had been hard to take in, when the knowledge hit him that she was growing up fast and wanted a husband.

Since her mother's death, Serafina had been a perfect daughter to him. From the tender age of eleven, she had looked after him. She had cooked for him, fed him, flattered his ego when things didn't go well. She had looked after his every need. But he consoled himself in the knowledge that although she would be leaving him to go away with her new husband, he would have a very capable replacement in his new daughter-in-law Emilia. He stood up from pinning the pouch, pudgy hand supporting the small of his back. Grillo invited the other guests to leave their gifts in the same manner, though he knew with a curious satisfaction that no-one there could hope to match his own financial contribution. The crowd laughed and chattered as the process went on, teasing remarks sometimes causing the brides to truly blush, at least in Emilia's case.

Grillo stood well back from the others, watching her. His pale eyes glittered as they rested on the high mound of her breasts. His breathing turned heavy as she laughingly bent over to smooth out the bedcovers which had become rumpled in the chaos, the cloth of her dress outlining the soft roundness of her buttocks. A trickle of saliva began to escape from between the rubbery lips and the eyes rapidly disappeared into thick folds of excess flesh.

His son Marco was a good-looking man, but he was no stallion, as innocent in the way of life as the day he was born. Grillo licked his lips greedily, as if in anticipation of some great treat ahead. Tonight, he knew, only the clumsy, fumbling lovemaking of the inexperienced would take place beneath those bedcovers, all over and done with in a minute or so. He smiled slyly to himself, his eager tongue now flicking furiously across his lips. He would have to make sure he didn't wait too long to teach this new daughter-in-law of his what a real man could do for her.

*

It was Sunday, just a few days later when the chance he had been waiting for presented itself. He, Marco and Tino had been working outside; Marco and Tino had set to mending and replacing fences and he himself had begun tidying up the outbuildings, ready for the lambing season, which would be upon them before they even knew it.

Emilia had gone to visit her family; she had seen the unhappiness in Tino's eyes and was riddled with guilt. Soon, in just a few more days, he would be gone from her life for ever. She wanted to tell him she was sorry for everything, sorry they had listened to Papa. They should have known better than to think he would break a promise to his sweetheart. She wanted to talk to her sister, ask her advice about the best way to approach him, without dredging up bad memories all over again. And there was something else on her mind too. As it happened, Carlotta was alone in the house with Lena, when she got there.

'I feel so bad about Tino,' she confided to her sister.

'We all do!' Carlotta tucked a wisp of stray hair back under her headscarf and sat down at the table opposite her sister. It was quiet, Lena had stopped singing for once. But her eyes were fixed on the girls, watching every move. 'But what about you? Are you settling in Grillo's house?'

Emilia smiled but a troubled expression crossed her face. And it didn't escape Lena's scrutiny. 'It's Marco's house, too,' Emilia chided her sister. 'And mine.'

'Yes, but… what I'm trying to say is, are you happy?'

'Of course!' she replied brightly and a little too quickly for Emilia's liking.

Carlotta was sure from her sister's expression that something wasn't quite right, but she couldn't put her finger on it. 'Emilia, it's me, your sister, you're talking to,' she pleaded. 'If there's anything wrong, I want to know. Please, tell me!'

Emilia's head bowed. 'I'm not sure,' she faltered. 'I don't even know if anything's wrong, or if it's my imagination.'

'Go on.'

'It's just that Grillo – the way he looks at me, it makes me feel so uncomfortable.' She paused, eyes downcast. 'I mean, he always has made me feel awkward, but it seems to be worse now that I'm living there.'

They hadn't noticed, but Lena began wringing her hands, a sure sign that she was agitated. She listened intently to the conversation, and she was frightened for Emilia. But as much as she wanted to join in, to tell them of her own thoughts and feelings about Grillo, it was impossible. Her lips moved, but not a sound escaped; nothing would come out. Instead, her mind in turmoil, she began humming quietly again.

They spoke for some time of their concerns about Grillo, Tino and the bad thing Papa had done. At length, Emilia got up with a sigh. 'Thank you for listening to me, sister, but I have to go now.' She hugged the other girl. 'I'm so glad I have you to talk to.'

'You know I'll always listen, at least while I'm still here.' Carlotta smiled. 'And you can always send messages to me. But you must try not to worry too much about Grillo. After all, he hasn't actually done anything, has he? If he does, then you must tell your husband. He would soon put a stop to it for you.'

Emilia went over to her mother, kissing her gently on the cheek. 'Goodbye, Mamma. I love you. And I'll be back to see you soon.' Tenderly, she straightened the shawl around Lena's thin shoulders.

'I'll come out with you, it's time to feed the animals again,' Carlotta sighed, picking up her own shawl from the back of a chair.

'What about Mamma?'

'She won't come to any harm for the sake of a few minutes, it won't take me very long.'

From the fireside chair, Lena could see outside through the small front window, and she watched silently as her two daughters left the house together. Soon, Carlotta turned left towards the barn and was quickly lost from sight. But Emilia, strode out in the opposite direction, diagonally across the fields towards Grillo's house. Lena watched as her daughter drew her wrap tighter, increasing her pace in an effort to combat the chill in the air. She smiled, remembering Emilia as a little girl, as she saw strands of chestnut red hair whipping around her face in the stiff breeze. Then a sudden movement behind the girl caught her attention. She strained her neck to get a better view. She drew in a sharp breath – she would recognise that fat, squat shape anywhere. He walked some distance behind Emilia, but his gait was fast and purposeful. He was quickly catching up with her.

Lena's heart began to beat faster, she was sure he was up to no good. But she was alone, there was no-one to turn to for help. Sobs began to gather in the back of her throat and with an immense effort, she put her hands on the arms of the chair and pushed herself to her feet. For a moment, she became dizzy and began to sway. Her legs felt like cotton wool and she was forced to hang on to the mantel shelf to steady herself. Then she looked to the window and saw that Grillo had now gained a considerable amount of ground on her unsuspecting daughter.

Lena murmured a prayer and a sudden surge of strength seemed to flood the frail body. Slowly, she made for the door, her legs stiff and slow. Laboriously, she shuffled one foot in front of the other. But as the blood began to flow back into the oxygen-starved muscles, it began to get easier, she was getting stronger with every step. Soon, her determination was rewarded and she reached the door. She stopped to lift something off a nail and went out, leaving the door wide open and swinging behind her. Grillo and Emilia were now out of her sight, but she knew the way to his house well, and purposefully headed in that direction.

Grillo still kept his distance behind the girl, he was a true hunter, a man who always enjoyed the chase as much as the kill. He was dribbling furiously, and feverish anticipation glazed his eyes. This one was worth the wait. He had wanted her for years. Why else would he have agreed to let her marry his son? While she was under his roof he could do what he liked and his skinny, pathetic son was neither bright enough nor man enough to stop him. His breath came in a series of heavy pants as he began to catch up with her. He imagined her in his son's arms and scoffed, filled with scorn. The purplish-pink tongue flicked out like a snake's retracting a fresh stream of saliva before it joined the rest already glistening wetly on his chin. He would show her what a real man was and he would wager a bet in a few weeks' time, that when she got used to it, she would be running after him. That scrawny boy of his would never be good enough to satisfy a lusty young girl like her, that was for sure. His breathing was getting heavier, and rougher. Oh, yes, she would enjoy what he had in store for her.

He waited, biding his time until he knew there would be no escape for her. He would make his move just before they reached the old ruined barn, just on the edge of his land. Far enough away from the house for no-one to hear their cries of passion or disturb them.

Emilia stopped and turned around. She felt uneasy, she was sure she heard a sound behind her. She couldn't see anyone, perhaps it was a rabbit or some other small animal. No snakes this time of year, and anyway, they moved too quietly. She carried on, moving faster now as fine rain began to fall and the light began to fade. There it was again. She spun around, but this time saw her father-in-law just a few yards behind.

'Oh!' she murmured, putting a hand to her throat. 'I thought I heard footsteps. I didn't realise it was you.'

'Who did you think it was, then?' he laughed deeply, revealing the few remaining teeth, some snapped off, others black and sporting a furry, green coating. He placed his arm loosely on her shoulders and squeezed his fingers into the soft flesh. Initially, she had been almost relieved that it was someone she knew; now she was having second thoughts and her reservations about Grillo were returning rapidly.

'I didn't know.' She remained rigid in his grip and the fingers on her shoulder tightened as they neared the old barn.

'What's the matter with you, girl?' He sounded angry, although the words were quietly spoken and his lips were curled into a parody of a smile. 'Not afraid of your old father-in-law, are you?' he wheedled.

She shook her head but the action belied her feelings. She was trembling and he could feel himself getting excited. He liked it even better when they trembled. He would have to teach her a lesson, show her who was in charge in the Grillo household, once and for all.

'Look, it's starting to rain heavier,' he remarked. 'I think we should shelter, see if it stops. We're still a way off from the house.'

'I'd rather carry on, if you don't mind.' Alarm bells were ringing as Grillo's fingers dug even deeper. There was no-one out here to call for help, the sooner she got back to the house the better.

'Well, as a matter of fact, I do mind.' Grillo's voice was as firm as his grip when he guided her towards the barn. It was darker inside, but dry except for a few patches where holes in the roof let the rain flood in. At the back, a few sheaves of old corn lay rotting against a wall. 'Let's go and sit over there, it's dry at least.' He was trying a different approach now and his voice did not sound too unkind. He didn't want to scare her away like a frightened little rabbit – not just yet, anyway.

They sat down on the ground and began talking, first about nothing in particular and Emilia began to think she had been worrying about nothing. But then the talk became more intimate.

'You are a very pretty young thing, you know,' Grillo said. 'Do you like the things that my son does to you in bed?' he asked, and she could see the beady eyes glittering even in the dimness of the barn.

'I don't think you should be asking me things like that,' she ventured quietly.

'Oh, come on now! Don't play the innocent with me, I know you're no virgin.' He paused to savour the words and leaned towards her, his face inches from hers. She recoiled as the fetid breath stung her nostrils. 'I've heard all that grunting and groaning coming from your bedroom; you're just ripe for the plucking. And I can show you a few tricks your husband isn't man enough to know.'

His hand reached for her breast and started squeezing, roughly palpating the soft flesh, hurting and bruising the delicate skin. She was more frightened than she had ever been and tried to push him away, but the harder she struggled, the more determined he became. She clawed his face in panic, dragging her nails and leaving a series of parallel red gouges down the length of the fat jowls. But her resistance only served to excite him and he laughed at the futility of her attempts to thwart his attack. She could feel the hardness of his body as he tried to climb on top of her and pressed himself tightly against her leg.

'Oh, yes, that's it! Go on! Fight me!' he grinned. 'I don't like the quiet ones much, I prefer the ones like you, the ones with a bit of fire in their bellies.'

'Get off me!' Emilia's eyes were wide with terror as one huge, calloused hand shot out to pin her wrists above her head, while the other roughly tore the shawl away from her shoulders, ripping the thin fabric of the blouse beneath from shoulder to waist, leaving her breasts bare and exposed to his hungry leer. She could hardly breathe as his immense body weighed heavily on hers, but still she tried to struggle, anything to get away from this revolting man's hold. His lips dropped to her breasts, leaving behind a slime-trail of silvery saliva in their wake and she gagged as the urge to vomit overwhelmed her.

Emilia sobbed as he turned his attention to her skirts, dragging them up high over her thighs. His grip held firm, she was pinned down with no hope of escaping and she writhed and turned in a desperate attempt to keep her lower body covered, but she didn't stand a chance against his superior strength. All the while, with every move she made to fight him off, his excitement increased to unimaginable proportions, his tongue lolled, his eyes glazed over and his breath came in short ragged rasps until he could stand it no longer. With her skirts high above her waist, exposing the lower half of her body, he couldn't resist the promise of the creamy-gold flesh another moment.

In his twisted mind, he was convinced she wanted it as much as he did. He reached a hand into his trousers and his intentions were unmistakeable. Emilia gritted her teeth as she waited for the final humiliation, the moment when her own father-in-law entered her body. She knew there was nothing more she could do to prevent it, but she was determined to keep the last remnants of dignity. She made up her mind not to plead any more, she knew it would do no good. Nor would she move, she would lie still, motionless, do nothing that might enhance the experience for him.

Then, the unexpected sound of a loud explosion echoed inside her head and hurt her ears. Without warning, the tension went out of Grillo's body and he slumped forward, still and limp on top of her. For a moment, nothing made sense, the girl had no idea what had happened. Then a warm, sticky substance began to flow over her hands and trickle between her fingers, running through them and staining the parts of her body he had rendered naked. Raising her head, she could just make out the bright red of Grillo's life-blood as it poured freely from what remained of one side of his head, the last vestiges of consciousness seeping away in its flow. A dark pool bubbled and spread crimson beneath him.

Then the screaming began. Loud, endless screams, shrill and piercing, cutting through the still air like a scythe. It was only the sudden realisation that her own lips, teeth bared and wide with horror, were the source of these animal noises, that shocked her into action. Terrified, she began to struggle in a frantic effort to drag herself from beneath the dead weight that lay on top of her. With one final burst of strength fuelled by fear, she finally managed to extricate herself. She wanted to get up and run, but the trembling legs refused to support her and she sat helpless on the ground, sobs racking her body.

But the horror didn't stop there. She became aware of a shadowy figure standing just in front of her and she looked up in disbelief. A second series of shocks tore through her body as she recognised the frail silhouette. Then the frightened gaze dropped to her mother's hands, where a glint of light caught the silver-grey object she held. At the same moment, the sound of running footsteps and shouting came from outside the barn and Lena turned momentarily towards the door. Tino and Marco came into view first, followed quickly by Raffaele. For a split second, there was total silence as they struggled to make sense of the horror before them, the scene of carnage a bloody tableau, frozen in time. But the peace was soon shattered.

'No!' Emilia's scream was drowned out by the report of a second gunshot that ripped and echoed through the barn. Then all hell broke loose.

Chapter 20

TINO WAS NOW more determined than ever to return to England. He made up his mind that they would leave as soon as the funerals and inquiry were over. With his Mamma gone now, there was nothing left for him here. There had been little before, but this recent tragedy had made him begin to question whether there was some evil curse on his family.

After the horrific events, Emilia had been distraught, and so had her sister-in-law Serafina, but their emotions manifested themselves in very different ways. Emilia felt dirty and ashamed. She had the constant urge to wash herself, scrubbing mercilessly at her body until the skin was raw, as if the act would erase the bad memories. She could never bring herself to face the world again if everyone knew what her own father-in-law had tried to do to her. The recollection of those rough, pudgy hands roaming over her bare flesh sent a shiver down her spine. The shame of having to share that knowledge would drive her out of her mind.

Serafina too was ashamed, but she didn't cry when they gently told her about her father's fate. They put it down to shock, the weeping would come eventually. But still the tears refused to be shed. No-one could understand this apparent lack of emotion. She was running around smiling, laughing as if nothing untoward had happened. Then one night, Tino challenged her, as they sat side by side on the high bed in the Grillo house. He too had been puzzled, shocked even, by her apathy. He had always thought she was close to her Papa. Tino had never liked Grillo, and Emilia's horrific experience at his hands confirmed that his instincts had been right. But there was more to this than met the eye and he was determined to get to the bottom of it.

'What is wrong?' he asked his wife. 'What your father did to my sister was unforgivable, but…'

She turned abruptly to face him, her eyes searching his face. 'Don't you know?' she cried incredulously, her voice shaking with emotion. 'You, my husband. And still you haven't guessed.'

Tino shook his head. 'Serafina, you're talking in riddles. Just tell me!'

Serafina began to laugh. She laughed until tears streamed from her eyes. But this was no ordinary laughter, this was born of hysteria. Tino panicked. He didn't know how to react and slapped her hard across the cheek. Still she didn't stop.

'You are so funny, Tino!' she accused through the giggles. 'You must be blind! As blind as anyone could be.' Without warning, the laughter stopped. She dropped her voice to a whisper, the black eyes staring hard into his. 'Even after what happened to your own sister, and you still can't see! Why do you think I'm like I am? Why do you think I have such a bad reputation around here? How do you think I got to know so much about men?' She fired the questions at him in quick succession, willing him to understand.

The colour drained from Tino's face as the terrible realisation hit him. Grillo had been a disgusting, vile man, but his own daughter? Surely not?

'Serafina, what are you saying?' His grip was tight on her shoulders. 'Surely you don't mean he did to you what he did to Emilia?'

She began to sob, quieter this time and nodded.

'Oh, God! How long had this been going on?'

'Not long after we lost Mamma.' Serafina paused, swallowing hard. 'In fact, it started some time before that, but at first it was just touching, kissing. But after Mamma died…' She shuddered at the memory, then turned to Tino with pleading in her eyes. 'Tino, please believe me, I didn't know it was wrong, not for a long time. He told me all fathers did it. It was a way of showing how much they loved their little girls. And he said I must be quiet, I mustn't tell anyone, because it would make other men jealous and they would want to do it too. He said if I promised not to tell, he would get me whatever I wanted.' Her voice dropped even lower. 'Including you.'

Tino could not believe what he was hearing. He was beginning to understand now why she had always acted so provocatively, so womanly. When other girls of her age were still playing childish games she was taunting and teasing anyone who would watch. 'It gave Papa a thrill, he liked to see other men lust after me,' she explained quietly. 'But he got tired of me. That's when he set his sights on Emilia, he used to watch her and Marco together and I could see him getting excited. Can you blame me for not mourning him, Tino?' She paused for a second, then added with a vehemence that astonished Tino, 'I'm glad he's dead.'

Tino didn't love his wife – how could he, he was still in love with someone else. But he had never felt closer to her than he did at that moment. It was little wonder she had turned out the way she had, and his heart went out to her. She had suffered enough. His heart would always be with Mara, nothing would change that. But he made up his mind at that moment to try to be a good husband to Serafina, he owed her that much at least after everything she had been through.

It was Tino who had first ventured the idea of not giving the whole truth away. After all, because of the tragic nature of the events, no-one had yet pressed them for a full account. That would be kept for the inquiry to be held later. Tino had gone over to the farm to confront Raffaele.

'Why should we bring shame on Emilia? She is terrified that people will only say she must have encouraged Grillo. We will have to learn to live with the stigma of Mamma shooting him, but at least, everyone knew she was sick in the mind. There's no point in dragging Emilia into it, she's innocent in all this.'

Raffaele lifted his head from his hands. These were the first words his son had spoken to him for some time, but they were out of necessity, not love for his father. With Grillo and Lena gone, Raffaele had had time to reflect on his actions, wrestled with the voices in his head. He came to the conclusion that he did not like the man he had become. He would have given anything to change things. But it was too late for that now.

Tino had already left him in no doubt that he blamed him for everything – if he had not let greed colour his judgement, he would not have sacrificed the happiness of his children. And Tino was sure that if he had been a more supportive husband, and treated Mamma with love and compassion instead of ignoring her as if she didn't exist, she might even have recovered in time. After all, hadn't she seen what they had missed, although it was under their very noses?

'So, *figlio mio,* what do you think we should do?'

'*Figlio mio*?' Tino flinched. 'Don't you dare call me your son! You are no father of mine,' he spat out. 'I just want to do what's best for everyone concerned.' He stopped for a few moments, composing himself, though the pulse at his temples throbbed visibly. 'We should just say the truth, that Mamma was sick; she followed Grillo, shot him then shot herself. No-one needs to know any more and it will protect Emilia. Think how it would affect Marco if the truth ever got out about the kind of man his father was.'

Raffaele nodded slowly. 'It makes sense. We've all been through enough and I don't want Emilia having to go through that.'

The funerals had been and gone and the inquiry was conducted as expected. They concluded that events leading up to the deaths were very clear. Lena had been ill for some time, the doctor testified to that. In her confused state of mind, she followed Grillo. It came out that the guns hung freely behind the door – a small hand pistol and a larger shotgun. Lena knew how to handle a gun, she had been taught from an early age. It was essential in this wild territory where wolves and wild boar roamed freely. And many years of practice had made her an excellent shot that would rival any man. No-one would ever know what went on in her mind before she shot Grillo then turned the gun on herself. Everyone was sympathetic, it was just an unhappy tragedy. Only the family would ever know the truth.

It was the day before Tino and Serafina were leaving for London. Raffaele had been turning the events of the past years over and over in his mind. He could not come to terms with what he had done to his family and he seemed to have aged in a matter of weeks. In one last desperate attempt to make reparation with his son, he went over to the Grillo house. Turning squarely towards Tino, he stared him straight in the eye. 'Tino, can't you find it in your heart to forgive me? Don't you think I haven't ripped myself apart over this again and again? I know now I was wrong, everything I did was out of pure greed. And, like a fool, I allowed Grillo to fuel that greed.' He paused and his voice dropped to little more than a whisper. 'But after Mamma became ill, things got worse, I didn't know what to do. The woman I loved, spent my life with had become a shell, a total stranger. My only consolation was to take my mind off it with other things, material things – and power. I admit I've always wanted a bit more than we had, but it became an urge, an obsession. I had to have more, more, more.' He banged his fist on the table three times to emphasise his words. His voice shook and he had to swallow hard before he could continue. 'And now, too late, I have finally woken up to what I've done.' Tears blinded his eyes. 'Please?' he begged. 'Can't you forgive a foolish man?'

Tino remained cold and unmoved. 'You've ruined too many lives, mine included, for me to ever call you Papa again. You are the one who has to live with yourself for the rest of your life, not me. When I go from here with Serafina, it will be the last time you will ever see or hear from me again. I can never forgive you. Or Francesco. He should have known me well enough to realise I wouldn't have let Mara down. Instead, he betrayed me.'

Raffaele turned away, tears running down his cheeks. 'Then I wish you luck and happiness. And may God go with you,' he whispered, then added even more softly, so that Tino did not hear, '*Mio figlio*. My son.'

The following morning, Tino and Serafina walked away from the house to the bottom of the hill where a donkey and cart already laden with their belongings awaited them. Carlotta was with them, she had asked if she could travel with them to London. Tino was not angry with his sisters any more, or with young Michele; they too had been victims of their father's power-hungry mind. They had heard from Giuseppe, he was more than happy to have them back there and Tino had resolved to look forward from now on, not back.

The partings had been tearful. Marco and Emilia, still pale after her ordeal, had seen them off with a promise to keep in touch, but Tino had deliberately kept away from his father's house. He had no desire to speak to his father again or Francesco. Instead, he had seen young Michele the night before at the Grillo house, giving him strict instructions to look after Tidillia in particular. Now that Mamma was not around she would need someone to give her lots of cuddles and stroke her fur. The boy had nodded, he too needed something to care for. The past few weeks had been really hard for him.

But the main reason Tino avoided going to the place he had once called home was that he couldn't bring himself to say that final goodbye to Mara. He couldn't have borne looking at her, speaking to her, knowing it would be for the last time ever. As they turned the last bend in the track, he couldn't resist a swift glance backwards. He didn't know whether it was a trick of the light or his imagination, but he would have sworn that just at the top of the ridge, he could see a slim figure with a halo of golden hair, a hand raised in sad farewell.

Chapter 21

IT WAS SOME days later that the locomotive steamed into a London station with a roar and a squeal of brakes. Tino gathered their luggage together and led the way outside. He had never thought he would be so glad to be back, but he was oblivious to the looks of dismay that darkened the features of his wife and sister. They turned to each other, crestfallen.

'I didn't expect it to be like this at all,' Carlotta murmured. She looked very close to tears.

'Don't worry, we've got each other.' Trying hard to put on a brave face for her friend's sake, Serafina managed a weak smile. It was nothing like she had imagined either, and she had been shocked by the dark, grimy atmosphere that seemed to hang heavily all around them. But then, she had nothing left in Italy to go back to. In fact, the further her homeland had disappeared behind them into the distance, the better she had felt. Anything to help take away the awful memories of her childhood and the more recent events that she feared would be imprinted on her mind for ever.

Giuseppe had arranged to meet them in Piccadilly Circus. He had business to attend to there and would bring the horse-drawn cart. The area was bustling, filled with people, traffic and street vendors, a riotous confusion of sound and colour. Pigeons with neck feathers that changed from purple to green and back again fought over the liberal crumbs and scraps of food that littered the pavements. The girls marvelled at the sights, turning their heads this way and that as they tried to take in as much as they could of the dizzying scene before them. Tino pointed out the fountain with its shiny aluminium statue rising high into the air above.

'That's the Shaftesbury monument,' he told them, proud of his superior local knowledge. 'It's new, only built a few years ago.' He turned quizzically to Carlotta. 'Do you remember our cousin, the one who went off to be an artist's model? He was about your age…'

She thought for a moment. 'Yes, I do. I remember that man, the sculptor, coming to the village, saying how handsome our boys were. Classical, or something, I think he said.' She paused momentarily, as if in thought. 'Didn't he offer him a good amount of money to go to England with him as his model? I remember Papa saying he thought it was all a bit odd and he didn't think he would have let his son go off to a foreign country like that with a stranger.'

'Well, there was danger out there in Italy, too.' The note of cynicism didn't escape his wife and sister. 'Anyway,' he went on, 'Zi Giuseppe told me they modelled that statue on him.'

'No!'

'Yes. Yes, it's true.'

It was true, there was a resemblance to their cousin, but perhaps that was how the rumour started. They watched as a few grubby ragamuffins ran around the fountain, playing some kind of chasing game, their thin, threadbare clothes hardly adequate for the time of year. They looked on to see one little girl grab the sleeve of an older boy as she caught up with him, shouting in glee as she caught her prey. The dull sound of thin, cheap fabric being torn apart followed, as the sleeve of the shirt came clean away at the shoulder.

'Now look what you bleedin' gorn an' done! It's me best shirt an' all!' the boy wailed, clipping the girl soundly across the ear. 'Jus' wait til I tell Ma, she'll 'av yer guts fer garters!'

Tino grinned broadly, forgetting for a moment the others couldn't understand what the children were saying. Even if they had understood English, he doubted they would have coped with this strong accent, it took a while for ears to become accustomed to it.

The little girl began to cry and Tino took a step forward to comfort her, but at that very moment, he caught sight of Nero pulling the cart. It looked different without the fancy awning which had been removed for the winter. The ice-cream paraphernalia had been removed too, leaving the back of the cart free for his passengers.

'Tino! Carlotta!' Giuseppe drew the cart expertly to a stop right alongside them and Nero gave a soft snort as he recognised his old friend. Giuseppe alighted with the grace of a man years younger. He threw his arms first around his niece, then turned to Serafina. 'Your new wife?' He smiled at the girl, but turned meaningfully at Tino. He knew the full story. Tino felt he and Janey were the only people he could trust with all the sordid details and had written to them some time earlier. Giuseppe had taken the opportunity to break the news of Tino's marriage to Kathleen too. She had been inconsolable when she realised she would meet him and his new wife; but she would put on a brave face, for his sake. But Donato had seized on the chance to be there for her with renewed hope, listening to her problems and wiping away the tears from her eyes. There might be a chance for him yet.

'Yes, my new wife. Serafina,' Tino reiterated quietly.

Giuseppe bowed his head and put his lips to her hand.

'You have a very beautiful wife, Tino,' he said, then releasing Serafina's hand, he wrapped his arms tightly around his nephew. He wanted to tell him how sorry he was for everything he had been through, how he sympathised with the way he had been being tricked into marrying the wrong girl. But the words caught in his throat as he imagined how he would have felt if someone had come between him and his lovely Janey.

Tino's eyes were damp as he and his uncle finally separated. 'I am pleased to be home, Zi Giuseppe,' he murmured and the lump in Giuseppe's throat seemed to swell to twice the size.

It was nearing the end of 1899, Tino, his wife and his sister had been in London for some months. It had taken them a while to settle in to this alien way of life, and at first, Carlotta in particular had questioned the wisdom of her decision to come to this country. But she had struck up a friendship with Beppe, they were of a similar age and it soon became clear that the companionship was beginning to take a new turn.

The new century was imminent and Tino had been giving a lot of consideration to his future. News had come via Emilia that Mara and Francesco were expecting their first child and that had cut Tino to the core. He had left the house that morning, angry and upset. It should have been him at her side, he should have been the father of her children. Carlotta picked up the crumpled note from the grate, where he had carelessly tossed it. Her hair shone softly in the firelight as she laboriously traced the words. It wouldn't do for Serafina to see this. She crumpled it up again and threw it into the heart of the flames. It was the acceptance that Mara was now truly bound to Francesco. The finality of her expecting this baby caused Tino to question what he really wanted from life. He needed something to aim for, a focus, and an embryonic idea began to formulate in his head. He decided he would discuss it with his uncle at the first opportunity.

But Giuseppe beat him to it. One evening, he took Tino aside in a quiet corner of the house. He felt the time was right to confide in his nephew – he was an intelligent and down-to-earth young man, he would value Tino's opinion of his plans and ideas.

'I'm getting older, now,' he explained, 'and I think it's time I began to look ahead. What do I want to be doing in the next few years?' The question was rhetorical, and short of nodding his head in encouragement for his uncle to go on, Tino remained silent. 'The thing is,' Giuseppe continued, 'the ice-cream market is becoming flooded here in London, just like the organ-grinders. You go to a pitch, there are dozens of others there already, beaten you to it and all competing for the same customers. For a long time, I always thought I would go back home, back to Italy but – well, after all that's happened, I won't be going anywhere, now. So, that leaves me with the four boys, Kathleen and not enough trade between them. And there's you, of course.'

He pondered for a moment, but Tino could see he was buzzing with suppressed excitement. The dark eyes, not unlike Tino's, seemed to light up and the strong features became animated with his next words. 'The future is in this lodging house!' he announced, slamming the flat of his hand onto the table. 'This is where the money is, I'm sure of it.'

Tino's brows drew together. 'The lodging house?' he said, immediately conscious of repeating his uncle's words.

'Yes. It's always full these days I've had to turn people away lately, and that's no good, turning business away like that. But,' he paused, savouring the moment before he finally laid bare his plans, 'there's this big house, not far from St James'. Tino, the previous tenants were kicked out, evicted and the lease is up for sale. I've been to see it, it would be perfect.' His eyes shone. 'It would be perfect – not as a lodging house, but a proper hotel. With a small café, as well.'

His excitement was contagious, but Tino still had some

reservations. He didn't want to dampen his uncle's enthusiasm, but there were many practicalities to be considered before any real decisions could be made.

'Zi Giuseppe, can you afford it?' he asked, concern forcing him to be open with his uncle. Places like that didn't come cheap and he was worried it would be out of his uncle's league. 'And what about staff? You and Janey couldn't run a place like that on your own, surely?'

'No, no, no, no!' he chided, this time bringing a fist down onto the table with a thump. 'Tino, don't you understand? I've thought it all through, I've been saving up for a long time and I've got more than enough money put aside. The boys can come with me, and we can take on some more staff. I'm not talking about some scruffy little back-street place here. I'm talking about a real hotel, with good, high class clients.' He reached across the table and grabbed his nephew's hands excitedly. 'Tino, I want you to be my partner in this business. I know we can make it work.'

Tino was taken aback. He had quite a bit of money saved, but he knew it would be no match for Giuseppe's contribution, and he said so. Apart from that, he had already come to a decision about his own future. And it didn't lie in London.

'Tino, don't be so quick to say no! Give yourself time to think this through, it could be a golden opportunity for you,' he begged. 'Please, don't go making any hasty decisions – you may regret them later. At least wait until you've seen the place, then you can tell me yes or no.'

Reluctantly, Tino agreed, but he knew in his heart it wasn't what he wanted. For a start, he was beginning to feel uncomfortable in Kathleen's presence. She was often close by, hanging on to his every word, while Donato brooded quietly, watching from a distance. She was forever making snide remarks about Serafina too, though luckily, she had not been as quick as Carlotta to pick up the English language, and most of the comments went over her head. He couldn't live like that for long, sooner or later his wife would begin to realise the animosity the other girl felt towards her. But above all, he didn't want to go through life owing everything to the generosity of his uncle in offering to take on a partner whose contribution could only be a fraction of his own.

No, it was time for him to take control of his own life, be his own man, make his own decisions, make his own future – even make his own mistakes. He wanted independence, to be able to choose his own direction in life. He needed to prove to himself that he could be a success – not through twisted, bitter greed like his father but through sheer hard work, determination and a flair for business. True, Zi Giuseppe was tight, close with his money, but he was more of a role model and mentor for him than his father had ever been. A man who had come to London with nothing and built himself up into someone who was well-thought of and respected by everyone, rich and poor alike. Tino wanted to be like him, with a lovely wife and a little girl just like baby Angela. A picture of Mara with a golden-haired baby nestling in her arms came into his mind and pangs of regret washed over him. She was in the past, his future now was with Serafina. He might not have loved her in the same way as he'd loved Mara, but he'd accepted her and had a certain amount of admiration for her, after all that she'd been through. She was a good, dutiful wife who tried everything to make up to him for what they had both endured. This new Serafina was a world apart from the shameless siren who had seduced him on the night of his return home. But now he understood why, and he had found it in his heart to forgive her.

True to his word, Tino went to see the house with his uncle and Janey. It was big and impressive. It would have been easy for Tino to accept his uncle's offer. But then he thought of his own need to prove himself and of Kathleen's growing antagonism towards Serafina and his mind was made up.

'Zio, you know I have every respect for you,' he began. Giuseppe's heart sank. He knew what Tino's answer was going to be even before he uttered the words.

'You're not coming into the business, then?' The hurt expression was plain as day on his face and Tino felt slightly guilty, but he kept to his resolve.

'No, I'm not,' he replied quietly but firmly. 'Zi Giuseppe, I thank you from the bottom of my heart, you have been a father to me, not just an uncle. But I need to make my own way in life. You know how we are, from our part of the world…' he stopped, smiling at the older man. 'We are a proud people. We have pride in ourselves, pride in our achievements. I want to provide for my family myself, to start my own business.'

Giuseppe's forehead creased. 'Then what is it you want to do?' he asked, perplexed.

'Start my own business!' Tino replied firmly. 'An ice-cream business. Just like you.'

'But I've already told you, there are too many people in the game now.' He nodded his head, intending to adopt a look of superior experience and wisdom but reminding Tino briefly of Nero when he was waiting to be fed. 'You'll never get on here.'

'Ah, but that's it!' he grinned. 'I don't plan on staying here.'

The older man's eyebrows shot upwards with surprise and were lost somewhere in the hairline of the thick dark mop. 'Not here?' he asked incredulously. 'Then where?'

'Wales!'

There was a stunned silence. 'Wales?' Giuseppe uttered. 'Wales! Of all places. Why there?'

'You remember Antonio, we used to meet up with him in the ice-house? Antonio, with the bad leg.'

'*Si, si!*' In consternation, Giuseppe had reverted to his native tongue without even realising it, then swiftly added, 'Yes.'

'Well, I was speaking to his son recently. It seems there's a big call for ice-cream down there.He's only been there two years and already saved enough to get a small shop. He doesn't even need to go out with the cart any more.' He paused, waiting for his words to sink in before dropping the next bombshell. 'Zi Giuseppe, you won't be needing Nero or the big cart now, not with the hotel. I will buy them from you, they will be the first step to starting my own business. We can even keep the D'Abruzzo name on the cart!'

Giuseppe wasn't convinced and threw up his hands in dismay. 'But where will you stay?' he shouted, his arms flailing around in frustration. 'You'll have to have somewhere to live, you'll need somewhere to make the ice-cream. And as for Nero and the cart, well, I'll still need to go and get provisions, with a place that size – I'll still need them.'

Tino was trying his utmost to stay calm, but in the face of his uncle's agitated response, it was not easy. 'First of all, Zi Giuseppe, if you're going to open up this hotel, you're going to have to start thinking big – of course you won't need Nero and the cart, the tradesmen will deliver to you.'

Giuseppe muttered something unintelligible under his breath, then added loudly, 'Well, yes, I suppose you're right, I hadn't thought of it like that,' he conceded and Tino had to stifle a smile. Not to be outdone, Giuseppe suddenly burst out. 'But what about a place to live? I bet you haven't worked that one out yet, now, have you?'

'It's already arranged,' Tino's voice was quietly determined. 'Antonio's place is big, he's got spare rooms, he said we can rent from him until we get up and running. He's even got a shed out in the back yard, with one of those new ice-cream machines. The big, mechanical ones.'

Giuseppe made no comment, but his whole countenance was serious, and Tino realised he would have to work hard to convince him of the wisdom of this exciting new venture which was becoming more and more important to him with every passing moment. The new century was fast approaching, he wanted this to be a memorable start to the next phase of his life. 'Zi Giuseppe, Antonio is a good man. I trust him.'

'Won't you be working the same patch?'

'No, that's the beauty of it. He's concentrating on the shop now, he's too busy serving up ice-cream, and pies and fish and chips and things in the shop to go out any more.'

Giuseppe heaved a sigh. 'Well, you're a man now, you know your own mind.' He knew when he was beaten, and Tino had inherited the determination and sense of adventure that had brought him and Raffaele to London for the first time, all those years ago. 'And you can have Nero and the cart.' Tino opened his mouth to protest, but Giuseppe knew what was coming and raised the palm of his hand to halt the unspoken words. 'They will be my gift to you,' he said, and before Tino could reply, added, 'and would you throw a gift back in the face of your old uncle, eh?'

Tino grinned. He knew from Giuseppe's smile that he had finally won his approval, but he was still reluctant to go on. 'There's one other thing,' he hesitated, unable to meet the brown eyes that watched him intently. He took a deep breath. 'Beppe and Carlotta want to come with us.'

He waited with bated breath for his uncle's reaction. He knew his uncle had planned to take his friend and sister on in the hotel. There was a long, agonising wait as Giuseppe considered this news.

'Then they must go with you!' he replied slowly. His

lips curved in a smile beneath the thin, waxed moustache. 'And you had better have one of the small handcarts too, if you're going to earn enough to keep you all out of the workhouse.'

Tino heaved a sigh of relief, and his hand thumped his uncle's back vigorously.

'*Grazie,* Zi Giuseppe. *Grazie*!' Suddenly, life seemed good again, he had something to work towards, something to look forward to. His own business! He could hardly believe it. He was going to have his own business. Perhaps life was not so bad after all!

But Giuseppe's next words brought him down to earth with a bang. 'Tino, son, don't go expecting too much too soon. You should know better than most people, life has a nasty habit of thwarting even the best laid plans. But I promise you, I wish you luck and happiness! And of course, you know where to find us, if you ever need anything.'

Chapter 22

The New Year and the turn of the century had been and gone. Giuseppe had been frantically buying new furnishings for the hotel, though a few of the armchairs had come from the second-hand shop down the road. They were good quality and he didn't see the point in spending money for the sake of it. Janey had taken one look at the old-fashioned, horsehair-stuffed monstrosities and raised her eyes to the heavens.

'Still the same mean, stingy ol' bugger as always,' she muttered to Tino. 'Anythin' ter save a few pennies. An' the man who sold 'em to 'im, 'e was a right mis'rable ol' sod – 'e knew a sucker when 'e saw one. Do yer know, when I started to say about the leather bein' all cracked, he 'ad the cheek to turn to me with a look on his chops that would've soured milk.' Tino turned away from his uncle, working hard to stifle the bubble of laughter that rose in his throat and making a big pretence of inspecting the room.

He had to admit, though, the hotel looked wonderful, it had been redecorated from top to bottom and looked to him like a small palace. There were only a few weeks left now until the grand opening.

Gianni had visited again, laden with treats, and was greatly impressed by this new venture. He was genuinely enthusiastic about Tino's plans too, offering advice and encouragement. He was fond of the boy, and genuinely wished him well. He had not been surprised when he had learned how Raffaele had tricked Tino and it had made him even more supportive of the boy's venture. But it was his news from home that had affected

Tino most. He had tried so hard to bury his feelings, hoping that time would heal the raw wounds. But he knew in his heart the past was still very much alive, and his reaction to Gianni's announcement that Mara and Francesco were now the proud parents of their first child, a baby daughter, confirmed it.

'Your Papa is desperately sorry for what happened, you know,' he told Tino gently. 'Though I can see why you don't want anything to do with him. But you know, Tino, he wasn't well at all. Your mother's illness and Angelo's death took its toll on him too. Now, he's a broken shadow of a man, painfully thin and hunched over, like he's aged twenty years in just a few months. He's missing your mother badly, you and Carlotta, too. He told me he wants to build some kind of shrine, some monument, to try to make amends. All he wants now is forgiveness.'

But Tino was resolute. 'Then he'd better ask God for forgiveness,' came the unrelenting reply. 'Because he's not going to get it from me.'

It was April when once again, the residents of Bramley Mews turned out to say their farewells to Tino. It was a cool day and a little damp, but the pale sunshine of spring battled successfully to penetrate the grey skies, so that even the drab houses and dingy cobbled streets seemed to take on a more vibrant appearance. This time, though, Tino wasn't leaving alone, and Kathleen stayed sullenly at the back of the crowds, watching the proceedings in silence. Tino couldn't help but notice the wan and unhappy face. Concerned, he pushed his way through the crowd to get to her.

'No more tears, *piccina*!' He used the familiar term of endearment, while dabbing at her cheeks with a clean handkerchief. She didn't know what it meant, but it sounded comforting anyway. 'It's not that bad, I'm not going to hell, just Wales! It's not that far, you can visit sometimes, you and Donato.'

She gave a watery smile and turned to the priest who was standing next to her. Her lips trembled as she fought back the tears. 'Father, you better tell 'im off, talkin' about 'ell like that! I fink that's a blast-fer-me!' She stumbled over a word Janey always had trouble with too.

'Blasphemy,' the priest corrected, laughing. 'And so I will, my child,' he added, feigning an icy glare in Tino's direction. He looked down from his great height, and sympathy for the girl softened his sharp, craggy features. It seemed Tino was the only one present who had always been unaware of her feelings for him. But she was a good Catholic girl, Tino was married now and she would have to learn to live with that – resign herself to the fact that he wasn't for her, no matter how hard it would be to endure. But too many people had been hurt lately. Donato still followed Kathleen around with unshakeable devotion and loyalty. One day, when she woke up to it, she too would find a good husband right there under her nose. Usually, these Italian people married whenever they could with their own kind; Giuseppe and Janey had been one of the few exceptions. Giuseppe had to admit, he'd had his doubts, especially since Janey hadn't even been of the True Faith to begin with. But hadn't they proved how well these mixed marriages could work? Father Delaney cast a glance towards Kathleen's mother. He knew as his eyes met Bernadette's that the same thoughts were going through her mind too. He would have to pay her a visit soon and talk to her about it.

They were travelling by rail from Paddington and waited patiently until the familiar sight of the deep Brunswick green locomotive, followed by a snake of rich chocolate-brown and cream carriages, steamed and hissed to a screeching halt alongside the platform. They had little baggage, Tino had arranged for Nero and the cart to be driven there ahead of them, along with the bulk of their belongings, so everything would be ready for them when they arrived. Beppe would be following on his own in a few weeks' time. He had decided to stay on to help Giuseppe with the grand opening of the hotel.

Tino helped the two young women aboard and settled down opposite them for the long journey ahead. The gentle rocking motion and the measured, thrumming sound of the wheels as they rolled over the tracks proved to be an effective soporific and before long, Serafina and Carlotta had both fallen into a deep sleep, heads resting together, hats skewed to one side where the brims touched. They had both been eager to try out the fashions of their adopted country and Janey had been more than happy to accompany them on a shopping trip. They had each ended up with a best frock and another, cheaper one for everyday use; a hat, a skirt, two blouses – one to wash and one to wear – and an assortment of undergarments, some practical and others trimmed with an abundance of frothy lace. These had made the girls blush furiously, especially when the shop assistant shamelessly held aloft a pair of fine lawn, lace-edged bloomers for their approval. And all this finery was provided courtesy of Giuseppe!

'A parting gift,' he had said, and Janey began to fear she was finally succeeding in turning her husband into a generous man. But despite their very English clothing, the girls' origins were undeniable as soon as they opened their mouths.

It brought a smile to Tino's lips as he watched them breathing softly, cheeks dusted with the blush of slumber, shiny black hair tumbling over rounded shoulders mingling with dark tendrils that had escaped from beneath the flower-decorated hat of the other girl. He sat quietly, contemplating the sleeping forms, and felt a deep pang of affection towards them both. But what surprised, even startled him, was the sudden rush of tenderness for Serafina that enveloped him. She had been through so much. Tino stared out of the window, deep in thought as the train pushed its way slowly and wheezily out of London. He watched, fascinated, as hazy-edged fields and towns swept past and disappeared from view, to the accompaniment of a series of blasts from the train's shrill whistle. Wide columns of steam shot skywards and swirled around, thinning and mingling until they became indistinguishable from the cool, damp air.

The few days before had been wet, and fat drops of rain had clung to the layer of grease and dust on the windows, drying out to leave behind a grimy, semi-opaque film that clouded Tino's view. It brought something Janey had said to mind, a comment that had made him laugh at the time.

'GWR?' she'd said, her face deadpan. 'God's Wonderful Railway. Course, there're those who'd say otherwise.' She paused, and Tino knew that the wicked glint in her eyes meant she had something else up her sleeve. 'Like Great Way Round an' Goes When Ready. It ain't the most reliable an' I reckon you might just get ter Wales via Italy, if yer lucky. They likes takin' the scenic routes.'

The girls slept on as they slipped through the stations – Reading, Swindon, Bath. Tino's spoken English was good now, if heavily accented, but he needed more practise with his writing and reading. Spelling out the names on the stations was a good way to learn and it helped pass the time too, though his pronunciation of Reading caused his brows to draw together in confusion. When they reached Bristol, he knew it would not be too many hours longer. The girls had drifted in and out of sleep but now, they were finally beginning to come round as the train steamed out of Temple Meads Station. Tino pulled down a wicker hamper from the luggage rack above them.

'Time to eat!' He deliberately spoke in English, trying to pass on his own knowledge to Serafina in particular. She was finding this new language confusing and illogical, and often lapsed into her native tongue. But despite her protests, Tino argued she would have to learn, for her own sake, or she would never fit in. He handed out the bread, cheese and meat which Janey had lovingly packed for them. They were all hungry, they had been travelling for hours now and began to eat avidly. Serafina yawned widely, trying to shake off the last remnants of sleep.

Then everything went dark, save for the dim lights inside the carriages and the there was a subtle change in the noise as the train ploughed on through the blackness outside the windows.

'What is it?' Serafina sat up sharply, though still not fully awake, and glanced around nervously. 'Why has the night come so quickly?'

Tino laughed and reached over to pat her hand. 'It's not night time,' he grinned, showing off his white teeth.

'Then what?'

They had been through other tunnels and viaducts on their way from Italy, but Tino had forgotten to warn them about this one. It was fairly new too and saved a much longer detour around the countryside. 'It's only another tunnel. A long one, I know – Zi Giuseppe said about seven miles – but that's all it is. It's called the Severn Tunnel.'

'Is that because of its length?' Carlotta asked.

Tino was thoughtful. 'I'm not sure. But I don't think so, I believe the spelling is different.' He tried to impress them with his knowledge, but spelling was not his strong point, so he quickly changed the subject.

'We'll be in Newport soon. And that's Wales!' He could speak now with renewed confidence; he had made a point of finding out about all the main stations on the route.

'Another country again!' Carlotta remarked. 'Where then?'

'Cardiff, then we're really on our way to Swansea.'

'I wonder what it's like.'

A strange combination of excitement and apprehension fell over the little group as they neared their destination. The landscape was beginning to change, they were leaving behind the flat, endless miles of the English countryside and soon, the gentle slopes of hills softened the horizon. They brightened up at the sight but their hearts sank again as they passed through the heavily industrialised areas around the main towns. It was a rollercoaster journey of highs and lows. Soon, Tino realised they were nearing their destination. His spirits dipped at the sight of the scarred, pitted landscape, tall chimneys belching out hideous bursts of smoke and towering mountains – not the green mountains of home, but shiny black slag-heaps looming dark and menacing against the sky, a legacy from the metal industries that provided jobs and food for the town.

Antonio had given strict instructions to carry on after the Landore station to Swansea High Street. He said he had to go into the town on business anyway and he would pick them up from there and take them directly to his shop in Morriston, a few miles away. In any case, it would save them getting a cab. As they pulled into the station Tino was determined not to let his first impressions daunt his spirits and he joked and teased the girls as they got off the train, trying to cheer them up. His eyes eagerly scanned the faces of the throngs of people on the platform, hoping to catch a sight of Antonio. But there was no sign of him anywhere.

'Let's look outside,' he said, leading the way along the platform towards the exit, hardly noticing the fancy scrolling and ironwork. He saw a few people heading for the waiting area, with its long, shiny wooden benches. 'Better still, you go in there and sit down, while I see if I can find Antonio.'

Outside, rows of horses and traps waited for their passengers, along with a few carriages and various motor cars. The latter made Tino very nervous indeed, he'd seen how they had increased in number in London of late and he had had a few close shaves with them himself. 'If people were meant to move at such a ridiculous pace on a regular basis, we'd have been born with wheels, not legs,' he had remarked indignantly. It just wasn't normal.

But Antonio was still nowhere to be seen. Tino paced up and down the street, hoping to catch a glimpse of the older man. The buildings were close together and tall, but somehow, the street still seemed to allow the light to filter through. He passed the Mackworth Hotel on the High Street, a big, imposing building with tall columns fronting the entrance. He began to think they might be passing the night there, if Antonio didn't turn up soon. It was late afternoon, he certainly didn't want to be hanging around here when it got dark, especially with the two women to look after. By now, he was also desperate to answer the call of nature, but was worried in case he missed his friend. However, he could see the lavatories, just a few yards away. He had correctly guessed what they were after watching several bowler-hatted men disappearing into their depths with a strained frown on their faces, and reappearing a few moments later, frowns replaced with a look of smiling relief. He decided he couldn't wait a moment longer and ran across the street, dodging various forms of transport until he reached the tall, ornate railings situated precariously in the centre of the road. Tino found he had to go down a series of steps flanked by white-tiled walls, with several of the tiles cracked or chipped, before he could relieve himself. The deeper inside he went, the more dismal it became, with only thick, frosted-glass tiles above allowing some hazy light to filter through. There was an overwhelming smell of disinfectant mixed with stale urine and it reminded him of the time Zi Giuseppe had taken him to the public baths in Little Italy, in the Holborn district of London. He was momentarily overcome with a wave of nostalgia, a longing for the safety and familiarity of his uncle's old lodging house. Curiously, the urinals were situated directly beneath the road and Tino was a little disconcerted to hear the sound of motor cars and carts as they rumbled ominously overhead. More comfortable now, he ran back up the steps and hurried off again in the direction of the station, where he was pleased and relieved to see the small, familiar form of Antonio limping eagerly towards him.

'Tino!' he yelled breathlessly, impatient that his leg wouldn't allow him to go as fast as his mind told him to. 'I'm sorry, there was a bit of a fight further up the road, someone's cart had been in collision with some fancy carriage.' He grinned widely. Some of the Welsh accent had rubbed off on him and the result of this coupled with the Italian accent resulted in a curious intonation that brought a smile to Tino's lips. 'There were vegetables rolling all over the place, and all the housewives in the street came out like a shot, gathering up the lot in their aprons – potatoes, turnips, carrots – everything,' he explained as he led the way back to his cart. 'And there was the old farmer, running round like an idiot, 'til one of the women called him a mean old bugger, begrudging them a few potatoes for their supper. Oh, Tino, you should have been there.' He began laughing out loud as he recounted the scene. 'She started pelting the potatoes at him, then all the others joined in. Oh, what a sight.'

'I wish I'd seen it,' Tino smiled, then as they approached

the entrance to the station added, 'I'd better go and get the girls, I left them in the waiting room.'

Soon, they were on the cart, heading for their new home in the small village on the outskirts of the bigger town. Antonio guided the horse expertly through the crowds in the area around the station. As they passed through the upper end of High Street, the congestion eased and he had time to point out anything he thought might interest his passengers. He showed them the Pavilion Music Hall, an oddly-shaped, almost triangular red brick building, which he explained was a theatre. 'They get some good turns there, too,' he commented.

Tino and the girls looked around. There was a small row of shops to the left, the proprietors' names proudly displayed either above the doors, or on signs that hung from ornate scrolled bars that stuck out from the frontage of the buildings. In just a few years, one of those doors would bear the name *Sabatino D'Abruzzo, Proprietor* written in gold script above. It would be his home for many years to come, bearing witness to many major landmarks in his life, a series of events that would take him to the heights of happiness and the depths of sadness – things that would shape the future for the whole family and the world beyond.

The small town of Morriston was nearer to Swansea than Tino had realised. Even by horse and cart, they were soon drawing up outside the door of their new home. He stretched and looked around. They were travelling through Woodfield Street, a long, fairly narrow street lined either side with houses, shops and public houses – the name of one of them, the Welcome to Town, seemed to be especially appropriate for them. He was particularly impressed with the huge Tabernacle Chapel, with its light stone exterior and flight of steps leading up to impossibly enormous doors, and his mind went back to the tiny little church in Picinisco. It was a stark contrast. He remarked on it to Antonio, who shrugged his shoulders.

'It's a good, strong building,' he conceded, 'But, of course, that's not where we Catholics go. They have started taking mass in an old Baptist chapel not far from here, but it's not much more than a battered corrugated shed. So we still go to St Joseph's, in Greenhill. It's further away, but – well, I'm sure God is pleased by our sacrifice.' He gave a wide, toothy grin, stopping the horse and cart just a few yards further down the street, with a loud cry of, 'Whoa, boy!'

Tino smiled, helping his wife and sister onto the pavement. The shop frontage was on the right, only a few doors away from the Tabernacle. It was bigger than Tino had imagined and above the door, as with the shops they had passed in High Street, no-one was left in any doubt as to the name of the shop's proprietor – Antonio Secchi. The building was three storeys high, tall and gabled, constructed from whitewashed brick with a shiny grey slate roof. The woodwork had been painted dark brown and on the ground floor, a huge glass window stretched almost the full width of the frontage, except for the door in the middle. It was filled with an assortment of treats, beautifully displayed on lace doilies to tempt the unwary passer-by. Two casement windows jutted out from the first floor, with a third one set neatly into the gabled section of the roof above.

But he caught his breath as Antonio led the way in through the door, he had the impression of being surrounded by polished wood and glass that sparkled in the soft light. But he didn't have time to fully appreciate the surroundings, for despite his limp the older man was moving at quite a pace to an opening at the end of the counter, where a brightly-coloured beaded curtain separated the shop area from the living quarters. Behind was a kitchen, with a large black range and sturdy wooden table.

'This is where we do most of the cooking, but we eat here

too,' he explained. He led them through into another room, which he told them was their main living quarters. Behind this were two further rooms, these were the family bedrooms. 'One for us, one for our son, though he spends most of his time in London now, so Beppe might as well have it. They can always share, when he comes home.'

The house was like a maze, much bigger than anyone could ever have guessed from outside. It seemed to go back for ever. They went back into the narrow passageway between the rooms and Antonio turned up a narrow staircase, taking them to the first floor which housed Tino and Serafina's two rooms. Another even narrower staircase led to a small room at the top of the house, where the ceiling vaulted upwards into a high point at the centre, and dipped almost to the floor at the edges. This would be Carlotta's room.

Tino was amazed; Antonio must be doing very well to afford this. There was even a water closet in the back yard, which itself was narrow, but long. There were outbuildings along one side and Antonio walked down to the furthest one, flinging open the door.

'Nero!' Tino cried, running his hand down the familiar shiny black mane. The horse whinnied softly in greeting as he recognised the gentle voice of his master.

Antonio laughed at the reunion. 'Too soft, that's what you are,' he said. Tino's hand stopped the rhythmic stroking of the horse and his eyes clouded over.

'Papa used to say that,' he answered quietly.

'Then he was right! Now, are you happy with the rent, Tino? Ten shillings a week for everything. A bit extra for meals, but if you want to cook your own – well, you're more than welcome to use our facilities at no extra cost.'

Tino nodded. It was a lot out of his savings, but he and Beppe would soon be earning again, the girls, too. And they had a lot here for their money, the rooms were even furnished. It was old furniture, true, but perfectly serviceable and better than anything they'd had in Italy. He suspected Antonio could have charged a much higher rent, if he'd wanted to.

'Yes, it's fine. Thank you,' he answered. His sincerity shone through in the firm grip of his new landlord's hand, as they shook hands to put the final stamp of approval on the agreement.

'Good. Now, let me show you the ice-cream shed,' he suggested, a cheery note lifting his voice. 'And the water closet, too. I know it's out here in the back yard and not one of those new-fangled indoor ones, but it beats using chamber pots and buckets under the beds.

It was early in May when they first set out for Brynmill Park, in Swansea. Antonio told them it had always been a good venue for him, there were always plenty of customers and what's more, it was just a stone's throw from the beach too. They had left Carlotta and Beppe, who was now back with them after the very successful opening of Giuseppe and Janey's hotel, to judge the potential of a pitch on the beach, where they had taken the smaller cart.

The weather was fine and a pale, hazy sun penetrated the wispy cloud covering to bring the first real warmth of the year. Tino and Serafina drew up at the entrance. The park was surrounded by railings with pointed tops and a high wrought iron gate, framing a shrub-lined path. It seemed to be beckoning them forwards, inviting them to sample the unexplored delights inside. They turned and smiled, each understanding the unspoken words of the other. Serafina giggled as they ran hand-in-hand along the path at breakneck speed, only stopping when they reached a small lake, laughing and breathless. Tino pulled his wife down onto a wooden bench with intricately worked ends, resting while they regained their breath. They watched the birds on the lake – mating pairs of swans and ducks skimming along the surface. A bright splash of electric blue caught their eye and they watched entranced as a kingfisher dived into the lake, immediately resurfacing and curving skywards with its prey, a sizeable fish which wriggled and flapped in a futile attempt to escape its long beak.

'Well, I think we'd better go and earn some money to buy our supper,' Tino said. 'Otherwise, we'll be fighting that bird for the fish.'

She laughed at the idea and her smile suddenly made Tino go weak at the knees. She might not be his first love, and he knew she would never replace Mara in his heart or in his dreams, but she was still a beautiful girl and a good wife. Hard for any man to resist. He bent his head and dropped a light kiss on her lips.

'You are a lovely woman, Signora D'Abruzzo,' he whispered. 'And I'm a very lucky man.'

She shot a quick sidelong glance at him, but his eyes were cast down, staring at the elongated shadows the trees threw onto the ground. He often paid her compliments but not once had he said he loved her, and the dark eyes clouded black. It hurt to know that no matter what she did, she could never compete with his first love. How could anyone compete with a memory? She sighed, but put on a brave face as they walked back to the cart, commenting on the plants which were already in flower and others, bursting with buds, waiting their turn to flourish.

When they got back to the cart there were already customers waiting to be served. Little girls in frilled pinafores and dainty hats, a little boy in a sailor suit and their parents, all eager to try out the ice-cream from the colourful cart which now proclaimed to the world – *S. D'Abruzzo, purveyors of superior ices* and underneath, in smaller gold script, *The creamiest you will ever taste.*

Tino apologised for the wait and immediately lifted the lid on the freezer compartment, ready to serve. The ice-cream had stayed good and firm, and came out a rich buttery colour. He passed the small tasting glasses to Serafina to give to the customers, who in turn dropped coins into her hand. She had learned fast in the few weeks since they had come to Swansea and was soon giving out the correct change from the large pocket in her apron, under Tino's watchful eye. A buxom girl of about sixteen, dressed in a dark dress and frilly white apron, came bustling across the road with a big glass dish, asking for it to be filled.

Tino's dark handsome looks hadn't escaped her but it was to Serafina that she first spoke.

'My mistress is expecting, see,' she explained. With no further prompting other than the smile the exotic-looking Italian girl gave her, she went on, 'The master said she can 'ave what she wants an' she'd got this real fancy for ice-cream right now. So don't worry about filling the dish right up to the brim, she'll eat the lot, I bet you.'

There was something about this young maid that despite the strong Welsh accent, reminded them both of Janey and they couldn't help but smile.

'Well, tell her I hope she enjoys it,' Tino gave his brightest smile and the girl turned to jelly. 'And we wish her well. We should be here often now, so if your mistress likes our ice-cream, perhaps she would be so kind as to tell all her friends.'

Tino was usually a man of few words with strangers but on this occasion, he'd excelled himself and the soft, musical accent sent the girl's heart racing.

'Um, er, yes, course I will,' she stammered. 'Who shall I say said?'

'Tino.'

'Tino,' the girl breathed, unable to drag herself away from the mesmeric liquid eyes of this man.

'That's right, Tino. Short for Sabatino.' He had suddenly become aware of the situation and his eyes gleamed wickedly as he handed the now full dish back to her. 'And of course, not forgetting Serafina, here.'

'Serafina,' the girl repeated like someone in a trance, refusing to drag her eyes away from Tino's.

'Yes, Serafina.' He paused, waving his arm with a theatrical flourish toward the other girl. 'Serafina, my wife.'

The trance was broken as the girl shot a glance at Serafina's left hand, where an unmistakable glint of gold caught the sun's rays.

'Er, I'd better be gettin' back, now then. The mistress will be waitin'.'

She shot across the road, stumbling awkwardly as she struggled to straighten the heavily-beaded lace cover over the dish. Tino and Serafina watched her retreating figure and doubled up with laughter.

They sold out quickly and went back to the Slip, the part of the beach where Beppe and Carlotta had gone to sell their wares. The road ran parallel to the Mumbles Railway, the tramway that ran the length of the foreshore from the Rutland Station. They watched as one of the trams rocked and rolled its way along shiny tracks, marvelling that it didn't tilt over as it followed the camber of the rails like fish glue. All the carriages, up and down, were full to bursting: men, women and children packed in together as everyone made the most of this lovely day. As it swayed off into the distance, they saw Beppe and Carlotta appearing from the stone archway that led to the beach itself, across the road from the almost triangular Bay View hotel. They waved in greeting, and from the easy way they walked together, comfortable with the close proximity of each other's body, it was easy for anyone to see that their relationship had evolved into something much more than friendship. Carlotta's eyes shone as she looked up at him and Tino was pleased for them. He'd had his suspicions for a long time and Beppe was his good friend, he couldn't have wished for a better partner for his sister.

'We sold out easily,' Carlotta told them, eyes bright with excitement. 'It's really busy, children everywhere with buckets and spades. And a funfair and bathing machines too.' It was true, the sands were a hive of activity, and even from where they stood, they could hear the delighted screams of children as they slid down the gaily striped helter-skelter on a rough mat, or became deliciously giddy on the brightly-coloured merry-go-round. An old lady, face crumpled up like a piece of old parchment, sat on the steps beneath the railway arch, a large wicker basket at her side. She wore a fitted black bonnet and shawl which seemed completely at odds with the warmth of the day. 'Cockles! Best Penclawdd cockles!' she announced loudly, her voice rising up to a high crescendo on the last syllable. There were ices too, though none of them to match Tino's by far.

'Oh, and you can see the sea stretching for miles and miles and miles, and there's sand as far as the eye can see,' Carlotta continued excitedly. She deftly removed a shoe while standing on one foot to demonstrate, and a shower of yellow sand poured out in a never-ending stream. It was a new experience for them, they had never seen a beach quite like this before, the closest was when they had arrived at Dover, with its white, chalky cliff face. But that wasn't quite the same thing and they had only been passing through, anyway.

'You'd better do the other shoe too,' Tino laughed, 'or you'll end up walking with a limp, like poor Antonio.'

That night, they counted out the takings carefully, putting some aside for the rent and other overheads, as Giuseppe had wisely taught them. Tino was ecstatic, they'd made far more than he could ever have hoped for. It was an excellent start to their new venture. This would be the pattern for the next few years, and as their reputation for good ice-cream grew, so did their takings. But Tino was never satisfied; he always had to strive to do even better. He was determined to make a success of his life, in spite of how his father had treated him. It worried Serafina sometimes, for he seemed driven by a burning desire to prove himself. Or perhaps this wild ambition, working so hard that he had no time to even think, was his way of driving away the memories of what might have been.

'We can do better,' Tino promised himself as he carefully hid the money away with the rest of his savings. His thoughts were focused somewhere in the not too distant future, where he was the owner of a shop just like Antonio's and there were small children running around playing, or sat on his knee as he recounted endless tales of his life in Italy. There was one thing he wanted to do though, as soon as he could. This was his new home now, his new country. Although he still loved his homeland with all his heart, the people here had been good to him. What better way to show his appreciation and loyalty to the country and its people than to become a true citizens of Wales and Great Britain, with a piece of paper to prove it.

Chapter 23

IT WAS THE year 1904 and a big turning point for them all. Three years before, Queen Victoria had finally died. Tino had felt sorry about that, he remembered the frail old lady he had seen in the Diamond Jubilee procession, she had looked kindly enough. King Umberto the First of Italy was dead too, he had been assassinated and replaced by his son, Victor Emmanuel the Third.

News came from London that Giuseppe and Janey's hotel was proving to be a huge success and Donato and Kathleen had finally tied the knot. Kathleen would never really get over Tino, but she had come to love Donato in her own way and would be a good wife to him. Carlotta and Beppe too had married, as Tino had predicted, in the Roman Catholic Church of St Joseph's, where they had attended Mass faithfully since they had arrived. Everyone shared in their happiness that day, and shared too in their deep misery when Carlotta gave birth to two stillborn babies in less than three years. Tino was beginning to get worried too, for as yet, Serafina showed no sign at all of becoming a mother and he wondered whether he should suggest she should see a doctor. Then, just as he was about to broach the subject, Carlotta and Serafina discovered within weeks of each other that they were both expecting babies.

Tino wondered at first how he could have missed the symptoms, he had seen it often enough in his mother and in Janey. Serafina had been listless and pale for weeks and couldn't even bear to look at ice-cream without feeling sick. He was thrilled at the prospect of being a father, but worried not only for his wife, but Carlotta too. Hopefully, with luck and prayers, she would give birth this time to a good, healthy child.

But when the first excitement had died down, the practicalities of the situation began to go through Tino's mind. Already, Beppe and Carlotta were cramped in the small gabled room at the top of Antonio's house. Antonio himself had already voiced his reservations during Carlotta's previous pregnancies, grumbling that perhaps the rooms above the shop weren't the best place to bring up young children, and he was getting old, he liked his sleep now that his own children were grown up and out of the way.

Tino had recently been depositing more of his money in the bank on Woodfield Street. He had a plan, but needed to pay a visit to the bank to find out the exact state of his account, so he sent Beppe and the girls out on their own that day.

The clerk, dressed in a dark pin-striped suit, soberly perused a huge ledger on the desk in front of him, nodding and grunting here and there and muttering to himself. After what seemed an eternity, he looked up and gave a polite cough. 'A very healthy balance, if I may say so, Mr D'Abruzzo,' he proclaimed, his lips curling into a smile beneath the bushy moustache.

'Good,' Tino replied, satisfied. 'I thought as much. Now, perhaps you would be so kind as to advise me on another matter?'

The clerk proved to very helpful and Tino left in a mood of happy contentment. He began to walk towards Swansea, whistling as he went. Less than an hour later, he was standing in front of number 81, High Street. He didn't go in, but stood just across the road with his back to the red brick and cream Pavilion Music Hall, with its round cupola-style towers. Only recently, it had been given the grand new name of The Palace Theatre of Variety. He glanced across the street to the building, his eyes roving over it carefully from top to bottom, missing nothing. This wasn't the first time he had done this. In fact, for many months, he had stood here time and again, looking longingly, admiringly and covetingly, but each time he had walked away, despondent and disappointed. He knew it was out of his reach. He just didn't have enough money and sooner or later, someone would be sure to snap it up from under his nose.

But this time, with just a little luck, it would be different. It wasn't unlike Antonio's shop, double-fronted with a big window either side of the door. Heavy cream lace curtains, grubby with age, framed the casement windows on the floor above and even the attic room, at the top of the building had the same lace at its tiny window. There was an array of goods on display, like any other toy shop, but the proprietor was old and the bank clerk had told Tino he wanted to sell up as soon as possible.

But Tino didn't see the toys – he saw beyond them, to a future where the shop windows were decorated with strategically placed lacy doilies, just like Antonio's; where the glass shelves were filled with fancy chocolate boxes decorated with huge red bows, jars of colourful sweets and other tempting treats. He would serve his delicious ice-cream in summer and pies with hot peas and vinegar in winter. There would be something for everyone, they would all soon learn the name of Sabatino D'Abruzzo by heart for serving good food at a good price. And in case his name slipped their minds, it would be there right above the door to remind them, spelled out in bright gold letters. He would work from four in the morning to midnight, but he would make a success of this. This was his future.

Straightening his hat and loosening the collar slightly from around his throat, he crossed the road. A bell tinkled as he walked into the dark, dusty interior. It was untidy and crammed with toys, piles of boxes reaching almost from floor to ceiling. But it had potential, and if he closed his eyes, he could almost see the wooden partitions and gleaming shelves with lots of coloured glass and mirrors everywhere.

A noise coming from the rear of the room caught his attention and he turned to see a wizened, shrunken old man shuffling towards him. He walked with a slight stoop, and tufts of dusty looking hair stuck out.

'Can I help you?' He peered short-sightedly over round glasses perched precariously at the end of a huge hooked nose.

Tino gave a nervous little cough. 'Yes, please, Sir.' There was a slight tremor in his voice. 'I've come about the shop.'

The man, who Tino later learned was called Mr Carmen, nodded. 'Ah, yes. The shop. Now, what is it you want to know?'

'Everything!'

Mr Carmen seemed a pleasant old man and Tino's nervousness abated. He showed Tino around the shop and the living quarters and he soon realised why the man's hair looked so dusty. Everywhere, a grey film covered everything in sight, and fine particles rose into the air in shimmering clouds at the slightest provocation or movement. Tino spluttered and sneezed in response, but he hardly noticed, he was too excited. Despite the untidiness and general run-down appearance, Tino could see the possibilities amid the chaos of boxes and clutter. He had already made up his mind about the shop itself, and the size and layout of the living quarters, and the rear of the property, only strengthened his initial impressions. There was more than enough room for two families to live together harmoniously without getting under each other's feet. There was running water and a bathroom, with a sizeable back yard housing a separate coal shed and two larger sheds, one of which had, at one time, so Mr Carmen told him, housed pigs. Tino had already, in his mind, allocated this one to Nero and the second one would be ideal for making the ice-cream. The whole place would need a good clean and whitewashing, and although it was definitely the place for him, he knew he would have to be crafty, hold back at first. Giuseppe had taught him never to show himself 'too eager'. He would haggle on the price too, just as his Mamma used to in the market in Atina.

They had taught him well, for he secured the shop for seventy pounds below the original asking price. It was just within his budget; he could never have afforded it at full price. Of course, it would use up most of his savings, but even so Tino went back to Morriston whistling louder than ever and with a renewed spring in his step. He would make it succeed. The following day, he took his wife, sister and brother-in-law to see what was about to become their new home. Serafina burst into tears.

'What is it?' Tino was at her side in an instant. 'Don't you like it?'

'Oh, Tino!' She laughed through the tears and her voice wobbled. 'Of course I like it, that's why I'm weeping!'

He raised his eyes heavenwards. 'Women!' he cried. 'I will never understand them. When they are sad – they weep. And when they are happy – well, they still weep. I just don't understand them!'

He threw up his hands in a gesture of despair and the whole group began to laugh. They laughed and joked until their sides ached. It seemed Tino had made a good choice.

The following year, the Palace Café was up and running and trade was booming. It was situated quite close to the railway station, the local abattoir, as well as factories and shops, and they quickly gained a reputation for their excellent service, good food and beverages and above all, their delicious ice-cream. One of the more recent innovations had been the biscuit cones and wafers which were much more hygienic than the licking glasses, which were passed from person to person. Despite the fact that they were washed between customers, health officials had often raised doubts about their safety. Tino soon realised that people would be more likely to buy from the cart if they used these new edible biscuits and was one of the first to introduce the novelty to the seaside town of Swansea.

In 1905, Both Serafina and Carlotta became mothers. Carlotta gave birth first, to a son whose abundant hair had the same reddish tint as her own sister Emilia's.

'We shall call him Lorenzo, after our saint,' the proud parents announced to anyone who stopped long enough to admire their new, tiny scrap of humanity.

A few weeks later, Serafina and Tino's daughter was born. Unlike Lorenzo's, her hair shone jet black, curling softly into the nape of her neck. The proud father looked down onto his first-born child and all kinds of feelings crowded in on him – love, protectiveness and an overwhelming sense of the miraculous.

'Serafina,' he asked quietly when he saw her for the first time, and his eyes were as soft as his voice. 'Can we call her Angelina? Angelina, partly for my brother Angelo and partly for my mother, Lena.'

His wife's eyelids drooped heavily, her cheeks still flushed from a labour that had been difficult and protracted. She looked tiny and lost in the big wooden bed with its carved headboard and footboard, almost childlike herself. But now, with her baby in her arms, her eyes shone with love and pride.

'That's a good name,' she smiled wearily. 'Say hello to your Papa, Angelina!' She raised the baby's hand and waved it gently towards Tino.

He laughed and reached out to touch the baby's hand, and the tiny, yet perfectly formed fingers curled around his forefinger, grasping it tightly in response.

'She is as beautiful as her mother,' he whispered hoarsely. But his eyes seemed to focus on something Serafina couldn't see, as he wondered whether Mara and Francesco's child was just as beautiful; whether she was golden fair like her mother with haunting blue eyes, or dark like his brother. Flooded with guilt, and something else which he could not quite put a name to, he hastily swallowed the lump that came to his throat and made an excuse to turn away.

The next few years in the town were happy and prosperous for the family. They had regular news from London. Giuseppe and Janey had bought a second hotel, which Donato and Kathleen were running for them. Even Bernadette and Paddy were working for them now, living in cleaner surroundings than they had ever dreamt of, a far cry from the slums of Bramley Mews and its surroundings. And it was all thanks to their good friends.

Carlotta had sadly lost another two babies before giving birth to a bouncing, healthy daughter Teresa. Serafina proved to be a good, loving mother and gave Tino another two daughters, Adelina and Carla followed by Gio, the son they both longed for. Their happiness was complete.

The same year as Gio made his grand entrance, Antonio shocked them all with the announcement that he was returning back home to Italy. He had been homesick for a long time and now that he was getting older he wanted to end his days in his homeland, with his brothers and sisters. To Tino's surprise, he offered him the Morriston shop for a very reasonable price. It took a while for him to come to a decision – profits were good on the High Street café, so he didn't want to give it up. They liked it there anyway and had come to know all the regular customers. But the perfect solution had been staring him in the face all along. He would put up the money for the shop and his dear friend Beppe and sister Carlotta could run it for him. He would pay them a good wage, but even better, they would finally have a place of their own, a place they could call home. They were touched and pleased by the gesture and accepted Tino's proposal without even stopping to think twice. Their own small world was complete.

However, on a global scale, things were not going so well as they headed into 1914. There was unrest in the world, and Europe was on the brink of conflict. Tino and Beppe had been distraught to find that Italy was again in serious crisis, with mass strikes and dissent. Pope Benedict XV led peace initiatives in the events which were heading at breakneck speed towards a world war. In March, Giolitti, the prime minister was replaced by his rival, Antonio Salandra. But nothing could prevent the riots that broke out in Red Week, when public buildings were attacked and ransacked and lines of communication cut. The rioters included the editor of the socialist newspaper, *Avanti*. The man's name was Benito Mussolini; a name that in time would go down in history in a way that none of them could have foreseen.

'Where is this all going to end?' Tino asked Beppe one day. 'I keep thinking we are on a course to disaster.'

'You may well be right.' Beppe's voice was solemn. 'But it's hardly surprising, with what has happened.'

In June of that year, news came of the assassination of Archduke Franz Ferdinand at Sarajevo and the unrest deepened. This event proved to be the catalyst for war. Within two months, Germany had declared war on France and Russia, then went on to invade Belgium. Britain's response in turn was to declare war on Germany. The First World War was beginning to unfold.

From this point on, news of terrible loss of life and injuries came flooding back to Wales, with bloody battles fought in terrible conditions on foreign soil. On the home front, people were on stand-by, others already mobilised, with women taking over men's work as more and more soldiers were sent off to battle. Tino, due to his chest problems, was excused active duty and anyway, they seemed to be taking the younger men. Beppe too had been turned down.

It was summer of the 1915 when Beppe called to see Tino. 'Have you heard about Michele?' he asked. 'We had a letter from Emilia, saying he's joined the Italian army.' He followed Tino into the back room.

Tino nodded. 'Yes, we had a letter, too. And of course, we're worried about him.' He turned to Beppe and handed him a cup of strong, black coffee. Beppe sat down in the big armchair and crossed his legs, sniffing appreciatively at the thick tarry liquid. 'How did all this come about then, Beppe? I thought Italy was staying neutral.'

Tino was not very politically minded, and Beppe, who liked to show off his superior knowledge, relished in recounting his views on the situation. 'Well, yes, they were' he began slowly, 'though really, they should have been in it right from the start. After all, they'd signed the Triple Alliance which tied them in with Germany and Austria.'

'So how did they keep out of it for so long?'

Beppe shrugged his shoulders. 'Probably waiting to see the way the wind blew, I suppose.' There was a hint of sarcasm in Beppe's voice. 'Though there were two things, really.' He was enjoying this, and his chest puffed up with pride as

Tino focused all his attention on him. 'Italy said they'd only support their allies if they were attacked first. But as we know, it was Germany and Austria who did the attacking. And Italy was annoyed too that they weren't consulted when Austria attacked Serbia. Said it broke the terms of the Treaty.' He grinned widely. 'Squabbling among themselves, as usual.'

Tino nodded. 'Yes, I can see that. But it doesn't explain how Italy got dragged in at this stage – and on the other side too!'

'Well, give me a chance!' Beppe answered. 'It was down to Mussolini – he saw things in a very different light. Staying neutral wasn't an option. But he wanted Italy to go over to the other side, join forces with the Allies – Great Britain, France and Russia. It was all in his newspaper, *Popola d'Italia*.'

He sipped at the hot coffee before continuing. 'Anyway, by May, they were offered a carrot, the promise of some territory – Trentino, Trieste, I think – if they got involved. The Nationalists thought it would be a good move, so here we are. Mind you, it's hard to get excited about a few minor provinces when you're poverty-stricken and there's no food on the table.'

Tino nodded in agreement. 'Well, let's hope it doesn't go on too long, that's all I can say.' He heaved a long sigh. 'These politicians, they play with people's lives and what for? Greed! Power!' He smiled wryly as a vision of his father came unbidden into his head. Greed and power. The root of many evils.

By the end of the war in 1918, the full cost became apparent. Soldiers of Italy and Great Britain fought and died on the same side. Why it was called the 'Great War' no-one, least of all Tino, could ever fathom. Where was the greatness in thousands of brave soldiers dead and dying, missing and injured, some maimed beyond recognition bleeding to death in stinking, muddy trenches, several feet deep in rat-infested water, where the stench was so bad it burned the eyes and nostrils. Where was the greatness for the thousands of civilians left in poverty and chaos, their home lives shattered, their loved ones lost? There was no greatness or glory in senseless destruction.

It was a year later when Tino heard his younger brother, Michele, had returned home safely to Italy from the Great War, and he thanked God. Apart from the loss of weight that left his ribs sticking out of his body, and the loss of two toes, he had suffered little physical damage. But the mental damage had been incalculable and he had suffered from horrifying nightmares ever since, of mustard gas and bombs and seeing his friends dying in agony and not being able to help them. He would regularly wake up in a cold sweat when the sound of his comrades, screaming in his dream, merged with his own ear-splitting shouts of terror. Over and over again, he would yell 'The rats! The rats are biting my toes'.

Emilia had written about her concerns for him and asked Tino if he could stay in Wales with them for a while. Tino was overjoyed at the thought of his young brother joining them and immediately sent over the money for his fare. Michele had arrived in 1921 and never returned.

It was in the same year that Mussolini was elected a fascist deputy, along with thirty-four others. Soon, he was to become prime minister by a tiny majority, consolidating his position with a series of rigged votes and stamping out of any opposition. He moved quickly towards dictatorship by relegating the ministerial cabinet and removing the party congress. *Il Duce* had been born and fascism, a movement that was never really defined but hid under the cloak of 'patriotic nationalism,' was on the rise, in Italy and abroad.

Chapter 24

EVEN THROUGHOUT THE 20s and 30s, the shadow of the Great War still hung everywhere, immortalised in the people and sights around them. Just on the edge of Tontine Street, near the Palace Café, the familiar sign of three brass balls hung over the door, announcing to the world that this was the place to come to pawn their belongings when things got tight. It almost broke Tino's heart to see row upon row of medals awarded for bravery sold off for a pittance, simply to buy some food. There were the beggars, blind or mutilated, or both, some with missing limbs, crouched like bundles of rags in the doorways with a card tied around their neck, proclaiming to the world they were war veterans. Tino could never pass them by without pressing some money into their hand. He wondered how it was that they could be left like this, desperate, hungry and often homeless – men who had fought so bravely for the King and country. He had done his own bit on the Home Front whenever he could, his weak chest excusing him from active duties. But the little he had done was nothing to what these poor men had given. It seemed the world had gone mad.

Tino was also filled with concern for his good friend and brother-in-law, Beppe. During the past few years, he had started holding regular meetings in the back room of the Morriston café. On the surface these were nothing more than a get-together, under the flag of their homeland – an opportunity to eat, talk, play *scopa* and other card games, or billiards on the table which now stood in the room Antonio had used as a bedroom all those years before. Carlotta had confided in Tino that she thought there was more than that going on, but every time she tried to speak to her husband about it, Beppe would clam up and become even more secretive.

Tino waited his chance until they were alone one evening. Michele and Gio had gone to the Elysium picture house, a few hundred yards away, escorting Serafina and Carla to see the latest Laurel and Hardy moving picture. Carla, at twenty-eight remained unmarried, much to her mother's despair and dismay. Tino had been keen for her to work in the family business, but although she often helped out in the café when she was home, she was a single-minded girl who had stuck firmly to her intentions of becoming a schoolteacher, something she had announced to them at a very early age. Eventually, Tino had given in to her and now, he had to admit, he was very proud of her. She was a dedicated schoolmistress but it was difficult for female teachers to marry – they had to make the choice between a husband or their vocation. And Carla loved her work. She had yet met a man that she loved more. The other two girls, Adelina and Angelina, had married some years before, to two brothers they had met when visiting Zi Giuseppe's place in London. The Cerviti boys ran cafes there and the girls had moved there after their marriages, both now with children of their own. Beppe and Carlotta's daughter, Teresa, had gone to London to work in Giuseppe's hotel.

Tino deliberately closed up the shop earlier than usual, an unprecedented move on his part. He flipped over the sign that announced 'Open at 5am' to the 'Closed' position and began clearing away the remaining cups, plates and glasses off the tables.

It was still light outside, no-where near closing time and Beppe frowned. 'What's going on, Tino?' he asked, perplexed. 'You can't afford to close this early any more than I can.'

'I need to talk to you,' Tino answered simply. 'We can

go into the back room, it's quiet and we won't be disturbed in there. I'll just finish tidying up first, I can wash the floor afterwards.'

'What's all this about, then?'

'You'll find out in good time.'

Tino continued tidying up, slowly and methodically. The Palace Café was his pride and joy, won through sheer hard work, grit and determination. The sight of his name written in gold above the door, just as he had envisaged it all those years ago, still caused him to swell with pride. No matter how much he needed to talk to Beppe, he couldn't bring himself to leave the place looking like a pigsty. The wooden partitions gleamed with polish, and a faint smell of beeswax wafted upwards. The sun still shone in through the shop windows, illuminating the stained glass above the wooden booths and scattering kaleidoscopic colours across the marble-topped tables.

Tino's dark hair was now sprinkled with white, but for someone in his fifties, he still made an imposing and handsome figure of a man. The sun picked out the lighter streaks, turning them to silver as he carried a tray, laden with dishes and cutlery, over to the sink in the corner of the room.

'Come on, Tino, hurry up!' Beppe grumbled. 'I'm getting fed up of waiting.'

'I won't be much longer.' Tino's voice was kindly, but firm and steady, broaching no argument.

Beppe sighed heavily. 'Well, don't forget I have to get home, I know I have a motor car now, but even so…'

Tino rinsed out a cloth and proceeded to clean the marble counter, then wiped it over the bright silver and chrome of the coffee and tea machines that hissed and spat liked an angry cat when in operation. The metal containers and other implements they used for serving ice-cream would have to wait, he would do those later. A huge mirror dominated the area behind the counter, and rows of glass shelves held bottles of cordials and other soft drinks, dandelion and burdock, home-made lemonade and sarsaparilla, popular favourites along with the ubiquitous ice-cream sodas. Colourful jars of sweets and bars of chocolate of every description filled every space on the shelves – aniseed balls, hard boiled mixture and gobstoppers sat comfortably alongside Rowntree's Pastilles, and Five Boys and Fry's chocolate. Big boxes of chocolates, tied up with shiny coloured ribbon, were arranged cunningly to catch the eye of the young men who strolled in with their sweethearts before going to the music hall across the street. Finally, Tino took one last look around and, satisfied that he had done everything he could for now, pointed towards the door leading towards the room at the back.

They sat facing each other across a scrubbed wooden table, Tino struggling to find a way of approaching the matter diplomatically without causing offence, and Beppe just wishing he would get on with it. Eventually, Tino spoke.

'Beppe, Carlotta has been speaking to me. She is worried about you,' He paused for a moment and swallowed hard before going on. 'She is worried that you are getting involved in things that will bring no good.'

Beppe closed his eyes in exasperation and sighed heavily. 'Oh, not again! Tino, she doesn't stop going on about it and now she's dragged you into it too.' He leaned forward, pushing his face close to his friend's. 'I will spell it out for you, Tino. I – am – not – doing – anything – wrong!' Suppressed anger mottled his complexion purple-red.

'Then you won't mind telling me what is going on?'

'Look, I have a few friends in from time to time, our fellow countrymen. We play cards, we drink, we eat, we talk – what is wrong with that, eh?'

Tino cleared his throat. 'It's what you talk about that

concerns me.' Beppe opened his mouth to protest, but Tino put up his hand to stall him. 'You know you can't lie to me, Beppe, we've been friends for too long. And I know that man Marcello who is always hanging around was active in the London section of the Fascist Party.'

'So what if he is?' Beppe retorted. 'He is a friend.'

'That he may be, but we should choose our friends wisely. Good friends, not ones who are likely to get us into trouble.'

'You don't know what you're talking about!' Beppe's voice rasped out across the room. It was heavy with derision and anger.

Tino was taken aback. Beppe had never spoken to him like this before, he had almost revered him. From the day Tino had almost lost his own life, rescuing him from the beating by the *padrone,* he had been grateful and loyal, as if he owed him some debt.

'Beppe, can't you see? I'm doing this for your own good. For you, for my sister and your family. For God's sake, get out while you can, don't get involved. With all this talk of war again, it can only lead to trouble.'

An impenetrable expression had come down like a mask over Beppe's features and Tino knew instinctively he was fighting a losing battle. 'What is so wrong with Mussolini making us emigrants feel like we matter? To him, we are still Italians – Italians abroad. We are important to him, don't you see? None of the previous governments did anything for us, not like he has.' He stopped and the veil lifted from his eyes, but what was revealed there worried Tino even more, the gleam of determination was unmistakeable.

'Just look at what they've done for us – the schools they have set up, for the children born here to learn their real mother tongue, all the free outings every year, the chance for the children to go back to Italy, learn where they've come from. They have given us back our national pride! How can all this be bad?' He paused again, and a note of cunning persuasion softened his voice. 'Look, why don't you come to one of our meetings, you can see for yourself then what goes on. I promise you, Tino, I don't hold with *il fascio*, I just want the best for my family.'

Tino knew when he was beaten. Beppe had been well and truly indoctrinated. He didn't have a hope of showing him the perils of dabbling in things he didn't really understand. Beppe was a simple man, he could only see the obvious, the superficial things that were being done for them. And his friend Marcello, a self-confessed fascist who had been drafted in from Cardiff to recruit new members for the party, made a point of singing the praises of the positive things that had been achieved for Italian citizens. He failed to tell them about the thousands of Italian citizens at home and abroad who were being manipulated like puppets, courted and flattered with one purpose, to use them as political pawns in an uncertain future.

Tino sighed deeply, a sound that resonated in the heavy silence between them. 'I can see I'm wasting my time,' he said. 'Do what you like, but don't say I didn't warn you when things go wrong. And don't try and drag me into your schemes either. I'm not interested.'

Beppe got up to go, and straightened his trilby hat. 'Well, the offer's there, if you change your mind.'

'I won't.' He made one last effort to make Beppe think of the consequences of his activities. 'But what worries me most is my sister and my nephew and niece. Think of them, I beg you.'

There was no reply. Instead, Beppe led the way to the front of the shop where he drew back the bolt and lifted the latch on the door. He pulled it open and the bell tinkled merrily, an incongruous sound in an atmosphere thick with animosity and bitterness. Without a word, he went outside to where his burgundy Austin Ruby stood, a few yards further up the road.

Tino watched and a wave of immense sadness washed over him. He would have challenged anyone who would have dared to suggest that such a rift could ever develop between them. He loved Italy as much as Beppe did, but it had done little for him – everything he owned now he had worked hard for. He was a loyal and grateful citizen in his adopted country of Great Britain, and while Italy would always be held dear in his heart, he had found more in Wales than he had ever done in his homeland. He and his family had been welcomed, loved even, by the people of this little country which he now thought of as home. They had made good friends – friends who even included them in their special family occasions such as weddings and baptisms. Their customers treated them with admiration, respect and friendship.

While they had been talking, a heavy shower had soaked the cobblestoned road and the tramlines curved into the distance side by side, two long satin ribbons shimmering in the watery evening sun. A faint rainbow marbled the sky and Tino absently noted the long queue of theatregoers excitedly chattering as they filed into the Palace opposite. It was a popular venue and Tino often benefited from the custom of its patrons both before and after the show. Indeed, occasionally even some of the acts would turn up in his shop to buy a packet of cigarettes or some sweets, and the possibility of this happening encouraged even more customers.

Tino turned his attention back to Beppe, watching as he turned the engine over and the Austin spluttered into life. He settled back in the leather-clad seat and drove off without even a backward glance. Tino's slumped shoulders reflected his mood of defeat and above all, sadness. He had an unshakeable feeling in the bottom of his stomach that the whole, sorry situation was going blow up in their faces. And there was nothing he could do to stop it.

It was busy in the café and the whole family were rushed off their feet. It was a wet, windy day and the windows had steamed up so badly with condensation, it was difficult to see the street outside. Even Tino's glasses, which pride had made him refuse to wear for a long time, steamed up and he had to take them off, wiping them on the clean white apron. But bad weather was always good for business, working people wanted something hot inside them when the weather was like that. The most popular topic of conversation at the time was the prospect of war. A group of Tino's regular customers, friends who would often come into the back room after closing time for a game of cards and a chat, huddled together now in one of the booths, and the conversation was decidedly animated. One of them, a man in his thirties, was voicing his opinions in no uncertain terms. There was a marked silence between each phrase as he shovelled generous portions of hot mushy peas into his mouth, revealing a meat pie covered with flaky pasty hiding beneath the thick green blanket.

'You mark my words,' said the voice of doom, 'we will be fighting for our country all over again before long, just like last time.'

'Oh, come on, now, Dai!' The man opposite slurped at a mug of tea, then gulped it down loudly. 'It might not come to us down here, it's the big cities like London they'd be after.'

'Oh aye? Then how do you explain all this activity, Tom? All this bolstering up of the fire brigade and things? I'm telling you.' The last three words were accompanied by an emphatic stabbing at the air with the prongs of the pea-laden fork. It came perilously close to his friend's eyes, forcing him to duck nimbly to one side to fend off the onslaught. 'I'm telling you, give it a year or so, we'll all be fighting again, one way or another. Just you think about it, mun. What've we got here? Heavy industry, busy dockside – perfect for munitions. Not only making 'em, but there's the docks for distributing them. And what's all that mean for us? What's it mean for the town?'

All eyes were on him as he paused dramatically before answering his own questions. 'Obvious to any fool, in'it? Sitting ducks, that's what we'll be.'

'What do you think, Tino?' Tom asked, as Tino stopped near their table.

Tino shrugged his shoulders. He looked anxiously to where Serafina was filling a row of mugs with coffee, hoping she had not heard anything. He knew she was scared out of her wits already with all this talk of war, it was hard to escape it. She worried about the girls in London and her family in Swansea, not to mention Marco and Emilia in Italy.

'I don't know,' Tino answered non-commitally. 'I do think it will be hard for us to escape war, the way things are going. And there's that rumour going around about building emergency shelters, in case of bombs. But there again, who knows, the whole thing might just be stopped in its tracks.'

'But your boy signed up for the army recently, though, didn't 'e?' Tom put in. 'An' your nephew from Morriston too.'

'Yes. But that doesn't mean there'll be a war for sure.'

Dai was a born mischief-maker and couldn't resist the opportunity to give a sly dig. 'Oh, aye, signed up for the army, 'av they? An' which particular army would that be, then?'

Tino drew his brows together, confused. He had never

been very fond of Dai. He tolerated him because he enjoyed the company of his other friends, Tom and Lofty, but his question didn't make much sense.

'I don't understand. There's only one army.'

'No, two!' He sniggered nastily. 'Depends on where your loyalties lie.' He turned to the other men for support. 'Well, you got to admit, they could 'ave joined either the British Army or the Eye-tie one.'

'I should treat your question with the contempt it deserves, Dai.' Tino's voice was chilly. 'But I will remind you, we became citizens of Great Britain many years ago and our children were born here. My daughters' husbands too. And Michele there,' he nodded towards the counter where his brother was wiping dishes with a snowy white dish cloth, 'he might not have the papers yet, but he's as loyal a British citizen as any of you. And don't forget,' Tino wagged a forefinger close to Dai's face, 'I did my duty in the last war on the home front. I even tried to sign up, but they wouldn't take me anyway because of my bad chest.'

There was an awkward hush around the table and Dai realised he had got on the wrong side not only of Tino, but his other friends, too.

'Only joking!' he laughed sheepishly. 'No offence meant.'

Refusing to be drawn any further, Tino turned his back on the group and went back to the task of collecting dirty dishes, but his mind was in turmoil. At the moment, Italy had no quarrel with Britain, but Mussolini was not only a man hungry for power, he was dangerously unpredictable and his loyalties could change in an instant. He would have no compunction in changing sides if it suited him, even if he had previously denounced the idea as preposterous.

*

It was April 1939. Dai and his friends gathered in the café again for their usual dinner and talk. The air above the table shimmered with the heat of the steaming mugs of Bovril.

'Don't say I didn't warn you all, the signs have been there for anyone who goes round with their peepers open. Last year, the Eye-ties at it with Ethiopia, Chamberlain trying to get Mussolini on side in the Munich peace conference.' He laughed. 'The newspapers might love the man, but never trust a bloody Eye-tie, I say.'

'Aye, well, maybe we were all just hoping it wouldn't happen, Dai.' Tom was beginning to get annoyed with his friend, he was almost gloating. He glanced towards the counter, in the hopes that Tino and Serafina had not heard Dai's derogatory comments. 'An' anyway, it's only now they're starting to build all those public shelters, a long time after you said they would.'

'Aye, but building 'em they are. Five hundred or so in all, so I've heard,' Dai replied. '*Duw*, it's bloody frightening, mind. We just got our Anderson shelter too last week. The wife was playing merry hell, we had to dig up all her plants and bury the bloody thing four feet down. The only way I could shut 'er up was to promise to pile up the earth over the top an' replant her precious flowers over the roof. In the end, I got so fed up with 'er going on an' on, I asked her if she wanted me to sit there with a bloody fishin' rod and pretend to be a garden gnome.'

The rest of the group burst out laughing at the image of the dour-faced Dai doing an impression of a gnome and Tom spluttered a mouthful of drink all over the top of the table.

'Dirty sod!' Dai remonstrated, then went on. 'Have you seen them pamphlets, telling us what to do if there's an air raid? An' all the stuff you should get – torches, blankets, Thermos flasks, the lot. An' all the stuff for the blackout. Mind you, fat lot of good a bit of corrugated iron like an Anderson would do, if we got a direct hit.'

'Better than nothing, though,' someone remarked.

A third man who had arrived just in time to catch the gist of the conversation joined in. His contribution stopped Dai and Tom's discussion dead. 'Aye, but did you know they haven't got enough to go round, anyway?'

Tino was standing by their table, distributing piles of bacon and eggs to go with the Bovril. He too stopped and turned towards the newcomer.

'How d'you mean, not enough to go round?' Dai asked belligerently. He couldn't bear it if he thought someone knew something he didn't.

The man, all of five feet tall and known as Lofty, slowly removed his woollen muffler and flat cap. His face was grimy from his work in the metal foundry in Landore, an area nearby that was heavily industrialised but where now, many of the factories were ready to support the war effort. An incongruously clean area ran along Lofty's hairline, where it had been protected from the dirt by the brim of his cap.

'A little birdie told me,' he went on, tapping the side of his nose knowledgeably. 'They've got less than a quarter of what they need.' Lofty was deliberately hedging. He knew Dai well, he had worked with him for years and was enjoying putting one over on him immensely.

'Come on, mun, out with it!' Dai snapped. 'If you know something that concerns our safety, we got a right to know.'

Lofty almost gave in, but not quite. 'Well, you mustn't let this go any further, or you could get someone in big trouble,' he said, unable to resist the temptation to prevaricate for just a little longer. 'It's my sister's husband, he's on the air raid committee. He said they haven't got enough to go round.'

'So what the hell are the rest of us expected to do, then?'

Tom interjected angrily. 'Stand there and wave to the enemy crying, "Come and bloody get me?"'

'I don't really know. But there's talk of them taking over cellars and basements, like.'

'Taking them over?' Tino frowned. 'What for?'

'You know, requisitioning them. For public shelters, so people who haven't got their own can use them.'

Tino slapped his forehead with his hand. '*Mamma mia!*' Taking the roofs from over our heads, the cellars from under our feet. They'll be taking the bread out of our mouths next.'

'Well, I suppose we've all got to do our bit in wartime,' Lofty pointed out.

Tino nodded and sighed. 'Yes, you are right, I suppose. We'll just have to wait and see what happens, eh?'

They were to find out soon enough. In the following few months, activity on the part of the government became more earnest and the distribution of shelters was more widespread. Tino had again taken on the role of fire warden, but this time Michele was with him, and they went around with Air Raid Precaution teams, giving people advice and demonstrations. They became adept at throwing buckets of sand to the best effect in the event of a fire. Pamphlets and leaflets on how to protect the home in the unlikely event of a gas attack popped through letterboxes. The thought of a gas attack was the most terrifying and every man, woman and child would be issued with gas masks, rubber and Bakelite contraptions held in place by a tangle of adjustable straps. These would surely save them; the story was that there was no immediate cause for concern. These were merely precautions, just in case the worst should happen. But people were getting worried and the sight of more and more young men in military uniform gathering in small huddles at the railway station as they waited for trains, saying emotional goodbyes to damp-eyed loved ones did nothing to allay their fears.

Their fears were realised when, on the last day of August, a group of German soldiers masquerading as Polish citizens, crept into a border town called Gleiwitz and attacked their own German radio station there. With them was a German criminal, purposely removed from a concentration camp. That man's fate was sealed, he was shot and his body left behind, evidence of the 'Polish' assault on German soldiers. The ploy worked, Berlin informed the world about the imaginary incident involving the Poles. It was the ideal excuse to launch an attack. The following day, things began to fall into an unstoppable downward spiral. Germany, under the command of Hitler, marched into Polish territory and the black storm clouds of war began to gather ominously over the rest of Europe.

Sunday, September 3rd, 1939. It was a date that would etch itself into people's minds for years to come. Like many other families in the country, the members of the D'Abruzzo family who were left in Swansea, including Michele, Carlotta and Beppe, had gathered together in the room behind the café to listen to the expected speech on the wireless. So far, there had been no response to the Government's demands to withdraw from Poland and the deadline for the ultimatum was due to run out.

Tino shook his head. 'I think we are in for big trouble.' His voice held a note of sadness. 'When you think of all the lives lost, lives ruined in the Great War. And it seems like it's starting up again.'

'No!' Serafina was close to tears. 'It must not happen again, surely they won't let it!'

He turned to her and patted her hand gently. 'But they might not have any choice in the matter.'

'But what about the boys?' She paused tearfully to reach out to Carla, the only one of their four children that remained in Wales, gripping her fingers tightly. 'Our daughters and grandchildren too. If only they had come from London when we asked them, that will be the first place to be attacked.'

'Now, Serafina, we've already talked about that. You know what they said, they have good strong cellars under the Cerviti shops, they'll be safe enough there. And you know as well as I do, they wouldn't want to be stuck out there in Parkmill, miles from anywhere.' Some years before, Tino and Beppe had bought a tiny holiday cottage between them. It was meant to be somewhere to go to relax, but they had rarely found time to take advantage of it. Tino had already considered the possibility of using the cottage, but Parkmill was several miles outside Swansea, in the heart of the Gower countryside and he was quite sure they would not settle there so far from the town, regardless of safety.

'They should at least have let the little ones come,' Serafina persisted.

'But they wanted to stay together.' Tino had not repeated to her the exact phrase they had used in their letter: 'We live together, we'll stay together. And if necessary, we'll die together.' Tino twiddled with the knobs on the front of the wireless and it crackled into life.

'Shhh!'

The mood in the room was sombre as the voice boomed out.

'I have to tell you now,' came Chamberlain's ominous words, 'this country is at war with Germany.'

They gasped in unison, struggling to get to grips with the gravity of the dreadful announcement. There was a long pause before he continued, going on to justify his previous stance of appeasement. But they hardly heard what followed; the damning words, 'at war with Germany' played over and over again, echoing through their heads like a gramophone record that had stuck.

'You can imagine what a bitter blow it is to me that my long struggle to win peace has failed...'

There was a deathly hush in the room. It was heavy and oppressive, each person wrapped up in their own thoughts, and for a long time it seemed that no-one wanted to be the first to break the silence. Beppe was the first to recover his composure.

'Well, it seems there's nothing more to be said, then. We're at war.' There was something disconcerting about the expression on Beppe's face and it made Tino uneasy. It was almost as though he was pleased, excited even. He stood up and walked out towards the café. Tino followed, leaving the women alone together in the back room. Beppe stood with his back to Tino, hands dug deep in his pockets. Their relationship had never fully recovered since the day Tino had questioned the dubious friends he welcomed into his home. But he was determined to have his say, he couldn't stand by and watch his friend make the biggest mistake of his life.

'Beppe,' he began quietly. 'I know you won't welcome this, but...'

Beppe swung around. 'I hope you're not going to start lecturing me again.' His manner was hostile, and Tino could not help noticing his hands, which were bunched up into tight fists. But he gritted his teeth, he was determined to have his say, come what may. At least then, if things should go wrong, he would know he had tried his best.

'I don't want to lecture you,' his voice was calm and even. 'But if only for my sister's sake, I have to say this.' He swallowed hard and the noise was audible in the quiet of the empty café.

'Beppe, get out of it now, while you still can! Before it's too late.'

'Nothing to get out of!'

Tino threw his arms wide in an act of desperation. 'Please, Beppe! Stop those men coming to your house. Please. I'm begging you.'

The other man rounded on him, his face red with anger. 'What do you know about it, eh? Just what?'

'Enough to know you are putting everyone, including my sister, in danger.' The calm yet grave tones did nothing to alleviate Beppe's anger. On the contrary, it seemed to inflame it, and he began to pace up and down, clearly agitated.

'I am not!' The words were spoken with such a force that Tino visibly recoiled. 'Now look here, Tino. You know as well as I do, Mussolini has declared Italy is non-belligerent. Do you know what that means?'

'Of course I know, I'm not stupid,' Tino retorted. Beppe's obstinacy was beginning to make him angry too, but he knew he had to stay calm. 'But the fact that Italy is neutral now doesn't mean it will be neutral next year. Or next month. Next week, even. Mussolini changes his mind more often than I change my socks! Beppe, can't you see?' He grabbed the sleeve of his friend's arm and his dark eyes filled with a mix of fear and desperation. 'Can't you see the danger of associating with people who have shown allegiance to the fascist cause? If the wind turns, and Mussolini turns to Germany…'

Beppe's answer was to shake Tino's hand off his arm and put his own hands over his ears. 'Shut up! I don't want to hear!' he screamed. 'I know who my friends are, I don't need you to tell me.'

He rushed through the beaded curtain into the back room, and grabbed his wife none too gently by the elbow. Serafina and Carlotta began to protest, but the enraged yells drowned theirs out.

'Come on, Carlotta, we're going,' he announced loudly, then glaring meaningfully at Tino, added, 'I don't think I'm welcome in this house any more. If people can't live and let live, we're better off without them.'

As he slammed the café door after him, the first notes of an air raid warning siren wailed plaintively across the town. And that was the moment when the prospect of war became a reality. People scurried around frantically, scrabbling for gas masks long forgotten in the determination to believe that the effects of war could not possibly hit their shores again. They all remembered how the Zeppelins had caught the towns of the east coast by surprise in the Great War. London, too, had experienced the dreaded Blimps. Although it had not affected them directly here, who knew what new tricks the enemy might have up their sleeve this time?

They ran down into basements or Anderson shelters, or into public shelters. Families which were not so well-prepared trembled in little huddles beneath kitchen tables or under stairs. Anywhere they could.

Then just as unexpectedly, the all-clear sounded to the accompaniment of sighs of relief. No amount of practice, familiarising themselves with the sounds of the different sirens in preparation for the mere possibility of war, could have equipped them to deal with the inordinate feeling of terror that gripped them in the grim face of the truth.

Chapter 25

THAT FIRST SOUNDING of the warning siren, followed by the all-clear, set the pattern for the next few months. People were beginning to breathe easily again, it seemed the war might not touch their lives after all. There was derision, confusion and above all, anger. What right had the government to spend all those thousands of pounds on the issue of identity cards, Anderson and Morrison shelters and all the other precautions they had taken for a war that it seemed was never going to materialise? Surely, at least, not for those held in the safe arms of the British Isles, cut off as it was from the rest of Europe by that great expanse of water, the English Channel? This Phoney War was beginning to raise questions and there was a sense of unrest as people gradually began to go about their daily routine as normal.

Hitherto unfamiliar sights of uniformed people in their midst only served to agitate people even more. The ARPs, with their uniform and white armbands, and women dressed in trousers, something rarely seen before, had become an accepted part of everyday life. And now, the last straw was that supplies of everyday things were becoming short, and rationing of basic foodstuffs was well underway.

Tino turned worriedly to Serafina one day. He had been going through the café accounts and his face was grim.

'I don't know what we're going to do with the café,' he said. 'I'm seriously thinking of shutting shop, I don't see how we can go on.'

'Is there nothing we can do?' Serafina asked, placing a hand lightly on her husband's arm. Now well into her fifties, she was still a striking woman. The dark eyes retained their sparkle and the raven black hair still fell thick and lustrous, to her waist with just the tiniest hint of silver. But lines of worry etched her face. Things must be serious. She knew it would break Tino's heart to close the café. It was his life.

He shrugged his shoulders. 'If you've got any ideas, I'm ready to listen,' he replied. 'But I don't think we've got any choice. How can we make ice-cream, without milk and eggs and sugar? And with tea and butter and meat rationed – well, it doesn't leave much else for our customers. I called into Jones the butcher this morning, he's worried sick.' He managed a weak smile. 'Told me he's even thinking of sprinkling less sawdust on the floor, in case they start rationing that next.'

'Tino, I know things are bad, but have you talked this over with Michele?' Serafina asked quietly. 'We've still got things like Oxo and Bovril, and we've got a good stock of coffee for now, maybe we could keep things going a bit longer, but we just won't be able to offer our customers as much choice as usual.'

Tino patted the hand which still rested on his arm. Serafina had been a good wife to him all their married life but she felt compelled to make up for the way in which she had tricked him into marriage. But she had proved herself over and over again. His thoughts drifted to Mara. No-one could ever fill the void that Mara had left and even after all the events of the intervening years, he would often lie awake at night and find his thoughts turning to her. He would remember that early morning, with the cold, fresh air and star-speckled sky. And once more he would feel the soft strands of golden hair as they brushed again his face and her scent which filled his nostrils. Blue eyes, darkened with passion, locked with his own. He would reach out to touch her, but each time, she would fade into the distance and he would be brought back abruptly to the present with a deep sense of loss and longing and above all, emptiness. He would seek refuge in sleep, but even then, Mara's face would haunt his dreams. There was no escape.

But his eyes were soft as he looked down at his wife.

'We'll see, Serafina,' he said. 'I'll speak to Michele, see what he says. I think Carlotta and Beppe are in the same position, too. In fact, all the cafes, Italian or otherwise. At least everyone's in the same situation. You know yourself, the girls had to close the shops in London a while ago and as for poor Giuseppe, he is such an old man now, Janey tells me she thinks he is nearing the end of his days. He was good to me, Serafina, like a father. I will never forget that. In fact, they both were.'

Tino went quiet, lost in thought of times long past. Emilia had written to him a long time ago that Raffaele had been taken ill and was asking to see him, begging his forgiveness. But Tino had sent back a letter, wishing him well and no more. No visit, no words of forgiveness. The memory of the hurt he had suffered served only to strengthen his resolve. But Giuseppe was different. His imminent demise hurt him and he promised himself he would visit him before it was too late.

News came from Italy. Everyone there was fearful of what the future may bring, as the balance of control in the war was beginning to change. During the early part of 1940, Germany had gained ground all the time and they set their sights on victory. All the time, Mussolini watched the proceedings with interest. If Germany was going to win this war, Italy could gain far more by revoking its neutrality and joining them in the final onslaught. In April, the eyes of the world were turned back on *Il Duce* when Italy attacked Albania, furthering the fascist dream of taking over 'inferior' states, but causing a backlash which meant that England and France guaranteed military assistance to Turkey and Greece if they too should be attacked in the future. Already, Mussolini had made it clear in the preceding February that if necessary, he would not balk at the idea of a confrontation with Great Britain. The situation was volatile, but as yet, Swansea had seen no action and life went on with little evidence of attack from any quarter. The main concerns of the people were for their brave sons who had gone to war.

Tino had just returned from London, his mood sad and dejected. The train had been crowded and smelled of damp. He was glad he had travelled in daylight, the dismal blue lights designed to conform with blackout regulations, would have been unbearable. It was June 10th, 1940. There was a note addressed to Tino propped up against the clock on the mantelpiece. Tino took it down and unfolded it, smoothing out the creases between his thumb and forefinger. It was written in English, in his daughter Carla's educated handwriting. Tino had long since learned to read English as well as Italian and as Carla had grown up, she had taught him what she had done in school that day. Tino smiled to himself. He swore she'd been born a teacher, that girl. And hadn't she proved it, when she had become a schoolmistress? Now, though, things were changing, for many of the schools in the country were forced to close, as more and more of the pupils were evacuated to safer areas.

Dear Papa

Mamma and Zi Michele have gone to the Morriston cafe, Z'a Carlotta is not well and Mamma has taken some of her home cooking to try to tempt her to eat. I am going to Gina Rinaldi's first, her mother asked me over there to eat with them. We're together on fire watch tonight, so no need to worry about me. I've left some food out for you. See you later.

Carla xx

Tino's smile was cynical. Not so long ago, he would have driven Serafina to the café in Morriston himself – after all, he still owned the place. But now, he knew he wasn't welcome where Beppe was concerned and he hadn't visited for a long time. He made a mug of cocoa and sat down at the wooden table. The only sound was the loud ticking of the clock. For once, he was glad to be on his own. He pulled a small packet out of his pocket and carefully began to remove the thin tissue paper that covered it. The single light bulb overhead shone onto the object nestling in the palm of his hand, and small golden starbursts emanated from it in the pale glow. He turned it over in his hands and hot tears pricked the back of his eyelids. He had always admired Giuseppe's watch and now it was his.

He had got to London just in time. Zi Giuseppe, had had over ninety years of life – a life that, like his own, had known abject poverty then later, the rich fruits of his own labour. But now, that life was drawing to a close. His breathing was laboured and the fat had fallen away, leaving a semi-transparent film of grey skin stretched tightly over angular bones.

His last words to Tino had been, 'You have some years left to you yet. Your Papa has gone, it's too late for him. But don't blight your life with bitterness towards the rest of your family.'

His hand had squeezed his nephew's. The grip was feeble, he was getting weaker by the minute. 'Tino, please make it up with your brother Francesco,' he urged. 'His only mistake was to fall in love with your sweetheart. If your Papa had told the truth, it wouldn't have happened, Francesco would never have done that to you. He loved you too much. Tino, I've loved you too, like a son. For my sake, try and give some of that love back to your brother.'

The speech had exhausted the old man and his eyelids drooped as he fell into a deep sleep from which never awoke.

Janey handed the parcel to Tino after the funeral. She was older now too, but her features remained unchanged. 'He asked me to give this to yer,' she had said. 'He knew you always liked it. You 'ave to wear it an' think of 'im.'

He thought about what his uncle had said about Francesco. Giuseppe's death made him question his own mortality. After all, he was a man rapidly approaching sixty now. Maybe one day, he would find it in his heart to forgive Francesco, Zi Giuseppe's words made him see he had been as much a victim of Papa's greed as he himself had been. But now, with this war, it would not be possible to travel freely in Europe. Perhaps when all this was over, he could return to Italy and make it up with his brother. He laid his head on his hands and wept – for Giuseppe, for his only son, Gio, and his nephew, Lorenzo, gone off to fight in the war; for the loss of his friendship with Beppe; for the years of time he had lost with his older brother; and above all, the loss of his childhood dreams, his life with Mara.

He had no idea how long he had sat there, he thought he might even have dozed off. It was dark outside and it registered that Michele and Serafina were leaving it a bit late to come back; there were curfews in place as it was. He was disturbed by a sound coming from the front of the café. A thumping, banging at the door. He had bolted it behind him when he came in, it was either Michele and Serafina returning home, or failing that, someone was about to give him hell, because the light from the back room could be seen from outside through the bead curtains, as he hadn't yet pulled the blackout blinds down.

'All right, all right!' he yelled, as he struggled to pull up his braces, which had slipped down over his elbows as he had slept. 'I'm coming.' His eyes were puffy and red as he rose stiffly to his feet.

At that moment, he heard a clamour outside and someone shouted, 'Go on, mate. Kick it in, mun!'

There were several dull thuds in quick succession, followed by the sound of splitting wood as the timber-framed door of the café splintered into jagged-edged pieces. Then another sound, unmistakeable as large panes of glass shattered into a thousand lethal shards as they succumbed to the onslaught of heavy working boots and missiles – bricks, stones, anything that could be thrown, went through the windows and even the thick tape that criss-crossed them to protect against a bomb-blast could not withstand such a determined attack.

Tino's heart began to race with fear, but instinct told him he must get to the stairs at the back of the room. There was a telephone upstairs, if only he could get there in time. He had no idea what was going on, but he knew that whatever it was, it wasn't good. There was another crash as more broken glass hit the floor. As he reached the stairs, he looked back for an instant and his heart sank as he saw fragments of the coloured glass from above the wooden partitions littering the floor of the café, sparkling like multi-coloured jewels in the beam of a torch. From among the shadowy figures bunched together in the darkened room, he heard a voice say, 'Don't think there's anyone in'.

Someone else replied, 'Well, there's a light on in the back. I bet the Eye-tie bastards are hiding out there.'

'Aye, well there's time to get them later, let's do the shop first.'

'No!' Tino heard this and reacted with his heart rather than his head. He couldn't just stand by and let them wreck everything he'd worked for. He turned around, and ran back across the room towards the beaded doorway. 'You leave my café alone, you bastards! Leave it alone!'

The thought of them destroying everything he owned, the

business he'd built up from nothing, ignited a fire deep in the pit of his belly, galvanising him into action with no thought for the consequences. But his efforts were useless against this angry mob and he suddenly felt his arms being seized from behind and wrenched backwards mercilessly until he was convinced his shoulders would be pulled clean out of their sockets. Tino's glasses were knocked off his nose. They fell to the floor and shattered, immediately lost among the sea of glass already lying there.

A man's voice, rough and deep, rang out, drowning Tino's feeble shouts.

'Look, I got one o' them stinkin' buggers here!' he yelled gleefully as Tino wriggled futilely in his grasp. 'What d'you want me to do with him?'

'A good kickin' I reckon,' another voice leered.

'No, I got better plans for 'im.' With a shock, Tino stopped fighting and listened. There was something about that voice that was vaguely familiar. 'I reckon 'e's got a bob or two tucked away somewhere.' The man took a step towards Tino, who at that moment managed to free one of his arms. He twisted around and brought his elbow forward, then swiftly back with all his strength straight into the man's stomach, winding him and causing him to double up.

'You dirty Eye-tie bastard!' he croaked, gasping for breath as Tino seized the opportunity to run.

'Don't let 'im get away!' one of the men shouted.

'Don't worry about 'im, 'e can't go nowhere,' said the familiar voice. It seemed this one was the ring-leader, he was the one issuing all the orders. 'We'll sort 'im and 'is stinking family later.'

Tino fled, running towards the stairs. He reached the upper front room and bolted the door behind him, dragging a heavy sideboard over to barricade it further. He prayed to

God that Michele and Serafina didn't come back yet and walk straight into this. Carla, too, though he wasn't expecting her back for some time. He would telephone the police first, then the Morriston shop. He switched the light on, with complete disregard for the blackout regulations. With shaking hands, his fingers turned the dial on the Bakelite telephone.

'Police?' he asked frantically. 'Hello, is that the police?' The colour drained from his face. He pressed the earpiece to his ear and listened carefully. There was nothing, no sound at all. The men had done the job well, the line had been been cut. He was no coward, but he knew if he tried to confront them, he wouldn't stand a chance, there were at least seven or eight of them. He needed to stay safe as long as he could, not for his own sake but so that he could warn his wife and brother as soon as he heard them return. A feeling of terror washed over him as he tried to find somewhere to hide. A huge, ornately carved dresser ran the length of one wall and he rushed towards it.

They had only ever used the top part of the cupboard, a shelved display unit and a set of drawers. The cupboard below was empty, and easily big enough to hold a man. He could go in there, it would buy him time if nothing else. He climbed in and crouched in one corner, pulling the door behind him. He could hear his chest wheezing. It seemed to fill the inside of the cupboard and he hoped they wouldn't hear it. He began to pray as he had never prayed before. Pray that something would happen to stop these men in their tracks, but above all, pray that none of his family came home while they were still there. He had done nothing wrong, he had no enemies. Who were these men, daring to come into his home and smash it to pieces?

Before long, the voices got closer, they were in the back room downstairs. 'Where are you, you Eye-tie traitor?' someone screamed. The note of hysteria in the voice chilled

Tino to the bone and he drew his knees closer to his chin. They obviously thought he wasn't in the house alone and renewed fear for his family made the sweat stand out on his brow. 'Bloody cowards, the lot of you. Get out here an' face us.'

'No, they 'aven't got the balls for that,' a rough voice interjected. 'We'll just 'ave to root the buggers out.'

What were they on about, traitors? Tino was sure that whoever they were, they had confused him with someone else. If they found him, he would have to try to explain to them that he was innocent. He'd done nothing to deserve this. The unrelenting sound of furniture being upturned, and anything breakable being smashed into pieces was terrifying. But when the noise of heavy boots thumping up the stairs reached Tino's ears, it became unbearable. He listened as the doors of the other rooms on that floor were flung open, followed by the now familiar sound of the wanton destruction of everything he owned. But his terror found new heights when he heard the handle of the room he was in rattle as they tried to open the door. Tino was wheezing badly now, and he was terrified the rhythmic whistling would give away his whereabouts.

'He must've blocked it,' a muffled voice penetrated the thickness of the door.

'Well, don't just stand there! Kick it in, mun!'

Although the door was made of sturdy, solid wood, it splintered ominously beneath the insistent barrage of heavy, boot-clad feet.

'Where are you?' the familiar voice taunted in a sing-song, chanting the words like children in a school yard. 'Come on, Mr Hokey-Pokey man! Mr Bogey-Man is coming to get you.'

The others began laughing and joined in. 'Hokey-Pokey, penny a lick.' The voices of some of the men slurred the words of the childish rhyme and Tino realised with a sinking heart they'd been drinking – drinking heavily, too, by the sound of it.

'Hokey-Pokey, Penny a lump, Hokey-Pokey, to make you JUMP!' On the last word, the cupboard door was pulled wide open and Tino was dragged by the collar from the safety of his hiding place.

'Not so clever now, are you, old man?' and a hand shot out to hit him hard just above his ear, splitting the skin. Tino could feel a warm trickle as blood ran down his face. Then his head was being forced down so that he could see nothing but the boot-clad feet of his captors and the floor.

The familiar voice boomed out. Where had Tino heard it before? 'Oi! I told you already, mun. I don't want 'im hurt!' he shouted angrily. 'Not just yet, anyway', he added ominously.

'Sorry, boss,' came the other voice, recalcitrant. 'What shall I do with 'im, then?'

Tino heard an upright chair being dragged across the floor and the man went on, 'Sit 'im down there. An' pass me the bag.'

He felt himself being pushed, none too gently, into the chair. He had to say something, it was now or never.

'Look, I don't know what this is about.' His voice trembled and he was close to tears, not caring for his own safety, but terrified that his family would walk right into this trap. 'Please, I don't know what you want.'

'Don't know?' the disembodied voice mocked. Listen to 'im, boys, pleadin' ignorance now.'

'I really don't know,' Tino protested. 'At least, tell me what it is I'm supposed to have done.'

'As if you didn't know.' A hand came hard across his mouth and again, he could feel warm blood trickling out of the corner, but he barely noticed; he was trying hard to concentrate, to pinpoint that voice. The man had something over his mouth, maybe a scarf, muffling and distorting his voice, and it was obvious he was trying to disguise it. But even so, Tino was convinced he knew it from somewhere, he just couldn't place it. 'Don't you come it with me. An' anyway, it's not just you, it's all those other filthy buggers from the same country.'

'What do you mean?' Tino was genuinely perplexed.

'You tryin' to tell me you didn't know that bloody Mussolini's turned tail? The bloody traitor's gone and joined up with those other bastards, the German filth? Gone all pally with his ol' mate Hitler, and now he's declared war on us, too!'

The silence in the room was deathly. The stark realisation hit Tino, that with Italy at war against Britain, every Italian in the country would be in danger. But he had lived here since he was a young boy, he had even done his bit for the country in the last war, this one, too.

'I've done nothing! Nor has my family, we've been good citizens of this country.' His fear was turning to contempt for the ignorance of these people, making him bolder. 'Even my son is in the British Army, out there fighting for the likes of you scum.' He was angry now, enraged that he should be treated like this. 'This is what I think of people like you, you are vermin!' he shouted, and spat hard onto the floor. Some of it spattered over the man's boots, speckling them with thick, sticky droplets.

'Gimme the bag! I'm fed up of listening to this rubbish.'

Tino felt a piece of coarse cloth being pulled over his head, and dragged down firmly over his face and past his neck. The world went black, even the torchlight was obliterated. He was convinced his end had come as he struggled to breathe within the confines of the thick cloth. He felt the roughness of the thick hessian rope cutting into his flesh as someone pulled his arms behind the chair and bound his wrists together, tugging the knots tightly into place. Without warning, a heavy punch landed on his cheekbone, setting his head rocking wildly on his shoulders.

'Where's the money then, old man?' the ringleader shouted.

'I haven't got any,' came the muffled reply.

Another punch followed, this time to the stomach and he doubled up, gasping. He was finding it very hard to breathe and the wheezing was getting worse by the minute.

'Don't give us that. A liar as well as a traitor, eh?' Again, Tino almost grasped the name of the man the voice belonged to, but still it eluded him.

'I am not a liar, or a traitor,' Tino wheezed. 'I keep little money here, most of it is in the bank.'

'Well, I bet my idea of little money and yours differs quite a bit. Now, tell me where it is or I'll slice you from ear to ear.'

The touch of cold metal running across his throat sent a fresh surge of panic through Tino's body. He was desperate to go to the toilet, and was terrified that he would suffer that final humiliation.

'In the drawer, over there,' he gave in, tilting his covered head towards the dresser. It was true, that was all the money there was in the house. What he didn't tell them was that much of his money had been stashed away behind a loose brick in the cellar, a trick Giuseppe had taught him years ago. Even the bank had only a tiny proportion of his wealth.

'Take a look,' the man indicated to one of the others, who opened the drawer, and pulled out a thick wad of banknotes.

He let out a low whistle. 'Quite a bundle there!'

Just then, the sound of a man's voice drifted up the stairs from the café below.

'Tino? Tino?'

'Quick! Run for it!' one of Tino's captors yelled.

But the familiar voice couldn't resist giving one last dig before he left. 'Oh, and as for your brother-in-law in Morriston…'

The man had lowered his guard and with a start, Tino realised who the voice belonged to. He could hardly believe it, he had always thought the man was his friend. But any triumph he felt at recognising the voice paled into insignificance at the man's final words. '… we're on our way up there next!'

The men fled, almost falling over each other as they rushed towards the front of what was left of the café. The ringleader suddenly lost his balance and slipped on the marble floor, cutting his hand badly on one of the many shards of glass. Muttering a string of oaths, he was quickly pulled to his feet by one of his accomplices as they made a hasty escape, barging past the ARP officer as they did so.

'What the hell is going on?' he muttered to himself. He had only come here to speak to the family about leaving lights showing, and found himself in the middle of this chaos. He walked through to the back room and found it in the same state of utter devastation as the shop, with anything that wasn't fixed or bolted down destroyed beyond recognition. He heard a sound coming from above as Tino struggled to scrape the chair along the floor to attract attention, and darted up the stairs.

'Christ, what have they done to you?' There was a knife on the table and he swiftly cut the rope away from Tino's wrists, then removed the cloth bag from his head.

Tino rubbed his wrists, trying to get the circulation back into them. The full impact of the assault became apparent as Tom, one of Tino's café friends, shone the torch in his face.

'Oh, my God!' he cried when he saw the extent of his

injuries. Tino's face was a mass of dark bruises and swellings where the punches had rained down again and again.

'Look, they cut the telephone lines, I couldn't do a thing.' The words were forced from between swollen, bloody lips. 'You've got to get help, quickly. Get the police, he said they're going to the Morriston shop. Please, Serafina's there with my brother Michele. Beppe, too. But Carla's alright, she's out on fire duty.'

Tom nodded, his face grim. 'I don't know which bastards did this to you, but they should be shot.'

'Well, I know who it was.' The words were whispered and the voice trembled with sadness. 'It was Daï.'

Tom raised the alarm and called one of the first-aiders to take a look at Tino. He tried to persuade him to go to the hospital, but he would have none of it.

'I am fine, these wounds will heal,' he protested. 'But for God's sake, just get help to Morriston, I just want my family back safely.' He was clearly agitated and Tom tried his best to pacify him and keep him calm. He'd have a heart attack if he went on the way he was going, his face was bright red as it was.

'I told you, Tino, I've already notified the police.' He'd managed to salvage a few unbroken mugs from among the debris and handed one to Tino, keeping one for himself. 'Told them who the ringleader was too. Don't worry, Tino, they were on their way the minute I told them what had happened. *Duw*, I can hardly believe it. An' all the times he's had free food and drink here, and played cards with us – he knows as well as I do, you're as much behind our army as anyone. I know Dai's always been a bit of a miserable ol' sod, but I never thought he'd stoop this low.'

Tino raised the mug to his lips with trembling hands and

took a long drink of the steaming cocoa. Rationing was the last thing on Tom's mind when he shovelled several heaped spoonfuls of sugar into the milky-brown drink. The man was in shock, he needed it.

'I just wish I knew what was happening.'

'They shouldn't be long, now. Oh, and by the way, I've asked some of the boys to come around later, to board the windows and door up. Can't leave them like that, it's asking for even more trouble.'

The sound of a car drawing up outside interrupted the conversation and Tom went over to the window and pulled the blackout blind to one side, peeping down onto the street through the minute chink he had made. The street looked strangely eerie and he could just make out the faint white lines painted on the kerbs and snuffed-out lamp posts, there to guide people in the absence of proper lighting. Even the car headlamps wore makeshift little hoods, to give off the bare minimum of light. Nothing that could guide the enemy towards their targets must be allowed to show. He could just about make out three dark silhouettes alighting from the car, against the slightly paler background.

'I think it's the police,' he told Tino, and they heard sounds coming from downstairs as the remains of the café door were pushed to one side.

Tino went to rush towards the door, but a wave of nausea and dizziness made him slump back down onto the chair. Before long, Serafina appeared in the doorway, closely followed by his sister Carlotta. They were white-faced, their eyes red-rimmed, and it was clear they had been crying. The abnormally bright eyes and beads of perspiration standing out on Carlotta's forehead showed she was far from recovered from her illness. She had, in fact, come straight from her sick bed. They stopped in their tracks, shocked at the appalling injuries covering Tino's face and upper body.

'Oh, God!' Serafina rushed over to her husband and threw her arms around his neck. 'What have they done to you?'

'Don't worry, it will heal,' he said for the second time that night. He looked towards the door, where Tom was engaged in conversation with the police sergeant. Tom was agitated and gesticulating first towards the stairs, then to Tino. The sergeant scratched his head, then murmured something to Tom. They both looked towards the small group of people inside the room.

Tino would have frowned if he'd been able, but the widespread swelling and cuts that distorted his features wouldn't allow it.

'Where is Michele?' he asked anxiously. There was no sign of his brother and his chest began to wheeze more noisily again.

His wife and sister turned towards each other. The exchange of worried glances was silent but meaningful.

'They've taken him away,' Serafina sighed. 'Beppe, too.'

'No!' Tino struggled to sit up, but the beating he had taken had left him weak. He felt useless and ineffectual. 'Are you telling me Dai and his gang got there before the police? How could that have happened, Tom told them straight away.'

Sergeant Bob Bishop came into the room. He was a tall, well-built man who often frequented the café. Tino had often hidden him in the back room when he was still a constable, covering for him with his sergeant, when he wanted a quick cigarette or mug of cocoa on a cold night, 'You've got it wrong, Tino,' he said quietly. 'We got there to find the Morriston police there before us. And thank God, they did, because those bloody louts had just burst their way into the shop and begun throwing things around. The whole bloody lot, chairs through windows, jars off the shelves – pretty much what they did here.'

'So where are they? Why aren't they here?'

Bob Bishop swallowed hard. He wished he didn't have to say the next words. 'I don't suppose you heard the speech Churchill, our new leader, gave out on the wireless today?'

'No.'

Bob's feet were shuffling and he fiddled about with his hat. 'Well, it was about 'enemy aliens',' he began. 'They've been planning this round-up for some time, but when the news about Italy joining Germany against us came – well, Churchill's answer was "Collar the lot". Tino, they were saved from a beating by Dai and his gang, but they've been taken in by the Morriston boys for questioning. It's happening all over the country. Some of their friends who were there, too.'

'But what does that mean for them?' Tino asked. 'Surely they will let them go, they must know that they are no threat?'

His words were calm enough, but inside, he feared for Beppe in particular. If Marcello, a known fascist sympathiser who had signed allegiance to Mussolini a long time ago, had been among the group of men found in the café, anyone in his company was likely to be tarred with the same brush, regardless. Beppe's only crime was to be impressionable, taken in by the smooth talker who had taken advantage of his ignorance and simplicity.

Bob shrugged his shoulders and the reply was guarded. 'I don't really know, at this stage. It's likely some will be released, if they can prove they're no threat to the country. But others could be held in internment camps, while the government decides what to do with them.'

This was too much for Tino and he broke down, his shoulders bowed and shaking beneath the gravity of the news.

Bob Bishop patted him on the shoulder. 'To tell the truth,

Tino, I was supposed to have taken you in tonight, too. But I'll come back tomorrow, I'll tell them you're too ill to be moved. Anyway, if there's any news, I'll come and let you know.' He turned to go, but stopped as he reached the door. Gently, he asked, 'You did take out British citizenship, didn't you?'

Tino nodded, but it was Serafina who spoke. 'All of us.' The voice was sombre and held an element of defeat. 'All of us, except Beppe and Michele.'

Later, it broke their hearts when they found out what had taken place all over the country. That night, the scenes of Italian immigrants being dragged from their homes, or even their beds was a familiar one throughout the length and breadth of Great Britain – old men, young boys, few were spared. Others were subjected to attacks by gangs who smashed, looted and raided the properties of the people who had been their friends just hours before; people who sat at the same dinner table, talked about the same things, feared the same bombardments of war; people they shared their daily lives with.

'The press have a lot to answer for,' Tino remarked, realising that much of this hysteria had been stirred up by the daily newspapers. 'Some papers are worse than others. They have stirred up this hysteria, this, this…' he spluttered angrily as he searched for the right word, 'this xenophobia. And in a nation of people that were already living on their raw-edged nerves.'

Clement Attlee told Parliament the following day, 'There is no quarrel between the Italian and the British and French people.' But that night, more than a hundred and sixty people of Italian origin, from Tino's county of Glamorgan alone, were rounded up and detained. Any man between the age of sixteen and sixty was herded and many even younger or older; they weren't too particular about checking their age. In Swansea, several cafes in the High Street and other areas throughout the town were visited in the dead of night, their unsuspecting occupants bundled unceremoniously into vans which would take them to be questioned. In Morriston, the shops of at least four families of Italian origin in Woodfield Street alone were raided, without counting Beppe's. All familiar names, many from the same village as Tino. Now they were no longer just Italians, the friendly Hokey Pokey men – they were instead Churchill's 'Enemy Aliens'.

The following day, Sergeant Bishop returned. It was early morning, his eyes were bleary and he looked as if he hadn't slept all night.

'Tino, I promised to let you know what's happening.'

'Yes?'

'Well, there's good and bad news.' The man hesitated, clearly uncomfortable with his task. 'First of all, I've had special permission for you to be interviewed here, in light of your injuries. But I can't foresee any problems, it should be pretty straightforward.'

The older man nodded, wincing as the swollen, black and purple skin protested at the sudden movement. He waited patiently for Bob Bishop to go on, but the police sergeant seemed uncharacteristically hesitant.

'But the bad news is exactly that. Bad.' He paused, coughing nervously. 'They're keeping Beppe and Michele, sending them on to one of the camps – I don't know where yet. Although he's lived here for a long time technically, Michele is still a citizen of Italy. And as for Beppe,' he shook his head. 'Because of his association with Marcello, and his reputation, he didn't stand a chance of being released.'

By now the whole family had gathered in the room and a shocked silence followed. But worse was to come.

It was a few days later, on June 27th, the family were suddenly woken from their sleep by a deep, throbbing drone in the far distance. Half asleep, Tino reached for the torch he kept at the side of the bed and fumbled around on the dressing table for his pocket watch. Flipping back the cover, he flashed the light onto the face. Three-twenty. Then the wail of the air raid warning split through the night air and Tino ran to the window, unable to resist a quick look before running to the safety of the cellar. He could see the sky in the distance lit up by an orange glow as the first bombs dropped in the general area of the docks. A split second later, an almighty bang echoed across the town, rocking the floor violently beneath his feet. That was enough for Tino. Only stopping long enough to grab the two gas masks which hung side by side on the door, he pulled Serafina to her feet, tugging her hand and pulling her towards the stairs. They met Carla and Carlotta on the landing and all four ran for their lives. That night, six high explosive bombs had missed their target, the docks, less than a mile away from Tino's café, falling instead on nearby Danygraig Road, where the Rinaldis lived, causing some damage to properties there but by some miracle, no-one was killed. A further bomb which had been dropped on the slopes of Kilvey Hill behind, failed to explode. This attack was just the beginning, the precursor of many more to come. The war had finally come to Swansea.

But even the shock of these first bombs to hit the town paled beside the horrors that would beset the family in the coming weeks. It was July 1st, a ship carrying sixteen hundred men, including Beppe and Michele who had until then been kept in dire conditions in various internment camps, set sail from Liverpool docks bound for Canada. There were far more men on board than the four hundred or so passengers that the ship, a luxury cruise liner in peace time, normally carried. Instead of its usual brightly coloured livery, the hull was now painted in the dark muddy colours of the military and there were armaments to the fore and aft. More ominously, the promenade deck had been laced with lengths of barbed wire. Huge funnels belched clouds of steam, tall grey sentinels silhouetted starkly against the sky. The ship was the *Arandora Star*.

There was a mix of nationalities aboard – British soldiers whose task was to guard the German and Italian prisoners on the long journey. The Italian internees had been divided into two contingents, one lot sent to the upper deck, the other to the lower one. After being pushed from pillar to post, constantly moved from one internment camp to another in cramped, insanitary conditions, often dirty and usually hungry, Michele and Beppe had finally both been sent to the lower deck. It was crowded here too, and the men were to be allowed just forty-five minutes each day to stretch their legs on the upper deck.

Just a few days into the journey, on July 2nd, at seven o'clock in the morning, the ship was struck by a torpedo from a German U-boat. It rocked violently and there was a frenzied crush as the men below deck scrambled to reach the upper decks, Michele and Beppe among them. There they found men already desperately racing for lifeboats, cutting themselves to ribbons on the swathes of barbed wire in the process. But by the time they got there, many of the boats had already been launched, some tragically empty in the panic to get away from the dying ship. Others, in their terror, had jumped into the sea and already, bodies floated motionless on the grey, murky waters. They could see there was little time left, the ship was listing heavily towards the starboard side, the bows already partly submerged. She was in danger of succumbing to the lure of the water at any moment.

The two men threw their arms around each other's shoulders. It was an emotional moment. The words were unspoken, but they both knew their only chance was to dive into the water below. The ship creaked and groaned loudly in its final death throes. They found a gap in the barbed wire, where it had been torn away, and looked down to see the forbidding dark waters littered with huge splinters of wood. Thick pools of oil spread out like a shiny blanket, some on fire, sending shooting flames high into the air above. Their hearts raced with fear. Taking one last look at each other, they closed their eyes and jumped. The last thing they remembered was the sight of the water rushing towards them. They hit it simultaneously, as if they were part of some dark, mysterious dance, a frenzied tarantella where every movement had been cleverly choreographed down to the last minute detail. Even the waves seemed to gather force, conspiring silently together to form a wall as unyielding as brick. The two men lost consciousness and disappeared, sinking helplessly beneath the flaming waters of hell. Four hundred and eighty-six Italians and seventy-five Germans perished on that fateful morning. Beppe and Michele were among them.

Chapter 26

THE LOSS OF Michele and Beppe had come as a huge shock, the first casualties of war to hit the D'Abruzzo family. Tino and Serafina's son, Gio, and his cousin Lorenzo, Carlotta and Beppe's son, had been given a few days' compassionate leave despite the absence of bodies. It had been an emotional reunion, made even more poignant by the fact that the boys had already seen action abroad and were being sent back again immediately on their return. But no-one would tell them where.

The cleaning up of the café had been a long process, Dai and his gang had done their job thoroughly. But the one thing that had hurt Tino most ironically was the very thing that gave him the strength and the courage to go on. A few days after the attack, still sore and bruised, he'd gone outside for the first time to survey the damage to the exterior of the building, and it hit him like a thunderbolt. The gold script of his name above the shop door had been completely obliterated with white paint. In its place were the words, 'Go home, bastard Eye-tie traitors.'

'I know I thought about shutting up the shop,' he told the family and a few friends who had gathered together to see the boys off. The group included Tom, Lofty and Bob Bishop. 'But now, I am determined, we will open again, if only to show them we will not let them beat us!' No-one could fail to be impressed by this brave, dogged resolve, evident now in his proud stance and demeanour. 'We might not be able to give our customers everything we used to, but by God we will make sure we give them what we can.'

'Well, we'll do anything we can to help,' Lofty said, looking to Bob and Tom for support and they nodded assent. 'I might only be a five-foot tiddler, but I can fetch and carry along with the best of 'em.'

And that was exactly what they did. Between them, they nailed and sawed, fixed furniture and windows, mended the wooden doors and partitions, until it was hard to tell it was any different from before. The three men wanted to show the D'Abruzzos who their real friends were, desperate to make up for the indignities and devastation that not only Dai and his gang, but the British Government, had heaped upon him and his fellow countrymen. They were determined to help the family get back on their feet again.

After Dunkirk, and a narrow escape, Churchill continued to lead the country with rousing speeches designed specifically to boost the morale of a country at war. But no amount of talk of 'fighting to the last man to defeat the evils of the Third Reich' and 'blood, toil, tears and sweat' could stop the unstoppable. The German machine advanced mercilessly across Europe. Country after country fell into the hands of the enemy. Bombs had started raining down over British soil. The Blitz in the English capital, which began in September 1940, was to last far longer than anyone could have anticipated. It saw Londoners, rich and poor alike, suffer relentless attacks from German bombers which spread utter panic, chaos and devastation in their wake.

Every single week throughout that month, thousands of people were made homeless as their houses splintered like matchwood under the attack, and if they escaped a direct hit by the bombs themselves, the ensuing blasts and the fires were in themselves sufficient to destroy everything beyond repair. Worse still, incalculable thousands of civilian casualties and loss of life became a regular occurrence. Other cities were prime targets too: Bristol, Cardiff, Birmingham, Coventry – the list was endless.

Swansea, too, had its fair share – enemy planes had been successful in a daylight raid on King's Dock, leaving a dozen dead and more than twenty injured. The Girls' School and St James's Church in the Uplands area had been hit and in another raid, the Landore railway viaduct was damaged, together with nearby houses in Landore and Cwmbwrla. High explosives, petrol bombs and incendiaries rained down relentlessly on the town. Nowhere was safe.

Some of the more recent attacks had brought with them heavy loss of life and on the first day of September, Swansea suffered its first Blitz which raged on for hours. Over two hundred and fifty high explosive bombs and a thousand incendiaries dropped without conscience onto the helpless town below. People had emerged from the relative safety of their air raid shelters to find the sky had turned red with the flames of dying buildings, the broken shells of others silhouetted against the bright glare, while parachute flares still hovered silently above the scene of destruction like silent observers. That night alone, whole areas were flattened beyond recognition, leaving over a hundred people injured and thirty-three dead.

Around the same time, the work on the Palace café had been completed. It was business as usual and ironically, it was booming. Customers were flocking in, especially from the nearby ICI works in Landore, which had been taken over and was now heavily involved in the war production effort. Railway workers too would come in for a quick break from providing one of the country's so-called essential services. The takings were better than ever, well in excess of seventy pounds or more each week.

The nights were beginning to draw in, October was already

upon them. Tino's motor car, which had miraculously escaped the destructive force of Dai's gang, had long since been laid up. Now, there wasn't even basic petrol rationing any longer and driving for the general public had been banned, the reserves kept for emergency personnel only. The car languished, lovingly swathed in an old sheet and immobilised in the shed that had once housed the long-gone Nero. Trees shed their leaves like crumpled confetti. A distinct nip in the air made mist in the mornings, and damp, bone-chilling evenings proclaimed the imminent onslaught of winter to come.

There had been no news of the boys, other than a heavily-censored letter received shortly after they left Swansea. Tino worried too about the family and friends in Italy and London. He begged his daughters to reconsider his offer of the cottage. But they would not change their mind, no matter what he said or did.

After the end of October, there was finally a lull in the air raids over Swansea.

'Can't understand this,' Lofty remarked. He was sitting in the café with Tom and Tino. They smiled as they watched his little legs rise off the floor by several inches as he pushed himself upright on the seat, leaving them to dangle back and forth like a ventriloquist's puppet.

For once, the café was quiet and Tino seized the chance to sit down at the table and chat with his friends.

'They've got something up their sleeve, I can guarantee that,' he said grimly.

Tino shook his head sadly at the memory of a little girl he had found wandering in the middle of the town a few weeks before, during a daylight air raid warning. A small toy dangled from her hands, sawdust stuffing leaving a trail on the pavement as it escaped from a small hole in its neck. She looked up at him plaintively and his heart skipped a beat. She was crying because she couldn't find her mother and father. Crystal tear drops ran down baby cheeks, spilling over from wide sapphire blue eyes beneath a haze of golden hair. Even after all those years, it was the little things that unlocked painful memories of the past and Tino swallowed hard. Just then, the frantic mother and father came hurtling out of the Elysium picture house, now a designated air raid shelter, hurriedly reclaiming their little daughter who had become separated from them in the rush to get to safety.

'Tino, you're not listening to a word I'm saying!'

Tom's laughing rebuke brought Tino back to the present, and the café, with a sudden jolt.

'Sorry, Tom!' he apologised. 'What was it you were saying?'

Tom winked at Lofty. 'Only saying how you must be coining it lately, with all this custom, you lucky bugger.'

'Aye, reckon we should be in shares with 'im, all the effort we put in.'

Tino laughed and joined in with the good-natured banter. 'Well, if you're willing to get up when it's still dark outside, ready to serve up by five in the morning, and still on your feet at twelve in the night, then you're welcome!' His voice was still heavily accented even after all the years spent away from his origins, but it had now evolved into a peculiar combination of Italian with a hint of Welsh.

'Seriously, though. What I said was,' Tom went on, 'I think it could be the calm before the storm.'

'What makes you say that?'

Tom shook his head. 'Don't know. Gut feeling, I suppose,' he said. 'They're still at it everywhere else, you can't tell me they've finished with us yet. They're just playin' cat an' mouse with us, if you ask me.'

The bell on the door tinkled as a crowd of men and

women brought a blast of cold air into the room with them. They were wrapped up against the cold, damp day outside and were glad of the warmth in the café as they piled into the booths.

Tino pushed his glasses further up his nose. Odd, he got on better with these ones than the ones he'd had before. 'Better go if I'm going to make it to my first million,' he joked. The now white-sprinkled moustache twitched with humour, and Tino went over to the counter, ready to help Serafina and Carlotta with the impending order.

It was not long before Tom's prophecy was fulfilled when by January 1941, the bombardment of their home town began once again. Throughout the beginning of the month, there were several attacks and on January 17th, 18th and 19th, bombs rained down heavily on a town that inadvertently flaunted its existence with a covering of snow. St Thomas, nearby Bonymaen, which could easily be seen across the river from Tino's café, and the Hafod area, near Landore, were badly affected and again, the loss of life amounted to more than fifty. One bomb in particular caused amazement throughout the town, a topic of conversation for a long time afterwards. Not only had it passed clean through a fully-laden truck carrying coal, but tore through the thick steel axle and a rail beneath before burying itself twenty-five feet deep in the ground.

But despite the shock and ferocity of the January raids, it was February when things really climaxed for the people of the town.

'Papa, I'm going out tonight, see if we can catch the pictures,' Carla announced brightly. 'Gina Rinaldi, too. Those Germans, they're not going to spoil my fun.' She was brushing her hair and leaning back against the counter to use the glass-backed display to check her reflection. 'Oh, and did

I tell you, Gina's sister Lucia has joined the Land Army? She's a land girl now, somewhere near Newcastle Emlyn. Some farm out in the sticks, anyway.'

'Carla! I told you before, stop doing your hair near my counter!' Ignoring her latest news, Tino remonstrated crossly instead as he caught sight of the brush in her hand when he emerged from the back room. The truth was, he hated seeing her in those manly trousers and that modern short hairdo, it set his teeth on edge. Her hair had always been so lovely and now, she'd gone and chopped off the lot.

'Well, I'm on duty. With Lofty. Tom too, I think.'

' Oh! I thought it was just pairs?'

'Usually is. But with the past few nights like they've been, there are more of us on duty anyway. We're doing the town centre tonight,' he said. 'At least, what's left of it.'

Carla's hair swung softly about her fine cheekbones as she turned to face her father. She had grown up into an attractive woman, a softer, more subtle version of her mother.

'I can't believe the state of the town, they've wrecked it.' If she thought the damage already inflicted on the town was bad, it was about to get worse. Her expression became more serious. 'I wish this snow would clear, too. I know it's not a lot, but it's like a bloody beacon for the buggers.'

'You can cut that language out, my girl, quick as you like!' Tino replied, grinning quietly to himself; she often swore on purpose just to tease him. Judging from her face, though, she was deadly serious on this occasion. 'But you're right, it's not helping matters.'

They left together not long afterwards. At the door, Tino kissed his wife on the cheek.

'Now, Serafina, you must go down to the basement if there's a raid,' he warned her. She hated going down into the cellar, the dark made her feel claustrophobic. 'And don't think I don't know your little trick of hiding under the table. The cellar is much safer.'

'You worry too much!' she told him non-commitally, giving him a gentle push in the small of his back.

It was seven o'clock on the evening of February 19th when the first Luftwaffe bombs fell. 'Baskets of onions' from the first aircraft hovered over the bay of Swansea – flares that illuminated the town and transformed it into a guiding light for the aircraft behind, allowing them to release their deadly payload. For five hours, in the upper part of the town, Tino and his friends ushered people to safety, directing them to shelters. They tackled fires and evacuated those at risk from their homes. In another part of town, Carla was doing the same, abandoning the pictures in favour of doing her duty.

At the first sound of the siren, Carlotta ran to the safety of the cellar, but Serafina refused.

'I will not be scared out of my own home any more,' she insisted. 'I'm more frightened of being stuck in the dark down there than of any German bomber.' She laughed as she said it, but there was an element of truth in the words. When Tino was there it was different, she felt safe. But without him, the windowless cellar seemed to close in on her, bringing an unwelcome reminder of the times when she was very small, even before her mother had died and her father would come to her room in the dead of night and whisper that she mustn't make a noise or tell anyone, or the ghosts would get her. And she would relive the nightmares. She hated the dark.

The following night, Swansea took more of the same. The German bombers came back, and the events of the night before were played out all over again. And bit by bit, the town was being transformed beyond recognition, as houses and shops, schools and hospitals fell victim to the war.

But it was the third night, which was a Friday, when the

bombing reached its ultimate climax. Again, Tino and his friends were on duty. Carla and her friend Gina Rinaldi were due for a night off, but had swapped with two other girls.

It was approaching eight o'clock when the familiar wailing sound shrieked out into the night and everyone's heart sank. It was dangerous enough just patrolling the streets now. With only shielded torches and painted white lines to guide the way, there was a real possibility of tripping over the piles of debris that littered every street. Tino's group were close to the centre of the town and people began to file in to the old chapel that was now in use as an air raid shelter.

''Ere we go again,' Lofty muttered. 'I'm gettin' bloody fed up of these buggers, spoiling my nights in with my missus.'

'If you had a missus like mine, you'd be glad of the rest, mun!' Tom replied. 'She's a right miserable ol' sod, accused me of having the glad eye for that blonde across the road from us.'

'Well, did you?'

'What?'

'Have your glad eye on her?'

Tom grinned. His teeth gleamed white in the darkness, except for a few gaps where only brown stumps remained.

'Air raid shelter here, missus.' With a well-practised sweep of the arm, he directed a woman towards the entrance of the chapel, then turned his attention back to his friends. Even in the dark, his expression gave the game away.

'Had more than my bloody eye on 'er, I can tell you,' his wicked laughter was infectious. ''An' as God is my judge, I can tell you something else. She's a real blonde too. Not dyed like straw, like some of 'em. Cor, what a woman!' His eyes rolled back comically in his head at the memory.

Lofty almost choked with laughter. 'You dirty ol' bugger, you!'

'Aye, well don't you go telling my ol' girl, mind,' his friend replied. 'She'd cut it off for me, an' then I'd be no good to man nor beast. An' come to think of it, the blonde across the road would be none too pleased, either.'

'Shhh! Listen!'

A prolonged droning filled the air, the now dreaded throbbing sound as German bombers got close to their targets. Then without warning, a piercing whistle rent the air, followed closely by two deafening bangs that seemed to split their eardrums.

'Christ a'mighty!' Tom shouted. 'Quick, get these people down there now.'

Already, people were running for cover. One after another, the bombs fell and the ground shook beneath their feet.

'Blimey, that was close,' Lofty shouted as yet another explosion, even closer than its predecessors, sent a series of red and yellow flames shooting upwards into the crisp night sky. 'Looks like the town centre's going to get it again. I think we'd better take cover.'

'Mister, mister,' a young boy came running out of the chapel towards them. 'Can you come in a minute, my mother's not feeling too good.'

'We was on our way anyway, son.'

The shelter was almost like a home from home. People had become so used to it that they had brought torches and blankets with them, along with flasks of hot drink and packages of food. The omnipresent gas masks were slung over shoulders or in some cases, thrown carelessly on the floor alongside. But above all, it was the camaraderie that shone through. Despite rationing, they shared their food and drink with anyone they thought needed it more than they did. Someone brought out a brown packet, and offered it around. It contained a few slivers of paper-thin cheese which just about distinguished them as sandwiches and not as bread alone. Another woman, pale and thin with a haunted expression, shyly held out a bag of hard-boiled sweets which had stuck firmly together inside the cone-shaped twist of paper. Then someone began to sing.

'*Keep the home fires burning, While your hearts are yearning...*' The lone voice rang out loud and strong, and the deep rich sound resonated around the walls. A small, thin man sitting cross-legged in the corner was belting out the first verse of the song as if his life depended on it. He tipped the dark trilby to the back of his head as if somehow, the action would lend him strength. Then a pretty dark-haired young woman joined in, the sweet, high notes ringing out crystal clear. '*Though your lads are far away, they dream of home.*' Her eyes brimmed with tears. Who knew who she was thinking of as she sang the words so poignantly? One by one, they joined in, some harmonising skilfully with the main tune, others slightly out of tune, but it didn't matter. A young boy pulled a mouth organ out of his pocket and putting his lips to it, blew gently. The resultant sound was haunting. But still, the velvety notes of the first man rose above the rest.

Outside, ear-splitting whistles of countless bombs, screaming remorselessly towards their helpless targets on the ground, hurt their ears and sent shivers down their spines. The very fabric of the building vibrated and trembled violently with the force of explosions it seemed would never end. But the voices in the chapel rose louder and louder until they filled the room and hit the rafters, determined to drown out the sound of the dreaded planes and bombs they knew were systematically destroying their town, possibly even their families. But still they sang. Swansea might be falling down around them, but their spirit was indomitable.

Tino was full of admiration for the man who had started the singing. He whispered softly to his friends, 'It's hard to believe a voice like that can come out of such a small man. He looks as if you could knock him down with a feather.'

'Aye, well, that's as maybe,' Lofty replied. He had to swallow hard to get rid of the lump that had formed in his throat. 'But by God, he's keeping their spirits up!'

He looked down as someone suddenly tugged his hand.

'Come on! My Mam's over there!'

'Blimey, I'd forgotten about you!' Lofty grinned.

The three men followed the boy to where his mother sat on a folded blanket, her upper body hunched over her knees. As they approached, she looked up with pleading, amber-coloured eyes.

'Please, I need help,' she whispered, then doubled up again with pain. The fine, mousy hair fell forwards over her face, lank with sweat. She was small, with little spare flesh to cover her bones. But it was the distinct swelling of her belly that gave away the nature of the problem, precluding the need for any further explanation.

Seeing the expressions on his friend's faces, Tino took charge of the situation. He knew it would be difficult, if not impossible, to get medical help while the bombs were still raining down outside, he would have to think quickly. He blew his warden's whistle to attract attention above the singing, which had now developed into a rousing chorus of *Roll out the barrels*.

'Is there a doctor here? Or a nurse?' he asked, deliberately keeping his voice calm as he had been trained to, but inside he was quaking. His request was met with a low murmuring followed by a room full of shaking heads. 'A midwife, then? Anyone who can assist in a birth. We have a young lady here in need of urgent assistance.' Still no response.

'I'll help,' a woman in her thirties offered. 'But the only experience I've ever had is having my own little sods.'

'Me, too!' said another.

'Oh, my Gawd!' Lofty looked horrified at the prospect of the woman giving birth in his presence. 'I've never done any of this baby stuff before, have you?'

Tom shook his head. 'No! I just make 'em, mun!' He grinned wickedly despite the seriousness of the situation.

'Stuck in a shelter in the middle of a raid is hardly the best place to give birth, but we're going to have to deal with it, somehow, boys.' Tino was open to any suggestions as he watched another spasm of pain hit the woman. But the only suggestion that was forthcoming turned his skin white.

'Oi, didn't you say before you used to help on the farm in Italy?' Lofty asked accusingly.

'Yes, why?'

'Well, you're the answer to a maiden's prayer, then, aren't you?

Tino was perplexed and a frown passed over his features. 'Am I?' As the words left his mouth, it suddenly hit him what Lofty was hinting at.

'Oh, no!' he answered slowly, at the same time, shaking his head emphatically. 'I helped with lambs and goats, kittens even. But never babies!'

Tom broke in. He kept his voice low so that the boy and his mother couldn't overhear. 'Tino, I don't think you've got much choice, *mun*. What're you goin' to do, leave 'er to try an' give birth on 'er own?'

Tino's hands begun to shake. When he volunteered for ARP duty, no-one told him delivering babies was part of the job. Basic first aid he could cope with, but this was something else. 'No, I can't! I just can't!'

'You've got to!' Tom's voice was firm.

Tino looked towards the woman who, judging by the time between the pains, was not far away from delivering her baby. He swallowed hard.

'It seems I've got no option,' he murmured. 'Look, can you get some hot water sorted for me to scrub my hands? I think there's a stove over in the other corner there. Oh, and we'd better put some screens around, it's not a bloody peep-show.'

He turned to the woman, 'I'm Tino,' he smiled. 'This is Tom,' Tom nodded dutifully. 'And the little one over there is Lofty. Now, what shall I call you?'

'Mrs Jones is a bit formal, what with you being the midwife, so to speak.' She giggled at her own joke, despite the pain. 'You'd better call me Rosie.'

People in the room were happy to lend pillows to go under the Rosie's head. By some divine chance, someone had been on their way home from the laundry when the warning went, and had a bagful of clean towels with them. Between them, they dragged some of the pews across and up-ended them around the woman, draping them with blankets to form a makeshift screen.

Tino was trying desperately to stop his voice and hands from shaking. He looked more terrified than Rosie did. This would have been difficult at the best of times, but in the middle of an air raid with poor lighting and cramped conditions, it was bordering on the impossible.

'You needn't worry too much,' Rosie patted the hand of this kindly, gentle faced man. 'I've done it a few times before.' She nodded towards her son. 'The other three have been evacuated, but he broke his heart at the thought of leavin' me on my own, with 'is Dad away fightin' for 'is country.'

She stopped, gasping for air as another red-hot band seized her abdomen in a vice-like grip. As the pain subsided, she went on, 'Tell the truth, don't even know how this happened.' She pointed towards her stomach. 'He was only home a couple o' days on leave. He doesn't even know, I've only had one letter from 'im since, but by the time the censors got to it, there wasn't that much left. But there we are, it was meant to 'appen, I suppose.'

Soon, the pains became so close together that there was no telling where one ended and the next one started. Tino and the two women who had volunteered to help, talked to Rosie constantly, reassuring her everything would be fine.

Tino suddenly gave an excited shout. 'I can see the head!' he yelled. 'Rosie, it won't be much longer, the baby's coming!'

As the next spasm came, Tino assured himself all was well, then issued the order. 'Rosie, it's time to push.' He was kept so busy, all traces of nervousness had disappeared and his initial misgivings had given way to excitement.

She gritted her teeth and pushed with all her might.

'Good! And again.'

With one final push, the baby came out in a slithering rush, almost falling into Tino's waiting arms. Someone handed him a towel and he quickly rubbed the tiny form. His glasses had slipped down his nose again and tiny beads of sweat stood out on his brow. The gentle brown eyes filled as the baby gave its first cry.

'Rosie, you've got a beautiful baby boy!' His voice was thick with emotion. It took him back to the birth of his own children. Everyone in the room cheered and clapped as he made the announcement. In the midst of the horror of the bombardment and destruction that was taking place outside, this tiny new life seemed to be a symbol of renewed hope. Hope for their families, their town and their country; but above all, hope for future peace.

'Have you got a name for him?' Even Tom looked moved at the sight of the child in its mother's arms.

'Well,' she smiled. 'I'd never heard of it before tonight, but the name Tino sounds good to me. And maybe you'll be his godfather when the time comes?'

Tino was beaming. 'I would love to! But for now, you must rest, then we'll get someone to check you over and get you all home, as soon as we can.'

When the all-clear sounded, Tino couldn't wait to get back out onto the streets and tell everyone about Rosie's baby. The event had been like a beacon on a dark night, comforting yet at the same time symbolic, engendering feelings of elation and hope for the future. But his joy was short-lived at the sight that met his eyes. Whole areas of the town had been flattened and flames raged irrepressibly, leaping high into the blackness of the night sky. It seemed to him that the whole town was ablaze, a devil's inferno. The friends could have been forgiven for thinking they had walked straight into the depths of hell itself. The three men stood for a moment in silent disbelief, surveying the remains of what once was their town. Whole streets had been flattened from one end to the other and the skyline had changed beyond recognition forever. They went down the road, unable to utter a word. The heavy bombing of the last three nights had succeeded in reducing the town of Swansea to little more than rubble.

They walked the length of the town centre from Castle Street, just half a mile from the shelter, to the centre of Oxford Street and found it virtually devoid of buildings. Even the market building had crumpled like a toy beneath the sheer might and mercilessness of the raids. Nothing was spared and the wholesale bombing did not discriminate between houses or churches, schools or shops. St Mary's, the old parish church of Swansea, did not escape, nor, as they found out later, did the Roman Catholic Priory of St Joseph. The nursery school at St Joseph's was another casualty, along with Danygraig, Dyfatty, St Thomas and many others. The BBC studios in Alexandra Road, around the corner from the café, were flattened, together with the Food Control Centre in Rutland Street, near the Victoria Railway Station. Even hospitals hadn't escaped. Everywhere the men looked the signs of utter devastation and destruction shocked and sickened. On one side of the town, housing which lay high on the hill at Townhill and Mayhill blazed like a huge bonfire. On the opposite hill at Kilvey, it was the same story. The fires blazed as brightly in the suburbs as they did in the town centre and thick, pungent smoke hung oppressively in the air, blackening faces and scorching the lungs.

During the Three Nights' Blitz of the Swansea area, thousands of incendiaries and around eight hundred heavy explosives turned the place from a thriving, bustling town on the Welsh coast into a heap of smouldering rubble and debris. A black wasteland where hundreds of people died and others were injured.

Tino watched in disbelief as firefighters struggled to cope with the ensuing blazes. But the problem was compounded by fractured water mains and telephone lines that were no longer operational. Electricity, gas and sewers had also been affected, making rescue operations perilous for the brave men and women who risked their own lives trying to dig out survivors buried deep beneath the tons of concrete and brick. That was all that remained of flattened homes and buildings which were once a hive of activity.

'Oh my God!' The three men cried in unison, reeling at the sight of the giant hulk of Ben Evans, the oldest department store in Wales, with its once-proud façade silhouetted starkly against the flames. Now, it had been ripped apart, only the bare, empty skeleton bearing testimony to its former glory. It would only be in the aftermath that people would begin to question why no-one had heard a flurry of retaliatory gunfire over the town as it was being blown to bits. The guns had been almost silent.

'Oh, Madonna!' The tears washed unashamedly over the Tino's face as the immensity of the damage finally hit home. Then he remembered Carla. Oh, God, he'd forgotten, she had changed her shift. Instead of being safe in the cellar under the shop with Carlotta and Serafina, she was still out there, somewhere among this mess.

'I've got to go,' he told his friends. 'I've got to find out if she's all right.' He ran all the way up the road, pushing and shoving his way towards the wardens' post; they might have news. He was panting by the time he got there, his chest constricting and wheezing with every breath. But he had to find out. Then, as he reached the post, he remembered that the phones were out and a groan of despair escaped from between his lips. He barged through the doors, desperate for news of his young daughter.

But no-one there knew anything. Communication was almost non-existent, everyone was working flat out to get the fires under control and lead people to safety. A major rescue operation was underway, there were unexploded bombs to be dealt with and buildings to be made safe, and God alone knew how many casualties and deaths there were. Carla was just one among many. Tino went back on to the streets, frantic with worry. He walked for hours, asking anyone who would listen if they had seen his daughter. In the end, tired and exhausted, he admitted defeat. Trying to find Carla among the burning ruins and chaos was like trying to find a needle in a haystack; he would have to go home and sit tight. Sooner or later, she would either come home or… The alternative was unthinkable and he refused to even entertain such thoughts, burying them at the back of his mind.

With head and shoulders bowed as if under some great weight, he made his way towards Oxford Street but was forced to take a different route. Buildings burned so fiercely that even the firefighters couldn't get close enough to do anything, the heat being so immense. Everywhere, frantic attempts to bring fires under control continued, and where flames had been successfully doused, smoke and dust still rose thick and dark from the ruins. Ashes of papers, fabric and all manner of other things now burnt to a crisp, flew into the sky on a wave of intense heat, only to flutter to the ground again moments later in a whirlwind flurry of thick black snow. Tino was disorientated and it crossed his mind that with all the familiar landmark buildings flattened, it was hard even to tell which streets were which, any more. Some time later, tired and frantic, he reached the top end of Alexandra Road, opposite High Street station, just a stone's throw away from home. The buildings at the end near the street by the fruit market were burning fiercely. Collapsed walls laid bare their interiors, leaving them shamelessly exposed and naked to the eye of any casual passers-by. Here, too, desperate attempts were being made to bring the raging fires under control, their efforts hampered by yet another fractured water main. Everywhere, the smell of pungent burning – burning buildings, burning furniture and the sickly stench of burning bodies, those who had sadly been caught up in this hellish inferno.

The latter sickened Tino to the stomach and he kept his head low as he hurried towards home. He was just yards away from the café when he saw a dark shape come running out of the door towards him.

'Carla!' he cried and gathered his daughter up tightly in his arms. 'Carla, thank God! Thank God you are safe, I've been looking everywhere for you.'

'Papa, we've been searching for you, too,' she sobbed. She was trembling and he guided her towards the café with his arm tight about her shoulder. 'I went to the wardens' post; they said you'd been looking for me.'

They had reached the pavement in front of the Palace café when it suddenly struck Tino that something was horribly wrong. In disbelief, he took in the sight of the broken windows. The glass in the door too, was smashed.

'My God!' he breathed. 'Not again. They can't have done this to me again!'

'Oh, Papa!'

He shone his torch around the room. For the second time in less than a year, shards of glass littered the floor, sparkling like miniature chandeliers in the beam of the torch. He shook his head in despair; this latest assault had rendered him almost speechless.

'It's not what you think, Papa,' came a tearful voice. 'It wasn't the men who attacked you before who did this.'

He noticed the shadow near the beaded curtain and raised his torch. 'Serafina?' he asked. But it was his sister Carlotta whose tear-stained face stared back at him. She looked strangely ghost-like in the harsh torchlight as it threw dark shadows across her features.

Panic began to rise in the pit of his stomach. And it wasn't just the café. Something else wasn't right.

'Is it Gio? Has he been killed? Or the girls?' he asked, daring to ask the question but frightened of what he might hear. He paused for a few moments and took a deep breath. 'Has my son been killed? For God's sake, answer me, woman.'

'Papa!' Carla began to weep. 'It's not Gio, it's Mamma.'

Tino felt his knees go weak. Realising they wouldn't support him for much longer, he dropped onto one of the café chairs, stopping mechanically for an instant to sweep the pile of glass off its seat. It tinkled lightly as it fell, an incongruous sound in a silence that was heavy with foreboding.

'What is wrong with her? Is she ill?'

Carla began sobbing. It was Carlotta who answered. 'She's not ill, Tino. She's dead.'

'NO!' Tino's shouts of denial echoed through the eerily still atmosphere. But it was true.

Serafina had, as usual, refused to go down to the cellar when the warning sounded. But later, when the bombing was at its most fierce, there had been several direct hits on nearby areas in the Dyfatty district. The café shook, followed by a terrifying sound as the glass was ripped from the windows and blown out with the immense force of the blast. The tape had proved useless. When the all-clear sounded, Carlotta had found Serafina in a crumpled heap at the bottom of the stairs, her head bent back at an unnatural angle. Blood trickled from her mouth, ears and nose and a dark red pool spread out in a dark red halo beneath her head.

'She must have changed her mind after she heard the glass going,' Carlotta murmured. 'I heard it from the cellar, and it scared me half to death.' She stopped, realising the inappropriateness of what she had just said. But swallowing hard, she went on, 'We've told the police, but I don't think they'll be here for some time, not with everything else going on.'

'Where is she?'

'They told me to leave her where she was until they came.'

With renewed strength, Tino suddenly got up, pushing past Carlotta towards the stairs at the back.

'No, Papa! No!' His daughter and sister tried to stop him, but he pulled away from their grasp, he had to see for himself. He couldn't believe his wife was gone from him.

He knelt on the floor beside the body. Gently, he pulled back the blanket Carlotta had draped over Serafina. With a sob, he lifted her head to his chest, and cradled the lifeless form of his dead wife. He was overcome with feelings of affection, regret and a deep sense of guilt. He had loved her in his own way, but never a day had passed when Mara hadn't crept unbidden into his thoughts. Now, he realised that Serafina had known all along where his heart lay and yet she had accepted it. She had been a good woman. A thousand thoughts rushed into his head. What would he do without her? How could he carry on without her at his side? Who could he turn to for advice? The realisation of what he had just lost hit him full force and he let out a roar of naked pain. Life would never be the same again.

Although the war raged on in Europe for another four long years, it had ended for Tino the day his wife died. He went about his everyday tasks methodically but mechanically, like an automaton.

When the war finally ended in 1945, the only good news to come out of it was that his son Gio was safe; so was Carlotta's son, Lorenzo and soon, they would be home. His family and friends in London and Italy too, had somehow escaped and lived through that terrible war, and he thanked God for that.

In Italy as well as in Britain, battles had raged as the fight for supremacy went on. The Germans had occupied Picinisco and the surrounding areas from early on and many of the inhabitants had been forced out of their own homes. News came that Mara and Francesco and Emilia and Marco, together with their families, had been taken to Sora some miles away.

Centres had been set up for the evacuees, but food was in short supply and people suffered. They were always hungry, often tired and cold.

The abbey at Monte Cassino came under constant attack until it was finally taken from the grasp of the German forces in a devastating attack on May 18th, 1944, reducing the ancient monastery to a pile of smouldering rubble. The town of Cassino too, was razed with a huge loss of life and the destruction of irreplaceable ancient works of art and manuscripts forever.

And ironically, after the fall of Mussolini, and the Allied advance, Germany no longer fought alongside the Italians, but had turned on them as enemies.

As the war in Italy neared its end, people were told they could go back to their homes. But many found they had no homes left – they had either been destroyed by the German occupiers, who ripped doors and shutters off hinges to use as firewood; or by Allied forces who, determined to root out any rogue German soldiers who may have gone into hiding in the mountains, shelled farmhouses and barns indiscriminately and ruthlessly, leaving a trail of destruction behind them. There were whispered tales of murder, rape and other indignities carried out against the innocent people of the region, but many were afraid to talk, fearing they might be next.

Emilia and Francesco returned to the Grillo home to find it damaged, but not beyond repair. Some of the furniture had been smashed and everything was in total disarray, but little that couldn't be mended. Mara and Francesco, though, hadn't been so lucky. The D'Abruzzo farmhouse, Tino's home, had been shelled and attacked, and was now desolate and uninhabitable. The only things left standing were the lower parts of the four walls, the steps that had once led up to the door, and the small cappella, built by Raffaele in 1900, in an effort to make up for the dreadful things he had done to his family, especially his son, Tino. His shame and remorse had been genuine, and he had never been able to forgive himself. But the hardest thing of all to bear was that he could never make peace with his son.

A new decade was well underway, and people were eager to look ahead, ready to make a fresh start. Tino was now an old man, not as strong as in his youth, but still a man who bore the signs of distinguished good looks. Carlotta and Carla still lived above the café. To his disappointment, Carla had refused quite a few proposals of marriage; she was too involved with her work to find time for a husband, she told him. When the letter arrived from Italy, he recognised the handwriting straight away. The spelling was poor, she had never been as good a pupil as he had, but the writing was still strong and firm, and unmistakeable. He turned it over in his hand and went to open it. But he changed his mind and propped it up against the clock on the mantelpiece. Later. He would open it later.

But the letter played on his mind. He got up and went back over to the fireplace, picking up the white envelope and again turning it over and over in his hands. But this time, he slit it open and pulled out the thin piece of paper. He began to read.

Dearest Tino

I am writing to you after all this time because Francesco has asked me to. I don't think I would have had the courage myself. He is sick, Tino. The doctors tell us he has just weeks to live. Please, he wants to see you one more time before he dies. He needs to make his peace with you. And if you won't believe him, I can vouch once more for the fact that none of what happened was his fault. I feel I must remind you of the things we spoke about – how your Papa told us you were never going to come back from England

and how he said you had another sweetheart and had forgotten all about me. Francesco was not well, he needed someone to look after him and I had become fond of him too. I was so hurt, I hadn't heard from you since you left, though we all know now how your Papa hid all the letters. And your brother reminded me so much of you. Tino, you must see – we needed each other's shoulder to cry on. That was why we married. We were both sad, lonely and hurt. Please, I beg you – come and tell him you forgive him, before it's too late.
Mara

Tino sighed as he slid the paper back into its envelope. He sat in the chair for some time, motionless. What should he do? He thought back over the intervening years and all the things that had happened since the last time he set foot on Italian soil. His life with Serafina had been happy enough, he couldn't have asked for a better wife. But the war, and Serafina's tragic death, along with the deaths of all those other people who were dear to him, had changed him beyond recognition. He wasn't the same person any more. Riddled with guilt that he had not been able to love Serafina in the way that she had wanted, and worse, that she had known this all along. He didn't really know who he was any more.

He thought long and hard before coming to the conclusion that it was right what people said – life was too short for grudges and recrimination. Francesco had been yet another innocent pawn in his father's games, a victim of his lies and deceit. And yet, when Tino thought about it, perhaps even his father had been a victim to some extent. As a child, his family had been one of the poorest in the area and he had always longed to rise above that. Grillo had recognised that need, played on it, encouraging and manipulating Raffaele to do things that would never even have entered his head, let alone carried out. Tino was slowly but surely working his way towards forgiveness and peace.

Yet he let two more weeks pass before finally making up his mind. One morning, he got up quite suddenly from his chair, leaving the breakfast dishes littering the table. He was a tidy man by nature and this was unprecedented. He never went anywhere without clearing the dishes away first. He reached for his hat and coat from the peg behind the door. He didn't have far to go, the railway station was just a few hundred yards away, down the road. He would find out the times of the trains and work out an itinerary. Perhaps he could persuade Carla to come with him, she would have school holidays soon. Carlotta, too. Later, he would write a reply to Mara, asking her to tell Francesco he would be there as soon as he could. He was on his way. After all these years, he had finally found it in his heart to forgive his brother and he couldn't wait to tell him so, face to face.

Epilogue

THE TEARS FINALLY stopped and Tino sat on a big round stone in front of the cappella, wiping his glasses with a clean handkerchief. They had been right, there was nothing much left of the farm at all. Nothing but empty walls. Yet it was the first time he had seen the cappella. If only, he thought, he had the power to turn back the clock. Too late, of course, but he could see it all now. He should have forgiven his father a long time ago. In a way, Raffaele's unnatural obsessions were as much an illness as Tino's mother's illness had been. And Angelo's tragic death had only served to push him even further over the edge.

He had made up his mind to fulfil Zi Giuseppe's final wish and give Francesco the forgiveness he asked for. In fact, there wasn't really anything to forgive; all that had happened had been out of his control. They had all been pawns in the dangerous game his father had played with Grillo, every single one of them had suffered the consequences to some degree.

He had arranged to borrow a car from one of Marco's friends in Cassino on their arrival and he had gone eagerly to collect it. But it was already too late. A message was waiting for them when they got there. 'Go straight to the cemetery,' it said. Francesco had held on as long as he could, but not quite long enough to fulfil his wish of seeing his brother one last time. If only Tino hadn't prevaricated. He should have booked the tickets the same day he received the letter. He was devastated. Now he would never get the chance to tell his brother that he finally understood. That he loved him. That he forgave him. For it was only through that forgiveness that he himself could gain the inner peace that had eluded him for most of his life. If only…

His one small consolation was that at least he had written to tell Francesco he was on his way and that he no longer bore him any grudge. He hoped that it had been enough for Francesco, for he knew it would never be enough for himself, he would regret his actions until the day he died.

Tino was vaguely aware of a movement behind him and he turned in surprise as a hand gently touched his shoulder. His cheeks were still wet with tears as he raised his face to find Mara standing there. He had seen her at the graveside, but only from a distance. By the time they had got there from Cassino, the funeral had already begun and everyone was deep in prayer. He kept well back from the main group, reluctant to intrude.

Mara was older now, of course, but in his eyes, she hadn't changed a bit. She was as beautiful as ever. Their eyes met, and in that instant, the years of separation melted away as if they had never existed. The passage of time hadn't made an ounce of difference to their feelings for each other. Fresh tears poured down his face, but even as they fell, a slow smile curved his lips upwards beneath the moustache.

'Mara!' It was all he could manage to say, and he held out his arms to her. There was nothing improper in the embrace; after all, she had only just come from her husband's funeral. But somehow, she felt safe and comforted, and a sense of hope and belonging.

'*Nonna*, we're going back to the house!' A voice from behind caused them both to turn around.

'We'll join you soon, Attillio.'

'Your grandson?' Tino asked in disbelief as he saw a young man, probably in his twenties, approaching them. It was like looking at Francesco fifty years before, the young man was the image of him.

She nodded. 'And this is my daughter, Anna.'

For the first time, Tino noticed the woman standing behind him. If Attillio looked like Francesco then this elegant woman was even more like Mara.

'You are just as beautiful as your mother,' he smiled.

'*Grazie,*' she answered, returning his smile. She turned to her mother. 'Mamma, we've just met Carla on the road, we'll go back to the house with her.'

Mara and Tino watched in silence as the car rocked and bumped its way back up the rough track.

'So!' he said, suddenly feeling very shy now they were alone again. 'Your daughter is so much like you, Mara. I have a very beautiful niece and a handsome great-nephew.'

Mara shook her head solemnly. 'That's where you're wrong, Tino.'

'Wrong?' His brows drew together in a puzzled frown. 'But I thought you said Anna was your daughter, and...'

Her reply confused him even more. 'Yes, she is.'

Long lashes dropped down shyly over her eyes, almost brushing her cheeks. Her heart was racing like a trapped bird and she felt awkward, like a young girl. She didn't know how she was going to tell him, but somehow she had to find the courage. She took a deep breath.

'Tino, there's something you must know,' she began. She paused. 'When Francesco came back from the war, he was badly wounded. Very badly wounded.'

'*Si*. I know that,' he replied. 'His leg was injured, it got infected.'

'Yes. But it was even worse than that.'

Tino's brows drew together in an even deeper frown. He had no idea where this was leading, but he waited quietly until she was ready to go on.

'Tino, when he was taken prisoner, he suffered the most

awful degradation you could imagine.' She stopped and tears filled the blue eyes. 'Francesco was a good man, he didn't deserve what they did to him. Nor did any of the others, for that matter. They beat them, they put them to work, they starved them. Then they beat them all over again. He was so badly injured, it was a miracle he managed to escape at all.' Mara gave a long, shuddering sigh and paused a few moments to regain her composure. Taking a deep breath, she went on, 'Tino, there was one final humiliation for many of those who were captured.' There was another long pause. 'They mutilated and damaged some of these men so badly, it was impossible for them to father children.'

Tino said nothing, but his eyes were full of questions as he waited for Mara's final words. 'Francesco was one of those men.'

'No!' Tino was devastated. He found it impossible to take in the full horror of what his brother must have suffered. That they had done that to his own brother and that he had never even been aware of it. Never even bothered to find out! A confusion of thoughts vied for attention in Tino's mind. Then suddenly, the full implication of Mara's revelation hit him like a thunderbolt. His mind shot back to the morning of his wedding, the one and only time she had come to him, by the stream and everything began to fall into place.

'You mean my niece is not…?' he stammered.

The nod was almost imperceptible.

'And your grandson?'

'He's yours, too.'

It was too much to take in. For some moments, Tino was shocked into silence. He had no idea how he should react and a thousand thoughts fought for attention in his head. But in spite of his confusion, the future began to unfold before him – a future that suddenly seemed more inviting. Brighter, with the promise of better things to come. But then, something else occurred to him and he needed to know the answer.

'Francesco – he knew about this?'

She nodded again. 'He knew the baby couldn't possibly be his,' she explained, her voice little more than a whisper. 'I had to tell him, I had no choice. But no-one else knows, not even now.'

'And yet he accepted Anna as his own.' Tino's voice was incredulous, full of admiration and wonder at his brother's selfless act. He felt humbled and ashamed.

For a few minutes, he stood quietly, digesting this latest news. Then, with a gentle smile, he held out his arm to Mara. She took it without hesitation, as if it were the most natural thing in the world. She returned his smile shyly, and they walked in companionable silence across the fields that led to the Grillo house, each wrapped up in their own thoughts. Tino felt the first gentle stirrings of the true happiness that had eluded him for so long. It was too soon for her; he was no fool, he realised that. There was so much news to take in. But then, who knew what the future would bring? He was back in his homeland, with the woman he had never stopped loving at his side. He was a patient man and for now, that would be enough.